Of the Night

Book One
The Black Odyssey

Alexander Johnson

Vae Vivis

Woe to the Living

Of the Night is a work of fiction. Names, characters, places, and incidents either are the product of the author's imagination or are used fictitiously. Any resemblance to actual persons, living or dead, events, or locales is entirely coincidental.

Publisher: Self-published, Alexander Johnson.
Editor: Kimberly Schwartz

Self-published, Amazon KDP.

ISBN: 979-8-9922154-0-3.

Cover art owned by Alexander Johnson.
Cover art created by Santiago Schreiber. Instagram: @sannosferatu
Cover design by Alexander Johnson.

Map art owned by Alexander Johnson.
Map art created by Gloria Byrd of SirenSongsBoutique.

instagram.com/@officialblack_odyssey
www.officialblackodyssey.com

"The ugly fact is books are made out of books, the novel depends for its life on the novels that have been written."

Cormac McCarthy

Contents

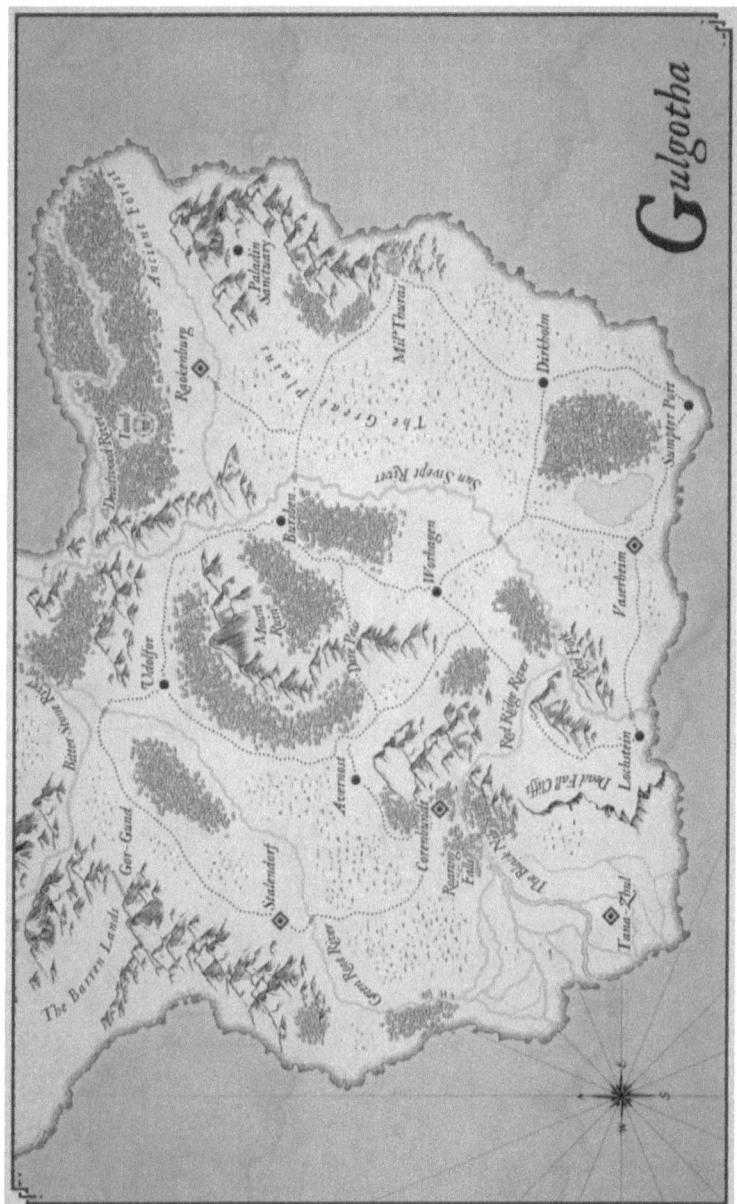

Gulgotha

Prologue:
The Storm

Kurodan stood upon the tallest wall of Mil'Thuras, gazing down into the darkness of the valley below. He stared at an army of death itself, knowing that what took place would decide the fate of the rest of the world—the battle that loomed could put into motion the very undoing of mankind. Few had heeded his warning that this moment was upon them. Yet here they all were, his brothers in arms, standing on these high walls. They stood ready to fight for their lives until their last breath while knowing full well that that breath drew ever closer.

The enemy's numbers were many—a horde with fangs, claws, wings, swords, spears, horns, and all manner of other treacherous forms. Each abomination eager to spill blood in all their savagery. Kurodan's heart ached, and his fury raged inside. He knew Toradin must have perished during whatever unholy ceremony had created this hellish army. He prayed that Toradin's soul now rested in peace. The enemy horde covered the entire valley. As they marched towards the city's front gate, they seemed to come from some other world, or the very maw of hell.

The sound grew louder and louder, until they came to a halt. Their being was immense. Kurodan had never seen such a force before. All became quiet, a final breath held in anticipation of the coming onslaught.

Then, a figure appeared in the center of the army, as if the hell around him had spawned him forth. The one that Kurodan had escaped from. The one that had slaughtered and tortured his kinsmen. The one that had awoken the Dark God, the true master of this demonic army. The one that Kurodan swore he would kill before his life was snuffed out.

The lone figure grew slightly larger as he walked down the open aisle formed between two ranks, making his way to the front of the army. Standing at the head, his dead eyes looked up at the city. His gaze scoured the immense wall that towered over him, and then appeared to fixate on Kurodan. At first Kurodan could not be entirely sure, but then their eyes locked in a brief instant. A chill calm seized Kurodan's soul as each recognized the other's presence. Each wanted the other's blood on his own weapon. Each would play his part in the battle with the hope of striking the other down.

The ebony armor the figure wore contrasted with his pale skin. He did not utter a word for he did not need to. The figure merely drew his sword and raised it high above his head. Standing there, with man and beast both as witnesses, he defied the world of men. The entire army around him erupted.

They began beating their armor and chests, bashing their weapons against shields, smashing spears into the ground, and stomping feet onto the earth.

The cacophony of sound echoed throughout the

valley and off the wall. Each warcry, scream, and hellish battle chant fought for dominance over the other. It was a horrifying and astounding display.

Kurodan could sense the dread and fear that spread across the men on the wall like a plague. His knuckles whitened as his hands clenched around his shield and sword. The men beside him grew tense and restless. The noise grew into a crescendo of rage and fury. In the blackness, from behind the army, the Dark God approached.

Chapter I:
Training Grounds

He awoke to the still cold in the barracks. Sitting up from his cot, he rubbed his eyes open. Kurodan looked around the barracks with blurred vision, trying to wake up. The other men that he had trained with for years slowly came into view. They were waking up themselves and attending to their equipment and weapons. When they had first started there were fifty of them altogether. Within the first four days, ten had quit, three had suffered injuries that had postponed their training, and one had been killed.

Their numbers dwindled over time, until the eleven men that had survived the harsh conditions had all formed a bond stronger than blood and would gladly lay down their lives for each other. That is how they had become successful in the training regime—working together as a cohesive fighting force was the only way to avoid failure.

This concept had been hammered into them since

day one by the paladin instructors. Acting and fighting as an individual always resulted in severe punishment.

All the men donned their armor and weapons and filed out of the barracks into the training grounds. Kurodan felt the sharp cold air slap him in the face as he exited into the open. Snow on the ground crunched beneath the weight of his armor. It was still dark, but a streak of light peered into the sky as the sun's rays began to awaken the world.

He stood shoulder to shoulder with the other initiates. His stern brown eyes peered out from his helmet, focused.

They came face to face with their instructors, who were awaiting their arrival. The instructors and initiates knelt; their heads bowed. In unison all recited the Paladin's Prayer: "This day we give our lives to perfection. Perfection in protecting the innocent. Perfection in slaying the wicked, destroying our enemies with utter ruthlessness and without remorse. We will not hesitate. We will be victorious, or we will die trying, with the holy light. This oath we take. Amen."

The instructors charged. "Shields!" shouted Toradin, one of Kurodan's fellow initiates and his closest friend. Upon finishing the word "amen," Kurodan sprang to his feet, drawing his sword and hefting his shield. They had come up fast, but the instructors came up even faster.

They always did. No matter how well prepared the initiates were, the instructors were always faster. Always ready to kill and fight at a moment's notice.

One of the initiates was not quick enough to get his shield up and was immediately targeted by two of the instructors.

One instructor smashed his shield into the initiate's weapon hand, making him drop his sword. The other

5

instructor simultaneously swung his sword, striking him on the shoulder, cutting open his armor, and sending him crashing to the ground. Warm blood spilled out, painting the fresh snow-covered ground red.

The snow on the ground made everyone's footing difficult. Five of the other instructors formed a shield wall facing the ten initiates.

Any man might look at this as a fight already won. Even with the one who had fallen, it was two-to-one against the instructors. Yet this was the scenario that they reveled in, outnumbered and odds stacked against them. This was also one of the ways they taught lessons about war. If the instructors could win under these circumstances, then so could the initiates. Lead by example, always.

"Move," shouted Toradin. In unison they all stepped towards their downed comrade, who was taking a severe beating from the two instructors. On hearing Toradin's command, the instructors simply stopped their attack on the now-bloodied initiate and stepped away.

"Bunker," Toradin's voice was loud and clear. They formed a shield wall in a circle formation around the downed man.

The instructors now circled the formation, looking for any signs of weakness. Thoughts of doubt began to whisper through Kurodan's mind. Were the men too tired this morning? Were they not using proper form in the shield wall? Would the downed comrade survive to the final test? These were all signs that the instructors could sniff out, like sharks smelling blood in water.

Simultaneously all seven instructors rushed the initiates. The first instructor smashed into Kurodan's shield, each man pitting his weight against the other.

Kurodan swung his sword low under his shield, trying to force the instructor off balance in the snow. His sword struck the instructor's leg, and blood began running down the gaping wound.

The instructor did not waver from the blow; using his sword arm, he forced Kurodan's shield down and smashed his own into Kurodan's helmet. The blow sent Kurodan spiraling to the ground. This was the opening the instructors needed. They immediately broke into the initiates' formation, smashing and cutting Kurodan's peers to the ground. Their formation had turned into an all-out melee. Men quickly fell until only Toradin and three instructors remained standing.

He managed to strike one of the instructors down before they overwhelmed him. Once Toradin was lying on the ground bleeding amongst the others, the instructors stopped the attack and all fell silent, except for their heavy breathing and the men wincing at their wounds.

The first initiate that had fallen was lying on his back, wheezing through his helmet. Some of his companions struggled to their feet and began to try and help him. Kurodan was furious with himself. His skull felt as if it had been caved in by a boulder. He slowly got to his feet, grabbing his shield and sheathing his sword. Every man was able to bring himself to stand, save for the first initiate to fall.

Maldin, the leader of the Holy Order, stepped forward. "Anyone unable to continue?" No one said a word. His eyes fell on the broken body of the initiate who no longer moved. The men stepped aside as Maldin approached.

His helm was similar in construction to the others, covering his head, nose, and cheeks, leaving his eyes and mouth exposed.

It differed, where he had crafted trophies to it. The helm had the horns of a beast, one on each side pointing downwards. Black horsehair tied in a ponytail atop his helmet blew with the wind. His plate armor and chainmail were heavily scarred and worn but shone brightly.

He carried a heavy steel shield that bore the paladin emblem: a hand imbued with holy fire. His weapon was not a sword like many of the other paladins, for he carried a war hammer that had previously belonged to an orc warlord.

Maldin was what every initiate hoped to become. Kurodan had put him on a pedestal, knowing little about him other than he was one of the most intelligent, respected, and feared men in the Holy Order. That, and he had served with Kurodan's father in the Great War.

Maldin knelt over the wounded man, who was now on the verge of death. Maldin hefted a large book, chained to his waist, and unlatched its pages. He laid his left hand on the initiate's chest and began to read from the book. A white light emanated from his hand, at first dim but growing ever brighter. He twitched and spasmed for a brief moment but then grew still. None of the men exchanged glances; all wondered the same thing. Would he live?

As Maldin's light faded, the initiate looked to be in a deep slumber. His chest slowly rose and fell. His most grievous wounds had been made whole. "So be it," Maldin said. He motioned, and two instructors carried the initiate away. Maldin turned his attention back to the remaining men.

"Your formation was sound in space and technique but was slow in forming. Had you all reacted faster, your first man would not have fallen so quickly," he said.

The instructors and initiates now attended to their own wounds. Kurodan sat as Toradin inspected his head.

"You're supposed to use your sword, not your skull,

you know."

Kurodan laughed. "Aye," he said. "You fought well this morning, Toradin. Perhaps I will have the chance to redeem myself in the next session."

Shifting slightly, Kurodan saw Maldin standing like a statue, watching them all.

He never saw to his own wounds in front of the others, though none had ever been successful in inflicting any too serious upon him.

Maldin's eyes scanned the men and locked with Kurodan's. Kurodan could not put into words the seriousness in Maldin's stare, but it froze him to his very core. In that brief moment Kurodan knew his life was about to change forever.

"Gather round, men," Maldin called. Everyone fell silent and walked to where Maldin stood. He removed his helm and eyed each initiate in turn. "You will face your final challenge today."

The men and even some of the instructors could not hide their surprise. Gleed, second in command, stepped forward. His dark skin matched his black beard and his long, thick, rope-like hair. His people hailed from Tana-Zhul in the wetlands. He was a bigger man than Maldin, and his skill with a spear was unmatched. "You think them ready?"

Maldin merely gave a slight nod.

"Right then," Gleed quickly said. "You will go eat and rest. Return here in one hour. Leave your armor and shields, bring only your swords. Understood?" He pointed to their weapons with the tip of his spear.

"Aye," the men responded. Kurodan turned with the rest of them and filed back into the barracks. His body and mind were overcome with adrenaline. None of them knew what the final challenge was. Only the graduated had that privilege.

The quiet that filled the barracks for that long hour matched each man's nerves. Some pretended to sleep, others read from the holy book or sharpened their swords.

Kurodan remained lost in his own thoughts. His heavy muscular frame was tense and sore as he slowly stripped off his armor. When he removed his helm, his shoulder length golden brown hair stuck wet and cold to his face. He stood tall but was not the tallest of the group and his body was built for soldiering.

As he stretched, his brown eyes looked up and stared at the banner of the Holy Order that hung above the door. A tapestry that was beautiful yet worn, it displayed the sacred hand imbued with flame. The constant reminder of why they were all here.

The paladins of the Holy Order were not only menacing warriors on the battlefield driving their foes before them, but they were also healers. They wielded the sacred light of the gods, having their weapons and armor blessed and anointed in holy rituals.

Among the grand weapons each paladin carried, the most important was his copy of the holy book containing writings and prayers of the gods that he had mastered. With these holy instruments each could use it to smite the wicked, or to mend the most heinous wounds.

When the initiates achieved the title paladin and joined their brothers' ranks, they too would undergo these rituals and receive the blessing of wielding the holy light.

Chapter II:
Purpose

The men stood in the empty courtyard. Kurodan could hear his heart pounding and the staggered breathing of the others. His palms grew cold with sweat and a lump formed in his throat. He closed his eyes and drew in a slow deep breath. He opened them to see the instructors leading men in chains towards them.

Some of the initiates exchanged confused glances. *Are these prisoners of some sort*, Kurodan wondered. The five men were shackled and had hoods tied over their heads. They were skittish and their bare skin flinched in the cold wind.

"Kneel," Maldin barked. The prisoners awkwardly dropped to their knees. The instructors removed their hoods, and each prisoner eyed his surroundings.

One began pleading immediately, "Please, good lords, I beg of you, release us."

Maldin moved and slightly lifted his hammer, so the massive weapon gently touched the prisoner's mouth.

He fell silent and Maldin turned to face the initiates.

"This will be your final test. Should you fail, you will never become one of us," he said.

Gleed stepped forward. "Each of these men is a traitor to you and to Mil'Thuras," he said. "Their lives have been condemned forfeit by the queen herself, their crimes unforgivable."

One initiate then stepped forward and spoke, "You would have us kill these men?"

"Aye," Maldin nodded.

Some of them could not hide the disgust on their faces. Kurodan fought to wait and listen if there was any other part to this "test."

"You would have us butcher these men, chained and defenseless? How do we know they are guilty of their supposed crimes?" another asked.

Kurodan watched as some of the men now grew angry. More voiced their concerns.

"I thought the Holy Order fought to protect the innocent, not murder those who cannot even fight back."

"There is no honor in this."

"Enough," Maldin shouted. "Each of you must prove that you are capable of killing! That is the test. No more, no less. These men have been tried and deemed to be put to death. Their lives are forfeit."

A sword clanged loudly on the frozen ground, as one of the men stood defiantly. "I will not," he declared. Others dropped their swords, three in all. Maldin motioned for those who defied the order to return to the barracks, almost as if he had expected some of them to refuse. This gave Kurodan further pause.

Before the ones who had refused could turn and walk from the courtyard, Lehm drew his sword, being the largest of the initiates, he covered the ground between himself and the prisoners in a mere few steps.

His cold blue eyes fixated on the nearest prisoner, who seeing the intimidating warrior approaching, tried to stand. Lehm reached the prisoner and hacked him down. Everyone froze. It was as if Lehm almost killed the man purely out of fear of failure, wanting to end the test quickly.

Unfortunately for Lehm, the prisoner did not have an easy death. The prisoner tried to protest his death by throwing up his shackled hands at the last moment, to stop the blow. Lehm's sword cut the man's arms away, completely severing one. The prisoner screamed in pain. The ones kneeling beside him fell away in horror. Lehm raised his sword and struck hard two more times, silencing the screams.

Lehm took a few steps back, breathing heavily, veins bulging on top of his bald head. He looked around. Maldin merely shifted his gaze from Lehm to the others, waiting. Another initiate stepped forward now. The nameless prisoner closest to him looked up, tears in his eyes.

"Please, I beg you," the prisoner began, then dropped his eyes and braced for death.

The initiate drew his sword and raised it to strike. But then the prisoner opened his eyes at the would-be killer. The initiate dropped his sword and quietly turned to walk away. "I cannot," he whispered.

With only four initiates now remaining, Kurodan watched as the others eventually made their decisions and killed, leaving him the last to choose.

Toradin surprised Kurodan to be the next to kill. His body flexed as he drove his sword into the chest of one of the prisoners. Unlike Lehm, he seemed quite calm as he pulled his sword free.

The prisoner struggled to live for a short time and then died with a whimper. Toradin walked over to Lehm and stood to watch the others, his face showed only determination.

Horad killed next. He was from Tana-Zhul as Gleed was, though his hair was cropped short against his skull, and he was slightly shorter than the massive instructor. Horad stood above one of the remaining prisoners, who started to beg and plead. "Lower your head traitor," he commanded.

The prisoner bowed his head lower, now on all fours and sobbing. Horad struck clean and true, severing the prisoner's head from his body. He gently wiped the blood from his sword and now stood with the others.

Kurodan and Bardu were the last two initiates. Just as Kurodan was going to draw his sword, Bardu stepped forward. Bardu was the shortest of the men but did not lack any in strength or physical prowess. He was bald like Lehm but had a long grizzled brown beard.

As Bardu approached the last two surviving prisoners, one remained silent and the other started to protest. The prisoner did not manage to get a full word out before Bardu decapitated the man and stepped aside.

Kurodan now moved to the last prisoner. All eyes watched them in anticipation.

The prisoner knelt in the center of the other corpses, their warm blood pooling around him, turning cold.

"What crime have you committed that would lead you here?" Kurodan asked. The question took some of the others by surprise. The ones who had made their kill may not want to hear an answer that could cause them doubt.

The prisoner was weeping quietly. In between sobs he spoke, "I … I did not … I swear to you I am but an innocent man."

"Very well, what is the crime you have been accused of committing? If it is truly punishable by death, I must know," Kurodan said.

The man wiped his face and quickly regained himself. "I have been accused of heresy, my lord."

"Heresy, how so?"

"My lord, false accusations and lies were reported to the queen in an attempt to silence me and end my life. I swear to you I am innocent."

"You did not answer my question," Kurodan drew his sword and pointed at the prisoner.

The man let out a heavy sigh as if his fate had already been sealed. "I have been accused of vampire worship."

A long silence took hold as each man weighed what he had just heard.

"That is one of the most serious of sins. How does one be convicted of vampire worship without proof?" Kurodan asked.

"My lord, I come from Dirkholm. I was witness to a horror that happened there just some time ago. I and others tried to warn anyone who would listen of the events that took place there. Soldiers came, orders were given to us to never speak of it again. I … we could not simply ignore what happened."

"What of the others that you speak of? What became of them?"

The man looked down at the butchered men next to him. "We are all here, my lord."

"What was it you saw?"

He looked up at Kurodan. "I fear that the Great War did not truly end."

"What did you see? Speak," Kurodan demanded.

"A vampire."

Kurodan looked from the man to Maldin. His leader's face was stone, his eyes fixed.

He continued his questioning, "And what

became of this vampire?"

"It took a girl, but that was not enough. It slaughtered many more and once it had its fill, it left."

"It just left, no one tried to stop it?"

"We tried, my lord. Those who did … died. I know not how it came to Dirkholm. Shortly after, soldiers came. We thought it was to hunt the beast down. How wrong we were," the prisoner sighed again.

"Tell me how wrong you were."

"They told us to never speak of the demon and what it had wrought. They said it would spread fear and chaos if word travelled that the vampires were not all but destroyed," the prisoner answered. "Soon after, I realized that there was no plan to find it and kill it … I believe it was to be kept secret."

"Kept secret? Secret from who?" Kurodan asked.

The man winced as if the very question had caused him physical pain. "I know not, my lord."

Kurodan met Maldin's stare once more. "You would have me kill him?"

Maldin spoke though his face betrayed no emotion, "The choice lies with you and you alone, now make it."

Kurodan's mind fought against itself. He wanted to know more about this supposed vampire, he wanted to know if there was any truth in what the prisoner had claimed. His grip slightly loosened on his sword and his mind flashed to his father. His decision had been made and he raised his sword.

"Know that I told the truth, paladin," the prisoner said. They locked eyes as the prisoner stated his defiance and Kurodan struck, splitting the man's skull and killing him outright. The body made a sickening thud as Kurodan freed his weapon and moved to stand with the others. He hoped he had made the right choice.

"At attention," Gleed ordered.

They stood at arms, shoulder to shoulder. Kurodan tried his best not to move, to still his body and become like a statue.

The time of taking on the title of paladin had finally come. His dream was coming true. He would serve among the ranks of the Holy Order, take on dangerous and exciting adventures, and one day become like his father had been.

Maldin stepped forwards. He spoke slowly and quietly despite the wind; he wanted each man to focus on the words themselves and not as much on himself.

"On this day you will never go back to a life of leisure," he began. "You will spend every day as a weapon and a shield. You will be the force and reckoning that is needed in times of war and in times of peace. The Great War is over but there are still battles to be fought and waged."

Maldin paused, but he had not finished, "Your war is just beginning. With your skills, you will continue to hone your craft and become victorious. The most difficult task you will come to face is not the battles themselves, nor injuries, nor the close friends lost in combat. It will not be the horrors witnessed that haunt your mind, whether you are awake or asleep."

At this, some of the men started to shift, perhaps with skepticism.

"No," Maldin continued. "No matter how challenging those moments may be, your most difficult task will be the mindset. The desire to always be ready at a moment's notice, never wavering, never dulling your sharp edge. It will be the wanting to wage battle when there is none to be waged or staying your sword when battle has begun but your services are required elsewhere."

Kurodan was puzzled by this. Why would he not be

called into battle if there was one to be fought? Why would he have to wait for battle when the world was so vast and there were still many enemies that needed to be quelled?

Maldin spoke again, "Remember, always keep your blessed weapons and armor with you. They are now an extension of your mind and will, just as your own limb would be. Without them you will still be a warrior, but you will no longer be capable of wielding the sacred light. Go forth, paladins of the Holy Order. Go forth and fulfill your oaths until death takes you."

As he was called a paladin for the first time, Kurodan could not help but feel an immense pride burning within himself.

"We will now travel to Mil'Thuras, and you will be recognized before the queen," Gleed said.

"Head to the Temple of Auras. After the ritual gather your things and prepare to leave at once. Some of you may never return to these training grounds. The queen will have the ultimate decision on where your services are needed."

Kurodan and his brothers filed back to the barracks to gather their belongings. Kurodan remained still for a moment. Troubled. What was the purpose of becoming a paladin if not for the glory of fighting and defeating their enemies, he wondered.

Realizing that he was the only one still standing outside in the courtyard, he quickly followed into the barracks. *But still*, he thought, *what will the queen require of us if we are not to fight?*

Chapter III:
Blessings

Kurodan, Toradin, Horad, Lehm, and Bardu walked behind the high priests, whose white robes matched the undisturbed snow freshly fallen on the ground. Their garb was embroidered with a yellow sun, signifying the highest-ranking clergymen and commitment within the Holy Order. Low tones and prayers were heard as these holy men swung their golden orbs on chains, smoke drifting from the fires they carried.

The temple door opened, and the candles within cast but a dim light against the immense interior. As they entered, silence took them all. They proceeded to the altar that stood tall in front of the empty pews. The high priests joined their fellow members along each side of the altar, turning to face the paladins. Kurodan and his brothers knelt. No one spoke.

More high priests entered the temple, bringing with them swords, shields, armor, and holy books.
One by one the paladins stood and moved to sit on the

altar, undergoing the sacred ritual of Auras the Light-Bringer, first blessed of the Holy Order.

Kurodan stood last. He sat upon the altar facing his brothers who now stood below clad in their shining armor. Each bore the runic weapons, blessed with sacred fire. The priests continued to pray in the ancient tongue of old. The sound of hammer and chisel cracked on steel as his blade was carved with runes marking its new power.

The priests wafted the smoking orbs about his body, armor, and weapons. They dressed him, carefully assembling each piece of armor to his body. His great helmet was gently placed on his head, and he rose from the altar.

His shield, bearing the sacred hand imbued in flame, was brought. The high priests knelt, and offered Kurodan this as his defense against those that would seek to destroy the world of men. Kurodan slid his arm through the handles. His mind envisioned the many blows that would strike against it and fail to overtake him.

Last, his sword was carried to him. Its craftsmanship and beauty were unmatched. One high priest knelt and raised it high above his head. Kurodan gripped the handle and felt its balance. The runes seared white hot along the blade at his touch. He raised it high above his head in awe. The runes faded and the ritual was over.

Chapter IV:
False Praise

Kurodan rode his steed among the long line of the other paladins and clergymen. Every graduation, the Holy Order would bring the new paladins to the capital of Mil'Thuras. The city celebrated when the queen formally recognized their new oaths. After the celebration the queen decided where throughout Gulgotha their services were required most.

Kurodan vividly remembered, standing next to his mother's side as a child, attending a handful of these ceremonies before the Great War and before the death of his father. He had seen his father and other paladins kneel before the king. His father was always in the same spot of the circle at each ceremony. The king would ask the new paladins to remain kneeling while the other older paladins would rise and form a giant circle in the great hall. The king would then draw his sword and touch each new paladin's shoulder with the blade.

He would then ask for them to all rise and state,

"The king of Mil'Thuras honors you as paladins of the Holy Order. Go forth and may you forever fulfill the oaths you have taken." Kurodan remembered how loud the cheers would ring out after that.

The king had not survived the war either, assassinated just before it ended. Rumors had spread that all would be lost after his death; his only heir to the throne had been killed as well.

The grief-stricken queen, however, had risen to the occasion and led the armies of men in what seemed Gulgotha's darkest hour. She was revered throughout the entire land as a hero. "The vanquisher," she had been called since that day.

Kurodan pondered how the ceremony would be different with the queen instead of the king. Pulling him from his childhood memories, Toradin rode up alongside him. "Are you prepared for this day?" he asked excitedly.

Kurodan smirked slightly, "I have waited all my life for this exact day, brother. I am more than ready."

"Good, I cannot wait to get my first decision from the queen. Hopefully, we will be going to the same place," Toradin said.

"With any luck we will all be going to the same place. To fight the remnants of the vampire scourge and the other enemies of Mil'Thuras," Kurodan replied.

"So eager to get into the fight are we, brother?" Toradin mocked.

"Are you not?" Kurodan replied almost angerly.

"I am, brother, but do not let your eagerness rob you of this day. You should be able to enjoy this moment and look back on it as a happy and prideful memory. Your father would be proud of you," Toradin said.

Kurodan opened his mouth to reply but fell silent

for a moment. He thought of what his father might have said to him. "You are right. We all should be able to enjoy this day. We have earned it."

The line of paladins broke out of the trees and into the open countryside that lay before the high walls of Mil'Thuras. As Kurodan's horse trotted a short distance to keep up, Kurodan stared at the capital city. The stone walls stood high, and they had guarded the people within for ages.

The city had been constructed into the side of the mountain called Thuras. Thuras meant "the king" in the ancient language. When the alliances of men were formed, throughout the world of Gulgotha, the capital was named Mil'Thuras, meaning "the king of men." The mountain was enormous and beautiful in its own right. To attack Mil'Thuras, an enemy could only advance in one direction, and to face the high walls was almost guaranteed suicide.

It was an impenetrable fortress. There were other great cities throughout Gulgotha, but Mil'Thuras was the strongest and most well-known. It stood as a beacon for all mankind and had never been breached since its construction.

As the paladins rode closer to the capital, the front gate came into view. It was massive and intimidating, like the walls themselves. The gate was one giant wooden door that lowered like a drawbridge. The chains that lowered the gate required immense mechanical machinations to operate.

Maldin, leading the single line formation, raised his war hammer high above his head. There were faint shouts high up on the walls. Then the sound came and echoed across the entire valley. The horn of Mil'Thuras, its sound was as much a triumph as it was a warning. The gate slowly began to lower as they approached.

Maldin halted the paladins in front of the gate as the massive drawbridge continued to drop. Kurodan had seen this many times, growing up, but it was always as magnificent as the first. The gate looked so powerful and overwhelming that it often left people in awe.

The gate reached the ground with a thunderous sound, and Maldin pushed his steed forward. As the paladins entered the city, the local citizens began to come out of their homes and shops, flocking to the holy warriors.

Maldin, having gone through this ceremony countless times, ignored them all. As he broke a path through the growing mob of townspeople, he grew impatient.

People began to cheer and applaud the arriving heroes. Kurodan could hear and see people shouting out praises to them from windows and doorways. He had imagined this moment for an eternity throughout his life, but he felt a rage building inside of him.

He recognized that the Holy Order and paladins had a long respected and feared reputation but found being on the other end of this parade infuriating. How can I be treated as a valiant warrior if I have yet to face a real enemy, he wondered. How can we be adored without having ever experienced the trials and hardships of combat? Let alone emerge victorious from them?

It was clear that his brothers did not share his thoughts. Toradin caught a rose that a local girl threw at him, grinning at Kurodan while holding it close to his nose and smelling its sweet scent. Yes, Toradin was truly enjoying the moment. Other paladins shook hands or bowed as they rode by.

Maldin led them through the winding stone roads of the city, going further upwards towards the great hall.

Kurodan noticed Maldin shifted in his horse's saddle and exchanged a few words with Gleed. Kurodan could not hear what Maldin had said due to the noise from the crowd. Maldin kicked his stirrups and forced his horse into a trot. Kurodan's and all the other mounts quickened their pace to keep up.

Most of the crowd followed the paladins through the city's streets, all the way to the entrance of the great hall. It was a big event and did not happen regularly. Often years went by without any appearances of paladins. The Holy Order had churches and clergymen of various ranks throughout Gulgotha but there were far fewer paladins.

Kurodan caught sight of a small boy standing at the top of a balcony gawking at the spectacle. Their eyes locked and Kurodan nodded. The boy smiled gleefully to be recognized by one who looked like a hero in a children's story.

As they reached the entrance, Maldin shouted, "Paladins, dismount!" One final cheer and applause came from the following towns people. As the paladins walked into the great hall, the queen, her council members, and the ruling elites stood waiting. The doors were closed behind them as the last of the paladins entered.

Maldin approached the queen, took off his horned helmet and knelt with his hammer. "I present the services, protection, and oaths of the Holy Order to the queen." All the paladins knelt.

The queen walked towards Maldin with her hands outstretched. "And the queen graciously accepts the Holy Order and its warriors into her company," she responded.

There was that word again, warrior. Kurodan thought, *we haven't truly earned that title yet. Maldin and the other "blooded" paladins had proven themselves in battle. I may be a paladin now, but I am still "unblooded" and have much to prove."* Maldin took the queen's right hand as she offered it and kissed the rings on her fingers.

Kurodan fought to not roll his eyes at the new formality.

Maldin rose, as did the other paladins. "The new graduates are ready, your majesty."

With the pomp and circumstance finished, all the blooded paladins formed a circle facing inwards around the hall. Kurodan stepped forward with the other graduates, standing in a line facing the queen.

Kurodan caught a glimpse of his mother standing outside the circle, crying. His throat grew tight, and he fought to control his emotions. He forced them back and still.

The queen drew her sword from its sheath. The grip and guard were made of solid gold, with a red ruby forged into the pommel. She raised it high, the blade glistening. It truly was a perfectly crafted piece of art.

Kurodan, and his brothers recited in unison the Paladin's Prayer. "This day we give our lives to perfection. Perfection in protecting the innocent. Perfection in slaying the wicked, destroying our enemies with utter ruthlessness and without remorse," they stated. "We will not hesitate. We will be victorious, or we will die trying with honor and valor. This oath we take. Amen."

The queen moved to the first paladin graduate, and he knelt before her. She placed her blade on his right shoulder, and then swiftly brought the blade back upright.

The paladin stood and the queen stepped to the next. This sequence repeated down the line. No words were spoken.

It was eerily quiet except for the movements of the queen. Toradin knelt before the queen next to Kurodan, who was last in the line.

Kurodan stared a hole into the wall in front of him, never breaking his bearing. He had waited his entire life for this exact moment. All the years of training, away from family and friends, following in his father's footsteps. He had taken Toradin's words to heart but could not shake the feeling that he was angry about the whole thing. His father had been a true warrior of the Holy Order, as were Maldin and the other paladins who had fought in the Great War. He was merely a new graduate who was beginning to think he might not ever see another war.

Toradin stood, and the queen moved in front of Kurodan. Kurodan broke bearing and locked eyes with the queen. It was as if her stare turned him to stone, not once breaking eye contact. She seemed to gaze deep into his soul. Kurodan could now recognize the calculated ferocity in her face.

He pried his eyes away, kneeling and felt the blade on his shoulder. The queen swung her blade back upright, and Kurodan stood. She moved back to the center of the circle. "I, Queen Delarona Valanore, the vanquisher, hereby declare on this day and henceforth, these men to be paladins of the Holy Order. May you serve me and my kingdom well!"

The blooded paladins, who formed the circle, saluted by making a fist and slamming it hard into their chest. The noise thundered through the hall. Cheers and applause erupted. The queen sheathed her sword, then announced, "Let us feast."

Immediately the room became a whirlwind of commotion. Joyful music played from string instruments and flutes.

Tables and food were brought out as family members and friends embraced their loved ones that they had not seen in years.

Kurodan turned to see his mother standing behind him. She had grown older since last he remembered her and was almost bawling. She threw her arms around him and pulled him in tightly. Kurodan hugged her back. "I have missed you," he said.

"My little boy," she said, cupping his cheeks. "Your father would be so proud of you. I am so proud of you!"

His mother pulled him aside and told him of all the events he had been absent for. "I have something to tell you that …" she trailed off.

"What is it?" Kurodan asked.

His mother hesitated, "Well, I remarried." Kurodan's mouth hung open, but his face quickly turned into a smile.

"When do I get to meet him?"

"Right now," she smiled. "He is a member of the queen's royal council." She motioned to a tall man approaching them.

Kurodan was surprised to see how well dressed the man was. Indeed, he looked the part of the ruling elite.

Kurodan's mother embraced the man, who offered his hand out. "Kurodan, my name is Arthur. I am thrilled to finally meet you."

Kurodan shook his hand, "The pleasure is mine. Please tell me about yourself, how you two met." Arthur and his mother told Kurodan that they had met one fateful day when they both had been at the market. The two of them could not stop smiling as they spoke of falling in love with one another.

Kurodan remembered how horribly his life had spiraled out of control when his father had been killed. His mother had plummeted into a deep depression, but seeing her now was almost like having his mother back before his father's death. He could not remember the last time she had smiled this much.

"Well, I am overjoyed for the both of you. I hope I will get to know you better in time." Kurodan said, shaking Arthur's hand again.

The rest of the evening the queen, her royal council, and the Holy Order all feasted and rejoiced in the great hall. The food was exquisite. Roasted boar, fresh fruit, and enough wine flowed to intoxicate all.

As the night continued, Kurodan stayed close to his mother's side, listening intently to her description of the new life she had been living. They seemed to be doing so well, it almost overwhelmed him with joy. Arthur asked about his paladin training, but his mother knew better than to pry. She was used to not knowing the specifics from her marriage to his father.

The queen suddenly stood, interrupting the festivities, tapping the back of a knife onto her chalice. The hall quieted to listen to her announcement.

"I unfortunately have other matters to attend to. But before I depart for the evening, I wish to make a toast."

She raised her chalice, "To the Holy Order and their long lineage of fulfilling their oaths to this great city!" Everyone raised their cups and cheered.

The queen gulped down the rest of her wine, bowed, and then left with some of her council members. The evening continued and people slowly began to make their way back to their homes, leaving the hall emptier and quieter.

Soon those who remained were the paladins who had no family members, lovers, or close friendships in the city. And Kurodan chose to stay, hungry for his purpose, his higher calling to fight like his father and those before him.

Maldin and many of the other paladins had refrained from indulging excessively in the festivities. Only now when they were amongst themselves did they begin to drink and become more at ease with their surroundings.

"We will meet with the queen in the morning. That is when she will decide where our services are needed the most," Maldin said.

"Or where we are not needed," Gleed retorted. Kurodan's head turned in surprise. Gleed was sitting in his chair, staring off into the distance as if in a trance.

"What is expected to happen? Surely you must have some idea of the queen's intentions," Toradin said.

"The queen is likely to have us remain here at Mil'Thuras. I would imagine she will require us to train more of her army," Maldin said.

Gleed snorted, gulping down a mug of ale. Small streaks of liquid fell into his massive beard as he wiped his mouth. "You will now become the instructors," he chuckled.

Kurodan was trying not to show his frustration at this answer. He waited to speak in hopes that there may be more to their new assignments.

"Are we not to go fight the remaining enemies?" Horad asked.

Maldin sat back in his chair, gazing off into his own thoughts but finally let out a sigh. "The queen and her council do not hold the same convictions as we do. They think our enemies as mindless beasts and unorganized, while simultaneously believing if we dare to venture outside these walls, we will all be killed. Even if our enemies were to mass together, it still would not be enough to bring down our forces."

"If they were to march against us, it would only afford us the opportunity to finish them off for good," Gleed said.

"So, they choose to remain in small numbers hidden in and around their stronghold in the mountain," Maldin added.

Kurodan finally began to speak his mind. "What of the vampires? The prisoner claimed there was one that still survived the Great War. Why not send us to do what we are meant for? To hunt them down and kill them!"

Maldin pulled out a long pipe and packed it, his fingers fidgeting through muscle memory. He lit the pipe and let out a billowing cloud of smoke from the corner of his mouth. Kurodan looked at Maldin for an answer but did not receive one.

Gleed downed his fourth mug of ale and packed his own pipe. Taking a large puff of it, Gleed looked at Kurodan. "The vampires are believed to have all been killed in the Great War."

"We all know that is a lie. Surely the queen does not believe it?" Kurodan blurted.

Maldin spoke with the pipe still in the corner of his mouth, "Kurodan, I commend your desire to hunt down our enemies. I share in that burning passion and agree with your thoughts. But you must understand our place in the world. Our calling. We are meant to destroy our enemies; it is what you have trained every day for. We do this to protect the world of men. In this service, we must obey and respect the ruler of Mil'Thuras. We may voice our concerns and consult with the queen and her council. We will do so tomorrow, I promise. In the end, we accept the decisions that are made, whether we agree with them or not. It is in the oaths we swear and keep."

"You will all begin to learn the customs and traditions of politics and how we suffer the decisions of people who will never step foot on the battlefield, nor should. It is a necessary evil, in order to maintain a balance for Mil'Thuras and its people," Gleed said.

Kurodan nodded, "I understand. I pray the queen will heed our council and perspective."

"You will all be present for the meeting and the queen's decision," Maldin assured him. "Though you are now paladins, you still have much to learn. None of you will speak, unless specifically addressed. Is this understood?"

Kurodan and the others nodded. Maldin exhaled another cloud through his nose. Silence filled the air around the group. Kurodan stared at Maldin. The embers of the pipe lit up his commander's face in the dark hall. He seemed to be somewhere else, as if awake in a nightmare.

Chapter V:
Politics

The morning's dawn slowly began to rise. The sound of the blacksmith's hammer and anvil echoed throughout the streets. Horses whinnied and cried as the stablemaster began the long process of brushing their coats. The smell of meat, fruit, and vegetables wafted through the air as the food market began to fill. The sound of moans and mugs clattering came from the local taverns as the late-night drinkers awoke. Finally, the church bell rang as the defining declaration that a new day was here.

Kurodan had been up before the sun. His mind would not allow the sweet release of slumber as he had stirred, restlessly thinking about what the queen would decide for his future. Maldin and Gleed's conversation had replayed itself repeatedly in his ears. He donned his armor and headed for the great hall from his sleeping quarters.

As he made his way through the labyrinth of halls

and corridors, he passed the multitude of servants hustling and bustling about their tasks. He had to dodge out of the way numerous times as people rushed past him. He slowed his pace, looking around curiously. *Is this how every day is waking up in the queen's servitude?* He chuckled aloud to himself. *Looks like I am in for quite the life.*

"What are you laughing at, youngblood?"

Kurodan paused, smiling as he turned and saw Toradin approaching from across the hall. "Just looking forward to our new future of housekeeping in the city."

Toradin pushed back his long brown hair and then rubbed the stubble on his face. "As am I, brother," He had spent the evening with one of the queen's council members.

"Yes, you seem to have already gained favor among the royal elite," Kurodan smirked.

Toradin bowed. "As a paladin, I must always be ready to render my services to those in need."

Kurodan rolled his eyes. "How supremely noble of you. Let us go."

As they entered the great hall, Kurodan noticed that almost everyone was already there waiting. Maldin eyed them, nodding slightly. The last of the queen's council entered and then, finally, the queen. Everyone stood, acknowledging her presence. "Let us be seated," she said, briskly walking to her throne.

The council members were on the queen's right-hand side while the paladins were on the left. No servants came with food and drink. This meeting was strictly for those who had earned a right to be in attendance of such a meeting.

The queen sat on her throne, and everyone else then sat in their chairs. "Now that we have gotten thepleasantries out of the way last night, we shall discuss the future of my city and its people," she said.

"Your highness, we are prepared to have the paladins take the lead in instructing your army. Their preparedness to fight on your behalf is paramount to the lives of our people," one of the council members said. He was a frail man with blonde hair and a small goatee.

"Yes," the queen responded. "The army must maintain a constant state of preparedness in the event any roaming war bands decide to mount an attack."

Kurodan turned to see Maldin staring off as if not even interested in the meeting. An awkward silence filled the hall. The queen stared daggers into Maldin as if he had somehow committed a great offense.

"Do you already grow tired of this meeting, Maldin?" she demanded.

Without even looking at her, Maldin spoke, "Your highness, your army is well trained and maintained. While we may be able to offer a few insights here and there on the art of armed combat, the leaders of your army are all veterans of the Great War. They are no strangers to violence and the ways of inflicting it upon our enemies."

Kurodan was startled at the lack of etiquette Maldin portrayed. *Maybe this is the side of politics Gleed was speaking of?*

"Your highness, what use are the paladins to you and your city if they cannot or will not carry out the task of aiding your army?" the blonde councilman asked. "Especially if it is as simple as they have made it out to be?"

The Holy Order has done more for Mil'Thuras than you could ever hope to achieve, Kurodan wanted to retort. But before he could make a fool of himself, Maldin spoke again. This time he stared directly at the councilman.

"Your highness, this is precisely why I believe the paladins are best suited for another task—" Maldin began, but the queen cut him off.

"Such as what, Maldin? You know as well as the rest of us that the orc threat is still a very real one. What do you propose instead of focusing your efforts on the army?"

Maldin now turned to her. "Korgath still lives, and as long as he draws breath there will always be a threat to mankind. His hatred runs too deep to simply be content with whatever dark place he has now made his domain. Let us seek his war bands out. Their numbers are small and scattered. We would only require a small regiment of troops—"

"Hah! Here we go again," interrupted the councilman. "You wish to go on these glory-seeking quests while simultaneously taking part of the queen's army, leaving the city vulnerable and exposed!"

Maldin ignored the man. "Your highness, if the orcs are truly as much a threat as you and your council propose, then we must deal with them sooner rather than later. The longer we wait, the more time we afford them to regroup, reorganize, and strategize."

"What if you go out in search of the orcs and never find them? What if Mil'Thuras falls under siege while you are away? What if you are ambushed and killed?" a new voice asked.

This time it was a woman from the council who spoke. "The risks are too great. We cannot put the future of the city in such jeopardy. If the orcs attack us, it should be on our own terms and with the defense of our city walls."

Maldin was about to speak but Gleed cut in, "The orcs will never mount a direct assault on the city. It would mean certain death for them. They are much more cunning and intelligent than that."

Many of the council members scoffed. One said dismissively, "The orcs are barbaric creatures with only the capability to think of slaughter. They do not perceive rational thoughts like we do."

Gleed was about to protest further, but Maldin motioned for silence with a wave of his hand. Then, lifting his hammer from his side, Maldin dropped it on the table with an obnoxiously loud thud. Its shaft pointed straight into the air.

"I took this from the orc warlord, Morglain, who held power prior to Korgath," he said. Maldin then raised a large skull that hung from a chain at his side, decorating his armor. "This skull belonged to Krashnik the Terrible."

Some of the council members startled at the mere mention of the vampire's name, sliding their chairs backwards away from the skull. Kurodan had only heard the name once, while eavesdropping on his father. Krashnik the Terrible was never spoken of. Kurodan stared at the skull wondering how Maldin had bested the vampire in battle.

"I ask you, which of these foes were more challenging on the field of battle?" Maldin demanded. An awkward silence grew.

"Do not lecture us on the merits of battle nor the enemy's thoughts. The orcs are just as much of a threat as the vampires are," Maldin said.

"Were," the queen corrected. "The vampires are no longer stalking the nights. You know that as well as I do, Maldin."

As he listened, Kurodan stared at the queen with his mouth open and his eyes squinted in complete disbelief —and it was noticed. "You there, paladin. You have something you wish to say?" the queen said, pointing at him.

The entire hall turned their eyes on Kurodan. Toradin, sitting next to him, slunk lower in his chair as if trying to avoid feeling guilty by association. Kurodan rose, slightly nervous at seeing all the faces staring blankly at him. Then he regained his composure.

"Your highness," he began, "my father served this city in the Holy Order during the Great War. He gave his life defending this—"

But the queen interrupted him, scolding, "While I am grateful for you father's service and sacrifice, do not for one second stand there thinking you can sway the minds of me and the council because your father did the duty he pledged and swore to uphold."

Kurodan looked into the queen's eyes again, witnessing her cold, harsh stare and felt frozen where he stood.

"Your highness, I merely do not believe that all the vampires have been killed. They are just as cunning as the orcs and the chances of one or a few surviving ..." he trailed off.

"What is your name, paladin?" the queen asked.

"Kurodan, your highness."

"Well, Kurodan, did you fight in the Great War?" she asked.

"No, your highness, but my father—"

"Yes, we heard you," she interrupted again "Your father did, but did you?"

"No, your highness."

"Ah, I see. Well then, let me make this perfectly clear for you and everyone else. You did not fight in the Great War, nor the final battle of it. I was there, as were some members of the Holy Order that are sitting here this day. I was there during the charge that day, Kurodan, and I will not have you spreading rumors and fear about something you know truly little about!"

She turned to Maldin, "While you may be able to throw your war trophies around to intimidate the council, Maldin, that holds little bearing with me. I know the enemies we face just as well as you do because I have faced them in battle just as you have."

The silence grew again. The queen was now standing, looking as if thunderbolts would spark from her eyes and eviscerate the paladins sitting there.

"Your highness, please forgive him," Maldin pled. "He is young and full of emotion. He merely wants the chance to serve you and the city the best he can. We all do. The best way we can do that is if we seek out our enemies and destroy them."

"Enough," the queen shouted. "I will reconvene this meeting at another time once I have made my decision. Dismissed."

With that everyone rose, bowed, and then turned to exit the great hall. Kurodan could not hide the look of shame on his face as he walked out.

Gleed approached him, placing his hand on Kurodan's shoulder. "The queen has the gaze of a witch, the tongue of a serpent, and the will of a statue. She is not to be trifled with. Know that her intentions are with the peoples' benefit in mind. Rule number one of politics, young paladin: Never take anything too personally."

Chapter VI:
Rank and File

Kurodan spent the next few days with the common army inside Mil'Thuras. Maldin had decided that it would be best to aid in any way they could while they waited for the queen's decision.

The quality of leadership among the army varied, as did the welcome received by the paladins. Some among the ranks were eager to learn as much as their minds would allow from the paladins, looking hungrily for their knowledge.

Kurodan found himself pleased to work alongside these soldiers. They were easy to communicate with and quickly tried to apply what they had learned in practice. When he could see his work bear fruit in the soldiers, Kurodan felt amply rewarded.

Yet others in the army were not so humble or eager to learn. Gleed made it very clear, after the queen's meeting, that the paladins were unwelcome among some of the soldiers. "Rank, authority, glory, and arrogance cloud the minds of many," he noted.

These soldiers believed that the paladins were no more than regular soldiers who had been placed high up on a pedestal but were not special or outstanding in any form. This resulted in Kurodan receiving the cold shoulder from more than a few, especially when some of the veterans of actual battles had found out that he was unblooded.

Kurodan could sympathize with them in some regard. *Why should a seasoned veteran be forced instruction from someone who had yet to test himself in real battle?*

The days slowly began to drag into one week, and then two. Maldin was ruthless and unwavering in his training regime for both students and instructors. Every day was spent going over the three levels of warfare: strategic, operational, and tactical. *And really*, thought Kurodan, *there were four if you counted the overarching level of politics.* The latter was why they were all in this current predicament.

After the morning lessons, they spent the rest of the day focusing specifically on the tactical level skills. These were the acts of individual soldiers and units on the actual battlefield. When Kurodan had first received lessons on war during his training, Gleed described it as "the actual fighting and dying."

While Kurodan initially put forth all his effort into this training, he quickly became bored, which eventually turned to anger.

He could see why Maldin had tried to convey to the queen and her council that the Holy Order was better suited for another task.

A real task, Kurodan thought.

He lay awake each night, not even knowing how much longer this routine would go on for. All he could think about was if the next morning would reveal the queen's decision.

Kurodan awoke groggily from a rough slumber that had not left him well rested. The morning lessons always started at daybreak. As he dragged himself out of his bed, he looked around his living quarters. The paladins had sectioned off a portion of one of the army barracks all to themselves. Such was custom among units that took comfort in taking care of their own and sometimes keeping to their own.

Maldin was pouring over maps on a table that were littered with lines, arrows, symbols, and terrain features. *I do not think I have seen him sleep once since we arrived at Mil'Thuras.* Kurodan thought.

As if reading his mind, Toradin whispered, "I don't think I have ever seen him sleep. Not once."

Kurodan grinned as he stood and stretched. "I don't think he sleeps at all. Sleep does not dare venture to a man so serious."

Toradin nodded in affirmation. As Toradin and Kurodan donned their armor, Gleed entered the barracks room. His face and armor were drenched in sweat, and the enormous spear and shield carried in each hand were menacing.

Toradin and Kurodan exchanged glances at the sight of him. Every morning Gleed would rise and practice his own personal training regime before the day had even begun for the rest of them. "This training is too mild for me," he had said in passing.

It had struck both Kurodan and Toradin, as well as the other new paladins, just how intense their seasoned comrades were. While they may have become paladins in the eyes of the queen and the others, their superiors were on a different level entirely.

"The queen wishes to convene with the council," Gleed said.

"When?" Maldin asked.

"The runner said immediately," Gleed responded.

"She has made her decision?" Kurodan stood up in excitement. Every paladin in the barracks turned and eyed him. Realizing he needed to work on separating his thoughts from words, Kurodan again felt embarrassed.

"Get everyone to the great hall at once," Maldin commanded.

"Come, let us spread the word to anyone already at the training grounds," Toradin said. Maldin walked out of the barracks while Toradin and Kurodan followed.

Gleed stopped Kurodan briefly for a moment. "A word, Kurodan."

Kurodan felt even more embarrassed and Gleed could sense it. "Kurodan, everyone here admires your will and eagerness for battle."

Kurodan could already see where the conversation was headed. "I know," he responded. "I need to control my emotions better. I sounded almost like a child just now."

Gleed chuckled. "You will become a great leader one day, Kurodan. When the tide of battle changes—and believe me, it does in an instant—that is when people will look to you for strength. Just remember war is never as you plan or envision. While our task at hand may seem dull right now, just know there will come a time when you will truly put your skills to the test. Be patient and learn."

Taken aback, Kurodan nodded. He had never heard Gleed speak so openly with anyone. With that, they both set off for the great hall. As they entered, Toradin caught up with Kurodan. "What did Gleed say to you?" he asked.

"That we, that I, need to be patient," Kurodan said.

Toradin laughed silently. "Does he realize that is the equivalent of telling a stubborn mule not to be stubborn?"

Kurodan laughed. "I do not think so." As they were entering the great hall, the council members also entered. A beautiful woman with red hair locked eyes with Toradin and smiled.

Toradin returned her smile with his own and a wink. "You need to learn how to enjoy the finer things in life, my friend," Toradin whispered.

Kurodan and Toradin made their way to their seats. "I cannot change what drives my passion and determination. It is what keeps me focused," Kurodan replied.

Then the entire hall fell silent as the queen entered. Everyone stood until she was seated on her throne. "You may be seated," she said.

Maldin had the same distant, uncaring expression on his face. The council, on the other hand, seemed all too eager to hear her majesty's words. Kurodan found himself more aligned with their emotions. *Keep your emotions in check*, he scolded himself.

"I have taken into account all concerns and information of the city's current situation. Given the current state of our enemies, it seems that there is much known and unknown. We know that the vampires were eradicated, but the orcs still remain a threat." She paused to look around the room, and then continued.

"It is thought that whatever remnants of their warbands are left have taken shelter on Mount Ruin, the old vampire stronghold. We do not know their exact strength in numbers, or their level of organization. It is believed that more orcs may still be in the Barren Lands."

Some of the council members nodded, showing their agreement with their queen. She ignored their affirmations, "We have heard rumor that Korgath has, or rather would be, the most likely successor as their leader. He is not to be taken lightly in the slightest. I ..." the queen trailed off.

An older man with long brown hair and a beard, dressed in a deep blue robe, entered the hall. His head was balding on top, and his stern eyebrows overshadowed his piercing brown eyes. His face showed severe seriousness and at the same time a lack of concern for anyone in the hall.

Some of the council members and paladins tensed as he entered further into the hall and stepped into the center between both great tables. The strange man paid them no attention.

The queen's face soured into a frown. "So nice of you to join us, Andazar,"

"I come bearing news of the very matters you speak of, Delarona," he said.

One of the council members stood, red in the face. "You interrupt this matter at hand, late no less, and then proceed to disrespect the queen in her own hall? Wizard or not, you will show some respect!" he shouted.

Kurodan and the other new paladins were intrigued by this turn of events. Kurodan had never seen a wizard, let alone attended the same meeting as one.

Turning to the council member, the man—*no, the wizard*, Kurodan thought—in the center of the hall rolled his eyes. "Silence your tongue before I silence it for you," he said and glared.

The queen squirmed slightly in her throne. "Andazar, you will not make a mockery of this hall. What is this news you came here to bring me?"

The wizard turned his attention back to the queen.

"My sources have conveyed to me that Korgath has consolidated the remaining orc warbands on Mount Ruin. He is indeed their new warlord. The neighboring villages nearest the mountain, have reported sightings of orc movement and—"

The same man on the council who had shouted at the wizard interrupted, "You came here to tell us exactly what the queen has already spoken?"

The wizard slowly moved towards the man who was still seated, glaring at him again. The man stood as if to hurl another insult, but the wizard threw up his hand. The man was flung backwards over his chair, as if pushed by some invisible force.

Kurodan and Toradin exchanged glances trying to contain their astonishment.

"Enough! What else have you come here to say, Andazar?" the queen scolded.

The man on the floor slowly collected himself while Andazar kept his gaze on him. "That it is only a matter of time before the orcs begin to raid and plunder around the mountain. With each attack, they will grow increasingly dangerous. Their need for vengeance will only escalate after their defeat in the Great War."

"How do you know they will attack, and what makes you certain it will be so soon?" the queen asked.

"The orcs are bred for conflict. It is all they have ever known and all they care for. They are cunning and treacherous creatures. The longer they wait, the more time we have to bolster our defenses and hurt their chances," Andazar said, still glaring at the councilman.

"Hurt their chances at what?" Maldin asked.

Andazar turned to address him. "That, I am still unaware of. My sources have not been able to accurately define what their main intentions are, but they have remained dormant long enough."

"Who are your sources?" Maldin asked.

The wizard laughed.

"Spies, cutthroats, bandits, rogues, the social elite. Pick one," a councilwoman said.

"Well, wizard, which is it?" Maldin pressed. Kurodan looked from the wizard to the queen. She had not intervened, and she seemed just as curious to hear Andazar's response as everyone else.

"Which of my sources does not concern you, just that you know they are reliable." Andazar replied.

"They concern me, Andazar, and you will answer," the queen demanded.

The wizard sighed as if this entire meeting was a nuisance rather than the queen and the council deciding the future fate of the kingdom.

Just as he was about to answer, a royal guard came bursting forth through the main doors. People on both sides of the hall rose to their feet. Kurodan noticed Maldin and Gleed immediately put their hands on their weapons as they stood.

"What is the meaning of this?" the queen shouted.

"My apologies, your majesty," the guard said bowing. He was out of breath and clearly looked concerned. Holding a note above his head, he continued, "I have news from a runner, from the town of Bursben."

The wizard quickly walked over to the guard, snatched the note from his hand and began reading intently. The guard seemed stunned, and the council members erupted in protest.

"Silence," the queen screamed, yet Andazar simply kept reading. Her face had now melted into a hideous scowl. "Andazar, since you have already read the news, would you care to share with us what the letter says?" She looked as if she were about to order the entire hall to be executed from all the frustration.

Andazar finished the letter and handed it to the queen. "It is as I predicted. The town of Bursben has suffered from an orc raiding party, and it appears they may have taken captives."

Hushed whispers fell across the hall as the queen furiously snatched the letter out of his hand. Kurodan and Toradin looked at each other but said nothing. Their faces had quickly turned from excitement and amusement at the wizard, to completely grim. Maldin motioned to Gleed, who then quickly left the hall with hardly anyone noticing.

"Why would they take captives?" one of the councilmen asked. "Is their purpose to use them for ransom?"

"Possibly, but we must find out for certain," Andazar replied. "I advise that we send a contingent force. Not an army large enough for full-scale war, but a detachment that is small enough for swift movement and gathering intelligence."

The queen looked around the hall. "Maldin, gather what men you think would best serve this mission. I want you and some of your best men to remain behind in case the orcs decide for all-out war. I want the ones departing briefed, supplied, and ready to take leave within the hour."

"As you wish, your majesty," Maldin said, bowing.

"Council, I want you to quell any rumors that our people are still at war. Control our peoples' perspective. The orcs are still a threat but reassure our people that we are carrying out a plan. Our people will not go unprotected, and the orcs will not go unpunished."

All the council members bowed.

"Dismissed." The queen said.

The great hall erupted into a frenzy of chatter, people rushing around, while Andazar remained still in the center. He and the queen had locked eyes.

Kurodan stood awkwardly and pushed his way through the crowd of people. Toradin followed and grabbed his shoulder.

"This is the last way I envisioned this meeting going," Toradin said. Kurodan simply grinned.

Chapter VII: Going to Battle

The paladins followed Maldin out of the great hall at a brisk pace. Maldin had not spoken a word since the queen dismissed the council. When they finally reached the barracks, soldiers were running around like headless chickens as Gleed barked orders.

"Gleed," Maldin shouted.

Gleed dropped what he was doing and walked over to them. "When do we leave?" he asked.

"We are not going anywhere. The queen has demanded I stay with some of the best, which includes you." He paused and looked back at Kurodan and the other paladins. "They are to leave within the hour."

Kurodan's blood ran cold, and his heart seemed to beat irregularly.

"We need to coordinate with the queen's soldiers who will be going," Maldin continued. "They are going to make up the bulk of the force."

"Who will we send that's blooded?" Gleed asked.

"We will send Aetholas along with them."

"Very well," Gleed said, turning to face Kurodan and the others. "Gather your equipment and meet me at the stables."

Gleed and Maldin walked back to the soldiers who were busy carrying food, equipment, and weapons, to their respective owners, leaving Kurodan and the others stunned.

"Leave us," the queen said. The remaining guards in the hall quickly found the nearest exit and shut the doors behind them. "What are we going to do? If we send them after the orcs, we will risk—"

Andazar raised his hand cutting her off. There was a long awkward silence between them. After what seemed far too long, he spoke in a hushed tone, as if someone might still be in the room with them. "I will accompany the contingent force," he said.

The queen raised an eyebrow in skepticism. "What will that accomplish? You joining the mission will surely raise some suspicion, and how is it that you will lead them astray? They will eventually make battle with the orcs unless they hide within the mountain, and even then—"

Andazar raised his hand once more. "Your highness," he began, but his tone was of one speaking to a child. "Firstly, I care not whether suspicion is raised on my behalf. I am a wizard. Nobody knows my business, not even the other wizards. Secondly, I will not lead them astray. That would be too obvious."

"So, you are going to make sure that the orcs are finally eradicated? If we are to go back on our pact and attempt to finish them … Should we not send a much larger force?"

Andazar sighed. "No and no."

The queen's face grew dark with rage. "Speak plainly. Andazar. I have no use for your antics and dramas," she said through gritted teeth.

"I will lead them directly to the orcs."

Her face darkened further. Then she whispered, "If we do this … It must be carried out with great subtlety. You must be absolutely certain none discover what we have done."

Andazar smiled. "Subtlety is my specialty. I would advise right before our departure you give notice that the contingency force is to be even smaller. Have your main focus still be on protecting Mil'Thuras. This mission, after all, is not to make battle with the orcs but to find out what is happening."

"And what, exactly, is happening?" she asked, but Andazar turned and made for the doors. She called, "Andazar."

The wizard stopped and turned slightly. They met each other's gaze. "Fear not my queen, I will resolve this little dilemma. You must trust me, after all, that trust is what made you queen did it not?" Andazar said.

The queen's face turned pale, and her hand reached out to grab part of the throne to brace herself. The wizard left without another word.

Kurodan and Toradin wove their way through the soldiers and townspeople. Each of them had dressed in full armor and weapons, with saddlebags slung over their shoulders. When they neared the front of the stables, Toradin gripped Kurodan by the shoulder and pulled him backwards, as three mounted soldiers came galloping out.

"Watch it," Toradin shouted. But the mounted soldiers were already gone.

Kurodan and Toradin entered the stables. Only a few

horses remained inside and unsaddled. The horses were nervous with excitement, whining, stomping their hooves, and snorting.

"Easy now," Kurodan whispered, reaching his hand out to gently rub the horse's forehead.

"Have you ever been to Bursben?" asked Toradin, as he hefted a saddle onto a horse's back.

"No, I have never been that close to Mount Ruin."

"The closest I have ever been is Worhagen. Although, I do not remember much as I was so young," Toradin said.

Kurodan paused for a moment to look up. "What do you remember?"

Toradin continued to saddle his equipment. "I remember having to flee from town to town, making our way here. My parents never let me out of arms' reach the entire journey. I never witnessed any vampires, but I do remember seeing orcs for the first time."

He knew Toradin had seen more of the world than he had. Kurodan grew up with a much more sheltered life, already having Mil'Thuras as his home.

"You had mentioned witnessing orcs before, I did not realize it was when you were so young. What else do you remember?"

Toradin cinched one of the saddle straps tight. "No longer am I the scared little child fleeing. I would, however, be a liar if I said those memories no longer haunt me. Make no mistake, brother, the orcs are not to be taken lightly. The queen is right in her concern of their threat."

Kurodan finished saddling his horse and threw his leg up over the saddle, grabbing the reins. "Make no mistake, brother, I have prepared for this moment my entire life."

Chapter VIII: The Warning

Maldin and Gleed stood waiting in the courtyard behind the front gate. Fifty soldiers of the queen's army sat saddled on their horses, waiting for the order to ride out. Kurodan, Toradin, Horad, Lehm, and Bardu pushed their horses through the formation. Aetholas stood at the front, clad in his own battle regalia. Kurodan and the others had had very little interaction with Aetholas. Kurodan had only observed him in passing while going through his training. Aetholas was a shorter man than some, but broad and athletic. He was one of the best horsemen Kurodan had ever witnessed. Kurodan hoped to learn as much as he could from the veteran warrior.

Aetholas eyed each of the new paladins warily and gave a slight nod. After throwing the reins up over his horse, he put on his helmet and effortlessly mounted into his saddle.

The sound of hooves clacked on the courtyard as loved ones and family bobbed and weaved about. Wives held out children for one last kiss or embrace, others passed flowers or other items and trinkets of affection. Kurodan paused, searching to find his own mother in the sea of people and animals.

His concentration was broken as the chapel bell rang loud and clear. All voices quieted to hushed whispers. The clergy and councilmembers filed into the courtyard followed by the queen herself.

Toradin reached over and nudged Kurodan, nodding his head in the direction of the stables. Andazar was sitting bareback atop a magnificent brown steed.

The horse stood a head taller than the finest horses the men had. Maldin and Gleed had noticed this new addition and whispered to one another.

"Hear ye, hear ye!" one of the councilmen cried out. All the townspeople huddled backwards, giving the soldiers more space for the queen and her elite. The council and clergy spread apart, creating a wide berth for the queen to approach. As she moved to address the crowd, the townsfolk all simultaneously dropped to one knee.

"I, Queen Valanore, hereby send forth these soldiers to the city of Bursben. Their mission is to assess the rumored orc sightings in that region and report back any findings at once. Due to the nature of this mission, I also command that the force be lessened in size by half the original number," she announced.

Hushed voices spread across the courtyard. Maldin and a captain of the queen's army both began to walk across the courtyard to address the matter. Kurodan looked back over to where Andazar sat on his horse. The wizard paid absolutely no attention to this spectacle. Kurodan could not tell if his face was pained with boredom, or deep in thought about some distant thing.

The queen ignored Maldin and the captain's

approach and continued. "This mission is to gather information regarding these concerns, not to conduct open battle. The swiftness of this matter is the ultimate concern."

"My queen," the captain began.

"Captain Bravmond," she replied.

"I urge you to reconsider this decision. We do not have an accurate representation of the orcs' numbers, or their whereabouts. If the force were to come under ambush ..." he trailed off.

"If the orcs mount an attack, these men will not return, my queen," Maldin said bluntly.

But the queen turned her attention back to the crowd. "You have your orders, now carry them out. I grant these soldiers the Queen's Rite of Passage; may you hold your oaths fulfilled."

Ignoring both men's concerns, she turned and made her way back across the courtyard, with the council members and clergy following ensuite. One man who had been trailing the queen's elite turned and approached the soldiers.

Kurodan watched as this man, dressed as priest, tried to converse with some of the soldiers, but they purposely avoided his attempts, treating him as if he were a beggar or leper.

The man was older with balding gray hair on top of his head. His long scraggly beard tried to hide his wrinkled, sun-bleached face. His brown robes were worn and ragged, the bottom hem covered in dirt. One hand clutched the book of Holy Works.

"Beware," said the priest. The soldiers acted as if he was not there, but the priest made certain that he would be heard.

"You must all heed my warning. The gods' warning!" the priest cried.

The man's eyes locked with Kurodan's.

Kurodan turned his head away quickly to avoid further attention from the man.

The priest pushed his way into the soldier's ranks, stumbling between the nervous horses.

"Get out of the way," one of the soldiers shouted. But the priest was now in turn ignoring them. Kurodan could no longer avoid the confrontation as the priest grabbed his horse's reins.

"Clergyman, you must move away–" Kurodan started.

"Hear my words, paladin," the priest said. His face was stern, but his voice was shaky and worried. "Your light, it is strong. Listen to me. You must know what perils lie ahead."

"You know about the orcs?" Kurodan asked.

"Orcs? No, orcs will be the least of your worries for you are a warrior of the light. It is your soul that is in question," the priest said.

"My soul?" Kurodan's face did not hide his confusion.

"The man is crazy," a nearby solder said. "Do not entertain his madness."

The priest turned sharply to the soldier who had hurled the insult. "Madness? My madness is the faith of the gods!" The priest turned back to Kurodan. "Your soul, holy warrior, will fall if you do not heed me."

"How?" Kurodan said.

The priest turned and nodded towards the front of the formation. "You depart with a devil."

"A devil? Who?" From atop his horse, Kurodan looked around as the priest motioned again.

Toradin leaned close from his horse. "I think he is talking about Andazar," he whispered.

The priest's eyes grew wide. "Yes, paladin. He has

gone by many names, that being one of them. If you gamble your futures with him, your soul will surely be lost."

"Why would the wizard be a threat to us?" Toradin asked, now interested in the conversation.

"The wizard…" the priest began and almost stopped. His eyes shifted from Andazar back to Kurodan and Toradin. A grim dread beset his face. He whispered now, "The wizard has walked in places no sane mortal man would dare venture. He has seen and done things that would taint even the most damned of souls. His powers and purpose are not of this world."

"Why would the queen trust Andazar if he was such a danger? Why would he be considered an ally?" Kurodan asked.

The priest let out a deep sigh as if his efforts were futile. "There are ancient beings that roam this world but are not of it. Do you understand?"

"No," Kurodan said shaking his head.

"Damn you! Listen," the priest raised his voice and his hands. "The wizard is not of this world and the other ancient beings that are not of this world share the same purpose."

"Spit it out, old man, what is the wizard's purpose?" Kurodan now raised his voice.

The priest now shook his head. "Theirs is power. It always has been and always will be. Their power allows them to play games with mortal men in pursuit of more power. Be wary and do not let yourselves become a pawn in their games. Cling to your souls, for if you do not, doom and destruction will seize you up in the jaws of hell."

The priest turned and walked away, as if his job was done and there was nothing further to speak. But he was stopped by a rider.

Andazar sat atop his horse grinning down at the priest, who now froze. "Priest, you truly do not know what you speak of," he said.

The priest appeared frozen, as if he could not decide whether to cower from the wizard or flee. Instead, he let out a long breath and stood his ground.

"I know all too well what I convey, serpent, for I am a holy messenger of the gods themselves!" the priest said, holding up his book as if he was fending off an evil apparition.

Andazar chuckled. "Now I remember you. I thought you looked familiar, but most of you little holy men do look alike."

The priest scowled. "You and I both know each other. We both know the war being waged that these men are blind to. You. Will. Not. Win."

The soldiers had turned in their saddles and many of the townspeople had inched their way closer, their curiosity growing. The two now had every eye of the crowd on them.

"And what war might that be? If my memory serves right, your conscience and character have been in question for some time. You were stripped of your title from the High Priest Council, no? In fact, it is my understanding that you hold no actual authority or divinity in the matters you speak of. Now you are merely a stray dog, wandering and begging for scraps. You cling to your former status by continued accusations of others," Andazar said.

"My accusations are not accusations at all. They are insights that the gods have bestowed unto me, to spread their warnings and save this world and its people from the devils that cloak themselves under the guise of men."

"Mathius, come now. We both know your accusations of myself, and many others, including the queen, have no merit whatsoever. It is a wonder that the queen has not publicly executed you by now, with how bold you have become," Andazar said, adding "At this point, it would be out of mercy that she put you down."

The jostling soldiers and citizens had quieted during this conversation. No one wanted to interrupt, trying to gather what it was these two were debating. *Most people have not heard a wizard speak, let alone this much*, Kurodan thought.

The priest stepped closer to the war steed that towered over him and the rider that now had to stare straight down to keep eye contact.

"I know what you are!" he screamed. Some of the other clergy members now approached Mathius to try and pull him away, but he threw them off.

"You will not win, I will not allow it," Mathius said with increasing fervor. Veins bulged in his forehead and neck, spit mottled his beard, and his eyes grew wide. His free hand pounded the air in a fist, while the other thrust forwards the book. He turned himself in a circle making eye contact with anyone that would dare glance in his direction.

"Heed me. This is no man, but a devil dressed as one. He will damn you. Damn you all!" Mathius screamed.

"Enough!" a clergyman shouted, and another tackled Mathius to the ground. It took three men to subdue the priest and drag him away. Andazar gently nudged his horse and cantered back to the front of the formation without saying another word.

"What in the gods' name just happened?" Toradin asked.

"Look," Kurodan whispered.

Andazar was laughing aloud to himself, amused and content at the sight of the priest having been forcefully removed.

He looked like a smug ruler who had just ordered the removal of some petty jester from his own courtroom.

Kurodan steered his horse into the rank and file. His eyes drifted about the men's faces who were around him. No one had made a sound after the priest had been dragged away.

A nervousness hung in the air. Each man appeared lost in his own thoughts of going forth into the unknown. Kurodan brought his gaze to the front, focusing on the enormous gate that now stood in between him and the outside world.

His mind tormented him, reeling with excitement, anger, and fear. His throat grew tight as did his grip on the reins. Sweat began to bead his forehead.

"Open the gate!" came a shout from high on the wall. The horses stirred and jerked their heads as the massive gate rumbled open, deafening and daunting.

"Forward," came the muted command. Kurodan gave a small kick of his heels to the horse, and they began to move.

"Wait," a cry came from behind the men. It was the plea of a woman.

Such was the brutal nature of war. The necessity to steel one's heart against all the sorrow and misery, Kurodan thought without looking back.

"Wait, Kurodan!" came the cry again. Kurodan spun in his saddle, trying to recognize the voice. He turned his horse from the formation to see his mother sprinting towards him.

She was carrying something. Toradin broke from the formation to see the commotion. Soldiers turned in their own saddles and struggled to catch glimpses of Kurodan as they continued forward.

Kurodan halted his horse as his mother had finally reached him, gasping for air. They locked eyes with one another and then Kurodan's eyes fell on the item she gripped tightly.

He was stunned. His mother fought back tears as she saw him in full paladin armor, mounted on his horse. As she fought to regain her composure, her face turned almost to stone. She raised the holy book up to her son.

Kurodan gripped the chain tightly and held the book at eye level, transfixed. "How?" he asked.

"I had it preserved," she said. "He would be so proud of you, son."

Kurodan stared at the name signed on the corner of the book's cover. Halaford. He had not seen his father's name in many years. He now fought back his own tears as his mother's face broke into a small smile.

"I hope I have made you proud," he whispered.

His mother reached up, clasped his hand, and kissed it gently.

"You have, son. Your father's faith has never led me astray. Let it give you strength. Now go. Go, and if you return, may you be still a warrior of the light."

Chapter IX:
The Plains

The soldiers all rode in silence as Mil'Thuras grew smaller and smaller behind them. The world around them opened up into the great plains.

Vast rolling hills of golden-brown wheat and grass seemed to have no end in sight. The wind rustled and gently swept across the landscape, gently disturbing it. The men watched from their horses as the grasses slowly rolled up and across the hills, almost guiding them through some golden shoreline.

The sun slowly crept along the edge of the sky, and their shadows grew longer. Finally, someone spoke. It was a soldier further back in the ranks.

"I still do not understand why the queen would cut our forces in half just before our departure," he said. The voice was soft, but the words were uttered with concern.

"We are just going as a scouting party, nothing more. With any luck, the orcs will have moved back into the mountains by the time we arrive," another spoke.

A third chimed in, "Luck be damned, the city of Raokenburg will send a detachment of troops to meet us. That way the orcs won't stand a chance."

Kurodan noticed a slight shift in everyone's body language as the murmuring started. Some men ignored the conversation, appearing stalwart in their silence or simply not caring. But others eagerly began to complain about their current circumstances. Toradin turned his head to see the soldiers talking.

"Why doesn't Raokenburg just send a larger detachment themselves instead of calling us to go scout for the orcs? They are at least a full day's ride ahead of us if not further," a fourth added.

"With their help we will be able to drive any orc raiding parties back," the third interjected again.

Toradin slowed his horse at this notion. "Do not be so assured in victory, for we have only just begun our journey."

The men conversing all stared at him as they continued to ride along.

"You believe this to be a folly mission, paladin?" asked the first.

"No," Toradin replied.

"Then what makes you so sure we wouldn't be able to drive the orcs back if need be?" asked the second.

Toradin strained his neck to look the men in their faces, but it was Kurodan who spoke this time. "The orcs are not mindless beasts as you men know all too well. They are cunning and deserve your respect as a worthy foe," he said.

The men began to chuckle at this. "The unblooded believes he knows what the orcs are capable of, but he hasn't even faced one in battle," the third said loudly. This cultivated heartier laughs from many of the surrounding men who were now listening.

"You would be wise to listen to the paladin, unblooded or not," Andazar said coldly. He rode his horse on the outside of the formation. Towering over everyone, he cast an imposing shadow from atop his saddle. The men fell quiet at the wizard's remark.

Kurodan and the wizard exchanged glances. Andazar's stare was menacing, a scowl etched onto his face. Kurodan merely nodded slightly and then faced forward again.

The wizard grunted as he kicked the large steed into a trot. Once Andazar was more than a few horses ahead another of the men whispered, "No one knows why he is here either."

"I am here to make sure the queen's orders are carried out to the letter, soldier!" Andazar shouted from his horse so everyone could hear.

The soldier looked shocked that this wizard had heard his hushed voice. Kurodan grinned slightly as the wizard made his way to the front.

The sun had fallen behind the sky, bringing the night. The weather had held so far, the wind only a gentle and cool breeze. The men halted their formation and began to set up camp.

Any kind of cover was welcomed as the plains were open and vast, so the men gathered around some larger rocks and two small boulders off the trail.

As Kurodan unsaddled his horse, he saw Andazar ride past the men. Captain Feore approached the wizard on foot. Andazar seemed to be doing most of the speaking and pointed further up the trail.

"I wonder what they are talking about?" Toradin whispered. Before Kurodan could reply, Andazar turned his mighty horse and rode off. Feore paused for a second as he caught the two paladins staring at him.

"Gather round, men," he said.

Feore removed his helmet from his head. His hair and beard were well kept as was his armor. His status clearly showed he was a cut above the other men, but he never seemed to let it cloud his judgement. The captain displayed confidence, and none had questioned his competence on or off the battlefield.

Someone had already started a small fire. The men gathered, staring blankly into the dancing shallow flames that cast shadows against the rocks.

"Andazar has agreed to ride further ahead in hopes of finding reinforcements from Raokenburg," Feore said. No one spoke. The mistrust of the wizard was written on everyone's faces, but no one wanted to be the first to speak their mind.

"Did the wizard say how far he would ride, or if he would return?" Aetholas asked.

"Andazar plans to make it to the crossing by sunrise," Feore replied. Some of the men murmured at this.

"If the wizard can make the ride that quickly, why send us at all? Why not just have the wizard scout Bursben and then return with whatever news he finds?" one of the men asked. It was the same man who had chided Kurodan and Toradin for being unblooded.

"If the orcs are truly there, we will have to make a stand. Andazar will be able to make the ride back to Mil'Thuras to notify the queen to send more troops," Feore said.

The same man scoffed. "So, we will be the first to die waiting for the queen to send more men?" he said. For a brief instant all that could be heard was the quiet crackling of the fire.

"It is our duty to fight the enemies of Mil'Thuras," Feore said. "Every man here has taken their oaths. If you do not wish to see yours fulfilled, then I suggest riding back home, Halthrow."

The man withdrew himself and sat on one of the smaller rocks. "Let us hope that Raokenburg can spare the men," Aetholas said.

"It matters not. If the orcs are truly still there, we can drive them back into the mountains. They are orcs. We are men of Mil'Thuras! I suggest you all start acting like it," Feore spoke loudly. "Get a watch going. Halthrow, you are first."

He pointed at the man sitting on the rock. The rest all turned to set up camp and their beds for the night.

Aetholas motioned the unblooded paladins closer with his head. They followed him a short distance away from the fire and out of earshot.

"Listen to me carefully. We will not see any orcs tonight," Aetholas told them. "They would not risk being caught out in the open on the plains. When we get to Bursben, there is a high chance that the orcs will have retreated to the mountains."

Kurodan felt his heart sink slightly. But Aetholas continued, "That does not mean any of you will become complacent. Is that understood?" Each of them nodded.

"The orcs are crafty; they do not seek a fair fight. Remember this," Aetholas warned. "If there is fresh sign of them, they will have seen us before we see them."

Then he dismissed them, and they made their way back to the camp and laid out their sleeping blankets. Each man quietly tended to his own equipment. The camp had three fires now as the men had spread out.

Kurodan sat quietly chewing on a piece of meat while staring at the fire. "Do you really think the orcs will have fled to the mountains already?" he asked.

Toradin did not move or even open his eyes. "Get some rest. You will need it if the orcs are still there," he said.

Kurodan chuckled but did not lie down. Instead, he sat watching the fire well into the night until slumber finally found him.

Kurodan awoke to the sound of men packing up camp. The sun had not risen yet, and the ground was cold and damp from the morning dew. Kurodan looked around to see where Toradin was but could not see him among all the commotion. He hurriedly rolled up his blanket and began to saddle his horse.

Their journey across the plains brought many scenes of beautiful landscape but also boredom. The ride was long but not arduous. Many of the men simply sat atop their horse, lost in thought or numbness. Some passed the time talking of home or distant memories.

Others regaled each other of battles and hardships long passed. Some spoke of friends lost, enemies slain, and victories celebrated. Kurodan listened to these men and caught himself daydreaming of his father, dropping his hand onto the book his mother had given him. His mind wandered through these imaginary but very vivid, hallucinations.

"Those orcs, damn them. They came and we held, we did. Not one man faltered in the wall that day!"

"Aye, we drove those heathens back. Had them running all the way to the Barren Lands."

"I lost count of how many orcs I killed that day."

"Aye, that was a glorious day, though I wish Captain Shaulders could have lived to see our victory."

"Aye. He gave his life that day spurring the hearts of his men in battle. He was a real leader, he was." The men quieted at this memory and Kurodan grew grim.

With all the memories of dreaming about his father slaying orcs, vampires, and beasts alike, he now remembered the nightmares that haunted him as a young boy. The dreams that left him jolting up in the middle of the night, screaming out, crying and covered in sweat.

No one had ever told Kurodan how exactly his father was killed. No one could even look Kurodan in the eyes when he asked. It was a dark cloud of pain and agony that followed him around, since he was ten years of age. Ever since that horrible day they had carried his father's body home after the final battle of the Great War.

Kurodan fought back a seething rage that almost consumed him. His hand gripped the book like the maw of a bear clutching its kill, and he shut his eyes. In his mind, he watched as paladin and soldier alike carried his father's body in a procession. His father still bore his armor but was concealed by a pure white cloth, draped over him.

He had wanted to run up and rip the white sheet from his father, to witness what had become of him. He had wanted—still wanted—answers.

What beast had killed him? How? Was it by sheer numbers? Kurodan could not stop the questions from rushing back into his mind. *Was it the unlucky chance of death that claimed him with a random arrow, flying only to find the right mark? Had he fought on as he died? Or was he killed outright? Who had been there with him, or had he perished alone?*

Kurodan's rage at not knowing never went away. Not entirely. It was always brooding, simmering on the edge.

In times of hardship during his training, Kurodan had let it fuel him. He could summon it like conjuring some great and terrible magic, turning his heart black and dead.

But on days like today he had to let it wash over him. He simply breathed until it passed, then opened his eyes and focused on the plains once more.

Toradin was eyeing him with some concern. "You all right, brother?"

"Aye, just weary from too little sleep."

"Aye, calming one's own mind can be the hardest mystery to solve."

As they rode on, Mount Ruin loomed up into the sky. The black mountain brought forth a beacon of menacing beauty and discomfort.

Chapter X:
The Wizard

The men settled into their routines and rituals of setting up camp for the fourth night. Most of them were eager to get some sleep before the next day's ride. The men spoke in hushed tones and seemed to listen more intently to their surroundings.

Fires were not permitted on this night and anymore to come. The watch was taken more seriously, while still a way from Bursben, the nerves began to tighten as they drew closer.

Some of the men had taken to discussing Andazar and just how little was known about the wizard. "How do we even know he is out doing what he claims he is? Wizards have always been known to have their own agendas," one said.

"Aye, have any of us ever truly come to know the wizard?" a reply came.

"How can one know a wizard? Their magic and being are so foreign to us mortals," a third spoke.

"Aye, I know the wizard," Regalt said. "He saved

my life." The men turned in surprise and one of them choked on a drink of water.

"Saved you? When?" asked Kurodan.

"During the Great War," Regalt replied.

"In the final battle?" someone interrupted.

"No ... before."

"Before? I have not heard anyone speak of knowing Andazar during the Great War. Toradin said.

"Aye, I did," Regalt sighed.

"So, you trust the wizard's judgement then?" Bardu asked.

"No." Regalt paused to see who was still listening. "I would not trust that being if he were to save me all over again."

Regalt was a broad man with great stature, but he was aged some. He was one of the most battle-hardened men that accompanied their party, having once been a member of the Iron Hooves. The Iron Hooves had been disbanded and its members distributed into Mil'Thuras's army after the Great War.

Kurodan had never understood the reasons or politics that went into making such a decision. They had led some of the most daring and heroic cavalry charges ever heard of, to the point of almost being suicidal, it was said.

Some of the men were too tired to listen or did not care to hear any more of the mysterious wizard who had accompanied them only to abandon them it seemed.

For Kurodan, Toradin, and others who knew little to nothing of wizards, they listened intently, as did a few soldiers.

"Well, out with it, Regalt! If he would go on saving you, why do you not trust him?" a man asked.

"He is ... strange," Regalt said quietly.

"Strange? He is a wizard! Of course, he is strange,

but strange how?" Bardu said.

"He does not abide by the laws of mortal men," Regalt replied.

"Nor do any magical creatures, neither wizard nor beast," Lehm said.

"Aye, but he makes his own laws and does not care for the world of men. He saved me and the other survivors merely out of convenience it seemed," Regalt said, shifting his body uncomfortably.

Aetholas walked over to the men and sat down. "Survivors? Tell us. I wish to know more about this wizard." More of the men approached now, curious about what Regalt would say.

"It was shortly after holding the defenses at Raokenburg. The vampires had launched an assault on their walls. We held for three days and three nights. Purging the demons back to hell. We had a few paladins with us to even the odds," Regalt stared at Kurodan and the other unblooded with his one good eye. A black patch covered the other.

"You speak of the famous Siege of Raokenburg?" Horad asked.

"Aye, they killed many men, but we held, nonetheless. On that fourth dawn we knew we had won. There were too few of them left to continue their siege on the fourth night. We wanted to end it once and for all, to be certain they would not return. I led a counterattack to hunt the beasts down."

"That morning, at daybreak, fifteen of us rode out the front gate chasing them down. They were crafty even in the daylight. They were prepared. They fled from hidesight to hidesight, only trying to expose themselves to direct sunlight for brief moments. Too long a time in the sunlight would have finished the job for us."

"Only fifteen of you?" Bardu asked in surprise.

"Aye, we could only count four, maybe five of the beasts left. More had retreated already. We rode hard and ran them down where we could. We managed to catch two out in the open. Their movements and power drained in the daylight. We decapitated their heads from their bodies and burned them to ash."

"Is that how best to kill them?" Kurodan asked.

"Aye, unless you have magic of your own. Again and again in the Great War that was the best way I saw it done. Cut off their heads and set fire to them until there is nothing left but ash."

"So how did Andazar save you if you rode the vampires down?" Horad asked.

Regalt paused and closed his good eye, as if remembering some terrible dream. "We grew foolish in our pursuit and bloodlust. We wanted revenge. The remaining three managed to flee. We rode after them, heading northwest until …" he trailed off.

"The ancient forest," Aetholas whispered.

"Aye," Regalt said.

"Surely you did not follow them in there?" Toradin asked.

There was a long pause. But then Regalt continued, "We did. We thought we could trap them close to the edge of the forest with how much daylight remained. We were wrong."

Every man now listened with great care. No sane man dared enter that forest. Kurodan had only heard snippets of stories of the Ancient Forest and those had always caused him great fear. It was said those who entered that dark place would never find their way out. They would remain lost forever until whatever sort of beast or creature lurked within claimed them.

"We dismounted and tied our horses up our horses on the forest's edge. We came close to the three wretches on our hunt. At times we could smell them, hear them. We were close. They would flee and we would give chase. Some of the men began to realize how far we had distanced ourselves from our horses, from our way out. That was what the demons had wanted."

"We decided to abandon our crusade. We thought we had enough daylight to find our way back. We were so dearly wrong. That forest … It was as if it swallowed the sunlight faster than any other place. As we made our way back, darkness quickly began to fall. We should have been free of the forest already, but we could not find our way."

"Panic quickly took hold. The men grew fearful and began to argue and bicker which was the way out. We could now hear the vampires coming for us," Regalt paused again, drawing in a deep breath.

"We became the hunted …" he whispered.

"They set upon us in a frenzy, just the three. Three she-devils, witches in the night. We tried to stand and fight but stood no chance in that godforsaken place under the cover of night. We had failed. We ran madly, trying to stay together, their hideous laughter tormenting us. All sense of direction was gone, our torches barely lighting our way. My men were picked off one by one. In all my battles and brushes with death, never have I felt more fear and hopelessness than that night."

"We ran. We ran blindly in that never-ending nightmare, until we came upon him. We had thought we had placed some distance between ourselves and the three. In truth they were now toying with us, taking their time with each victim they claimed. I still hear their screams shrieking in my ears."

"We came to a small opening in the forest. There was some strange large stone with symbols and writing on it. The presence of that spot was more dreadful than any other in that forest. It seemed to be a part of an entrance into the earth, or maybe blocking an entrance— I do not know—but there, standing out in the open, he was. He had no clothes on and stood smoking that long pipe of his."

"You mean to tell me he was stark naked just standing in the middle of that forest?" one man asked.

"Aye, no sane reason on how he came to be there, or what in the gods' names he was doing. The men and I were at a loss. At first, we did not know what to make of him. He stood there, seeming to study the stone and symbols. He paid us no mind. Not even the blood curdling cries of my men being torn apart behind us caught his attention."

"What did you do next?" Aetholas said.

"I called out to him. Still, he ignored us. Some of the men thought he might be a vampire, or some lost and damned soul, trapped just as we were. None of us dared approach him too closely. One of my men called out to him once more but the bloodcurdling cry from the last who was taken drowned him out."

"I told my men to leave him, that the vampires might feast on him and buy us more time. Before my men could argue, he turned. It was as if the mention of vampires drew him from his trance."

'Is that what hunts you and your men?' he asked me.

"I told him that was what would kill him soon enough if we could not find our way. He just stood there and chuckled to himself, smoking his pipe. Not a care in the world."

"'I know the way out,' he told us.

"Some of my men almost laughed at this notion. How could some naked madman know his way through that horrible place? We began to argue even more about whether to leave him or follow him. He merely stood and watched us, saying nothing. The screaming had been silenced. They were coming for us again."

None of the men spoke or asked questions at this point. Everyone sat in silence, not knowing how this nightmare had to end. Regalt paused and took a sip of water, before continuing.

"'How can we trust you?' I asked him and his face grew into a devil's grin.

"'You can't,' he said, and with that he started walking into the forest. We were set before a crossroad. Follow this deranged being or simply accept our fate and make one last stand. So, we quickly took the devil's gamble. We followed."

"He walked with purpose, never running, always careful of where he stepped. He knew, though. He knew that place intimately. For him it seemed as if he was going for a midnight stroll in his own personal garden. We urged him to quicken his pace, —to run— but he would not. To this day I do not know what divine or evil magic he used, but he led us out of that damned hell."

"It took us all night to reach the forest's edge. The vampires followed us but slowed their pursuit. It was as if they were now cautious either because the night was drawing to an end or … because of the man who now led our party. Alas, when we broke free from the forest only eight of us made it out, not including the wizard. We were faced with mountains, and we climbed. Higher and higher we went."

"We could see the vampires leave the forest below us. The sight of us climbing spurred them, I do not know why. I think they knew their time was running short and, like us, they grew foolish in their bloodletting. We could now see the first crest of sunlight break into the sky."

Regalt paused and closed his eye. "I will never forget that feeling, a shred of hope warmed its way into my heart," he said opening his eye again.

"Soon we could climb no further for the mountain side was too steep and treacherous. He seemed to care not, as he turned and stared down the mountain, watching them climb for us. He simply puffed on his pipe and waited. Fear attacked us again. Had the imbecile only drawn us into our own undoing? Aye, he had led us out of the forest but only to be trapped on the side of a mountain, like a goat waiting for a lion to claim it."

"The wizard said nothing, and it unnerved me. Our gaze fixed upon the mountain above us, watching the sunlight drift closer and closer towards us. Lower down the mountain the vampires still climbed, shrouded in the dark."

"It was as if we were caught in the center of the universe, directly between all the heavens and all the hells. As the sun rose just above, the three were almost upon us. I could see their eyes and fangs, that's how close they were. They paused as if plotting how to take us."

"I stood next to the wizard, sword drawn, shouting at the demons daring them to fight and cursing them to hell. My men clung to their weapons and readied themselves for death."

"The three charged and he raised that pipe of his high above his head, just high enough that a ray of sunlight struck the embers. It was as if a shooting star had struck us. Light erupted, blinding, treacherous, and beautiful."

"I fell to the ground, having no conscious thought of what had just taken place. When I stood, the vampires' charred corpses lay in ruin, broken before the mountainside. My vision was altered, and I felt the warmth of blood running down my face."

"Is that how you lost your eye?" someone asked.

"Aye." Regalt said, touching the black patch that hid his left eye.

"What happened next?" Kurodan asked.

"What took place next is what truly haunts me to this day. More than the screams of my men, more than the thought of never leaving that forest. He asked me and my men what provisions we had left. At first, I thought his mind was set on how to get back to our horses or on the journey back to civilization. I was wrong."

"He had us lay out our water pouches, scraps of food, weapons and anything else we had. He crouched over them, surveying them until he found what he was looking for. He snatched up one of the small water pouches and poured the water out. One of my men protested and he grew angry at this, silencing us with a darkened scowl."

"He then carried the empty pouch down the mountain towards the corpses. My men stayed where they were, not fully trusting that the vampires were entirely dead. I followed him, sword at the ready with the same caution."

"He paid me no attention. He bent over each vampire, sticking his face right up next to theirs, looking for something."

"When he came to the third vampire, its body was the least destroyed. He knelt next to it and then looked up at me and asked me for a knife. I thought maybe he was taking a war trophy of some sort, collecting the fangs of the creature. I tossed him my skinning knife and he snatched it out of the air with great dexterity."

"He eyed the blade's edge carefully, as if to see if it was a worthy blade. It must have been because he turned his attention back to the vampire. He opened the pouch and held it underneath the vampire's neck, and with the blade in his other hand, he carefully drew its blood."

"I watched in horror as he collected the vampire's blood. I asked him in a rage, by the gods, for what purpose he would need such a poison. He did not break his concentration, not wanting to spill even the slightest drop."

"'All the Gods' creations that exist, exist for my own iniquity,' he said and then he whispered two words to himself: 'Vae vivis.'"

That same night, Kurodan stood at the edge of the camp out of earshot, having volunteered for first watch. He had volunteered not out of duty but more so because Regalt's terrible story was still in his mind.

Captain Feore walked up beside him, slowly, as to not startle him. "Well, paladin, you seem ready for the first of the night's shift," he said.

Kurodan glanced at him. "Yes, captain."

Feore leaned in closer, as if someone might be listening. "If you see anything out of the ordinary you sound the alarm, do you understand me?" he whispered. Kurodan simply nodded his head.

"If the orcs are raiding these lands there is no way of knowing how far they have traveled and in what direction. Let us hope the night goes quietly, yes?"

"I haven't seen an orc before. The men seem to all have different opinions on them," Kurodan mused.

Feore paused as if he were waiting for a question, then finally spoke, "The men all have differing experiences with orcs and battle, yes."

"What is your experience with them, captain?" Kurodan asked.

Feore did not hide the surprised look on his face.

Kurodan noticed and quickly asked, "I mean, is

there anything you can tell me about them, to help better prepare me if they are truly still out here?"

Feore let out a heavy sigh and placed his hand on Kurodan's shoulder. "I have fought in many battles, paladin. I have had the misfortune to face orcs, vampires, and even other men. Vampires are truly the most dangerous because of the powers they wield. Men from other cities and lands are predictable because they think just like we do, but orcs … orcs may not have the power of a vampire, but they have the same amount of cunning as one, if not more. The smarter ones, their leaders and warlords, are unpredictable. If we are unlucky enough to find ourselves in the middle of an orc ambush, do not rush out to meet them. Take strength in numbers and a shield wall, then fight well and fight hard." With that, Feore turned and walked back towards the camp.

The moon had graced the night with some illumination. Kurodan could see the men's camp and trail clearly. He tried to calm his nerves and slow his breathing. His mind raced with flashes and visions of battle, and orcs running wildly at them. His head swiveled at every slight noise, almost growing dizzy as he played out these scenarios over and over in his head.

He took another deep breath and looked up at the moon. It had grown colder, and the wind had picked up slightly from the previous night. Then he heard the sound of hooves racing down the trail towards them. Kurodan wrenched his sword free from his sheath.

"Rider!" he shouted. The sound of swords and shields came alive in the camp.

"How many?" Aetholas shouted.

"I count one," Kurodan said.

The men quickly spread out around the camp, facing outwards, looking for signs of a threat.

"Stay ready, men!" Feore commanded.

Kurodan squinted harder through the moonlight. The single rider was dashing towards them at a breakneck speed.

"It's Andazar! It's the wizard," Kurodan shouted. Feore and Aetholas sprinted to where Kurodan stood on watch.

"Break camp! Three men on watch!" Feore ordered. The men immediately broke into a frenzy, packing up what little provisions they had set up.

The wizard finally reached their camp, his great horse breathing and snorting heavily. The men slowed their actions to focus on what news Andazar had brought.

"It is worse than we had thought," Andazar spoke without getting off his horse. "The orcs launched an attack on Bursben. We must send one messenger back with word. The rest of us must reach the town before dawn."

"What of Raokenburg? Did they not send any men?" Feore asked.

"They did," Andazar said.

"And?" Feore asked, mounting his horse.

"Mount up!" Aetholas shouted.

Just as Kurodan turned to run for his horse he heard Andazar answer, "They were slaughtered."

Chapter XI:
Bursben

The night's ride was long and vicious. Kurodan could not tell if the pounding in his head came from their steeds' hooves or his adrenaline. The countryside flashed by them as they rode on and on. The cool breeze had grown into a cold wind that whipped at their faces. A light rain began to fall from the sky, making the ride wet and miserable.

Kurodan could see his horse begin to strain as the pace took a physical toll on all the animals. His eyes darted back and forth looking for any signs of orcs or danger. The wind and the rain made him squint hard, and seeing any fine details in their surroundings was nigh impossible.

Andazar led the frenzied group further and further. He broke free of the pack, putting more and more distance between himself and the others. The wizard held his staff high and shouted against the wind and rain.

"Onward, to me."

His horse's full stride propelled them into the unknown.

Just as Kurodan thought his horse would give out from underneath him, he saw the river crossing far off in the distance. Andazar had already reached the bridge and halted his horse.

The riders slowed to a grinding walk. The horses snorted and gasped, worn down by delirium and exhaustion.

Feore held his fist in the air and made a motion, opening his fingers. The riders spread outwards looking for any sign of threats. The rain tore down from the sky now, and they could just make out the eerie outline of the town of Bursben. Mount Ruin now towered over them, cast against the night's torment.

Andazar motioned for them to move forward as he crossed the bridge. Kurodan and Toradin looked at each other for the first time since their ride had begun. Kurodan was going to speak, but Toradin's eyes were wide, and his jaw clenched.

Aetholas drew his sword from its sheath, and every rider instinctively did the same.

"This is madness," Feore said.

"When we cross that bridge, be ready for an ambush," Aetholas yelled, nudging his horse forward.

The sound of the horses' hooves clacked against the stone bridge but were muffled by the falling rain. The river underneath them tossed as the wind howled. As they all crossed the bridge, the town's details became clearer.

Many of the houses lay in massive heaps of rubble, showing only the skeletal structure of what once was. Hacked bodies lay strewn about in the mud. Andazar stopped his horse at a tattered flag that fluttered in the middle of the road.

The flag bore the emblem of the Eagle of Raokenburg. Its teal and gold colors were soiled with blood. The flag was attached to the end of a spear that was impaled into a corpse, lying on the ground.

Feore waved one hand out to his side in a swift motion. Immediately a group of the riders dismounted, passing their reins off to other soldiers. Kurodan was trying to hand his reins to Toradin, but Toradin pushed his hand back, shaking his head. He leaned in closer to Kurodan and whispered, "If the orcs are here, you will want your horse."

Kurodan said nothing.

Aetholas and Feore rode their horses alongside Andazar, who was staring at the flag.

"Damn them," Feore hissed as he approached the impaled corpse, whose helmet had been stripped, revealing a butchered face and bloody stumps where his ears used to be. "I know this man. He was a Lieutenant of Raokenburg."

Kurodan nudged his horse forward, moving his gaze from buildings to broken bodies, until his eyes fell on a child. It was a small girl, no older than seven or eight years old. She was lying face down in the mud, and the top of her scalp had been taken as a trophy.

Kurodan immediately shoved his reins over to Toradin, who again tried to refuse. Kurodan glared at him, but Toradin would not even make eye contact. Kurodan let his reins fall and dismounted. He slowly made his way over to the little girl, since the mud made it difficult to walk, and knelt beside her.

He rolled her over so that she was no longer lying face down. Her cold blue eyes were open and stared directly into his own. The mud and blood splashed sporadically on her body from the rain. Kurodan stood and drew in a deep breath. He started to make his way back to his horse.

"Search the town for survivors," Aetholas said.

"What survivors?" Feore replied.

"Help," a scream pierced through the night.

The entire troop immediately turned to the direction of the sound. It came from northeast near the trees. A man came stumbling forth through thick brush and tall grass. His shirt and pants had been torn to tattered rags. He wore no shoes. His body itself had been racked with wounds.

"Help, please," he moaned. "By the light, please."

Kurodan ran towards the man, sheathing his sword. The man clung to him with a grip so strong that Kurodan almost stumbled backwards.

"Help me," he pleaded once more. The man's face was bewildered as Kurodan strained to stay upright and gain control of him. The man's eyes closed, and he coughed up blood that splattered Kurodan's armor. He choked on the blood, making a horrible gurgling sound. His eyes snapped open in fear, as he struggled to breathe. Kurodan tried to hold the dying man up as he slumped to the ground. A black arrow protruded from his back.

"Orcs!" Aetholas shouted.

"At the ready," Feore ordered.

The men placed their backs toward each other, facing outward. Kurodan drew his sword again. His chest strained against his heavy breastplate.

"To the north," Andazar said, pointing further down the road. The men strained their eyes through the rain and debris and saw orcs sprinting across the road.

"Mount up," Aetholas said, forcing his horse down the muddy road. The men on the ground scrambled to their horses, but mud had caked to their boots and armor like quicksand. Some had to rip away the mud before they could fit into their stirrups.

"Ride them down," Andazar screamed and charged his great warhorse. Kurodan looked back down the road for his horse as men rushed past shouting battle cries. Toradin rode up to Kurodan with his horse in tow. He threw the reins at him.

"Hurry," Toradin said. Kurodan gripped the reins and threw himself up into the saddle as the horse kept trotting.

The men urged their mounts into a full gallop, their horses thundered forward, kicking clumps of mud and debris high into the air.

"For Raokenburg," Feore screamed. Orc war cries sounded in response and the sound of metal on metal rang clear. Kurodan could see their formation riding through whatever orcs were caught out in the open. But the orcs ran at them, accepting their fates.

The men swung their swords and plunged their spears as they charged past. Kurodan watched the chaos unfold, ready to kill the beasts or die trying. One orc was struck in the back of the head, its skull breaking apart as it turned to defend itself from the onslaught of riders. Another left its feet as Feore's sword caught it across the chest.

Andazar had turned his horse to rally the men back around for another pass. The riders' formation had begun to fragment in the fray. A handful of orcs sprinted, escaping into the trees and grass.

One lone orc had dragged a soldier from his horse and gutted him. The orc dropped the man's body and ran at Kurodan, the axe it carried still hanging with his victim's entrails.

Just as Kurodan was riding his horse to meet the orc, Lehm came into view at a full gallop and trampled it. Andazar urged the men to regroup.

The riders fought to control their mounts, pulling on

their reins in the directions they wanted.

Arrows flew from the trees like predatory birds catching their prey midflight. Kurodan's horse reared up, pitching him backwards.

"Shield wall," Feore barked. At this command, the men struggled to dismount and place themselves in formation, shoulder to shoulder.

One man was attempting to free himself, caught in his horse's stirrup, as the fear-stricken animal kicked and stomped him into the ground. Another was slumped over in his saddle as if the rider was sleeping and riding at the same time. Arrows protruded from his back and blood poured from the orifices of his face, his chin resting against his chest.

"Form the line," Aetholas shouted as he swung his legs from his saddle. Men flocked to close ranks, shield to shield. Kurodan stepped over a man lying on his back.

"Help me," the man shrieked, trying to reach up and grab his leg. An arrow had gone into the man's eye and out the back of his skull, yet he still drew breath.

Another victim, bent forward at the waist, his hands holding an arrow, the shaft sticking out of his stomach. He fell on all fours and vomited a vile black and brown liquid.

Arrows hammered against their shields. The men braced themselves hoping the enemies' weapons would not be strong enough to penetrate their defenses.

"Hold," Feore ordered. Aetholas echoed the captain, both veterans reinforcing the other's directives. The cries of the orcs grew louder in defiance.

"Their numbers are greater in the trees," Toradin said, raising his voice to attract Feore's attention. The arrows continued to strike their shields in sporadic cadence.

"Forward," Feore shouted.

Kurodan's throat burned as he and every man screamed the same word in reply.

"Move," Feore commanded.

"Move," the men repeated and stepped forward in unison.

Before they had the chance to take more than a few steps, Andazar rode his horse in front of the shield wall and into the hail of arrows.

Kurodan watched from between shields as the wizard raised his staff high above his head and let out a bloodcurdling scream. It did not sound like that of any mortal being.

A bolt of fire hurled down from the sky, lighting up the night and exploding the world in front of them. The ground shook so hard the men were thrown from their feet. The flash stole some of the men's sight, blinding them for an instant.

Then more bolts struck downward into hidden orcs. The trees and earth erupted skyward in a magnificent hailstorm of flames, splinters, and debris.

The ensuing fire and smoke fought against the rain. No more arrows flew at them. The men slowly recovered to their feet. Kurodan helped Toradin up as he watched for more orcs. Andazar still held his staff above his head, sitting atop his horse.

The treeline looked as if a battery of catapults had demolished the area. Whole trees and giant patches of earth had been eviscerated into pieces and flung in all directions; black smoldering smears remained of what was left in the gaping craters.

Chapter XII:
The Pursuit

The men slowly lowered their guard. Some tried to tend to the wounded. Feore and Aetholas stepped forward towards the wizard. He did not turn to acknowledge them, as if still searching for orcs or merely enjoying the destruction he had just wrought.

"The orcs take flight to Mount Ruin, we must follow," Andazar said. Kurodan's eyes followed the forest terrain higher and higher until they strained to witness the jagged peak. The mountain itself loomed over the entire world. The dark sky and rain raged around it as if the mountain called to some otherworldly evil.

It looks like a monument from some horrible forsaken land brought into our world, Kurodan thought.

"We must wait for reinforcements and regroup. Our numbers are too thin to pursue them," Aetholas said.

"There is no time," Andazar raised his voice.

Toradin motioned with his head for Kurodan to come closer. "If we follow, we go to our deaths,"

Toradin whispered.

"Why is the wizard so determined to pursue the orcs?" Kurodan replied.

"Because, paladin, this may be one of our only opportunities to truly locate the orcs' stronghold. If they are already this bold in their raiding, they are not far off from amassing even worse devilry," Andazar said, turning towards Kurodan, able to hear them through the rain.

"We simply do not have the numbers to follow," Toradin spoke openly now. Kurodan was surprised to hear him defy the wizard.

"Andazar is right," Feore spoke slowly.

The men grew quiet.

Aetholas began, "Captain, if the orcs are baiting us into a trap—"

But Feore interrupted, "We will follow them until we locate their main grounds. We do not engage in another fight. We will travel light and fast. Leave the horses and carry only what you can on your backs. If we can find where the orcs make their home, we can send word back to Mil'Thuras. We can end them once and for all."

The men stood staring at their leader. "We must do this," Feore concluded.

"Very well," Aetholas sighed. "If we are to go to our deaths this day, then so be it." Aetholas turned, "Gather whatever supplies you can carry but still be able to fight with. Lehm, Bardu, you will stay and heal the wounded. Once you have saved those you can, make way for Raokenburg. Give word of what has happened here and wait for instructions from Maldin."

Bardu and Lehm immediately went to work, kneeling over dying or already dead men. The prayers they recited from their holy books could only be heard faintly beneath the rain.

Feore turned to address the rest of the men, "Stealth is the highest priority from here on out, men."

Kurodan turned and walked back to find his horse since many of the animals had scattered down the road when the wizard's magic had struck.

Toradin ran to catch up with him. "This is a death wish," Toradin whispered.

Kurodan turned and looked at him. "We are paladins. We do not fear death," he said.

Toradin spotted some of the nearby horses and pointed in their direction. "I do not fear death, brother, but do not be so hasty to throw your life away."

The men grabbed food, water, and weapons from their saddlebags and met back at the massive smoldering craters at the forest's edge. Andazar dismounted from his giant steed and gave it a hard slap on the rear. The horse whinnied and raced off towards the other horses.

Feore walked up to Andazar and drew his sword. The sound of swords being unsheathed quietly cut through the storm.

"We must be swift," Andazar said, eyeing all the men.

Feore nodded and turned back to face them. He raised one fist in the air and opened it rapidly. The men spread out along the treeline. Then Feore turned to face Andazar. "Lead the way, wizard."

The wizard walked at the front of the formation, his sword and staff at the ready. Kurodan began walking at an angle uphill. The rain and terrain were difficult and some of the men struggled to spread out their formation. Kurodan bumped into another man by accident, his focus on Mount Ruin.

Kurodan looked to see who it was. Regalt's face was pale, and his expression carried a bleak appearance.

He simply turned and moved off without saying a word. Kurodan's gut sank for a moment, recalling Regalt's story of the wizard. The rain fell harder, and the wind howled.

The men climbed and the storm raged against the mountain. "The night is too treacherous," Feore said, trying to speak through the downpour.

"No, we must press on," Andazar said firmly and continued marching ahead.

Aetholas made his way back to where Kurodan, Horad, and Toradin were in formation.

"Keep your eyes sharp, lads," he said, and the three paladins nodded grimly. Then Aetholas muttered, "The tracks have vanished in this godforsaken rain."

"We must seek shelter to wait out the storm," Horad said.

"Aye, aye, we must," Aetholas replied. The four of them moved towards the front of the formation where Andazar and Feore still argued.

"If we lose the tracks now, this will have been for nothing," Andazar hissed.

Aetholas stepped between them before Feore could utter a reply. "The tracks are already lost, wizard," he said. "If we do not find shelter, and fast, we will lose more than that."

Andazar scoffed and turned to continue up the mountain.

"You can go on alone, wizard, but the men will follow us," Feore said.

Andazar paused for a moment, then merely continued further into the storm.

"Look for any sign of usable shelter. If we are lucky, we can find a spot until dawn," Feore ordered.

"Pass the word down the line, lads," Aetholas said, turning to the other paladins.

The group split up, making their way to the nearest soldiers.

"We are seeking shelter for the night, pass it on down the line," Kurodan tried to whisper in a hushed tone, but the wind and rain were too much.

The soldier he had spoken to held his hand up to his ear.

"Look for shelter. Pass it down the line," Kurodan said louder.

The soldier nodded and moved off. Kurodan kept his eyes on Aetholas and Feore, who in turn, kept their attention on Andazar. They continued up the mountain for some time, working their way across its side at an upward angle, for it was too steep to climb head on. All around them massive rocks and trees stood as if defiantly rooted in place against the rain.

Toradin made his way back to Kurodan as they climbed on. "What drives this wizard? What madness tears at his mind?" Toradin asked.

Kurodan watched as the wizard distanced himself farther from the rest of the group. Out of breath, he gasped a bit as he said, "Andazar has not slowed once the entire ascent."

"His magic gives him stamina," Toradin said.

Kurodan grabbed Toradin, stopping him. Toradin made ready with his sword, but Kurodan stayed his hand. Then Toradin's eyes followed Kurodan's finger up the side of the mountain. Just beyond a clearing of two boulders, there was an entrance to a cave.

"Go tell Aetholas," Kurodan said to Toradin. "I'll tell the others."

Kurodan waved down the closest soldier, making him pause. He pointed to the cave, and the soldier understood him. With that, Kurodan turned and began to climb almost straight up the mountain.

His fingers were numb to the bone as they gripped on to harsh rock and cold mud. The rain continued unforgivingly, creating small streams that cascaded every which way down the side of the mountain.

Kurodan reached the two massive boulders near the entrance. He turned to catch his breath and saw the men climbing up after him.

"Wait before you enter," came a voice. It was Feore. Glancing between the cave and back down the mountain, Kurodan saw Feore and Aetholas, but no Andazar. The wizard was not among them.

Approaching Kurodan and the cave, Feore gripped his sword with both hands and moved closest to the entrance. As more men finished their climb, they also pulled out their swords.

"Where is Andazar?" Kurodan asked.

"Leave the wizard to his own devices. Slowly now, lads, be on your guard," Feore said as he entered first. Behind him, the rest inched their way into the awaiting darkness.

The cave was dank and damp with a stench that was foreign to Kurodan. There was no light, and the men struggled to keep their footing as they crept through the shadows. The sound of small rocks being disturbed echoed around them. Feore froze and the men instinctively stilled themselves.

Kurodan could feel his own heart beating in his forehead. Water dripped from his armor, and his throat drew tight as did the grip on his sword.

"Aetholas, can you light the way?" Feore whispered. The sound of small rocks moving seized the groups' attention. Then a silence grew around them. Once the cave was still, Aetholas moved to Feore.

"Be ready," Aetholas whispered.

He retrieved a small stone from his satchel and

brought it to his lips. His hands cupped it as if he were trying to drink water from his palms. He drew in a deep breath and exhaled. The stone began to glow with a bright illumination that filled the cave.

The men's eyes darted all around, looking for any signs of movement. The cave was more like a large tunnel that only traveled roughly thirty yards or so. There was a small hole in the wall of the furthest rockface, where the tunnel ended. Aetholas stepped forward, the men slowly following him. As Aetholas reached the end of the cave, he knelt, still holding his sword at the ready, and lifted the stone up to the hole. It was large enough to fit an arm through, but Aetholas did not risk it.

Aetholas stared through the hole for what seemed an eternity. There were no sounds save the men trying to control their breathing and the torrential downpour that still raged outside. Finally, Aetholas stood and faced them. "The cave is deep and massive behind this wall. I cannot see any way through or down. It is as if a cliff into nothing is just behind it."

"The mountain runs deep," Andazar said.

The men whirled around. The wizard stood at the entrance of the cave, the glow from the stone casting his figure in a haunting light. The wizard's arms were full of broken wood and his staff.

"What is the wood for?" one of the men asked.

"A fire, of course, unless you prefer to stay wet to the bone," Andazar replied.

"We cannot make a fire from wet wood," another scoffed. Andazar sighed and made his way to the middle of the cave.

"The men of this world have little to no imagination," Andazar spoke more to himself than the men who questioned him. He dropped the broken wood onto the cave floor with a loud crash.

"Quiet, Andazar," Feore said sharply.

"Do not worry, captain, the orcs seem to be long gone," Andazar replied. "We have lost them in the storm, or rather they have lost us. With a little luck, the storm will break, and we will continue our hunt."

Aetholas moved towards the center of the cave, his stone still glowing brightly.

"We won't be needing that any longer, paladin," Andazar said, reaching into one of his pouches. He pulled out a smaller pouch and then an even smaller one from within the second. Pulling on its string, he poured a fine powder into the palm of his hand.

Andazar knelt close to the pile of soaking branches. "Stand back a bit," he said, waving the men back. The men drew away from the wood, watching the wizard intently.

The wizard held his hand out as if to blow the branches a kiss, and then did exactly that. The powder drifted across the wood and then ignited into a deep blue flame that sent sparks and smoke upward, reaching the top of the cave.

Some of the men gasped in awe as the cave was now completely alight. Others coughed as the billowing smoke fought to escape the cave.

Kurodan stared into the flames and wondered how long the wood would burn. The flames crackled to life just like any other well-tended campfire and eventually turned the color of a normal fire. As if Andazar could read Kurodan's mind, he said, "The fire will last the night. Set a watch, dry yourselves."

Feore motioned to two soldiers, and they nodded, moving to the edge of the cave.

"Stay on your guard," Aetholas called. He then exhaled onto the stone once more, and its glow slowly dimmed until it faded completely.

Chapter XIII:
The Cave

Kurodan sat warming himself by the fire as did the other men. He looked at some of their faces, staring into the fire's warmth. They had lost seven men to the orcs, either dead or too wounded to carry on. Two more had remained behind, with Bardu and Lehm to help on their journey to Raokenburg. That left sixteen, not including the paladins and the wizard.

They were exhausted. The night had beaten them down and snuffed out any hardiness remaining after the first sighting of the orcs. They were soaked to the bone, but the magical fire seemed to warm their spirits. The warmth radiated off the cave walls, making their current predicament bearable.

Toradin walked over to where Kurodan was sitting. "The soldiers have posted a watch. You should get some rest while you can." Kurodan nodded, staring into the flames, and Toradin walked back over to his gear and lay down.

Kurodan was still warming himself when Andazar pulled out a pipe and lit it.

"Is it wise to be smoking?" Kurodan asked. Andazar glared at him and let out a puff of smoke from the corner of his mouth.

"He is right, Andazar, the scent could draw the orcs here," Feore said. The men had all grown quiet, trying to bed down for the night. There was a long silence.

Finally, Andazar spoke. "The orcs have moved on. We have a fool's hope of finding a trace of them. Even if this storm breaks rather quickly, our chances are thin at best. They are not going to find us here."

Kurodan frowned. "You would put us all at risk on a whim?" he questioned the wizard.

Feore looked surprised at the boldness in Kurodan's voice. But Kurodan glared back at Andazar, who deliberately puffed smoke in his direction.

"Boy," he said condescendingly, "I have stalked, fought, and killed every living creature that has walked or crawled this world. Do not lecture me on the merits of risk."

Kurodan started to defend his concerns. "If the orcs—" But Feore quickly interrupted, "Kurodan, get some rest. We have a night's watch."

Kurodan nodded and lay down, still staring into the fire. As his head rested, his exhaustion finally struck. His entire body ached for sleep. The fire slowly danced in and out of focus as he fought to keep his eyes open for some unknown reason. The harder he fought sleep, the quicker it seemed to take him.

The last thing he saw was Andazar sitting there blowing smoke rings from his pipe. Kurodan watched as the perfect rings floated above the flames and rose to the ceiling of the cave, vanishing into nothing. He remembered what the crazy priest had said to him before they left Mil'Thuras.

You depart with a devil.

Kurodan opened his eyes to see that the fire had died down to mere embers. There was still enough warmth for comfort in the cave but not like it had been at first. Kurodan rubbed his eyes and began to stretch. The sun had not yet risen, and darkness shrouded the cave. The storm had finally ceased, and a stillness hung in the air.

Rocks. The faint sound of rocks being disturbed came from within the cave. Kurodan sat up quickly, training his eyes into the dark.

He strained to see anything as time seemed to stop. The sound had vanished. Kurodan sat staring, afraid that the second he took his eyes off the dark, empty tunnel, something terrible would happen. He let out a deep breath, realizing that he had been holding it the entire time, and looked around the campfire.

The men were still asleep. He looked for Andazar, but the wizard was not among them. He scanned the bodies lying about one more time but did not see the blue cloak. Kurodan looked at the entrance to the cave and saw no man standing watch. Infuriated, he thought, *The wizard has disappeared once more, and the night watch has failed its duty.*

Kurodan started to work his way over to Toradin to ask if he might have noticed when the wizard left, and who was supposed to be on watch.

Rocks. Again. Kurodan froze mid-crawl, his eyes trapped in the darkness. This time the sound was unmistakable. There was someone or something moving at the back of the cave. The tunnel was just long enough that he could not make out any movement. "Toradin," he whispered, but was met with silence.

The rocks again. This time there was movement. Kurodan's eyes grew wide with fear. He could now see some kind of faint light coming from the very back. It seemed to cast shadow upon shadow in the black stillness. Kurodan looked around wildly, wondering if the wizard could be stalking the tunnel.

"Toradin," he said again, louder. Toradin rolled over to see who had called his name. Upon seeing the terrified face of Kurodan, he shot up, making enough noise to stir some of the other men.

The rocks moved again. There was more than one person—or beast—moving. Other men sat up, exchanging worried glances with each other.

"Who is on watch?" Feore asked. No one answered.

"Where is the wizard?" Aetholas asked. Again, no answers from the men.

Kurodan stood to break the tension but rather magnified it. "Who goes there?" he cried aloud.

The sound of the rocks ceased, and the faint light was snuffed out. The men started to stand.

"Shield wall," Kurodan shouted. The men panicked, unsheathing weapons and attempting to don armor.

Orcs flooded into the cave tunnel. Initially, there was no sound except for their running feet beating on the cave floor. Kurodan drew his sword and stood his ground. In the fading firelight, they looked to be monsters emerging from shadow, deep from within some demonic world.

Their skin was dark shades of grey and green. Their eyes glowed yellow as if they could see in the dark like wild cats. Their mouths contained jagged teeth and small tusks that jutted forth from their bottom lips.

All manner of braids, locks, and manes covered their heads. Some had shaved down portions of their skulls to create an even fiercer image.

Most had painted their faces and bodies with what looked to be blood, ash, and mud. They carried primitive weapons: clubs, spears, and axes made from sharp stone and wood. Only a select few had weapons forged of real steel. Their bodies were covered in furs, hides, skins, and crude armor.

The first orc that rushed Kurodan wore a horrible sash wrapped around his torso that appeared to be fashioned from human skin and faces. Just before the orc reached him, Kurodan recognized something that was attached to the terrible web of human flesh. A small scalp of black locks. He remembered the village girl.

The orc swung a cruelly formed axe at the paladin. Kurodan sidestepped and swung his sword in reply. The blade sung in the cave and caught the orc in the bicep, severing the arm in two. The orc fell backwards, bellowing out a scream that echoed throughout the tunnel. The smell and sight of fresh blood seemed to urge the orcs into a frenzy. The mob clashed into the men. Weapons sounded on bone and flesh, and more screams echoed in the cave. In the middle of the fray, Kurodan cared not for his own life anymore, not even for the lives of the men around him. The sole thought that burned within his mind was to inflict the orcs' own atrocities back onto them.

He took a blow from a club on the shoulder. Intense pain radiated down his arm and into his back. He screamed not only at the pain but in defiance. He realized he had been screaming the whole time. While his mind focused on the killing, a small part of his thoughts recognized that he had never heard himself scream this way before. All of them were screaming. Orc and man, all sounded alike.

Kurodan plunged his sword forward, sinking it into the chest cavity of another orc. He fought to pull the blade back out, but the orc clung to the sword with its free hand. With the other, the orc raised its weapon to swing again. Kurodan's eyes began to glow white-hot as did his sword, and the orc now screamed. Smoke began to rise from the orc's hand and wound cavity.

"Kurodan, no!" Aetholas shouted.

But Kurodan's rage enslaved him. Light and flames erupted from his sword. The orc was eviscerated into smoldering body parts and ash. The flames roared in the cave, catching many of the orcs and soldiers around him. Kurodan's chest heaved as his eyes faded, no longer bright with holy light. His sword was coated in smoldering blood, burnt black. Both men and orc ran like rabid dogs in all directions, trying to put out the fire on their clothes and skin.

Kurodan ran at the nearest orc, who was hacking at a burning soldier with his own sword. Just as Kurodan raised his sword for a killing blow, a bright blue light appeared, hovering at the ceiling of the cave. All fighting ceased for a moment—even those who were caught with fire paused. As the light illuminated the scenes of horror, it painted them in a deep blue that shaped the carnage into something almost beautiful. There was complete and utter silence, as if the world had taken a deep breath before plunging into the ocean from a cliff's edge.

The light hovered and then shattered upon itself. A noise so loud and deafening came forth that it shook the very walls of the cave, throwing the men and orcs to the ground. The cave was cast back into darkness, and all remained motionless, save for one.

"Get them into the mountain."

Chapter XIV: Prisoners

Kurodan came to and tried to stand. His head felt as if it had been split by a sword. His world and vision reeled, and he fell back down.

"Get the ones who are awake," came a voice. Kurodan felt hands grip him and hold him down.

"Take the weapons that wield the holy fire," another voice growled. The sounds of chains and shackles rang in his ears and then he felt cold hard steel bind his wrists and ankles.

He fought the hands, but his strength had faded, and his vision was still blurry. His body was wrenched forward by the shackles. Finally, his vision focused. The cave was dark, save for two or three orcs holding torches. Bodies littered the ground.

His restraints chained him to his fellow soldiers. He looked for the other paladins. Toradin, he saw, was already in chains, an orc standing over him with a spear held to his throat.

Then Kurodan's eyes caught a body lying not far from them. Aetholas lay on his back, his body disfigured and burned. Kurodan gasped as his mind tried to fight off the terrible realization.

"Andazar, you traitor!" Feore howled. He continued flailing against three orcs who were struggling to restrain him as he yelled. He looked like some cave-dweller who had hid in the mountain his entire life. "You side with the orcs? You betray your fellow man? Why?" Feore's eyes bulged out of his skull as he raged, but then an orc struck him across the face, silencing his questions.

Kurodan watched as the wizard cloaked in blue moved towards Feore. "The age of men is quickly ending, captain. You will realize this soon enough," Andazar said.

Feore spit blood at him. "I will tear your heart out before this is over," he shrieked.

Andazar calmly wiped the blood from his face. "Get them up. Get them moving," Andazar said, pointing further into the mountain.

The orcs continued to shackle and chain any man who still drew breath. The men that were mortally wounded, were executed immediately, their corpses subjected to brutalization. War trophies were taken, hewn with glee. They were forced into a single file line, connected by their chains.

One orc emerged from the blackness of the cave, striding forth from the abyss that now awaited them all. His yellow eyes glowed, calculatingly, eyeing the prisoners. And his dark green skin flickered in the torchlight.

His face was scarred, and his mouth held a broken tusk. He wore a hooded chainmail shirt, and one hand clutched some kind of coiled rope. The other hand rested on a long dagger at his waist. A signal horn hung on the other side of the orc's hip. The men stared at the lone orc with a mix between hate and curiosity.

"I never figured you to be one to miss the bloodshed, Korgath," Andazar said, smirking.

The orc grinned wickedly. "The bloodshed is just beginning, wizard," he retorted. Then Korgath unfurled the long whip from his hand; it slithered onto the ground like some hideous serpent. All manner of jagged bones, thorns, and rocks had been woven into the braided rope of the whip.

"Move," the orc bellowed. His whip thundered and cracked, echoing across the cave. The men rose to their feet. Kurodan struggled to stay in step with the other chained men. They approached the back of the tunnel with the hole that Aetholas had inspected. The hole had been pulled apart; the wall now gave way to an opening deeper into the mountain.

As they passed through it, the cave opened into a massive chasm. Kurodan paused and stared off the cliff's edge. The blackness seemed to go down into a never-ending pit.

The whip cracked once more. "Move or I will cast you in!" Korgath orc yelled. Kurodan turned to his right. A small ledge hugged the rock wall, where men carefully crept their way forward. In the faint torchlight, Kurodan could see the winding ledge make its way around the cave wall and into another tunnel.

The whip sounded again. "Faster," ordered the orc. Kurodan followed the man in front of him and tried not to look down.

Some of the orcs remained in the rear, dragging the dead through the opening. Others gathered rocks and began piling them back up, attempting to conceal the carnage that had taken place.

The mountain seemed never ending. More tunnels

split off from their path, and more orcs emerged from within them. The tunnels burrowed deeper and deeper, as if they were walking into another world. The orcs were merciless, noticing the faintest sign of weakness like a shark smelling blood in water. The whip was the constant penalty for any man who could not keep pace.

The orcs had begun stripping the men of their armor during the forced march. As they removed it, they passed each piece down the line, examining the new treasures. A larger orc pushing a wheelbarrow in tow of the shackled line gleefully accepted them. Their leader who carried the whip could now strike bare skin and lashed accordingly.

At the beginning of the march, Kurodan had tried to conserve his energy, looking for any chance to start an uprising or escape. His mind had raced with each step, but the slow decay of time finally drained him. *The orcs do not seem to tire*, Kurodan noted. *Was theirs the same kind of magic that spurred the wizard?*

One of the men began to slow, which caused the entire line to fall out of pace. It was Halthrow, the soldier who had questioned their mission from the very beginning.

Instantly, the orc shouted at them to move, followed by the sickening crack of the whip. Halthrow screamed out in pain. Kurodan contorted his neck to try and see, but the chains made it difficult to do anything. The whip cracked again, and screams turned into a panicked shriek.

Another brutish orc approached. He was fearsome, standing a head taller than almost all the other orcs and carrying a massive cleaver like a demonic butcher from hell.

He gripped Halthrow by the throat with his free hand and lifted him off his feet.

The orc's muscles bulged as the man gasped for air, his fists batting at the orc's hand. "If you cannot keep up, human, I will peel your flesh from your bones," he said, raising the cleaver.

The whip cracked, this time striking the big orc. The orc turned in anger, black blood running down the side of his arm. The wound did not seem to upset him nearly as much as the interruption to his killing did.

"They will not be killed, Muglok. Each of them is needed," Korgath said.

Muglok released Halthrow, who fell choking and sputtering. Then he growled, "You challenge me again, Korgath and I will wear your skin instead of the humans."

"You threaten me openly?" Korgath barked.

Kurodan noticed that the orcs all paused in excitement and anticipation at this confrontation. Just as the two orcs appeared ready to tear each other to pieces, a voice came from the front of the line.

"We have no time for your pathetic squabbling. We must keep moving," Andazar commanded.

The orc with the cleaver turned and began walking away. The whip cracked again, and the imprisoned men were back on the move. Kurodan futilely tried to turn and see where Toradin was, but he could not keep his eyes off the man in front of him for too long, for fear of bringing the whip down.

All sense of time was warped and lost. Kurodan felt they would soon reach the other side of the mountain and have nowhere else to go. But he was wrong. The pace began to slow as the orcs sensed the exhaustion of the men.

Kurodan's mind focused on one thing over and over. *The orc had said each of them was needed.*

Kurodan wondered, *Needed for what?* His imagination now started to run wild at the countless horrible deaths that he was certain awaited each one of them.

The men noticed that they had reached a different part of the mountain's depths. The dirt ground had given way to stone. Not just rock, but stone of immense craftsmanship, Kurodan observed. *Surely the orcs did not create this*, he thought. Then statues started to appear, beautiful and terrible alike. They were statues of vampires. Some were clad in armor; others bore nothing except their godlike physiques. The tunnels gave way to larger ones that mimicked the great halls of a castle. The men could not comprehend what they were seeing. Slowing in awe, they stared at their new surroundings.

They came to a great black door, massive in size and construction. It seemed to be made from a form of stone or granite, but it was black as night with red markings etched into it. Kurodan could not tell what language or writing it was. The foreign markings were inscribed in a perfect circle, and in the center was a chalice. Instead of drink, the chalice was depicted holding flames that poured out of it.

Andazar motioned to some of the orcs, who then began to push on the door. The sound of immense stone grinding on stone thundered through the halls. As it opened, the black door split perfectly down the middle. Gasps—not of horror, but of amazement—could be heard from the men.

Before them lay a great hall that rivaled Mil'Thuras. Immense tables lined the open room. Torches lit up the splendor, and statues lined the back walls. The walls themselves were painted with murals that depicted fierce warriors of some ancient world.

Giant heads, that looked to be of monsters or

demons, were carved into some of the very walls themselves. They jutted out hideously, staring down at them all. The decorations all unfolded a drama or ancient history, but it was one that Kurodan had no knowledge of.

At the very head of the great room was a throne. Its magnificent chair appeared to be made from the same material that the black door was. The most skilled artisans in Mil'Thuras would have fought each other to examine its dimensions and beauty. At first, shocked that such splendor of this proportion and magnitude had been built under the mountain, Kurodan had not noticed the figure on the throne. But now he saw a figure, cloaked in black, rise from the black chair.

He stood and spoke. "Vae vivis."

"Indeed," Andazar replied. As the still bewildered men now stood in the center of the great hall, the whip sounded with a loud crack.

"Kneel," came the command. Kurodan and the others knelt but continued to stare at this supposed king.

The figure stepped down from the throne with an unsettling gracefulness. His head was bare and partly shrouded by a black cowl, which draped his body save his clawed hands and feet. His eyes were white and surrounded by sunken dark features, making them contrast even more. His face was starved and hallowed, yet strong. His pale white skin stretched taught over muscle and bone. His fingers ended in long black nails as did his feet, appearing closer to beast than man. The sword of a warrior was sheathed at his hip. Fangs protruded from his black lips.

"We have done as you asked, vampire," Korgath said, stepping forward.

"And we shall all be rewarded because of it," the vampire replied.

"Yes, if we are careful," Andazar cautioned. "I must make my way back to Mil'Thuras. I have much work that still requires my attention."

The vampire nodded. "We will continue our work here."

Andazar then turned to leave and walked towards the massive door, only to stop and turn again. "If you find it, you must wait for my return."

"Agreed," the vampire replied. Andazar then hurried back into the tunnel.

"That sword," Feore whispered.

"Quiet," Muglok shouted, walking towards Feore.

"I know that sword," Feore said, his gaze fixed upon the sword that hung on the vampire's hip.

The vampire slowly turned and met Feore's stare.

"Where did you get that sword, demon?" Feore asked defiantly, his face contorted in confusion and anger.

The vampire held up his hand, staying the orc butcher, and asked, "Where do you think I got it from?"

Kurodan and the other men hung on every word.

"Where is the rightful owner of that sword?" Feore shouted. The vampire laughed. Feore tried to stand but was held down by Muglok. "That is a weapon of the light. You are not worthy of wielding it."

"Yet it has killed many by my hand. Does that trouble you?" the vampire asked.

"Where is the paladin who carried it?" Feore demanded. But the vampire did not respond, and Muglok raised his cleaver above Feore, slaughter in his eyes. Before the blade dropped, Korgath stepped between Muglok and Feore.

"Move or be moved," Muglok said, his voice deep and booming.

Korgath remained still.

The other orcs again grew agitated in excitement, as if they had been anticipating this challenge for a long time now.

"I will not tell you again," Muglok warned, towering over the other orc.

The vampire stepped back and returned to his throne, clearly intending to sit and watch with the same curiosity as the others.

"You give no orders here," Korgath told Muglok.

"You are a false warlord. You make our kind look weak, bending the knee to the bloodsucker and wizard," Muglok replied. The other orcs pulled the prisoners back, clearing room for the two barbarians. Silence fell. Kurodan and the men were as captivated as the orcs were.

"The rank of warlord is mine," Korgath declared. Muglok spit on the ground. The orcs erupted into bellows and foul curses. Some began beating their shields and stomping their feet. The sound drummed louder and louder.

"You are not fit to be warlord," Muglok shouted. Korgath stripped off his chainmail and adornments, leaving only his dagger on his belt. Muglok did the same. The orcs screamed and shouted at the action. Scars and war paint marked both the orcs' bodies.

Korgath held out his hand as if beckoning for something. Neither broke eye contact with the other as another orc ran out and presented each with a shield and spear. Then the noise died down to silence again.

"I will have your head," Muglok screamed and ran at Korgath with such speed and violence that the men sat awestruck.

Korgath shielded himself from the heavy blows and replied with his own. The orcs' footwork and movement were impeccable. Each action appeared to be a killing blow, but neither orc could strike the other down.

The sound of their spears and shields crashed as the onlookers watched the two gladiatorial savages in their impressive display of combat. Kurodan instinctively knew these two orcs were skilled beyond years over the others. It was as if two titans had decided to go to war.

Then Muglok brought his shield down hard, shattering Korgath's spear. Continuing to press his advantage, Muglok stabbed wildly. Korgath appeared to be losing the fight quickly, having lost the ability to return strikes. Muglok bellowed and thrust his spear so viciously into Korgath's shield that it snapped in his own hand. Throwing the broken shaft to the ground, he rammed his shield into Korgath, pushing him back.

Before Korgath could respond, Muglok dropped the shield and drew his terrible cleaver. With the huge weapon in both hands, Muglok swung, trying to finish it. And Korgath's shield, heavily scarred and beaten, barely withstood the cleaver. Kurodan did not understand how the orc still held onto the shield at all.

Korgath sidestepped in between the heavy blows, dropping the shield, and with the swiftness of the blink of an eye, drew his dagger. Whirring and flickering, the dagger was wielded with such skill it appeared to be alive on its own. Black blood splattered as Korgath's dagger claimed its kill like a hungry wolf running down a newborn fawn.

Muglok dropped to one knee. His hand clutched his stomach, trying to hold in the entrails where the dagger had found its mark. His other hand still gripped the cleaver. Screaming, he swung the cleaver again, still with the strength to hack a man in two. As Korgath danced away from the strike, his dagger responded in kind, like a coiled snake, striking at just the right moment.

Muglok's hand fell, still clutching onto the massive weapon. The orc let out another scream, more in a rage at losing the fight, than over any pain from his grievous wounds.

Korgath stood over him, relishing the moment, but Muglok would not accept defeat. With his remaining good hand, Muglok seized Korgath by the throat, trying to strangle the life out of his enemy.

Korgath ignored the choking pain and grabbed a fistful of Muglok's hair. With his weapon hand, Korgath began to carve Muglok's neck.

Some of the men had to look away. The dagger sawed back and forth, its edge holding sharp. Muglok's screaming turned to a sick gurgling sound. Even as he was being decapitated alive, Muglok did not break eye contact. Finally, his grip fell away empty and Korgath raised his opponent's head high above his own. He bellowed a hellish war cry, worthy of legend.

The orcs cheered at the final spectacle of defiance and victory. The vampire applauded the sight as well, clapping his hands.

"Are there no other challengers?" Korgath yelled. His stare fell upon his fellow orcs, who grew quiet. One orc knelt and bowed his head. Almost in unison, the others did the same.

"Most impressive, Korgath," said the vampire. Korgath dropped the severed head to the ground, and the orcs stood.

Turning his attention to the throne, Korgath said, "Tell me, nightwalker, what is stopping me from claiming your head as well?"

The vampire laughed. "You know as well as I do that I am needed just as you are. The prophecy does not lie."

"Prophecy or not, these are my prisoners.

We captured them, not you," Korgath snorted.

"Indeed, you did. What will you do with them now?" the vampire asked.

"I will leave some of my warriors here. They will oversee the mining. I will take the others and call upon the remaining tribes," Korgath replied.

Looking at Muglok's decapitated head, the vampire said, "I suspect you will have little trouble recruiting them under your banner, warlord."

Korgath turned and motioned to the prisoners. "Get them up!" shouted an orc. The men were grabbed and pushed once again until they stood in a single line.

"Crunok, Orgron, Atroc, stay your warriors. The rest will come with me," Korgath commanded. Three orcs stepped aside and motioned for others to join them.

Before Kurodan could get a good look at the orcs chosen to remain behind, he was forced to keep pace with the chained men in front of him. Back out the giant black door and into the tunnels they went. They walked deeper and further into the mountain.

At last, they arrived at a heavy wooden door with a small, barred window. There was an orc standing guard, alone in the blackness.

"Who goes there?" the orc challenged.

An orc pushed his way past the men to the front. "I am Udal, of the Bone Eater Tribe. These are Warlord Korgath's prisoners."

The guard eyed him and the band of chained men warily, then asked," What does the vampire command?"

The orc called Udal grew angry at this question. "The bloodsucker does not command us or these prisoners," he said.

The guard stood silent. He looked more like an executioner than a guard with his black hooded mask and large polearm.

Udal pointed his club at the other orc. "These prisoners are to be kept in the dungeon and used for the digging,"

This is the second time an orc has mentioned digging. Digging for what? Kurodan wondered. The guard unhinged a set of iron keys from his belt. Leaning the large blade of the polearm against the tunnel wall, he turned and faced the door.

One of the orcs passed his torch up to the front, but the guard shooed it away. "The light hurts my eyes," he said. The orc found the key he was looking for and fit it into the keyhole. Using both hands on the large key, the orc turned it hard. There was a loud thud, and the door slid ajar. The guard grabbed his weapon after returning his keys to his belt.

"Get them in," Udal ordered. The men were led through the door and down stone steps. The dungeon, as it were, was merely a large room with a stone floor. Shackles lined the walls and floor. The men were being lined up to their new restraints, Kurodan began to take mental note of who had survived. Of the paladins, Toradin, Horad, and himself still lived. Feore, Regalt, and six other soldiers remained of the regular army. As Kurodan counted the men, he froze.

A man already chained in the corner of the room sat staring at them. Yet he remained quiet as the orcs placed each prisoner in new shackles, chaining them to the walls or floor. Then the guard came around and checked the restraints, one by one. Kurodan had to admit that these orcs were thoughtful in their actions and did not leave anything to chance.

The orcs left with their torches, and the guard shut the door behind him, locking it with the loud thud.

Darkness and stillness claimed everyone in the room. No one spoke.

None could find words to match the gravity of their situation.

No one spoke save for one, "What year is it?"

Chapter XV:
Dead Men

"The year is 1163, the third of the Evening's Fall," Feore said.

There was silence, then Kurodan could hear muttered numbers. The man was quietly counting to himself.

"Who are you?" Feore asked. The man either ignored the question or did not hear him. But when he stopped counting, Feore asked again.

"I am Uthrol, son of Uthrod," he said.

"I know that name," Feore replied. "Uthrod was a lieutenant during the Great War,"

"Aye," Uthrol said.

"How did you become a prisoner here?" Feore asked.

"You are a captain; I recognize you now," Uthrol said, ignoring the question.

"You ... you know me?" Feore asked.

"How can you recognize someone in this

blackness?" one of the men asked.

"I can see you, hear you, smell you. If I can, the orcs can, too."

"How long have you been here?" Kurodan asked.

"Long … too long," Uthrol whispered.

"Where do you hail from, Uthrol son of Uthrod?" Toradin said.

"I come from Vaserheim. My family traveled to Mil'Thuras when I was but a child. My father joined the king's army. I was raised to follow in his footsteps."

"You and your father both fought in the Great War, did you not?" another asked.

"Aye, my father gave his life during the last battle," Uthrol said.

"We won that battle and the war. How is it you fell prisoner?" Feore asked again.

Uthrol laughed, a raspy sound. "If we won, captain, how did I end up here? Why was I not rescued from this torture and captivity?" His voice grew louder. "Why are you all here now beside me? We did not win."

The orc standing guard pounded on the door and everyone grew silent. After a time, Uthrol spoke again in a hushed voice. "We merely postponed their quest."

"What is their quest?" Kurodan questioned. "What is this mining the orcs have spoken of?"

"The orcs are searching for something here within the heart of the mountain. What it is, I do not know," Uthrol said.

"Do you know the tunnel's layout? If you have been here long, have you any idea of a way to escape? How many others are prisoner here?" Feore asked, his tone almost panicked.

Uthrol grew angry again. "Do not be so bold, captain. The last men who tried to escape used to sit where you are now. I am all that is left."

"What happened?" Horad asked.

Uthrol began to weep silently. An awkward silence swelled, as the new prisoners did not know what to say to this broken shell of a man. Uthrol finally gained control of his emotions, choking them down.

"We planned for what seemed an eternity. Every inch, every tunnel, every orc, every possibility. There were only two outcomes: freedom or death. But we were ready. We were going to be free," his voice waned.

"What went wrong?" Kurodan said.

"The orcs were also ready," Uthrol's voice was barely above a hiss, as if the orcs were listening to his every word. "We fought our way tunnel by tunnel, killing the orcs and taking their weapons as we went. We were so close but—"

"But what?" Kurodan interrupted.

"The vampire," Uthrol spoke, but then stopped as his voice faded.

"He carries a holy weapon," Feore said. "What happened to its first wielder?"

Uthrol seemed to ignore the question about the sword. "He is no mere vampire, like the ones we purged during the war. He … he is a devil."

The men grew quiet except for some of their chains rattling.

Uthrol continued, "He moves as if he owns the very shadows, breaking them under his will. He fights, not to kill but to maim. His torture is the most sadistic I have ever laid eyes on. He takes great pleasure in it."

"So do the orcs," Kurodan said.

"His cruelty rivals that of Krashnik the Terrible," Uthrol whispered.

"Surely this one vampire, that no one has heard of, is not so great a threat? As you yourself admitted that many of their kind perished in the war." Toradin said.

"The stories alone of Krashnik the Terrible are too much for any sane man to comprehend," another responded.

Feore grew angry now. "You still have not answered me. What of the man who carried that sword? What of the men who shared this dungeon with you?"

"Do not ask questions you are not prepared to hear answered!" Uthrol snapped.

"Are there any survivors elsewhere in the mountain?" Horad could not stop himself from asking, hope evident in his voice.

"Have you not heard me?! Have you listened to nothing I have said? You will all beg for mercy and a swift death! I'm talking to dead men," Uthrol shouted. "Dead men," then started to sob uncontrollably, sounding more like a chained animal than man.

The door thudded open, and an orc was heard slowly descending the steps. The men could only hear the next acts unfold.

"No! Please! By the light, no," Uthrol screamed. His voice held sheer terror, like a panicked rabbit squealing in a snare. The orc said nothing, but Uthrol's shackles clanked open. The sound of his screams became piercing as he was dragged across the stone floor. It was too much.

"Enough," Kurodan shouted, standing to his feet.

Feore also stood, calling out, "Release him!"

In response, Kurodan felt a blow strike his head and was knocked to the ground. The orc carried the screaming mad man up the stairs and slammed the door behind him. The lock sounded loudly, leaving the men trapped. The screams of Uthrol were now muffled as he was carried back into the tunnels.

The men sat in darkness and silence for a long time. Kurodan tried to find the words to speak, to spur his brothers into action, but his thoughts were sporadic, unfocused. His head reeled from the blow and Uthrol's screaming still haunted him. Many of the men seemed to have accepted their new fate. While in the vampire's throne room, Kurodan had counted eleven that remained, not including Uthrol. They were prisoners, slaves to be used and most likely slain.

Toradin was the first to speak. "Whenever the orc returns, we must fight. It is the only way. We wait for the chains to be unbound and then strangle it quietly. Once the orc is dead, we will take the keys from it and free ourselves."

Toradin's plan was met with a long silence, each man weighing their odds of survival. "This will work," Kurodan said in agreement. If we can find where they have taken our blessed weapons and holy books, we will have better chances of fighting our way out."

"There is only one orc that guards our cell. We kill it, and we can make our escape," one of the men said.

Feore laughed quietly, angering and frightening some of the men. "I admire your unbreakable spirit, paladins," the captain said. "What do you suggest we do when we have the key and escape this cell? Wander aimlessly in the dark and right into more orcs or the vampire?" He laughed again.

"It is better than sitting here waiting to die," Kurodan raised his voice.

"No, this plan will not work," Feore said.

"What do you suggest then?" Toradin spoke with disdain now.

"If we are to survive this place ... this hell ... we must plan," Feore said slowly. He continued, his voice growing stronger as he gave the speech of a leader, "We must memorize our surroundings the best we can. Discover the orcs' patterns. Where they sleep, where they eat, where they shit. We need to know if there are any gaps or breaks within this mountain hold, somewhere we could possibly signal any who may have come looking for us."

No longer angry, Kurodan acknowledged the captain, saying, "Agreed."

Feore added, "The two orcs that fought one another—their culture is one of constant war even among themselves. If we can possibly find a way to turn the remaining orcs against each other and cause inner turmoil, that could be our chance. We must bide our time and survive. Rushing blindly headlong into a fight will get us killed. We plan and, most importantly, we keep each other alive."

"Aye!" came a few responses.

"What is our first step?" Horad asked.

"We need to learn what it is we are truly being kept here for. What they are searching for within this mountain," Feore said.

More time passed. The men drifted into sleep and exhaustive thought. For hours, they could hear nothing save for their own breathing and the chains rattling with their tosses and turns.

Footsteps. Some of the men sat up. Footsteps could be heard approaching the cell door. "Wherever they take us, go willingly," Feore whispered. "Remember everything I have said. Concentrate, and do not lose hope."

An orc's voice could be heard talking to the one on guard. "The vampire requests one of the holy warriors to be brought to the hall," he said.

Kurodan felt his blood run cold. Kurodan thought,

Will I or one of my brothers be bled dry by this monster? Is this my fate? To not die in glorious battle but as a slave to feed some vermin vampire.

The orc on guard did not reply but began to open the cell door. As the door opened, torchlight blinded all those inside. Kurodan tried to look past his hand shielding his own vision, but the light was now painful though he desired the flame's warmth. The men sat chained with their gazes focused on the ground, hoping to avoid drawing any unwanted attention on themselves.

The two orcs walked up and down the men, eyeing them carefully. "Those three," the guard said, pointing at Kurodan, Toradin, and Horad.

"The vampire only requested one," the orc with the torch said. The orc on guard stood staring, seemingly impatient, at the other orc.

"I guess I'll just pick one then," the other finally said. The orc held the torch over Kurodan. He recognized the orc as the one called Udal.

Udal's face and ears were pierced with sharp, stunted bones. *Hence, the Bone Eater Tribe,* Kurodan thought.

"You there, stand up. You try anything, I mean anything, human, and I will bring the vampire your head," the orc said, hefting his axe and resting the blade's edge on Kurodan's neck. "Understand?"

"I understand," Kurodan said.

Kurodan's shackles were removed from the dungeon's floor and checked for their integrity before the orcs pushed him up the stairs.

After the door was shut and locked, leaving the men in the pitch black once more, and the footsteps grew faint, they whispered to one another.

"Why would the vampire request one of us be brought to him?" Horad asked.

"Interrogation, torture, feeding, take your pick," one of the men replied.

"How will we follow our plan if they simply torture and kill us one by one?" Horad said, angrily.

"Calm yourselves, men, we do not truly know the intention of this summoning. We must keep hope, no matter how dire our situation becomes," Feore said.

"The captain is right. Trust me, Kurodan's will, and valor go unmatched to a fault," Toradin said in praise of his friend. "He will be able to endure whatever lies in store for him, and if something good can be brought forth from this, he will make it so."

The men grew silent again. Each pondered their own hopes, doubts, and fears.

Once they exited the dungeon cell, a hood was roughly pulled over Kurodan's head. Struggling with blurred vision, his stumbling footsteps followed the now dim torchlight. His thoughts were swirling. *Why did the vampire want a paladin brought? Am I to be tortured to see what information I know? Or will I merely be bled dry for the vampire's amusement?*

Shaking these thoughts from his mind, Kurodan forced himself to focus. He tried to count his footsteps, taking note of the tunnel's direction and elevation, what turns he was led down, and what sounds, smells, and sights he could take in despite the hood. At one point, he thought he heard the sound of picks or shovels striking rock.

He feigned exhaustion and stumbled to stall his captors. Falling onto his stomach, he listened. He was right. The sound of digging echoed from some unknown distance down a nearby tunnel. The orc known as Udal jerked violently on Kurodan's chains. "Quit stalling, human."

Kurodan again portrayed signs of weariness, struggling to stand. "Forgive me, please."

Udal gripped Kurodan by the throat and slammed his back against the tunnel wall. The other orc moved aside. Udal tore the hood from Kurodan's head and brought his own face close to his. Kurodan felt cold sharp steel pressed against his cheek.

"Did I not warn you, human?" the orc growled. "Did I not say I would have your head?"

Kurodan was breathing heavily as he felt the axe slowly bite into the side of his face, just enough to draw blood.

"You did, you did," Kurodan whispered. "If you leave the hood off, I will be better able to keep to your pace."

Udal's grip began to tighten, "Do not try my patience again." The orc placed the hood back on Kurodan and shoved him forward. "Move!" he ordered.

At last, the ground gave way to the stone floor again and Kurodan knew they had reached the vampire's hall. He could vaguely make out the shapes of the great statues and the throne. A swift kick to the back of his leg painfully forced him to kneel, and once again the hood was torn from his head.

Kurodan's eyes rose to look at the throne and the vampire he was summoned to, but the great chair was empty. He began to look around, curious as to why the vampire was gone. Udal struck him with a closed fist. "Keep your eyes down," he commanded.

Blood began to trickle from his nose and mouth. Kurodan brought his chained hands up to wipe away the blood.

"Let it bleed," came the vampire's voice from a dark corner. The creature stepped out as if birthed from the shadows.

"Leave us," he spoke, waving its hand dismissively. The orcs backed away quickly as if they were just as nervous to be in the vampire's presence as Kurodan was.

Kurodan kept his head down, staring at the stone floor. A single drop of blood finally fell and gently stained the dark stones. The vampire drew in a deep breath and let out a sigh of pleasure.

"Ahhh, intoxicating. You may raise your head and look upon me, mortal."

Kurodan lifted his gaze and met the cold dead eyes of the monster that stood before him. The vampire's face was expressionless, like stone that had been unchanged since the beginning of time.

"Why have you brought me here, vampire?" Kurodan asked.

"Why is it you think I have summoned you, paladin?" it replied.

Kurodan shifted his weight and looked around the throne room. He feigned bravery but knew that he did not wish to keep looking into the vampire's dead eyes. "I would wager it is not to waste either of our time by playing guessing games, creature. You wish to better know your enemy, no? Or do you wish to merely gratify your cursed existence and feed upon me?"

The vampire's face turned into something that hinted at a smile. "I know my enemy more intimately than you do yours, paladin. And what better way to endure eternity?"

"So that is it then? You really did summon me here to play games?" Kurodan said.

"No, I did not. I have brought you here simply to converse with you."

Kurodan laughed out loud, still portraying a false confidence. "You truly think me to be this daft? That I would entertain the devil by conversing with it?"

"I make no mistake of what you know me to be,

paladin," the vampire replied.

If you are going to kill me, get it over with, Kurodan thought.

"Damn you. Damn you and your petty attempts at conversing. Speak plainly, demon, for I am in no mood for riddles or mere conversation," Kurodan spat on the ground, his confidence now believable.

Now it was the vampire who laughed aloud, "No? I thought you to be in a more forthcoming mood, considering your current circumstances and how little you know of them."

"I grow tired of this. State your purpose and be finished."

"Very well. You and your men are my captives in this mountain. All I require of you and your companions is that you dig when and where you are instructed. If your men do this, I will see to it that your suffering is ... eased."

Someone screamed in the distance, a piercing shriek of agony. Kurodan's attention turned to the direction it came from. A brief moment of silence resumed, and then another scream. The sound was horrible.

"You believe that my men will trust your word? When, in this exact moment, some poor soul is being tortured—"

Another scream cut Kurodan off.

"Disobedience will bring about severe punishment," the vampire warned. "As I said, if your men follow the commands given to you, you will be rewarded."

"Rewarded? Rewarded with what, exactly? What is it you vermin dig for under this mountain?" Kurodan demanded.

Another scream.

"Even if you find what I am searching for ... its true purpose will be unknown to you," the vampire said dismissively. "The important task is that it is found."

"And if we refuse? If we merely waste away and refuse your so-called rewards? What then?"

The screams grew in a crescendo, and Kurodan's ears could not dispute the pain of the owner's suffering.

"I assure you, paladin, you do not wish my wrath."

"Your wrath?" Kurodan questioned, but he tried to press his advantage. "You need us alive. You need us to search for whatever it is that is buried here. You and the orcs may—"

The screams turned into sobs that were too overwhelming to ignore any further. And then Kurodan realized the weeping was familiar, and he thought he recognized the poor soul being tortured.

"In time, you will see."

"I see nothing, save for the rats that hide within this mountain, helplessly searching for their own filth," Kurodan retorted. "If you wish for my obedience, you will bring that prisoner here and cease whatever pain has been inflicted upon him."

The vampire stared at Kurodan. "Very well." He strode to the door leading to the tunnel from which the screams had emanated. As he opened the door, the orc standing guard on the other side was startled at the vampire's presence.

"Bring him," he instructed. The orc at first glance did not seem to fully understand who the vampire referred to, but another scream called out and the orc understood.

The vampire walked back to Kurodan and stood watching the tunnel. They remained in silence until the orcs could be heard bringing someone. As Kurodan had suspected, it was the prisoner who had been waiting for them in the dungeon cell, Uthrol.

With absolute horror, Kurodan looked at the

evidence of the torture inflicted upon the man. His scalp was gone, and blood ran down his bruised and cut face. His hands were mangled, and several fingers were missing. His body bore the cruel marks of whip lashes down to the bone. The orcs dropped his torn body in front of Kurodan and the vampire.

"He is no longer useful," one of the orcs said.

The vampire said nothing but sniffed uneasily. Its mouth hung slightly open, revealing pointed teeth. Kurodan was unsure why but wondered if the vampire was struggling to control his own bloodlust at the sight of such carnage. Uthrol wept and gasped for air in between his sobs.

"Is this your reward you speak of vampire? If you wish for my men's cooperation, you will end this torture," Kurodan said.

"As you wish," the vampire replied. As he walked over to Uthrol, the man met Kurodan's eyes.

Uthrol's stare froze Kurodan to his very core. His gaze then looked up in panic to see the vampire who seized him. Kurodan watched as the vampire forced Uthrol to stand. Uthrol's entire body trembled, and he tried to call out for help.

Kurodan charged. The orcs, all too eager, struck him down before he even had a chance to stand fully. He paid dearly for the act of bravery.

The vampire drew his sword and readied it to kill Uthrol, then paused. Staying his sword, the vampire dropped Uthrol to the ground.

"No, no," it said. "I shall prolong your suffering, mortal. Take them."

The men had broken their silence and begun to argue once more as their nerves got the better of them.

"He has been gone far too long; he is not coming

back," Halthrow said.

"Silence yourself, Kurodan will return," Toradin replied.

"What if this is how we all die, one at a time. Tortured and alone," another said, almost asking himself more than the others.

Feore stood, struggling against his chains. "Enough! We do not know what has happened, so until we have proof, he is still alive. Understood?"

The men all grew quiet. A short time later footsteps could be heard from outside the cell door. The voices of orcs could be heard beyond the door, but no one could make out what they were saying.

The door was unlocked and opened. The orcs marched Kurodan back down and chained him to the floor. Uthrol's broken body was dragged in and chained next.

"Any two will do," one of the orcs said. Horad and Regalt were selected and marched back up the stairs and into the tunnels. Once the door locked behind them, Feore spoke first.

"What have you learned? What did that vampire want with you?"

Chapter XVI:
False Pretenses

Maldin, Gleed, and Captain Bravmond ran towards the throne room, their armored boots thundering on the stone floor and echoing through the halls. The guards standing watch at the door barred their entrance.

"Move aside, soldier, we have business with the queen," Maldin ordered.

"The queen has given specific orders to—"

"Let them in," came a voice from the other side of the door. The guards exchanged an odd glance at one another and stepped aside.

The three opened the doors to find the throne room was empty save for the queen and Andazar standing in the center. Their faces were both grim, almost distraught.

"What word do you bring, wizard? Why have the others not returned?" Maldin demanded.

"We were ambushed, set upon by the orcs. We gravely miscalculated their numbers and strength."

"You did not answer me," Maldin said.

"Where are the others?"

"Most of us fell in battle. Some tried to flee, though I do not know if they were captured or survived. Others defiantly made a last stand."

"And you, wizard? You fled?" Gleed asked. Andazar's face was unchanged at the insult.

"I tried to take command and rally our party, but the orcs were swift in their attack. They had us outnumbered and were waiting for us."

"Where did the orcs lay ambush?" Maldin said.

"They destroyed the town of Bursben. When we arrived, there were no survivors."

"And Raokenburg? Did they send no reinforcements?" Bravmond asked.

"The reinforcements reached the town before we did, ending in the same fate."

"Andazar believes the orcs are claiming Mount Ruin for their own," the queen told them. "We must send word to the other cities and make them aware of this new threat."

"Your highness, send word, yes, but you must rally your army. Others will join us, but we must strike, and we must strike now," Maldin pleaded.

"No," the queen shouted.

"If we risk all-out war, we will only give the orcs the chance they are so desperately seeking," Andazar said.

"Risk? Your highness, war is here, and war is a game of risks. If we do not act, we will only allow our enemy to gain power in territory and numbers," Bravmond said.

"We will decide on a course of action when we have word from our nearest allies. Has word even made it back to Raokenburg? Do they know the fate befallen of their men?" the queen questioned.

Gleed spoke, "So we are supposed to remain idle?

Do nothing?"

"Give your men orders to double the watch in case of an assault. If our allies answer our call, we may devise a battle plan," Andazar said.

"And since when does the wizard give us our orders, your highness?" Maldin asked.

"These are my orders, Maldin," she scolded. Then her voice became imperious. "If you wish to no longer follow them, then by all means, disavow your oath. You may leave my city and go die in whatever matter you deem fit."

Maldin scoffed. He turned and left the room without another word, the other two men following in suit.

As the three men walked in silence, Maldin's anger grew.

"So do we remain here, waiting for the orcs to attack whenever they please?" Gleed spoke.

"No," Bravmond said. "I have a plan."

Stopping, the two paladins both turned to the captain. "I will take my men under the cover of darkness to Mount Ruin. I will hand select them. They will be sworn to secrecy, as will you. No one will know we are gone."

"Gleed will go with you," Maldin said.

"No."

"I would be of much help to you," Gleed persisted.

"Aye, your skill would be most welcome, but I am afraid that a paladin's presence might jeopardize our mission. If we come across townsfolk, they may grow suspicious of our party. Not to mention if the queen calls upon your members and you are elsewhere. The soldiers I select will be up to the task, trust me."

"And how do we know the queen will not call upon you?" Maldin asked.

"I am a mere captain. There are many others who may answer for me or on my behalf," Bravmond said, smiling.

Maldin shook Bravmond's hand. "Then we are in your debt, captain. Send word the moment you find any knowledge of the ambush, or by the gods any survivors."

Chapter XVII:
Crune

Crune awoke to the brisk night air. His fingers, ass, and toes had already grown numb, and he could see his breath even in the dark. "This is going to be a long night," he muttered, as he crouched on one knee, leaning against the great tree he had fallen asleep on. The ground was hard, and the work would be tiresome.

He peered into the dark that now covered the cemetery in the distance, like a heavy warm blanket in bed. The night had become a comfort for him. Hiding him, protecting him. The days had become increasingly difficult.

Just as Crune's gaze was drifting through the maze of tombstones, lost in his own thoughts, movement caught his attention. The groundskeeper, Hamlith, was making his last round. His faint candle-lit lamp, a dim glow floated above the graves. Crune peered around the tree, to get a better look.

There was someone with Hamlith. "Interesting,"

Crune whispered to himself. Ever since they had been found out, rumors had started around the town like wildfire. "Graverobbers steal body," had been the front-page title in the common paper.

How self-explanatory, Crune had laughed when he read it. Since that little incident he had been forced to expedite his plans for promotion, and the groundkeepers must have doubled the nightly watch.

His so-called peers were careless, some even downright stupid. Most had a sliver of cleverness and the skill of a common thief or gutter rat. They were all, however, short-sighted, impulsive, and of course detestable. However, this last trait defined Crune better than any of them. His mind wandered again, to his life before he had thrown in his lot with some of the worst wretches in all of Gulgotha. But that was back when his dreams had no possibility of becoming reality.

The pain-stricken failures of his life had plagued him at every turn. He felt cruelly fated to become nothing more than a mere peasant, toiling endlessly and meaninglessly until death would finally bestow mercy upon him. That was until he had decided to descend with the degenerates who kept his current company. If life would not bestow any bounty upon him, then he would strangle it into submission and take it himself.

Rustling off in the distance behind him drew his attention. He instinctively drew the dagger he kept concealed. He crept to a better vantage point, slowly moving into a thick part of vegetation, trying not to make his own racket. *Sound always travels further at night*, he reminded himself.

The sound grew louder and louder, and he could now hear the harsh whispers of a man and a woman. "It's so cold we won't be able to dig up a damned thing," said the woman.

"Shut yer mouth. Yer gonna get us caught," the man replied.

"So what? If someone finds us, we can just kill 'em."

Crune wanted to kill them both for their lack of discipline but that would make the night even more arduous.

"Over here," Crune hissed. The two stopped, making a rather loud commotion before silence filled the air once more.

"Who was that?" asked the woman.

"How in the hells should I know?" said the man. The two made their way towards Crune, now with much more tact. They picked their steps carefully and moved slowly, watching for any signs of movement.

The man was average looking, slimly built with red hair. His face held a stubble of growth, and his clothes were that of a stall hand such as Crune. He held a pickaxe and carried a shovel tied around his back. The woman was attractive, petite with long blonde hair and wearing a dress that was ill suited for creeping through forests at night. She carried a small lantern in one hand and a shovel in the other.

Crune sat still, letting them get closer and closer until they had walked right past him. They reached the large tree that had been his original vantage point. They stopped and looked around trying to find him, but the two groundskeepers had started to make their way towards the noise.

"Shit, put that out," the man ordered. The woman carefully lowered the lantern to the forest floor and blew the candle out, leaving them in the dark. The two watched from either side of the tree. The groundskeepers had reached the edge of the cemetery and the edge of the forest.

138

"If you're out there, announce yourself," Hamlith said. The woman made a step as if she was about to reveal herself, but the man gripped her arm. They exchanged angry looks at one another but said nothing.

"We know you're out there. Show yourself and no harm will come to you," the other groundskeeper said. The couple looked at one another, and slowly the man nodded.

The woman placed her shovel against the tree, adjusted her dress in a more revealing fashion and then stepped out into the open.

"Please help!" came her plea. The groundskeepers both instinctively drew their short swords.

"I'm so, so lost."

She began to walk but faltered and pretended to rest against the tree.

"State your name," Hamlith demanded. The two groundskeepers approached her, one raising his lamp. She merely slid down the tree and slumped onto the ground.

"Please, help me," she whimpered.

"How is it you came to be here, young lady?" Hamlith asked.

"I was being followed by two men coming home. I thought if I hid in the trees, they would not find me. They chased me. I ... I ... lost my way," she said in a halting matter, wiping feigned tears from her face.

Crune rolled his eyes and fought the urge to boo her sloppy performance. The other groundskeeper sheathed his sword and stepped forward to help her up.

"It will be all right, dear."

The man with the pickaxe moved. "Wait!" Hamlith shouted, but it was too late for him. The man rounded the tree, pick raised and brained the man just as he was turning.

The woman jumped to her feet, screaming and clutching Hamlith, trying to hide behind him.

"Damn them," Crune said. He left his hiding spot and walked out.

The man who had just committed murder, Jagard, looked over his shoulder. "So nice of you to join us."

"Please! Those are the men that chased me," the woman claimed, still hiding behind Hamlith.

"Not one step more or I will kill the both of ye!" Hamlith shouted, sword pointed at them. Jagard was still trying to remove the mining tool from the other man's skull.

"What part of subtle do you two not understand?" Crune said, disdain oozing in his question.

"Please do something," the woman begged.

"Well, you weren't helping any, were you?" Jagard said. He placed his boot on the man's neck and ripped the axe upward with a wrenching sound.

"Drop the axe," Hamlith demanded, at the same time trying not to vomit.

"Please," she cried. "Arrest them,"

Crune looked past the groundskeeper with an expression of utter boredom, as he bent down to grab the fresh corpse. "Enough already," he said.

Hamlith's face turned from anger to confusion. Shannara simply shrugged and drove a knife into his neck. Hamlith dropped his sword and lantern, clutching the blood flowing from the grievous wound.

He fell onto his back, coughing and gagging as he died. Shannara stepped over him and began digging through his coat and trouser pockets. Crune and Jagard were dragging the other body back into the forest.

"We are leaving," Crune said. Shannara ignored him as she pulled a small coin purse from Hamlith's shirt.

"What else do you have for me?"she muttered more

to herself than the dying man.

"Why are we leaving?" Jagard asked. "We just got here."

Crune dropped his half of the body, and the man's broken head bounced on the frozen ground with a sickening thud.

"We were supposed to retrieve bodies and remain unseen," he said through clenched teeth. "Unnoticed."

"Right. Didn't really go that way now, did it?" Shannara said. She had bored of pickpocketing Hamlith's still dying body and walked over to the two arguing. "It's easier this way."

Crune turned to her in shock. "Easier what way?"

"Now we don't have to spend all night digging, right? Just take the groundskeepers and we'll be set," she said. Her voice carried a cool casualness for someone who had just cut a man's throat and watched him die.

Crune clasped his hands together and put them to his mouth, as if trying to find the words. "You two cannot be this daft, can you?"

"She has a point, Crune. Woulda taken us all damned night, not to mention probably just of gotten the one body by sunrise. Now we got two," Jagard said, still dragging the body.

"Yeah, two is better than one, right?" Shannara said smirking.

"And what happens when these two don't show up for their relief? Hm? What happens when the day watch comes looking for them? Now instead of Avernost being worried about a measly graverobber, they will be on the lookout for a murderer."

Shannara quickly dismissed Crune's angst. "So? People get murdered every day."

"Not groundskeepers on watch. This will raise not only suspicion, but this news will reach Corenbundt. We will not be able to just keep paying the town's guards to turn a blind eye. They will send soldiers down here to deal with this. Real soldiers, not some band of freelance thugs who care only for coin. Murder carries much more weight than robbing a grave."

"What in the damned hell is this mess?" came a voice. The trio turned to face the cemetery. A large burly man with an ugly face and balding head was pointing at Crune. Two other men were not far behind, carefully moving about the graves.

"Hello handsome," Shannara said, walking to him. The bald man had brigand and bastard written all over him.

Crune's face twisted into a cross between sneer and hate. "Your whore and her little plaything made so much noise that the groundskeepers walked right to us."

Shannara and Jagard both returned hateful looks at the insults. "He didn't even help, handsome." Shannara stood on her toes to go in for a kiss, but Rignor pushed her aside. Jagard grew tense at the exchange.

"This is the last time you fail me; do you understand?" Rignor said.

Crune stepped forward. "Did you not just hear me? These two are the ones who failed. Had it not been for them, the groundskeepers would still be alive, and our business would go about as usual."

"This was your idea. The blame falls on you."

"My idea! You are correct," Crune mocked. "Once again, I was the one who conjured a plan in order to fulfill the demands. You simply sat back and did nothing."

"What did you say?" Rignor asked, drawing a knife.

Crune did the same. "You claim to be the leader here, and yet you really have not done anything of merit, have you? All you do is drink, and whore, and reap the benefits that come with the title of ringleader."

"Are you challenging me, Crune? You want my title?" Rignor held out his arms, beckoning for a fight. Crune spat on the ground.

Shannara was at Rignor's ear. "Do it. Kill him." Her mouth stretched into an eerie smile. Rignor took a step forward but one of the others stepped in between them.

"Enough. We need to leave, now."

Shannara's face contorted into frustration. "Kill him and then we will leave."

"No, our numbers have been dwindling with all the in-house fighting. There will be no more," the man said, looking at Crune.

Crune sheathed his dagger, but Rignor was still pointing with his. "Mark my words, I will gut you, you little bastard. You and Jagard get the bodies back and prep 'em."

"Got it, boss," Jagard said, bending down to grab Hamlith's corpse. It had finally stopped gurgling and twitching.

"Do it yourself," Crune said. The man who had stepped between them stood in Crune's face.

"Your insubordination has gone far enough."

"So has your petty bootlicking, Thrass."

At the insult, Thrass struck Crune hard, knocking him to the ground. Shannara and Rignor laughed.

Crune got back to his feet and spit blood, almost grinning back at them. He had been laughed at his entire life, the sting was gone and only numbness remained.

Rignor turned, grabbing Shannara by the waist, making her laugh more. They walked back through the cemetery, leaving Crune and Jagard alone with the dead. Jagard watched Rignor and Shannara holding each other as they walked.

"You know she is never going to love you the way

you love her," Crune said, taunting Jagard.

"Shut up."

"Why do you follow her like some pet when she leaves you for him every time?"

"I said shut yer mouth," Jagard said and raised the axe.

Crune shook his head. "Right, have it your way. Before we depart let us try and clean up your mess, leave less of any sign for the day watch." Jagard stood watching the others leave until they were out of sight.

Crune wiped the cold sweat from his brow as they placed Hamlith on the rotting wood table. The two of them had managed to get both corpses back to one of their hiding places unnoticed. Though Crune knew it was just a matter of time before the other groundskeepers would patrol the cemetery and see the blood they left behind. Crune damned Shannara and Jagard silently to himself.

"What?" Jagard said.

Crune hadn't even bothered looking at him. His mind was racing with all the tasks that still needed to be completed. The real challenge would be moving the bodies after they had been prepared. That required finesse and a delicate touch. Something all his peers utterly lacked.

"Nothing, you may leave."

Jagard paused, "You don't need help preppin' 'em?"

"No, Jagard. You have helped far too much as it is."

Jagard's face soured. "Yer welcome fer movin' 'em, you little prick."

Crune looked at him then and gave a sarcastic smile. "I'll prepare them, you may leave me to my work."

"Gladly." Jagard turned and made his way up the cellar steps but stopped and turned near the top.

"You know, you think yer better than me an' everyone else."

Crune just stared back.

"You aren't better, you just hate everything."

Crune turned his back to Jagard and faced Hamlith's corpse again. "Jagard, I want more than you could ever dream of. I intend to make my vision a reality."

"And what is that?"

Crune turned over his shoulder and looked at Jagard. "Mastery."

Jagard turned and left with a slightly puzzled look on his face. Crune closed his eyes and let out a long exhale.

The room was dank and damp. It was under a barkeep near the south side of Avernost. The owner had allowed Crune to utilize the cellar with the understanding that Crune needed another job aside from his daily one.

It was a simple job: stocking, cleaning, and organizing the inn's products and goods during the night. Something simple but at night, to earn another measly wage to add to his other measly income.

Crune had been careful, picking nights that were less crowded and busier than others. He had specifically chosen this place of business as it was not the most popular establishment, especially compared to The Laughin' Maiden or even The Broad Barrels. Those were finer taverns with a much steadier clientele.

No, The Broken Cup was much smaller and not as frequented. Of course, there were the regulars every night, but it was a much quieter inn.

Though no matter how quiet, every tavern had a flair for drama. The Broken Cup was still no stranger to brawls, whoring, and drunkards who tried to skip out on their tab.

Crune had worked this nightly occupation for weeks now. Only recently had he slipped up, having an almost catastrophic failure.

He had cursed himself ever since, always his own harshest critic. Crune had prepared the last corpse they had used. He had done everything perfectly. Cleaned every inch of the cellar. Carefully washed all the blood and grit away. He had almost broken his back lifting the body from the table and into one of the largest ale barrels. He had even figured out the right amount of salt and herbs to put in the barrel with the corpses to preserve it and to mask the smell. The barrel weighed a ton and had to be strategically placed before adding the concoction of salt and the dead.

But alas, his exhaustion had finally bested him. The unrelenting toll of working the armory and horse stalls during the day, then digging up the dead at night while pretending to work the cellar, had pushed him to the point of delirium. That night, Wurshmere, the owner, had asked Crune if he needed the night off at first glance of his appearance.

He had formulated the excuse of fighting off a slight illness. But Wurshmere had pressed him hard, explaining that he did not need anyone sick touching all of his perishables and then serving them to his clientele. Crune had almost panicked at that moment, knowing a body was right outside the back of the tavern. In his weariness he did not know where he would hide it, if not in the cellar. He begged and pleaded that he needed the nightly wages as meager as they were.

Wurshmere had taken pity on Crune that fateful evening and was rewarded with it being his last night alive.

The irony, Crune had thought.

He was just walking up the cellar steps as Wurshmere closed the bar.

Dawn was only a few hours away, and Crune was already dreading reporting for his stable duties, his body and mind wracked with fatigue.

"By the gods, Crune, you look like a damned ghoul! Take yer leave and get some bloody rest," Wurshmere had said to him. He handed Crune his earnings for the night, giving him more than the agreed-upon wages. Crune had thanked him and assured him that he would return the following night much better rested, knowing it was a complete lie.

Wurshmere had begun inspecting the cellar just as he did at the close of every night. "I have to admit Crune, yer an organized bast–what's this?"

Crune had felt his blood run cold and the hair on the back of his neck stand straight.

Wurshmere had walked to the back part of the cellar towards the barrel. "Looks like ye finally slipped up," Wurshmere laughed.

Crune had feigned a laugh and asked what Wurshmere meant. But inside his head, he was screaming to get away from the barrel.

"You forgot to label this one," Wurshmere said, pointing at it. Crune had instantly begun apologizing, trying to make his way in between Wurshmere and the barrel.

Wurshmere had only laughed at him and told him to leave, saying that he would label it and then lock up. As Wurshmere reached the barrel, he stopped, almost gagging.

"What is that smell?"

Need to add something to the salt, Crune had thought. Wurshmere pried off the lid to the barrel and looked inside.

"Holy Light," he shouted as he looked upon a flayed skull, its blackened eye sockets staring back at him through the salt.

Crune brought the knife down hard, aiming for the back of his neck, but he was tired and slow. Wurshmere had spun to face him, taking the knife in the top of the shoulder. They screamed at each other as they fought. Wurshmere was a portly man, but he was burly as well, having dealt with many drunken fights in his day.

Wurshmere gripped Crune's knife hand in place as he struggled to rip the blade free and stab again. With the other he began to pummel Crune's face and head. Crune took the punishment, blow after blow, trying to strike back with his free hand. The struggle for life and death now took full hold. Desperation set in.

Wurshmere beat him to the ground and sat atop him. Crune could feel his blood, wet and warm, seeping into his eyes, nose, and ears. Tasted it in his mouth. He could no longer tell if it was his tears or his blood that blurred his vision. He was done for.

Wurshmere was now strangling him, and he could feel his life slipping away. *Yet another failure*, he thought, all but ready to embrace death and finally end his miserable existence. But something within him stirred, deep inside.

No, he thought. Then said it aloud. "No!"

Struggling at his own boot, Crune's fingers found what they were searching for—a boot knife about the size of a small scalpel and just as sharp. With a rage that scared even himself, he drove it into Wurshmere. The man reeled back in pain, falling over.

Crune now in turn, climbed on top of him. He stabbed wildly. Again and again, over and over. Not even being able to see what he was stabbing or the wounds he was inflicting. Not caring. Not caring that the screams might alert someone. Not caring for the life he was snuffing out. Not caring for the lives he had selfishly claimed and brutalized before this one. Not caring for the lives that he would take in the future. He only cared for one thing. His one goal.

By the time Crune had caught his breath and ceased the carnage, he could not even stand. He sat atop the bloody mess beneath him, closed his eyes and exhaled. Just as he had done now. Focused. Calm. Calculated.

After a moment he had left, not bothering to clean the cellar or hide Wurshmere's carved corpse. Crune simply cleaned himself and reported to the stalls. His face was still a wreck from the assault, which raised questions and brought ridicule from the soldiers and other aides.

Crune simply ignored them. He went through that day as if he were already among the dead he worked on, save only one thought.

Soon he would be the master of his own fate.

Chapter XVIII: Facade

Crune envisioned all of his tasks in his mind's eye. Then his eyes slowly opened and directed his movements. His hands and fingers found their home, tightly gripped around the tools he had carefully laid out. His body was tired but relaxed, his mind focused but at ease.

The work demanded he be diligent and meticulous. He felt truly alive in these solitary moments. *Funny*, he thought. *Why do I feel more alive with the dead than with the living? Is it the work, or what I'm working towards? The future fruit of my labors, forbidden and unknowing. That is it, perhaps. Knowing the unknowing.*

Crune washed his hands and arms, changed his clothes, and turned to walk up the cellar steps. The bodies were no longer hidden in barrels. There was no need now that Wurshmere had suddenly disappeared from the town.

Crune had impressed himself preparing both bodies

in the amount of time he had before the sun came up.

No longer having to hide the bodies allowed for more time to prepare them. That, and he was becoming more proficient. Crune recognized this. His hands worked with a familiarity now that had astonished even himself. Repetition.

Against Crune's advisement, Rignor had declared himself the manager of the now vacant establishment. Rignor's reputation had become bolder and more well known in Avernost. But alas, Rignor did whatever the hell he pleased, everyone else be damned.

It had not mattered much anyway, as Rignor rarely frequented The Broken Cup. Management meant work. Rignor was much better suited to delegating tasks, rather than completing them himself. So, he had appointed Jagard to be the face of the bar.

Jagard was a useless human being. His entire existence revolved around gaining the attention of one of Rignor's whores, Shannara. Everyone knew this and at first Jagard had initially refused the offer, out of his spite and contempt for Rignor. Then Shannara had but mentioned her excitement of the idea of ownership and he changed his mind in an instant.

The fools, Crune thought. All of them trying to play each other. Trying to get what they wanted, and in turn being played. Rignor believed himself to be the mastermind, that he was untouchable. Crune knew that when the opportunity arose, Rignor would no longer be able to stand in his way. No one would.

Crune made his way out of the cellar and into The Broken Cup's main entrance. He counted three drunkards still trying to polish off their mugs before daybreak. Four if you included Jagard, who was serving himself behind the bar and was already drunk.

Another of his useless qualities.

Anytime Shannara left him to be with Rignor, he spiraled into a drunken stupor.

"Finished?" Jagard slurred as Crune walked past him.

"Yes." Crune was in no mood to pay any attention to Jagard, but he reached out placing his hand on his chest, stopping him.

"Rignor was here …" Jagard said, taking a large gulp from his mug.

"And?"

Jagard leaned closer, "He said to have the two bodies in the forest by nightfall, tonight."

Crune turned to eye the three regulars to see if they were within earshot. "Tonight? What about the final task? That will need more time if we are to—"

Jagard interrupted, "Rignor's orders. He said the wizard is going to be there tonight. He is going to—"

Crune now silenced him, "Who is to do it, if tonight?"

Jagard downed his mug and gave Crune a stare that was identical to the ones the dead gave him. "Who do you think?"

Tamerill sat at the closest table to the bar, half pretending to spill his mug's contents down his beard and shirt as he continued to drink. He was careful not to even look in their direction, but he could still hear them. *Tonight*, he thought, and he had definitely heard them mention a wizard. His work was finally beginning to pay off.

Tamerill watched as the "owner" poured himself another drink and took a swig. *This poor bastard could drink an entire troop under the table*, Tamerill smiled to himself.

The other one was different. He was not like the

typical bandit that Tamerill had observed and kept tabs on. He did not drink or gamble or whore, so far as he could tell. He carried about him a crafty intelligence and his eyes appeared like those of a cold-blooded killer, predatory and dead inside.

He spent long spans of time down in that cellar. *It's funny*, Tamerill mused. *He always appears tired except when he exits that cellar. Just now he appears refreshed after a long stint down there.*

Tamerill had planned to break into the cellar if given the opportunity but alas, that had not come to fruition yet. He watched the two men from his periphery.

The calculated one leaned closer to the drunk and whispered something so quiet that now Tamerill was unable to discern their conversation. The drunk's expression changed to surprise and even worry. He began to shake his head, declining whatever the crafty one had said.

He said something else, and the owner's face grew angry. Tamerill was able to make out just three words: tonight, kill, and Rignor.

Tamerill knew Rignor was the groups' leader or appeared to be anyways. They were going to try and make their move on him.

He watched as the crafty one walked past and out the front entrance, leaving behind the owner, who had suddenly stopped drinking. "Alright lads, time to finish your drinks and pay yer debts,"

Tamerill stood up too quickly, filled with adrenaline about what he had just heard, as much as the drinks had impaired him.

He paid his coin and made his way out the door looking for the one who had just left. Tamerill did not know how, but he felt it in his bones. That was his man. The one who would unravel this entire devilry and bring it into the light.

Crune made his way through the town heading northeast to the soldiers' quarters. There, just beyond the town, a small barracks with an armory, a horse stable, and a small training grounds provided space for the soldiers to practice. Though the men who lived there were more professional guards than soldiers. The castellan, Lord Dramington, had been appointed over Avernost by Tharfern, Duke of Corenbundt.

There really had been no need for Avernost to have any permanent quarters for soldiers, as Corenbundt was just to the south. Corenbundt was where the queen's furthest army reached, save for Stalendorf. Stalendorf was much further north and almost completely isolated.

Despite all of this, Lord Dramington was a keen individual. He had worked his way up the political ladder by proving his competence in all matters he touched. He had personally requested that a small detachment of soldiers be stationed at Avernost.

When Duke Tharfern had declined, Dramington put into effect a personal guard and had their quarters built. This way it did not require an official part of the army to be stationed there.

The men Dramington hired, jumped at the chance. Better wages, living quarters, treatment, and—most desirable—no direct supervision. They could operate as force unto themselves unless directly summoned by Dramington himself.

This had created a unique situation among the men that served as the guard. Just like the regular army, there were those who were honor bound, dutiful, and professional warriors. Then there were men who were merely there because they simply had no other profession—discipline and honor be damned.

Crune had worked at the barracks and living quarters for the better part of his adult life. His existence there was mundane at best. Cleaning the horses, the stalls, the weapons and armor, preparing meals, more cleaning. Crune had come to see it as the life of a slave.

As he approached the front entrance of the barracks, two men eyed him.

"You're late," one said.

Crune smiled at both the men, "My apologies, gentlemen. I was more occupied this morning than I had anticipated." He tried to make his way past them, but the other put out his hand.

"This is the third time, Crune? Or the fourth? You keep this up and you won't be around much longer, ye hear?"

Crune's mind's eye watched as the man's face began to melt, his skin oozed, and his blood bubbled and burned like acid. The man's smoldering skull shrieked and begged for mercy.

"I," he started, then paused and began again. "You are right. It will not happen again. I need to simply wake up earlier it seems." Crune still wore a gentle smile, hoping the guise would be enough to end the conversation.

The first laughed, "You need more discipline if you are ever going to make something of yourself in this world. Is it a wonder you could never make it as a soldier?"

Crune felt the rage, the hate almost brimming over. His face slightly twitched, his facade almost faltered but he remained calm. He was used to this sort of chiding from them. From everyone, really.

"If you excuse me, I must be getting to the horses now. I know there is a riding expedition scheduled for today."

"Riding's been cancelled. We are training in the pit today. Feed the horses, clean the shit in the stalls, and then get the water and food ready."

"Right away," Crune nodded, making his way into the barracks.

Some of the men were sitting at the tables still eating breakfast. Most did not pay him much attention as he quickly walked past the dining hall, the living quarters, and out the back. The horses' stalls were actually the largest building of the station.

Forty horses could be housed inside, though there were only thirty right now. Two horses per man and only fifteen men. That still meant thirty animals to feed, brush, saddle, unsaddle, and then clean up the shit. It was not an easy task, day in and day out, on top of the other trivial tasks that filled Crune's day.

Crune tried to mentally prepare himself for the long hours ahead of him at the pit. While he understood the training behind the pit, he also knew that it had turned into more a gladiatorial practice for ego and sport. And after he would be doing the cooking and cleaning for their meals that evening.

As he entered the stalls, a voice called out to him.

"Riding's been cancelled."

Crune turned to see Oslav, the only other servant who worked at the barracks.

"I heard," he responded. "Changed to another bout at the pit it seems."

Oslav was much older than Crune. He was wiry but strong. He walked with a limp on his left leg, but in his prime he could outmatch every man in the barracks. He had been a soldier for his entire life until he could no longer keep pace in his aging years.

He was less of a servant and more a mentor to the soldiers. The only reason he helped with the servant duties was that, like Crune, he was a perfectionist.

"Aye, I've already prepped the supplies. Help me load them," Oslav said. The two loaded the carts and then followed the men to the training grounds.

Not far from the barracks, Tamerill stood on the corner of a dirt road and watched. He could not make out the men's faces, but he could still identify his man by the way he moved. As the guards arrived, they began dismounting. The older man with the limp left the wagon and began barking orders at the others to offload the wagon. The one Tamerill was tracking started to unload all the equipment.

Their training grounds were not large, but they had everything they needed. There were human silhouettes made of wood, dressed in old gambesons and stuffed with straw. Some even had armor on them. There was a lane on either side for the men to practice fighting from horseback. And at the far end there were archery targets with bullseyes painted on. In the center was a circular ring, wooden posts driven into the dirt and thick rope tied all the way around.

The men lined the rope and placed their weapons and armor at their feet. The old man motioned for Crune to bring up supplies. Tamerill watched as Crune made trip after trip, bringing wooden swords first. After, he carried water, food, and other miscellaneous items.

The old man barked again, and each guard started limbering up. Some jogged in place, others reached for the sun and then touched the grass. After a few minutes, every man turned to his right and started jogging around the ring. This warm-up continued for some time, but the training did not concern Tamerill. He was there for one man and one man only.

Eventually some of the men entered the ring,

brandishing wooden swords. At the command of the old soldier, they commenced fighting while the others watched. Crune stood by the pile of supplies he had organized and watched as well.

Tamerill could not discern his facial expression but had many years practice at reading body language. *No matter how strong willed*, he thought. *The body always betrayed itself.*

Tamerill did not know how much time had passed. Judging by the sun, he estimated at least two hours. The men were relentless, or rather the old man who oversaw them was.

He was what Tamerill had always referred to as the "old breed." Born at the right time to serve in the many wars that had ravaged the world. The Eleven Years War, perhaps? Judging by the man's age, most definitely the War of the Dukes and the Sack of the North. Tamerill wondered if the man, with his age, had fought much in the Great War. Very few ever lived through one if not all these atrocities. That was the reason the few who had, were called the old breed.

As time went on, the training began to increase in intensity. The men traded out their wooden swords for real ones. They donned their armor. Duels yielded to groups of men entering the ring at the same time. While Tamerill enjoyed the spectacle, which reminded him much of his own training, he kept his focus on the man. He had not seemed to say or do much of anything at all.

He merely catered to the men with water, helping them with armor and weapons before and after the bouts. The men almost completely disregarded his presence.

He is cunning to hide in plain sight, Tamerill told himself.

When the guards were fighting and not resting, the man just stood and watched.

Tamerill wondered if he was paying attention to the training or was lost in his own thoughts.

Chapter XIX: Memories

Crune had grown bored of the fights. He had witnessed them so many times before. *The men are good at what they do, but the excitement of it all fades quickly once accustomed to it,* he thought.

His mind began to wander as it so often did. Gnawing at him, pulling him into the thick of his own subconscious. Events of the past, tasks of the present, and possibilities of the future. It plagued him.

He thought of everything that had gone wrong in his life, starting from childhood. True, his upbringing had not been horrible compared to others. His parents had not been rich, nor utterly poor. So, he had been raised among the commoners and townsfolk.

He had received some schooling at a younger age, and his parents had traveled to Mil-Thuras when he was still a young boy, to manage some business affairs in the capital. Crune envisioned that great bastion. The vision was clear as glass. *Funny, how some of the best memories in life are just as fond as the worst*, he thought.

He had been lucky, Crune's parents told him. Upon entering those colossal gates that seemed to tower over the entire world, Crune saw *him*.

Everyone saw *him* where he stood in the courtyard. The aura around him demanded attention, and the city's populace demonstrated a respected reverence at his mere presence. Even the king and queen seemed to obey it, whether out of fear or unknowing he could not say.

Crune was drawn to the being and the feeling, even more than the others in the courtyard. That feeling, he could not dare even try to bring to life with words.

The man, if he could even be called by such a common word, mounted the largest steed Crune had ever laid eyes on, and began to ride the beast out of the city. His fierce eyes met not a soul, save for him. As the being passed by, his gaze turned ever so slightly, locking eyes for an instant with Crune.

Crune had not even the slightest notion of why him, but it was him, nonetheless. When their eyes had met, he had a vision, be it a dream or nightmare, he could not say. But in that look, the being had shown Crune the faintest potential of the powers he possessed and conveyed, that one day he could learn the same. Magic.

After he watched the gates close behind the rider, Crune heard whispers that confirmed his vision. It was a wizard. Rumor had it he saved a small contingent force from the city of Raokenburg who had been stalked by vampires in the Ancient Forest. The king and queen had summoned him to Mil'Thuras, to bestow upon him their personal gratitude and verify the account.

Crune had immediately become obsessed with all things considered magic from that moment forward. He had begged and pleaded with his parents to stay in Mil'Thuras.

The city had quite possibly the largest accruement of books, tomes, scrolls, and writings ever kept in one location: the Sanctum, where almost every facet of life, from the minor and unimportant to the most serious, had been documented.

After harassing his parents, as children do when they become fixated on certain things, they allowed him to visit the enormous library. Crune had never felt such excitement in his life. His parents admired their child's pursuit of knowledge but felt pursuing magic was a complete waste of time—and possibly evil. One could not make a living in the world from magic, they had vainly repeated.

But they relented and took him to the Sanctum, thinking if they humored him a little, sooner or later Crune would realize that one does not just simply read a book and learn magic. In fact, no one really knew how magic worked, or even if one could learn it. There were no schools, no concrete documentation. Only stories, tales, myth and legend. The few wizards that had been rumored to walk the world had never shared with any mortal the ways they had learned their powers.

Crune searched desperately, hopelessly. Any piece of paper that had the mere mention of magic, he had to consume. As he grew older, to his parents' dismay, his obsession only grew worse. He tried everything to try and return to Mil'Thuras. To return to the Sanctum in hopes of stumbling upon new information. In hopes of crossing paths with the wizard, or any wizard, or any person who claimed to know anything about wizards.

On one fateful day, Crune had the opportunity to return to the city, whether he had willed it into existence or simply outwaited time itself it seemed. He was much older now, well into his years of becoming a young man.

His father scheduled another trip for business and

secretly hoped his son would gain a new interest in his older age.

Crune remembered his father suggesting that he might pursue work at the Sanctum itself. To ask the bookkeepers if he might be able to obtain an apprenticeship. Crune had almost laughed out loud at the notion. He had no real interest in the books themselves, only the knowledge that they possibly possessed.

When they finally arrived, they passed through the main gate, which was just as large and magnificent as Crune recalled from childhood. He immediately abandoned his father and headed straight to the library.

The streets were a cacophony of people and activity. As Crune made his way through the main marketplace and in so doing, witnessed an event by mere accident.

A common thief had made the mistake of trying to steal some food from one of the local traders. Crune had been standing not two feet from the assailant when he committed the crime.

Crune thought that the thief may have gotten away with the petty crime had he been more patient, but alas he had not. The trader had turned his back to the thief when asked a question about a specific fruit he had in his inventory. When the thief had made his move, attempting to pickpocket the trader, he had already turned around and witnessed the act.

The thief tried to turn and run with the small sack of coins, but the trader cried out in anger and leapt at him, grabbing him and wrestling him to the ground. This drew the attention of quite an audience and Crune slowed down, both due to the crowd and his own curiosity.

The two fought each other briefly until the thief produced a knife and stabbed the trader in the belly.

Letting out a scream and letting go of the thief, he lay on his back holding the knife that was still protruding from his stomach.

The thief panicked and ran, pushing his way through the crowd. Men shouted for his capture and women cried aloud. Crune watched as men swarmed and piled onto the thief, pinning him to the ground. A group of soldiers came running to aid, but one of them was different. He did not wear the usual insignia of a soldier of Mil'Thuras.

His armor was scarred but clean. He had a long beard and carried a shield which bore the emblem of a hand imbued with fire. Crune's interest piqued at the sight of this strange soldier.

The others made their way to detain the criminal, but this man made his way to the injured trader, lying almost at Crune's feet.

"Help me, please," the man begged. The warrior knelt over the trader and laid his shield beside him.

"Look away," he instructed the trader, removing his horned helm. The trader looked directly up at Crune. Crune watched as the warrior carefully pulled the knife from the man's belly.

The trader screamed again in agony, claiming, "I am a dead man."

But the soldier calmly dropped the knife and placed one gauntleted hand over the bleeding wound. Crune assumed it was to apply pressure on the wound to try and slow the bleeding. He was wrong.

With his free hand, the soldier opened a large book and whispered something to himself. The words were undiscernible, but Crune thought it sounded like a prayer.

A form of light began to glow from the warrior's hand. Then, as quickly as it had appeared, it faded away. The injured trader sat up, then looked down in amazement at his belly.

He leapt to his feet and then fell back down on his knees.

"By the gods, it is a miracle! By the Holy Light you have saved me," the trader cried and tried to kiss the man's armored boots. But the man brushed him off and stood, donning his helm and shield.

In complete awe, Crune blurted out, "How?"

A shout from the crowd erupted, "Blessed be the paladins of the Holy Order!" But the soldier or paladin seemed to all but ignore the man he had just saved and the people around him. He turned and began to walk away, saying not a word.

Crune surprised himself when he stepped in front of the mighty warrior. "Please, I must know," he said.

The warrior stopped and glared at Crune.

"You must know what?"

"How? How did you learn to do that? How did you learn magic?" Crune asked frantically, unable to hide his desperation for knowledge.

"I am a paladin of the Holy Order. We wield the blessed light of the gods. We are the protectors of Mil'Thuras and the realm of men."

"How can I learn your magic? Please I must know."

"If you must know, you must become one of us," the paladin said. With that, he turned and pushed his way back through the sea of people. Cheers erupted over and over, and the other soldiers marched the thief, now bound and gagged, to the executioner's square.

Crune followed, watching as he was brought forward and declared guilty of attempted murder. He was decapitated directly after the sentence. Crune then rushed to find his father and tell him about the events that had just taken place. To tell him that he was going to join the Holy Order.

Chapter XX:
Shattered Dreams

As the guards continued their training, Crune's mind wandered even deeper into his memories. He remembered his parents' excitement at the notion that their son would be pursuing a most noble goal, and that his future would be in the life of soldiering. It had pained them some, knowing how dangerous that particular life could be, considering the horrors of the Great War. But the Great War was over, and the world of Gulgotha now knew peace, or at least the most peace it had known in ages.

Crune threw himself into his own hell. He began an excruciating physical regimen, training himself to the highest standards. He consumed all books on military history and strategy. He had found his new goal, his new purpose. His excitement was all the more real when he found that there was real information at his fingertips. No longer did he spend his time in search of knowledge and only finding empty rumors and myths.

The Holy Order was real; he had witnessed it. Their recruiting, while held sacred, was not entirely secret. Any able man who was deemed fit and worthy could enlist in their training. Crune had learned that the training to become a paladin, or "unblooded," was the most rigorous and long of any armed profession.

If one were to fail this trial, their life was deemed bound by contract to serve in the army of Mil'Thuras. Crune had not given this notion much thought, his mind had already been made. He would not fail.

Crune joined the ranks of other initiates that were just as eager to prove themselves worthy of earning the title of paladin. The training was horrendous. Crune thought himself mentally and physically up to any task, but the rigors and challenges were extreme. The forced marches with little to no sleep, food, or water. The unrelenting standards for perfection. The physical toll of practiced combat against each other and the instructors.

He did not quit, in fact he absolutely refused to. He made up his mind that he would achieve his goal or die trying. There was no second option.

However, to his surprise there was another challenge—an interview he did not know how to prepare for. At a certain point in the training regiment, after the initial portions that had wounded and scared off all the weak and the timid, the ones who truly were not prepared, the ones who could not grit their teeth and press on, came a different type of challenge. It was to be conducted by the same paladin whom Crune had witnessed that day in Mil'Thuras, Maldin, the most formidable of the instructors. Each initiate was spoken to in person with the great warrior, alone.

When it was Crune's turn, he stood at attention facing the paladin. He remembered sweating and the feeling of exhaustion taking hold but also feeling proud for the first time in his life.

Maldin simply asked, "What is your true purpose here?"

Crune assumed many gave the answer of protecting his fellow man, to become like Maldin, great warrior, or to vanquish the terrible foes that threatened all way of life. Not for Crune. When he was questioned, his mind fixated on the vision the wizard had shown him. In so doing, Crune answered the warrior honestly. "I seek the power and understanding of magic," he said.

Maldin seemed to grow curious at this. "What purpose does learning magic have to do with becoming a paladin?"

Again, Crune answered honestly. "I have seen your magic, and this is the only way I know how to attain it," he had said. Yet his honesty became his undoing, Crune always thought. His face turned into a scowl as his mind replayed the events and the pivotal moment which led him to his current misery.

For this answer, he was removed from the training and stripped of his title of initiate. He protested as much as he could, of course. He had not understood why. He had not failed, not quit, not given up, not become too wounded, not been killed. He was simply told that he was not to become a paladin, now or ever. He was banished from the training grounds and forced into the standard army.

Crune stood by the horse cart, staring blankly at the small flame on the tip of a match he had lit, his thoughts now trapped in his own torment.

Instead of preparing the lantern, Crune watched as the flame slowly descended the match until it singed his fingertips, the burning sensation causing him to smile slightly. Crune quickly looked around to see if any of the others had noticed. To his relief, none had, and he struck another match to ready the lantern.

His obsession with magic did not fade. It was a plague that clung to him as flies cling to the dead. His training among the common troop was difficult but nothing compared to the rigor of the paladin training he had become accustomed to. Now without the end goal being achievable, there was no point, at least not to him. He grew bored and increasingly angry. He lashed out at anyone who tried to help him and especially those who stood in his way.

Soon he became blacklisted with those whom the army had also deemed untrainable. There was a place for those who fell into this category: the very bottom of the barrel. If the individual would not learn or improve, if the army could not train him, he would live the life of a servant. He was still bound under oath to serve in the military, regardless, and serve he would.

Having earned no rank, no respect, and no merit and now forced to go about the most tedious and lowly duties, Crune plummeted into a deep depression. He stopped caring all together. He no longer cared for life itself, as his own seemed futile, and he often contemplated ending it.

Eventually he found himself surrounded by similar people. *Misery loves company*, he often told himself with a pain wracked smile. His newfound company drove him deeper and deeper into the dark. All his morals faded and gave way. *If I ever truly had any to begin with*, he thought.

He became acquainted with the criminal underworld and all the scum who inhabited it. The beggars, thieves, murderers, prostitutes, swindlers, and the deranged and depraved. Rarely did he ever personally partake, but he was witness to it all. Until one night he had overheard the whispering that set him on the path before him now.

One evening, while Crune was cleaning up the tables and kitchen quarters at the barracks, the soldiers were staying up into the night drinking. They had recently thwarted an attempt on Lord Dramington's life.

As best Crune could tell from their loud boasting, Dramington had just foiled an attempt on his life. The lord had taken most of the men on a business trip to Corenbundt. While he was conducting business in the city, one of his spies reported that there was to be an assassination attempt. Lord Dramington, being clever, concluded his business and headed back to Avernost, hoping to draw out his pursuers.

To his credit, the contract killers had taken the bait, attempting to strike while Dramington and his men were on the road. Even more to Dramington's credit, he had sent some of his men out ahead to scout the roads well before him ever leaving Corenbundt. Their plan was to find suitable chokepoints and in turn ambush the assailants.

His plan had evidently worked flawlessly, and the men had all fought bravely, or so Crune had heard that entire evening. Lord Dramington, pleased with himself, his men, and the slaughter of his murderers had given the men a much-needed night of reprieve.

He had ordered barrels of ale, mead, and wine brought to the barracks and sent finely cooked meals from Avernost's greatest chefs. Women from the local whorehouses paid their visits and left. The men indulged until only a few remained, halfway conscious in a drunken stupor. Two of the men still regaled each other with the events that earned them their night off.

"Ya shoulda, did ya seen the look on ther faces?"

The two men burst into laughter, "I bout thought they was gonna throw ther swords down and give up!"

"Aye, they fought till the end, they did. I'll give 'em that!"

"Theys didn't know what to do, we had 'em surrounded!"

"Aye, aye. Ran righ' into me sword, tryin' to get away." More laughter followed by more drinking, and then silence for a moment.

Crune thought the two had finally passed out in their chairs or on the floor like many of the other men. But then he heard their voices, hushed and curious. He slowly made his way out of the kitchen quarters, sidestepping the drunk bodies that hindered his movements. Pretending to clean up around the men, he inched his way closer.

"They wasn't just tryin' to kill Dramington," the first one said, as he reached into his pocket and produced a small piece of parchment.

"What da mean? Ye think they was tryin' to rob all us too?"

"No. I found this on one of 'em," the man said, sliding the note across the table. The other man's face grew still as he read it.

"Did ye tell Lord Dramington 'bout this?"

"Not yet. I think he might already know."

"So, the rumors are true, eh?"

"Maybe. Could be just a bunch of bandits makin' 'emselves out ta be worse than they are."

"Aye, but if 'em rumors are true," the second halted, then continued, "if they are a bunch of devil worshippers, what then?"

"Aye, then we don't know what kinda foul magic we might face, if they try again."

The two men fell silent and turned to look at Crune.

"What rumors?" Crune politely asked. The man with the note returned only a sour expression; the other clumsily stood to leave.

"Why would I tell you anything, house rat?" Crune laughed at the insult. But his obsession flared, and he continued, "I heard you mention magic. Only curious."

The second man who awkwardly stood up, made his way to the sleeping quarters.

The first man with the note stared at his drink and then downed it. "That matter doesn' concern ye. Cleanin' these mugs do." He pushed the empty cup towards him.

Crune was now the one who stared silently, with a blank look on his face. "You are right," he finally said, a false attempt to break the tension. The man was about to stand and take his leave, but Crune stopped him. "However, if you believe it wise to hide something so important from Lord Dramington, maybe I should advise him certain men under his employ are keeping secrets."

The man now stood and placed his hand on the hilt of his sword.

"Maybe, just maybe," Crune ventured, "Lord Dramington would not be so keen on his trusted men hiding information, especially after an attempt on his life."

"You little rat! I'll gut ye—" the man began stepping towards Crune and drawing his sword. But he was stopped by the sharp edge of steel against his throat.

"Move, ever so slightly," Crune whispered, pulling the man closer so that their eyes had nowhere else to look except into one another's. He pressed the short blade down harder but not enough to break the skin. "Please … give me a reason."

The two stared at one another for a brief moment. Crune saw a man, drunk, angry, and scared. He wondered what the man staring back at him saw.

"If ye kill me, ye will hang," the man said.

"Aye, but maybe I kill you and take the note to Lord Dramington. Say you attempted to take my life when I overheard your ... little secret. Say you were actually part of the group of assassins, and I was just defending myself against you."

The man fell silent, his mind fighting his own drunken stupor and his current predicament. "What do you want?" he muttered.

Crune smiled, "I want to know what that note says. I want to know any knowledge you have of magic or people that know how to use it. You tell me that and we can forget this ever happened."

The man let out a sigh. "Deal," he said and handed Crune the note.

It turned out to be a set of instructions. The so-called assassins did not, in fact, want to kill Lord Dramington. They wanted him kidnapped and taken alive to a certain location. There was a red marking, a symbol of some sort at the bottom of the note. Crune had never seen it before. The soldier described the symbol as that of a vampire marking.

He believed the assassins were vampire worshippers—a cult that kidnapped and sacrificed people to the devils in hopes that if the vampires were to ever return, their dark angels would spare them or even turn them.

Crune questioned the soldier about magic. Had he seen or heard about anyone using it. The soldier laughed in his face.

"Have ye not heard a word I've said? For someone who is cunning, ye are a bit daft," the man said. "The human sacrifices, vampires—it is all dark magic. Devil magic."

Crune quickly grew more and more disappointed as the conversation went on. It must have been obvious.

"We done?" the soldier asked.

"No. Where is their meeting place?" Crune asked.

The man laughed but then stopped. "Ye can't be serious?" After a moment of silence, he said, "By the gods, lad, do ye have a death wish?"

"Do you know or not?"

"Some have said it is in the forest to the northeast."

"Where in the forest?"

"No one knows. The forest ends at the mountains and then ..." he trailed off.

"Mount Ruin," Crune said, eyes alight.

"Aye. Why? Why do ye seek this lad?"

"Does the note say when?"

"When, what?"

"When their meeting is to take place."

"Ye do have a death wish don't ye." More silence. "Tonight."

Crune left the man, even after his warnings. The drunk soldier finally gave up, probably thinking that he would never see the fool again. Crune was frantic, adrenaline was coursing through his veins. There was not much time left and he most likely would not make it into the forest before sunrise, but he had to try. He sprinted to his quarters and hastily packed some supplies. His mind raced and his breath deepened as he watched his hands grab at what he thought might be needed for a trip.

He set foot outside the barracks and onto the dirt road, able to see the forest's edge, far in the distance. Beyond the forest lay a mountain range, its peaks rugged and beautiful against the night sky. Deep within that night sky loomed Mount Ruin.

It towered over everything; its mere existence was

difficult to put into words.

When Crune reached the forest, his excitement ramped up once more. The sun was only beginning to rise, and all was quiet. He crept along the forest floor, being most observant where he stepped, as to not disturb his surroundings. His movements and focus were that of a hunter stalking his quarry, looking for any sign that would guide him further, closer.

As the sun now broke past the world's edge and its light brightened the sky, the forest began to awaken. Crune could now hear and see the forest's inhabitants stir. Birds chirped and fluttered from tree to tree, singing at the new dawn.

Crune continued further and further into the forest, now able to stop and admire its calmness. His hunter's pursuit had quickly turned into a nature walk. His goal still remained the same, trying to seek out this so-called cult, but the harsh reality had sapped his vigor. He was wandering aimlessly with no resolute destination. The longer he walked, the more frustrated he grew with himself until he found a fallen tree to stop and rest on.

Sitting there on the tree, he was left completely alone with himself and his thoughts, thinking about the odds that he would actually, by chance, come across this meeting place of a cult so secret he had questioned its very existence.

He cursed himself for being so brash and even downright stupid. His actions were normally methodical, calculated. After some more internal battle, he gave up and headed back. He would return, he told himself. His efforts were not over, they had merely been postponed.

So Crune returned to his duties, suffering his day-to-day existence once more. But he began to formulate a plan to return to the forest when he could sneak away.

He purchased a map and began to mark the locations of where he had scouted. He eavesdropped on everyone he could, asking others about any rumors they had heard of cults or vampires. His methods produced very little results, if any at all.

It was disheartening, but he told himself it was only a matter of time before he would find something new. Some new piece of information, a new person of interest, a cult member, or their meeting location. His patience and diligence were rewarded sooner than he had originally anticipated.

Chapter XXI:
Schemes

Tamerill sat alone in The Broken Cup once more in the evening hours of the night. He nursed his drink and tried not to draw attention to himself. He had watched the man from the training go down in the cellar. He knew something had to be down there. Something that would bring all this out in the open. The others he had suspected to be party to the murders were in the bar as well, including the redheaded barkeep who seemed to have a certain affection for the blonde.

Her attention, however, was directed at the big lumbering man who portrayed himself as a leader, or at least demanded the others' attention. As the night went on, the inn became less and less occupied. Soon, it was just him and the people he was hunting. The three of them, if you did not count the man in the cellar. From eavesdropping and stalking the group, Tamerill had discovered each of their name's overtime.

"Well, friend, best be on your way, we are closing

for the night," Jagard said.

Tamerill pretended to protest, "This early? The night is still so young. Can a man get one last drink?"

"We're closed," Rignor gruffed.

Tamerill stood from his table and downed his drink, "Well, if you lads won't give me another, I guess I'll have to take my money elsewhere."

Before the barkeeper could reply, the bald man stood, turned, and grabbed Tamerill by the shirt.

"You deaf? I said we're closed!" He shoved Tamerill backwards and pointed towards the door. Tamerill held up his hands as if he was innocent of an accused crime. He quickly placed his coin on the table and left.

Crune exited the cellar to find the establishment empty, save for Shannara, Jagard, and Rignor. *How I loathe them all,* He thought

"Right, you two ready to get to it? You have got a lot of work ahead of you tonight," Rignor said.

Crune sneered, "You prepared to let us do everything once again? How kind of you."

Rignor and Crune stared at one another, both wanting to end the other's life but not having the right opportunity to do so.

"If we are to move the bodies and capture him, it will take more than Jagard and I. You know this," Crune said.

"You are the one who works in the barracks, you said you could pull this off," Rignor replied. "What, you got cold feet now?"

"Thrass and his men will have to move the bodies that I have already prepared. This will allow us to focus on the matter at hand, unless you have realized we need more time?"

"Thrass can move 'em, sure, but we are doin' this tonight. The wizard gave specific instructions."

Crune nodded, thinking. Then he spoke, "I know where he sleeps and who will be on guard duty tonight. I will need help." It pained him to say it, especially to the three of them.

"Exactly, you got Jagard to help you," Shannara said.

"I will need more than one lookout. This will require tact and stealth, unless you want this to turn out like your brilliant display with the groundskeepers," Crune grinned.

Shannara was about to protest, but it was Jagard who spoke first, "Crune, you can distract the guards. Rignor and I will sneak in and do the nabbing, Shannara you can be the lookout in case anyone comes snooping. Taking him alive will be a two-man job, and Rignor, you are the strongest here."

The group was a bit stunned at Jagard's plan, mainly because it was sound.

Rignor mulled it over a bit. "Right, which room does he sleep in?"

"The furthest one upstairs, on the west side," Crune answered.

"How are we supposed to sneak through the entire barracks without anyone noticing us?" Rignor questioned further.

"His room has a window you could enter using the roof." Crune answered.

"Any guards in his room?" Jagard asked.

"There are two guards always on duty, both posted outside his room."

"We supposed to break through his window without waking him or the guards right outside?" Rignor sneered.

"There won't be any guards outside the room, I'll

make sure of that," Crune assured.

"Still a loud racket trying to break in a window in the middle of the night," Shannara said.

Crune paused and wracked his mind with options. *This would not be an issue if we had more time,* he thought. "I could try and get inside his room, leave the window unlocked. However, that opportunity may never present itself to me tonight."

"How hard would it be for us to just go through the front door?" Jagard asked.

"I would have to distract both guards long enough for you to enter, subdue him, and exit. That is too much time," Crune said.

"Not exit, just enter," Jagard said.

"You distract both guards, we come in, grab him and leave through the window on the roof," Rignor nodded.

"Unless we can come up with a better idea and soon, that will have to do," Shannara said.

"I'll leave you with a spare key, but how will I give you the signal to enter once I have the guards occupied?" Crune asked.

"You won't. We are gonna have to do this fast. We will give you some time and then come in. You'd best have 'em distracted," Rignor demanded.

Crune laughed aloud. "And if you enter at the wrong moment, be it too soon or too late? What then?"

Rignor smirked, "Then I guess you and Jagard will be preppin' a lot more bodies tonight."

Tamerill watched The Broken Cup from further down the dirt road. There was a cold chill in the air and the sky had darkened with clouds.

He hoped it wouldn't start raining, or at the very least that they would move soon. He hated having to wait in the cold and the rain, it would make for a very long night. He wondered if they were going to actually try and kill the big man tonight or if he had heard them wrong.

They could be moving on him in the tavern right this very instant, he thought. He took a deep breath and tried to calm his nerves. They were planning something all right, and he would find out what. Even if he had to sit there all night, even in the rain.

To his surprise the door opened, and the group filed outside, including Crune, who had been in the cellar. They stopped in front of the tavern, whispered to each other for a brief moment, and then all dispersed in separate directions.

Damn! Have I been found out? Tamerill thought. Crune was now walking down the road directly towards him. Tamerill quickly surveyed his surroundings, looking desperately for any hiding spot. He had left himself completely exposed.

Crune walked at a brisk pace, his eyes darting, searching for anyone who might still be awake at this witching hour. A man a short distance up the road, seemed to be lost or looking for something. As Crune walked closer he recognized him as one of the men who had been frequenting the inn recently. Crune didn't know anything about the man and that made him wary.

The man appeared to be stark raving drunk. He stumbled and spat on the ground, drool hanging from his mouth. "Ya … ya still closed fer tha' nigh'?" the man asked.

Crune sidestepped him and looked back a short time later. The man was still slowly making his way down the road, stumbling.

He made his way through the streets of Avernost until he was standing at the front door of the barracks. Crune closed his eyes for a brief instant and inhaled deeply. He opened the door and stepped inside.

It was dark, save for the few candles that were still lit, and quiet. The guards on duty at this very hour were Haslforth and Wilderum. Haslforth sat alone in the dining area reading some parchment when he looked up at Crune. "Why are ye arriving at such an hour?"

Crune made his way past the man heading towards the kitchen. "Thought I would get an early start on breakfast; sleep has eluded me."

"Well keep it down, the men won't be awake for a few more hours."

Crune nodded as he went into the kitchen. His forehead and palms began to sweat from his adrenaline.

How am I supposed to distract both guards without waking all the others? he thought. He feigned interest in the various foods and ingredients in the storeroom. He picked up a pan as if to make some noise, and possibly get the attention of at least Haslforth. He set the pan back down nervously and let out a deep sigh.

Think, his mind demanded.

As if to answer his prayers, or rather his nightmare, he heard the front door begin to open. *Time! You were supposed to give me more time,* he screamed in his head. Crune almost darted out of the kitchen. Haslforth was standing with a candle in his hand. He looked at Crune nervously, "You expectin' anyone?"

Crune stared into the dark towards the front entrance. Wilderum descended the stairs, hand on the hilt of his sword. "What is all this?"

The door made a quiet sound, as if someone had tried to silently shut it behind them. Haslforth stepped forward raising his candle. "Who goes there?" he called.

Silence filled the room.

Haslforth and Wilderum drew their swords and slowly crept towards the door.

Crune was almost in a panicked frenzy.

He knew it was only a matter of seconds now before they discovered Jagard and Rignor. The fight would be on, the other men would wake, and they would be slaughtered or worse.

Tamerill had backtracked very carefully, cursing himself for being so careless. He followed Crune, making sure to remain unnoticed. He still did not know where the others had gone but that was all soon answered. Crune had made his way to the barracks and walked inside. Tamerill watched as the others approached the front door and stood there. They spoke in hushed whispers, but their body language showed disagreement. The big one, Rignor, seemed particularly displeased about something.

Wonder if the one I followed was supposed to have waited for them before entering? Tamerill thought. Their quiet debate went on for a short time until Rignor produced a key and opened the door. The two men stepped inside and closed the door behind them, leaving the woman standing out front. She made her way to one of the corners of the building and stood very still as if waiting for something to happen.

Tamerill weighed his options. If he left to try and alert anyone, he could miss his chance. *Who would I alert anyway*, he thought, *it's now or never*. Tamerill made his way to the barracks. As he drew closer, the woman's attention was drawn solely to him and not whatever was happening inside. She waited to see if he would turn in a different direction but intervened when he was just a few steps from the front door.

"I remember you. You won't find anything to drink in there," she said. Tamerill paused pretending to look around as if surprised she was talking to him.

"What do you mean?" Tamerill asked.

"Are you lost? This isn't an inn. Last I saw you, you were trying to get another drink."

"Ah, no. I live here."

Shannara raised an eyebrow. "Really?"

"Yes. I … I just got hired."

"Little late to be out drinking when you've just found new employment, isn't it?"

"Was just celebrating is all," Tamerill said and reached for the door but stopped. "What are you doing here? I don't recall seeing you around this place."

Before Shannara could reply, shouting erupted from inside. She drew a dagger, but Tamerill was faster. He grabbed her and threw her to the ground. She struggled to cut at him, but Tamerill forced the knife from her hand and stood pointing it at her. "Stay down," he shouted.

Screams and the sound of steel on steel rang out from the other side of the door. "I am Tamerill, agent of the Silver Wardens. You are detained, pending crimes against Avernost."

Glass shattered from the rooftop, and both Shannara and Tamerill looked upward to see what was happening. Lord Dramington climbed through the broken window followed by Crune. A cry of agony poured out as the front door burst open. Rignor and Jagard stumbled out, Jagard held one hand against a grievous wound on his stomach. The guards ran behind them, attempting to hack them down as they fled.

Rignor shoved Jagard out of his way as he ran, leaving his cohorts to fend for themselves. The first guard didn't know what to make of Shannara and Tamerill, other than to assume they were all a part of this treachery. Tamerill threw the knife to the ground and shouted, holding up the small silver emblem each agent possessed.

Dramington's men had been attacked in their own garrison and were raging into a frenzy. They ran at Jagard, butchering him until he fell. Shannara scrambled for the knife on the ground and a soldier kicked her in the face. Yet the silver emblem stopped them from attacking Tamerill. The first soldier held him at sword point. A shout came from inside.

"Dramington is gone! Spread out and find him."

"Hurry, my lord," Crune pleaded. Lord Dramington paused to catch his breath, leaning against a tree. They had entered the nearest forest, but the village was still within eyesight. Dramington turned back to see if any pursuers followed them. Crune was trying to keep himself collected but his anger and adrenaline were at a collision. *Those fools*, he screamed in his head. Dramington held up a hand as if he could hear Crune's thoughts but needed quiet.

"I think we should try and backtrack," he said. "If we can reach my men, we have a better chance with more numbers."

"My lord, we do not know how many are out there. They attacked us, attacked you—in your own home," Crune said. "There could be many more. Some of your own men—"

Dramington drew his sword and pointed it at Crune. "You think my own men conspire against me, Crune? Tell me, are you among these traitors?"

Crune threw his hands up, feigning shock and fear, "No, my lord! I saved you. I am still trying to save you."

Dramington lowered his sword but did not sheath it. "What is your plan then?"

"I know of a secret refuge deep in the forest. It is a hideout that is not known to many."

"How do you know of it?" Dramington asked.

"I heard some of your men speaking of it," Crune ventured.

"If my men know of it and you suspect them to be traitors, how is it safe?"

Crune was losing his patience and his lies. *It would be easier at this point to carry his corpse there, but the wizard was very specific*, he thought.

"My lord, I … I do not know if it is safe. I just believe it to be safer than returning to the very spot you and your men were just attacked."

Dramington let out a heavy sigh and looked back again. "Very well, Crune. Lead on."

Chapter XXII:
Cloak and Dagger

Kurodan felt the cold weight of the chains that bound him. The men were quiet, only their breathing could be heard in the dark cell. The dull silence, fully encapsulating the immensity of their dire circumstances. He knew every man felt what they dared not speak. This was it.

They had made good on their promise and kept each other alive, even Uthrol. His wounds had been severe, but the ragged prisoner had clung to life like the rest of them had clung to hope. The twelve of them had made it this far. Kurodan had felt guilty that he truly knew little of half the men, but the guilt vanished knowing he would gladly lay down his life for any of them.

They sat in silence until finally the orcs came to retrieve them for another digging excursion. The silence now churned into a dreadful tension. As the orcs fumbled to open the door into the dungeon, Feore whispered, "Easy does it, lads."

The orcs made their way down the steps. "On your feet, humans," the first said. Each man stood, awaiting the orcs' ritual of exchanging one set of chains for another, setting them free from the dungeon walls and floor only to be chained to one another.

"Move," the other orc barked. The men slowly made their way up the steps and into the tunnel. Only two orcs carried torches. The sound of their chains and feet echoed in the dark tunnels. Kurodan fought to control his anxiety, his fear. It clawed its way from deep within, climbing its way up, heavy on his chest, and choking in his throat. He pushed it back down, forcing himself to remain focused, fearful the orcs might sense something.

They descended into the labyrinthine heart of the mountain. Its complexity and immensity still amazed Kurodan. *We must be careful and quiet*, he thought.

The orc leading the way with the torch paused at a fork in the tunnels. He raised the torch up to each. *Left. Go left,* Kurodan thought. The orc went left. The men fought to let out an exhale of relief.

Finally, they reached their destination. The men moved to face the rock wall, again awaiting the orcs to adjust their chains. The orcs were diligent in their cruelties, never ceasing. After their chains had been checked, one of the orcs gave the command, "Dig."

Kurodan hefted the pickaxe in his hands, its cold hardwood handle biting into his blistered fingers. The sound of metal striking against the mountain rang loud and heavy. Kurodan felt his fear mauling for control once again. This time he channeled it into the work at hand. He brought the tool down hard, feeling the shock of the blow ripple through his hands and into his arms.

Again and again, he hefted it high above his head and brought it down like deafening thunder. The men were all working in unison, with what seemed to be a new resilience, a new hate. The orcs watched the men intently, unfazed by boredom or weariness. There were five of them including the one with the torch.

One more than we wanted, but the orcs are being cautious. They need more guards when they make all of us work at the same time now, Kurodan thought.

Each man was vigorous in his labor, until one began to slow. Toradin began to take longer pauses in between swings. He breathed heavier. Kurodan watched Toradin out of his peripheral. The orcs took the bait.

"Work, human," the orc closest to them said. Toradin acted as if he did not hear the orc, or blatantly ignored his order. This angered the orc, and he stepped closer. Toradin picked up his cadence and rhythm once more. This satisfied the orc, and he returned to his original spot.

Not close enough, Kurodan thought. The work continued. A few of the orcs muttered to each other and then nodded as if coming to an agreement. One of the orcs with a torch began to leave. Darkness crept all around them as only one torch remained among the group. Kurodan paused to let his eyes adjust. *Now! Now or never, and be damned*, he thought.

The men picked up their rhythm once more save for Toradin, who slowed. The same orc took notice.

"You will be the weak one this time. I'm surprised, I thought paladins had more grit," the orc said as he approached Toradin. In the three paces it took the orc to reach Toradin, every man in unison, paused. It was, Kurodan knew, the slightest hesitation with the most strained sense of instinct. The instincts of killers.

Toradin turned and swung the pickaxe with such force that it shattered the orc's head, sending brain, bone, and blood into a fountain of beautiful gore.

The other orcs charged weapons at the ready.

The torchlight grew brighter as the orc that had left heard the commotion and sprinted back towards them. Kurodan swung, his strike missing the closest orc's head but catching him in the neck. The orc's body crumbled to the ground; the head almost completely severed.

Feore was strangling an orc from behind, the wood of his pickaxe bending and almost breaking against the orc's throat. The fourth had remained at the ready until the torchbearer returned. Another pause hung between the men and the two orcs.

"Stay, and if any break free kill them," the torchbearer commanded, then turned and sprinted back into the tunnels.

The men began to madly strike at the links that chained them into the ground. Kurodan and Toradin's chains broke free. They rushed the remaining orc and slew him without hesitation. Kurodan ran into the tunnel chasing the torchlight. Toradin remained to break the others free.

Kurodan's heartbeat thundered in his head, his eyes watered, and warm black blood wet his grip on the tool. "Run faster, damn you!" He was talking to himself out loud. Kurodan commanded his body into a mad dash. His cold feet felt as if they would shatter with each step slamming into the hard, unforgiving dirt. He could see the orc now turning to face him. They ran at each other. The orc's sword struck the tool just below its head, shattering the axe into splinters.

Kurodan tackled the brute. The orc brought the small sword to bare but Kurodan stayed the blade, gripping the orc's weapon hand with all his strength. The orc beat Kurodan about the face and head with its free hand. When Kurodan was unfazed by the assault, the orc tried to gouge out his closest eye.

Kurodan ripped his face from the orc's grasp and at

the same time, freed the blade.

He stabbed wildly, displaying none of his skill at arms, only unfettered primal rage. The orc fought on, taking the wounds.

Kurodan felt his grip slipping with the black blood staining over him. He stabbed again and again, the blade slicing his own hand. He stabbed and stabbed until the short sword broke in the ribcage of the orc. Kurodan dropped the handle and pushed his back against the tunnel wall. His breathing was sporadic.

He stared at the orc's corpse that now lay in the tunnel as if in a trance. The torch lay next to them. Its faint light flickered and illuminated the horror that Kurodan had inflicted. The sound of movement somewhere in the labyrinth brought Kurodan back, quickly grabbing the torch he slunk back into the tunnel with the broken blade.

He fought to slow his breathing, trying to control his heartbeat. He paused and listened; the silence revealed the men creeping up the tunnel. He revealed himself in the dark. No one spoke. Kurodan quickly motioned them to follow.

They moved slowly, sound now the highest priority. Each man carefully stepped over the torchbearer's body. As the men made their way through the tunnel, they could hear orcs coming towards them. The sound of their fighting obviously had drawn attention. Kurodan motioned the men into a tunnel to their right.

Each of them pressed themselves into the tunnel's walls, gripping their weapons and tools, holding their breath, forcing themselves to melt into the shadows. Two orcs hurried past their position. Kurodan could feel his veins bulging in his neck and face as he fought to hold his breath and fear.

Kurodan eased himself out into the open and could

hear the orcs continuing in the direction away from them. As he motioned for the men to follow, he heard a faint shout from one of the orcs. They must have found the body. The men swiftly made their way to escape. Feore took up the rear, his head on a swivel, watching for any orcs behind them.

Kurodan led them through the labyrinth. All of the men knew the immediate layout of each tunnel. Their goal was to reach the makeshift armory the orcs had built. They were all aware of the major risks with their plan. The armory was located just past the throne room. Kurodan knew there would be many orcs in and around those tunnels—not to mention the vampire. And whatever orcs were guarding the armory would have to be taken loudly, there would be no other way around it. He prayed their blessed weapons had been kept there.

But before they arrived, any orcs that were dispatched would have to be done quietly, so as to not alarm a swarm of them. Kurodan thought of all these variables as he inched forward in the dark. Every few steps he froze and listened closely, as did the rest of the men. Orcs could be heard coming back up the tunnel from behind the group.

"They have found their dead," Toradin whispered. "We must hurry."

Kurodan nodded.

Just up ahead lay the entrance to the throne room. Kurodan took a step forward and then quickly pulled himself back, halting the men once more. A group of orcs opened the throne room entrance and began to close the massive doors behind them. Toradin gripped Kurodan's shoulder as the orcs coming up the tunnel grew louder. They were trapped like rats in a maze.

"The bloodsucker … he does nothing but give orders and sit atop his throne," one orc said.

The other grunted in approval.

"We orcs should be the ones giving orders, not some filthy nightwalker."

Kurodan could not help but be interested in the orcs' conversation. *The enemy of my enemy*, he thought.

The orcs slowly began to walk into the tunnels. Kurodan motioned the men to follow. They were now stalking the small group of orcs. As the men passed the throne room doorway, Feore paused. The orcs behind them seemed to be doing the same.

Kurodan watched as the three orcs in front of him continued their stroll. As they came to a split in the tunnels one parted to the left, leaving two. It appeared the remaining two were going to the armory as well. To signal Toradin and the men behind him, Kurodan motioned with the broken blade, pretending to cut his own throat. The men nodded and crept forward.

Feore waved one of his arms in the air, trying to motion the others, as the orcs behind them shouted something. Their party froze as the two orcs, just a stone's throw away, turned to face them.

"Kill them," Kurodan shouted.

The two orcs were quickly overtaken by the men and hacked to pieces. The third orc now rounded the corner and gave the alarm, "The humans are escaping!"

"Run!" Feore shouted as he looked back to see orcs giving chase from behind.

The men made a mad dash up the tunnel. The third orc ran at Kurodan, who sidestepped his blow. Kurodan plunged the broken blade into the orc's chest and left it resting there, continuing the charge weaponless. Panic set in. The men ran past the armory now in a race for their lives.

Gone was their plan of sneaking out of the mountain

armed and leaving a trail of dead orcs behind them. Gone was the backup plan of making a final stand in the armory until either all the orcs lay dead, or they did.

They raced onwards; every man fighting exhaustion and panic. No one dared look back. No one, save Feore. Kurodan led them, frantically turning left and right into tunnels, hoping his memory did not fail them now.

Kurodan rounded the long corner of a tunnel that led to the chasm—that terrible chasm they had skirted when they first were forced to march into the mountain. The path was slowly steepening into an incline. His legs burned with agony and his cold sweat chilled him to the bone.

The orcs were now in a full frenzy after them. Their shouts and bellows filled the tunnels. Kurodan pushed all thoughts aside—every doubt, every fear. Being chased so closely by death, he had the clarity of a single thought: *Survive*.

And so it was that, spurred on by his faintest hope, he ran and led the men. Their party, like a pack of game animals and the orcs, savage beasts running them down across the plains. As the tunnel grew steeper and steeper, their strength was strained.

Kurodan brought them to the final ascent. To the right, the tunnel continued further into the depths of the mountain. To the left, the climb along the chasm. Kurodan had not forgotten how narrow and treacherous the path was.

"Stay together," his voice echoed within the pit.

Kurodan edged out of the tunnel and onto the cliff's edge. Some spots were wide enough to face forward and run on. Others forced him to embrace the mountain's rock like a newborn clinging to its mother's bosom. Kurodan poured all his focus into each step, and the men followed his lead.

When the orcs reached the same path exiting the tunnel, the sight of their captives fleeing enraged them. The orc in front hefted his spear and hurled it at them as others pushed on. Some of the men hesitated, almost falling as the spear crashed and splintered by their feet.

"Do not stop," Feore urged.

He was still holding the rear, ever defiant, ever resilient. He spurred his men onward. "We are free, lads. Fight for it!"

The men responded in kind, keeping their composure in the face of insurmountable odds. Kurodan's concentration broke for a fraction of a second as he looked up at the arduous path that lay before him. Then he looked back at Toradin and past his men at the orcs, still relentless. He gritted his teeth and pressed on. *I will not fail*, he thought.

At the rear, Feore paused, readying himself for the first orc that would inevitably catch them. Steeling his nerves, he prepared to throw himself and every orc within grasp into the pit of hell. But the orcs had slowed their pursuit, almost stopping. A grin broke across Feore's face as he wondered if their captors had finally given up.

Then his grin died and disfigured into a grim expression of terror. "Brace yourselves," he called. Each man froze in place, turning over their shoulders to witness what horror now would play its hand for their fates.

A black mist of dead ash floated out over the chasm, rising ever higher towards them. It held no true form, but it did not need form to convey the devilry of its ancient death magic. Magic, born of those who bathed in blood.

"Vampire!" Feore shouted.

Some of the men tried pushing forward while others froze, either readying themselves to fight or merely accepting their fate. To end the madness, the suffering, the fear—end it all.

Toradin gripped Kurodan's arm and pushed him forward. The formless haze darted forth like a dagger's tip. It struck directly in the center of the men. The impact shook the mountain. One fell, never to be seen again, his screams crying out as the belly of the mountain swallowed its victim.

The vampire emerged from the mist, taking his true form. He wielded the holy sword of the dead paladin, his movements crossed between acrobat and demon. The closest man tried to strike out, but the vampire vanished into the black ash, and the attack cleaved nothing but air. Then the vampire took shape again and replied in kind.

Kurodan watched the men cower at this unholy act as Toradin tried to push him up the path. The men were now divided. Feore was caught between his men being slain by the vampire and the orcs slowly drawing closer.

As he watched the vampire wield its blade of sacrilege, Kurodan birthed one new thought. It was no longer one of survival, but of killing.

He pushed his way past Toradin and the remaining men scrambling to get clear of the demon's wrath. *If I wield that sword, I will strike you down*, Kurodan thought, making a charge with no weapon of his own.

Toradin instinctively took the lead but could not help turning back to see Kurodan marching towards his own death. Frozen to inaction and dumbfounded in awe, Toradin watched as his brother in arms committed this act of untold heroism and stupidity.

Just as Kurodan lunged for the sword, the vampire

dissipated away, only to crash back into the wall of the mountain. The shock forced the men to cower and cling to the cold cliff face.

None fell but some of the men had thrown themselves down onto the narrow path, hoping the nightmare would end. Kurodan and Toradin were on their stomachs for fear of falling.

Feore hung suspended from the cliff's edge, having caught himself at the last possible moment. The orcs crept closer, staring down at him. The other men, only ten survivors in all, merely stood frozen in place, not knowing what to do.

The vampire took shape at the furthest point ahead, cutting off their escape. They were trapped. He held up the paladin's holy weapon, now covered in the blood of men. His face was that of an angered god.

Uthrol's saddened gaze met the eyes of Kurodan.

"No … no, no, no!" Kurodan screamed. But Uthrol cast himself into the blackness.

Feore's eyes followed him downwards until he was nothing. As he looked up, he met the cruel smile of an orc leering over him. Almost, the thought overwhelmed him to let go, but his hatred for the orc made his hands bite harder into the cliff.

"Do it!" Feore bellowed, challenging the orc.

The orc happily obliged the captain, stepping on one of his hands.

"Enough," shouted the vampire, and his rage made the orc recoil in fear. "Restrain them. Now."

The command spurred the orcs into a hurried panic as they grabbed each of the nine remaining captives. Some of the men continued to fight, just as panicked as the orcs.

Feore was plucked from the precipice and in so doing, threw the first orc that grabbed him off the cliff.

"You will keep them alive," the vampire demanded.

The closer the vampire approached, the harder they fought until he brought the sword to Kurodan's chest. They stopped. Kurodan and the devil stared into one another's eyes, neither displaying fear, only hatred. The men were placed in shackles once more, the cold iron bite on their skin all too familiar.

"Udal," the vampire said. The fearsome orc stepped forward, carefully moving around orc and man, so as not to fall. "You claimed these were your captives, did you not?"

"They are Warlord Korgath's captives."

"Ah," the vampire said. "And did he not place them under your care?"

"Yes."

"So, you are to answer for this utter failure?"

"Failure?" Udal repeated in a questioning tone. "None of this would have happened had it not been for your futile crusade searching for the goblet!"

The vampire's grim stare turned into a scowl as he plunged his sword through Udal's stomach, the blade tearing out his back. The orc spat and coughed his own blood.

"You will know the true meaning of failure," the vampire said, removing the blade with a quick wrenching motion, disemboweling the orc. Udal screamed and staggered, falling to his back.

The vampire struck the sword into the ground, wrapped and tangled in the orc's intestines. Udal vomited blood as the vampire knelt over the orc and began to cannibalize him.

Kurodan and the others watched in horror as the orc weakly tried to fend off the monster.

The vampire buried its fangs into the orc's guts, chewing and drinking with a vile slurping sound, until the orc fell silent, and the vampire had its fill.

Chapter XXIII: Riddles

Regalt paused to wipe the sweat from his eyepatch and brow. He could feel the nearest orc staring at him, so he began again. He swung the pick with a lazy effort. He no longer tried to conserve his energy after their failed attempt to escape. Feore steadily worked next to Regalt, neither speaking to one another.

Horad, Kurodan, and Toradin were left in the dungeon cell. The other six had been taken for the digging excursion.

When selected for digging, the men were kept in pairs of two. Each pair was taken to a different location. Whether to avoid another attempted escape or because there were only so few of the men remaining, it mattered not.

The strike of the axe reverberated in the cave tunnel. His hands and arms were numb to the exhausting work, accustomed to the long sessions of abuse. His mind no longer wandered and dreamed.

He could no longer delude himself with the hope of escape—that one day he would free himself of this terrible existence and be rid of his captors. No, he would die here. He had accepted that. He now welcomed that death as a final release from his physical torment.

His axe hit something hard, something dense. It immediately gave off a different sound. The impact almost wrenched the tool from his blistered hands. The orcs approached curiously.

"What was that?" one asked.

Regalt paused to look at the orc that addressed him. "I do not know, probably just a boulder buried here."

"That was no boulder, human. These tunnels you are standing in—we dug them. We orcs know what digging sounds like."

He lifted the axe again and struck the same spot. This time the tool did fall from his hands. "See. It is but another rock face."

The orc pushed him aside and bent to examine the spot he had struck. Then the orc picked up the axe and began to dig with it.

Regalt was surprised at the orc's mastery of the tool. The impacts echoed as the orc continued. The orc stopped and looked closely at his handiwork. "This is no rock face."

A second orc stepped closer in anticipation, "Is it what the nightwalker spoke of?"

The first nodded, "Go tell the others. Bring the others here to dig at once." The orc shoved the tool back into Regalt's hands. "Dig, human, as if your life depends on it."

The four other men were lined up next to Regalt and Feore. Regalt swung with purpose, his adrenaline causing him to gain a sense of renewed strength.

He did not care if he drew the attention of the orc slave masters. But he did still fear bringing down the orcs' wrath on any of the other men.

Before long, some of the others were brought. Regalt exchanged a few quick worried glances with them. No one fully understood what they were digging for, save that it could not be of any comfort to them.

As they all struck deeper into the wall of the mountain, Regalt was surprised as they began to uncover a portion at their feet. The orc had been correct—this was no boulder or rock face.

It was the same form of craftsmanship that he had seen in the black door that led to the vampire's throne. Regalt did not understand if it was another door, or maybe a wall of sorts. *The throne room had depicted many murals and art.* Regalt almost had to hide a smirk as he thought, *that is what they are searching for you imbecile. Long lost artwork.*

"Widen your line," the closest orc commanded. Regalt and the others increased the distance between themselves slightly and continued their labor. Regalt's swings no longer struck the hard midnight material beneath the earth. In fact, he was striking something soft altogether now. He swung again. This time his pick sunk deep into the tunnel wall, so much so that he struggled a bit to pull it back out.

"I think … I think I found something else," he said. The orc stepped closer as Regalt swung again. The axe sunk deep, only this time Regalt could not pull the tool free.

When he tried to, a strange shrill moan came from beneath the dirt, almost as if someone or something was alive.

Everyone paused.

Regalt pulled again, but the shrill grew louder and

the wooden handle shook violently. Regalt fell to the ground and watched in utter terror as the earth around whatever foul thing was buried before him began to fall away.

It's a person ... or may have been a person at some point, Regalt thought. A human form emerged partly from the tunnel wall. It appeared to have been burned terribly or buried for an eternity. Its wretched form was the color of ash. Its eyes were sunken black sockets, and its mouth bore no teeth or tongue.

The thing seemed to still be half buried into the wall from the waist down. Regalt's pickaxe had pierced clean through its chest and out its back. Its hands gripped at the tool, struggling to free itself.

"What wickedness is this?" Regalt asked.

One of the orcs turned to another, "Seek out the nightwalker."

The thing began to twist and writhe. Screaming, it tried to free itself from the axe. Its screams thundered within the tunnel, deafening and terrible, until the wall around it began to give way.

"Run," Feore shouted. "It's coming down." The men awkwardly scrambled away in their chains as the orcs quickly distanced themselves.

As the wall crumbled, abomination after abomination reared up from the earth, as if birthed from a hideous nest hidden within the mountain. All of the beings were caught, trapped in the wall. Some only managed to free portions of their bodies. Others, like the first that spawned forth, had almost their entire torso free. Each of them began to cry out. The men knew not whether it was in agony for their mere existence, or for some more insidious reason.

Before them lay a solid black door and the walls on either side swayed with the contorted beings.

"By the light," Feore whispered.

"Quite the opposite," Andazar said, approaching the door.

"What is this magic, wizard?" an orc asked. Andazar ignored the question for a time, lost in either curiosity or admiration at the sight that lay before him.

Another voice arose from the shadows. "It is a crossing," the vampire said.

"No, not a crossing," Andazar corrected. "A chamber. And within it lies what I have been seeking." Andazar appeared transfixed by the door. The twisted moaning bodies seemed to cry out to him, to all of them, but the wizard did not heed them.

"What are they?" an orc asked.

"A warning," Andazar said. The men tried to back away further, but the orcs kept them in check, no longer sharing the same fear, emboldened by the wizard and the vampire.

"Do you know how to open it?" the vampire asked.

Andazar walked closer and placed his hand on the door. The abominations clawed towards him as if he had just committed the greatest act of trespassing. Half-buried faces fought to shriek, limbs danced and lunged. But their attempts to reach him were in vain, as the door was so large, and they still could not free themselves.

Andazar turned slightly, a wicked smile on his face. "You, you are the key," he said to the vampire, his hand still touching the door.

The vampire stepped forward. "What must I do?"

"You feed on blood, and yours is what will open the way," Andazar said, removing his hand and motioning for the vampire to offer his own. "You must simply offer your blood and touch the door."

The vampire held his dead white hand palm up as Andazar produced a knife from his belt.

Andazar slowly sliced into the vampire's palm. The abominations reacted as if the very fires of hell were burning their already blackened skin. Their cacophony grew so loud and thunderous that the orcs and prisoners fought to cover their ears.

"Hurry!" Andazar shouted.

The vampire stepped forwards, his hand dripping blood from the wound, but remained an arm's length from the obsidian structure. The bodies contorted themselves into a frenzy trying to reach him. Pausing as if fearful for the very first time, the vampire raised his blood-stained hand and struck the door.

The shrieking forms froze as if turned into statues, their silence now more petrifying than their suffering. The vampire now began to scream. He fought to pull his hand free, but an invisible force kept it pinned there. He fell to his knees, pulling on his arm with his other hand. The door illuminated with bloodred markings, and a great heat radiated off its surface, until the vampire's hand and the markings themselves began to burn and sear. The markings grew until the entire door appeared as if it had been stained in burning blood and fire, then instantly faded to black.

The vampire fell clutching his hand, the wizard pulled him aside, and the door began to open. A perfect split formed down the middle and gave way to the inside. As the door opened, an awful stench of death and decay swarmed the air.

Andazar stepped closer to the door, through which only an impenetrable blackness awaited. "We must enter," he whispered

"All you, step through. Now," the vampire demanded. The orcs began to push the men forward, though they were hesitant enter themselves.

A dim light grew from Andazar's staff until it was brighter than the torch an orc still carried. The light revealed that the group had entered some hellish chamber. It opened into a large circular cavern, as if someone or something had hollowed out another section in the heart of the mountain.

The ground, walls, ceiling—every inch, save one patch of ground that was unmolested by the damned, where the group crowded together, was covered by the terrible ashen souls. The cavern appeared to have been built out of their very beings.

There must be hundreds, maybe thousands, Regalt thought. Their stillness gave the impression that a great artisan had carved each horrible being out of the cave itself.

Once the last of them crossed through, the door began to shut on its own. Regalt looked from Feore to the others, all of them stricken with panic save the wizard and the vampire. But it was too late, the door had closed.

Regalt felt a pit in his stomach, he was sweating and nauseous from the stench of death.

"What now?" the vampire asked.

Andazar held up his hand, but it was unclear if he was listening for something, or if he did not want something to hear them.

The orc holding the torch was trying to nudge his way to the rear of the party. He reached the door behind them and began pounding and pushing on it.

"Stay yourself," Andazar shouted.

The orc ignored the wizard's command. "I will not die like this," the orc yelled. As the orc beat on the door, his torch burned one of the closest beings trapped in the wall.

The damned came back to life.

Everyone pushed closer together on the barren patch of earth, but it was too late for the orc. The figure that was burned had been close enough to seize him. The orc tried to free his axe from his belt but dropped it. He punched and kicked, bit, and bellowed curses, but all in vain. The orc was torn from the party's safety and dragged up the wall, each form hoisting and pulling at him.

Soon the orc was dangling from the ceiling, his screams echoing, until at last he was held above the very center of the cavern.

The sea of the damned below writhed, looking up at the struggling orc. They reached upwards, crying out to him. Their screams now drowned out their victim's. Regalt watched in terror as the orc was released. He fell into the pit of the damned, his body consumed and torn apart, buried in the sea of souls and now gone forever.

From the wizard's light, the party could see a great hole in the ground where the orc had fallen, as if the sea of the damned had parted, dragging the orc down into despair. The ground trembled as if the mountain had been awoken and fed. A fountain of blood and flame erupted forth from the hole, reaching almost the height of the cavern. The fire illuminated the horrendous scene, then as quickly as the fountain had burst forth, it died and flickered into smoke. A being emerged from within the deep.

The ground and sea of the damned gave way further and a great demon appeared. Its waist down remained hidden by the ashen figures, as if trapped in place just as the damned that surrounded it. It bore four massive arms, four great horns, and four nostrils. It had no eyes and no skin, only bloodred tissue and muscle exposed. Its gaping mouth contained a thousand teeth and a forked tongue like that of a serpent.

It raised all four arms, outstretching them, its immense form filling almost the entirety of the now tomb. It sniffed with its four nostrils, as a beast would catch the scent of its prey. It spoke, its voice deep yet clear and concise.

"I smell you," it said. None dared reply. "One wielder of magic." It slightly leaned forward. "One neither living nor dead." It sniffed again. "And mere mortals."

"By the gods, may the Holy Light protect me," one of the men spoke.

"Gods?" it said, as if almost puzzled. "I am no god."

"What are you?" the vampire asked.

"I am a guardian of the ancient. Savior to some, devourer to others."

"We seek what you have guarded here for eternity," Andazar said.

"What you seek is not the question, magic wielder." It leaned forward, its four terrible hands supporting itself, crushing the damned beneath them. "Will you be able to claim it from me?"

"I will have my prize," Andazar declared.

"Which prize? There are two I guard."

"Two prizes?" asked the vampire.

Regalt tried to cover his ears at its laughter.

"Seek you the book or the goblet?" it asked.

"Both," Andazar replied.

"Ambitious, magic wielder."

"What book?" the vampire hissed, his fangs flaring. "We came here for the goblet—for the ritual."

"The book of the dead," answered the demon. "The magic wielder seeks the book for himself. You both seek one or the other. You both will have to answer, and a third. A third will have to answer."

"What must we answer?" Andazar asked.

The great demon leaned back, folding all four arms. "None have bested me in battle, your answer must be of the mind. The magic wielder, the undead, and a mortal. Each must answer."

"If all three of us answer correctly, you will give me what I seek?" Andazar asked.

The demon's great mouth widened in a smile showing its teeth, its four hands coming together as if slightly amused. "If you answer correctly."

"And if our answers fail?" the vampire questioned.

The demon arched back, looking up into the air. Taking in a deep breath through its four nostrils, smelling again. "I have not tasted the flesh of an adversary in some time."

"Very well. Ask and we shall answer," Andazar said.

"Wait, wizard, do you not think we should—" but Andazar held up his hand, silencing the vampire.

"Eager, this magic wielder," the demon said mockingly. "Very well, you must answer first."

"I am what you seek but attempt to shun, I live in every man's heart but poison his mind. I can hide in plain sight, even in the light of the sun. To the devout I bring ridicule and fear, for they need only see themselves in the mirror. I am the truth and a lie. Others embrace me and thus forever seal their fates as they die ... What am I?"

"Sin," Andazar said, as if matter of fact.

Regalt stood stunned at the wizard's confidence and lack of hesitation.

"Good. Very good, magic wielder. Let us see if the undead will answer correctly."

As the vampire stepped forward, Andazar's voice betrayed him for the first time and said with a hint of fear, "I cannot answer for you, if you answer wrong—"

"Be silent!" the demon hissed. "I will only offer the question once. The undead will only answer once."

"Ask me then," the vampire said.

"I am both weak and strong. Many hide behind me, claiming to have never committed wrong. I can be found and lost, tested and shattered. Some spend a lifetime searching to never find me, others die believing theirs is the only ones to have mattered ... What am I?"

The vampire paused, muttering and repeating the words to himself. All eyes stared at him wondering how long until he would answer, and what would happen after.

"You must answer—" Andazar began.

"None shall speak save for the undead!" the demon roared. It stood defiantly as if it had already won the wager.

At last, after the silence and anticipation were almost too great a burden to bear, the vampire answered, "Is it… faith?"

The demon laughed, deep and booming. "Though your answer lacked it, very good, little undead. Now which mortal will answer the third?"

Andazar and the vampire turned to face the prisoners and orcs. "None of the orcs," Andazar said.

"The prisoners are exhausted and on the verge of delirium," replied the vampire. "You trust their minds?"

Feore looked into each one of his men's faces until he looked at Regalt. *I must do this for them*, he thought. Before Feore could speak, Regalt slightly grinned.

"I will answer," Regalt yelled, taking off his eyepatch and stepping forward.

"No," Feore shouted, but the orcs held him in place.

Regalt now stood between Andazar and the vampire, facing the demon. The demon took a deep breath through its nostrils. "This mortal has more courage than most."

"Ask your riddle, abomination," Regalt said.

"So be it, mortal."

"I am the home to many, both ancient and young. I have claimed warriors, scholars, heroes, and transgressors. All around me, praises and horror are sung. None escape me. Not the mighty nor the meek, king nor slave. I am the ultimate goal for the ultimate prize. I am both eternal and ending. No matter the victor, I am all mankind's demise... What am I?"

"You are death!" Regalt screamed.

The demon lunged forward, its four arms crashing down. One clawed hand seized Regalt, who began screaming as the demon lifted him up. It held him taut by each limb above its horned head, and then tore him apart, its great maw devouring him whole. Feore sobbed in a horror-stricken rage.

"Be silent!" Andazar commanded.

"His flesh and bones are now mine," the demon said, blood still dripping from its teeth.

Feore fought and pushed his way to the front, but Andazar barred his way with his staff. "You will not hinder me from this task," the wizard said.

"This is your doing," Feore screamed. Grabbing ahold of the staff, he tried to push the wizard to be eaten next but was struck to the ground by the vampire.

"He was under my charge. These are my men," Feore said, getting on his feet again. "Take me, monster. Take me! But you will spare the lives of my men."

The demon sniffed, laughing. "This one—this mortal—seeks to save the others. Well, mortal, will you save them?" the demon hissed.

"I will answer," Feore continued boldly. "But if you take my life, you will let the others leave, prize or no prize."

Andazar's face contorted into anger. "You do not make the wagers here, worm." He struck Feore with his staff.

"Enough," the demon said. "Mortal, you will answer. But if you fail, it will save no one."

"If I win?" Feore asked.

"The artifacts I guard will be revealed," the demon said.

Feore laughed hysterically, growing louder and

louder, as if he were mad.

His eyes and jaw snapped open until he regained some composure, wiping the spit from his mouth. "That holds little value to me, devil."

"Answer or I shall devour you all," the demon demanded.

"If you are not death," Feore spoke slowly, "you are war."

The great demon bowed its head. Its upper two arms clasped each other's hands and raised above its head. The lower two arms remained outstretched at its sides. The damned souls now clawed at the demon, pulling it back down into the hell from which it spawned.

The damned screamed and wailed under the monumental task of imprisoning the demon. Their bodies lunged and shifted, breaking upon themselves. The demon's hands remained clasped together, jutting forth from the dead, the rest of its body dragged below the sea of the damned. Some of the ashen figures between the group and the demon lay flat and formed a narrow pathway.

Andazar was the only one willing to brave stepping forth onto the horrid figures. As he approached the demon's hands, the damned bodies clung to one another, forming steps that brought the wizard within arm's reach of the demon's great clutches. The party stared in awe and wonder at the diabolical spectacle. Andazar simply struck the enormous monstrous hands with the butt of his staff.

The two palms opened like the petals of a flower and a puff of smoke poured out, as if a fire had just been put out.

Cradled in one, stood a golden goblet rimmed with bloodred rubies. The other palm held a large book. The cover was black and large thorns protruded from it.

The pages appeared to be trapped shut by overlapping pieces of jagged bone.

"They are here. They are here," cried the wizard.

Chapter XXIV:
Man's True Nature

Kurodan thought that their existence had broken them down into mindless slaves. He looked at Feore, who had once maintained the willpower to rally the men's hope but now appeared utterly destroyed. He no longer spoke to anyone. Kurodan, Toradin, and Horad attempted to question the other men about Feore's state or Regalt's whereabouts, they too refused to answer.

As time seemed to no longer exist, the men continued to waste away. The measly scraps and portions of food and water were just enough to keep them alive but barely functioning. The long periods of digging had ceased which left the men to slowly suffer in their despair.

Horad broke a long silence, "Why do they no longer speak?"

"Maybe they are under some type of spell or curse." Toradin said.

"Feore, please you must tell us what has happened." Kurodan urged.

Silence.

"One of you must answer, now." Horad demanded, his voice raised.

One of the men began to speak, "It … It just took him. He answered wrong and it …" The man began crying.

Before any of them could question further, the dungeon door opened, and orcs began walking down the steps. The three paladins all stood. "Not you," one orc said.

"We are the only ones fresh enough to work in the mines, orc. If you take any of the other men, they will merely waste your time," Toradin said.

Kurodan thought the orc would have to agree since the other men could barely stand. Some did not even bother to stir from their slumber when the orcs arrived.

"We choose who stays and who goes," the orc replied. Kurodan felt the orc's hands working his chains and restraints. Next to him, Toradin now stayed silent. If he were to protest again, it would only result in injury.

Then Feore was stood up and chosen as the second. He and Kurodan were led up the stairs and into the tunnels.

While the men had grown weary and lost much of their hope, the orcs had grown complacent as well. Feore and Kurodan were no longer placed in the hooded sacks, and the orcs used torches quite often now to move from tunnel to tunnel. They were, however, still diligent in checking the chains and shackles. They also never let up on the harassment of their captives when orders were disobeyed. *Likely due to the mere satisfaction of inflicting pain, rather than anything else*, Kurodan thought.

As they rounded one of the tunnels, Kurodan and Feore began to make their way out of habit towards a makeshift ladder that led down a hole into another maze of tunnels. The orcs grabbed and pushed them in another direction, grunting and pointing.

"Not this time," the orc said.

Kurodan tried to exchange glances with Feore, but he looked upon a walking corpse instead of his once fearless leader. *Where are we being taken now? Have the orcs begun mapping out another section of tunnels deeper in the mountain?* Forcing himself to be aware of their surroundings, Kurodan soon recognized where they were being taken. The vampire had called for him once more. *But why was Feore brought with him?* The vampire had never spoken to more than one of them at any given time, if at all.

Feore had come to the same realization as Kurodan. He began to slow his pace and even tried to stop. Kurodan could not hide the shock on his face.

"No, no do not take me back there." Feore pleaded.

One of the orcs gripped Feore by the back of his hair and shook him violently. "Move, human."

Kurodan's dread grew as his imagination took over. *What happened? What terrible event had taken place to cause so much fear in Feore?* Kurodan thought.

Both the men were brought to the throne room and forced to kneel. The vampire stood up from his chair and approached them, motioning for the orcs to leave. They knelt in silence for some time. Kurodan eyed the vampire and his surroundings carefully. Feore merely stared at the ground.

The vampire looked at each of them in turn and then, walking to one of the great tables, called, "Come, join me."

Kurodan slowly stood but Feore remained motionless. The vampire chuckled. "Please, sit." Feore finally rose, though keeping his gaze on the floor, they both reluctantly moved to the table.

Kurodan and Feore sat on the stone bench that lined the massive table. The vampire sat down across from them and gently intertwined his clawed fingers together. His dead face betrayed no emotion, save maybe boredom. An awkward silence grew until Kurodan had had enough.

"Why have you brought us here?" Kurodan demanded.

"I have simply grown bored, to be perfectly honest," the vampire said. "The orcs, while great warriors, make incredibly dull conversationists."

"Do you honestly think we will believe that you brought us here because you are seeking more entertaining company?" Kurodan asked.

Feore remained still, head sunken down, like some whipped slave too frightened to move.

"What happened to him and the others? Why do they all of the sudden cower and refuse to speak?" Kurodan raised his voice.

Before the vampire could answer, a door opened, and the smell of fresh-cooked meat wafted into the great hall. Kurodan felt like a rabid dog at the scent.

Orcs brought a heaping portion of what appeared to be slain wild game and placed it in front of them on a large shield. A chalice was placed in front of either man, then the orcs simply walked out as if they were part of the queen's professional chefs.

The two men looked up from the feast to the vampire and back to the food.

"Please, eat."

Feore grabbed a fistful of meat, but Kurodan pinned

his arm to the table. "What is this?" he questioned. "Do you make a habit of dining with your captives?"

"Paladin, if you do not wish to eat, you do not have to. As you both know, I do not partake of these meals any longer."

"Has the food been poisoned?" Kurodan asked. Feore gently placed the meat back onto the shield at the question.

The vampire's lips smirked, slightly revealing his fanged teeth. "If I were going to kill the two of you, why would I go through all this trouble? The food has not been tampered with; I assure you. While the orcs are not to the liking of a royal kitchen, they make do."

Kurodan slowly grabbed some of the meat and brought it to his mouth. He bit into the suculant meat, the warm juices running down his chin and fingers. It tasted delicious, almost melting in his mouth as he chewed.

Feore suddenly grabbed the meat with both hands and began to devour mouthfuls at a time, struggling to not choke in the process.

Kurodan did not realize that the chalices were full of fresh mountain spring water until he needed something to wash the food down with. As he raised the chalice and began gulping, Feore did the same. Then both men returned to eating. After a few minutes, the rate at which they consumed the food began to slow. Kurodan's focus drifted to the vampire. He had merely remained silent and watched the two of them eat, unmoving.

His stillness was unnerving. Kurodan broke the silence once more. "Surely you did not want to just watch two starving prisoners gorge themselves. What is it you truly want?"

"What do you believe will happen to you after all of this?" the vampire asked.

Kurodan paused for a moment, then answered, "You

and your kind will fail in the end. Many may perish, but the world of men prevailed through the Great War."

"Ah, but my kind has also prevailed. Here I sit in front of you as," the vampire opened his arms and again he smirked, "living proof."

"If there are any survivors other than you, the vampires are still scarce," Kurodan said. "The orcs may be many in number, but they are scattered and fight amongst themselves just as much with the world of men."

"All that can change. Do you believe that your world of men is any different? That it is immune to the struggles you see in your enemies?"

"You will fail because there will always be men who will stand against you," Kurodan said. "No matter the odds, no matter how dire. There will always be men who will rise and stand against the evil that plagues this world."

The vampire laughed aloud, sounding almost elegant and human. "And here we arrive at the true meaning of all this. Very good, paladin. I applaud your bluntness. Please stand and take a bow but not for the cause you so valiantly defend."

Kurodan hesitated. "What cause would I bow for if not for the one I speak of?"

"Evil."

Feore awkwardly squirmed at the word. He had not looked up after the two of them had stopped eating.

"Evil? You already admitted that I defend the opposition of evil, the adamant defiance of it," Kurodan said. He raised his voice, "What reason do I have to bow to it?"

"Evil is a mere perspective, an outlook cast upon those who defy oneself and one's nature," came the vampire's forthright response.

"You are wrong," Kurodan challenged. "Evil is palpable. It is tangible as is righteousness. They are both defined in the purest of actions one makes or does not make."

"Action has nothing and yet everything to do with it. If you act upon your cause and strike me down right this very moment, you would be righteous," the vampire said. "If I were in turn to destroy you, it would be no different."

"Your cause is one of evil," Kurodan shouted. "You would slaughter and feed on the innocent, enslave entire peoples, destroy entire kingdoms. Our causes are vastly different. If you cannot see that, you truly are blind to evil, vampire."

The vampire answered as if speaking "Evil exists forevermore. It is undying, eternal, uncaring. It has no beginning and no end. It is indifferent to race, kindred, or beast.

Before the birth of man, evil lay in a shrouded veil, waiting for him. The apogee of man's truest potential."

"You are lost beyond saving," Kurodan returned. "Proof your kind is incapable of existing in this world without committing atrocities. I may not know what the future will bring, but I do know one thing. You will die by my sword before this war is over."

The vampire began to laugh but was interrupted by Feore.

"I know who you are," the captain said slowly. "I did not recognize you this entire time, but now it is so clear to me."

Kurodan snapped his attention to Feore, his mouth hung open, and his eyes were wide with astonishment.

"Dear captain, I wish to speak with you further," the vampire said pleasantly. Dismissing Kurodan, he said, "You may be excused, paladin."

But Kurodan was transfixed, looking at Feore, waiting for him to speak further.

"How? How did you fall to this?" Feore whispered, his face contorted into a cross between sadness and disgust.

"Please, sit and eat more if you desire."

"How do you know this creature?" Kurodan asked.

Feore turned to answer Kurodan, but orcs entered the throne room and seized them both.

"Leave the captain," the vampire said.

Rage and courage overtook Kurodan. He tried to pull away from the orcs, "I will slay you! Every devil and beast that crawls within these pits will be purged by my own hand," he screamed and thrashed as the orcs dragged him away into the tunnels. Kurodan felt a swift blow to the back of his head, and the sight of Feore and the vampire faded.

Kurodan awoke chained in the dungeon room and noticed two torches hung on the walls, casting dimly lit shadows among the men. Only Toradin and Horad noticed him sitting up. "How long were we gone?" Kurodan asked, looking around in the dark room.

"The orcs brought you back unconscious some time ago. What happened to Feore?" Horad asked.

Kurodan looked around frantically. "Feore has not returned?"

"No, just you." Toradin answered

"The vampire wanted to keep speaking with him," Kurodan said. "I think he grew tired of my threats."

"You threatened the vampire?" Horad asked. The three paladins looked at each other.

"Yes." Kurodan admitted, and the three men began chuckling.

Their laughter grew louder until tears were in their

eyes and they were gasping for air. Some of the other men stirred. Laughter had become a foreign sound. None of them had laughed since their incarceration inside the mountain.

Kurodan wiped away his tears and regained some composure. "Before they took me, Feore he said something. He said he recognized the vampire."

"What?" Toradin asked.

"Feore asked the vampire how he had become the way he was" Kurodan said and noticed the other men were all awake now and listening.

"Feore knew who the vampire was in life?" Horad questioned.

Kurodan's voice grew somber still not knowing what happened to Feore. "I believe so, though he did not say a name or anything before I was taken away."

"Why did the vampire summon you two in the first place?" Toradin asked.

"The vampire feigned that he merely wanted to converse with those who are not orcs," Kurodan responded. "He fed us, thinking us to be daft and unsuspecting of his insidious intentions."

"Fed you? What kind of food did he offer?" One of the men asked, his voice waning at the thought of eating.

"What did you speak of?" Horad questioned, focusing on the heart of the matter.

"He asked us what we thought would happen after all this. How the war would end. When I answered he began to lecture on the evil nature of mankind," Kurodan said with disdain in his voice.

"This vampire sounds like a strange creature," Toradin concluded. "Intelligent but strange. We will have to question Feore when he returns."

"I hope for Feore's sake that he does not say anything as daft as I," Kurodan said, rubbing his head.

Some time passed and sleep began to quickly take the men. It was a respite from their torture. Kurodan lay on his side, waiting for his mind to slip into a dream. He wanted to fall asleep, but his head still ached, and he could not shake the anticipation of Feore's return. He wanted to know more about his enemy. *Who had the vampire been in life? What had Feore and the creature continued to speak about?*

Just as his eyelids began to droop, the dungeon door opened. This time, all of the men awoke and sat or stood.

Feore stood at the top of the stairs unchained. His hair, wild and unkept, hid most of his face. The orcs did not follow him into the room. There was no urgency in his movements. In fact, it was the opposite, Kurodan observed, almost as though Feore were sleepwalking or daydreaming.

Their captain slowly stepped down the stairs and sat down in his original spot on the floor. The door was shut. Confusion and panic were etched on all the men's faces.

"Why are you no longer bound? Did you fight your way back?" Toradin questioned.

Feore's response was low and quiet. "I no longer need to be bound."

"Why did they not chain you? Are we to be set free?" Toradin kept asking.

Kurodan interrupted, "Captain, what did you and the vampire speak about?"

Feore was silent at this, staring at the ground in front of him. Kurodan could not make out his face as he bowed his head.

"Captain," Kurodan said again. "Before I was taken away, you said you recognized the vampire. Who is he?"

Feore crept closer to Kurodan, his movements now sudden and startling as he crawled. His face was horribly disfigured and had an expression of eerie excitement. His eyes were black, blood oozed from cuts on his face. Saliva drooled down from his open mouth. An inhuman bite marked his neck.

"He… he is my master."

Chapter XXV:
Woe to the Living

Kurodan and the others reeled back in their chains at the whispered admission of their leader.

"Feore, what happened? What did he do to you?" Horad demanded.

Feore turned towards his voice to answer. "I have been... saved. My master saved me. I—"

"Saved you? You have been plagued with undeath," Toradin interrupted.

"No. I am to become as my master."

"Your master is a slave as are you," Kurodan said. "You no longer have free will."

Feore grew quiet.

"What do we do with him?" Horad asked. No one answered.

"Why would the vampire do this and then return him to this dungeon?" Horad pressed, fear wavering in his voice. Again, no one answered.

Feore took a few steps towards the far wall, turned

around and sat so that he was facing all the men. Everyone studied him. Kurodan felt the men's panic was palpable.

"Why has your master sent you here?" Toradin asked, now trying to speak with the spell subjugated servant.

"We are not safe with him here," One of the men declared.

"Safe? We have not been safe this entire time." Another bickered.

"Should we kill him?"

"No," Kurodan said loudly over the conflicting voices. "There still may be a chance to save him."

"Save him? We cannot even save ourselves."

"If he is now connected to the vampire, he may know a better way out. We might be able to use him," Toradin said. This made the conflicting voices pause.

Feore said nothing to indicate if he was listening to the conversation of how to decide his fate. He simply sat there looking as if he were a common street beggar, ridden with sickness, who was shunned by society, and did not show his own sympathies in return.

His silence made the group wary. *Maybe the orcs will come take him away, or the vampire will summon him back to the throne room*, Kurodan thought.

Regardless of the men's patience, Feore did not move. He seemed to be either deep in thought or have no thought at all. He did not look at any of the men but merely stared blankly at the dungeon floor.

Kurodan realized that Feore had not blinked once since he had returned. This was probably due to the captain's missing eyelids. Now that he studied him closer, he also realized he was not breathing.

"Feore, do you know the way out of this place?" Toradin asked. No answer, just the blank stare.

Kurodan inched closer, "Feore, we need to get back to Mil'Thuras. You remember your home, do you not? If we get you back home, we can get you the help you need. We can save—"

Toradin cut him off, "Feore, does your master know a way out of this place?"

Feore slowly raised his head, looking at the men. His wretched face split into a smile that petrified them to the bone. "No one will leave this place. You are needed."

One of the men whispered, "It is hopeless. The second he comes closer; we should finish him."

But Toradin continued his questioning. "Needed for what, Feore? What purpose does your master need us for?"

"All of you… will be the instruments…"

"Instruments for what purpose?" Toradin pressed. Feore's only reply was a ghoulish smile.

"For what purpose?" Horad demanded

"For the Dark God," Feore said, laughing and began to stand.

Feore shook as he stood but he was no longer plagued by the daze that had clouded his mind. His sickening smile decayed away into a fiery expression of fury and wrath. "All those who defy him will suffer and torment," he screamed. "Vae vivis!"

Feore ran at them, his scream harsh and wild, echoing in the dungeon.

"Look out," Horad shouted.

"Kill him," cried another.

Feore clashed into Toradin, seizing him in a frenzy. But Toradin struck a mighty blow across Feore's face, spraying blood across them both.

"Vae vivis," Feore repeated, his fingers clutching around Toradin's throat with deranged insanity.

Kurodan struggled to reach Feore's back but the

chains that bound him were spaced too far.

"Vae vivis."

Toradin fought like a rabid dog caught in a snare, his panic and fear palpable.

"Vae vivis."

"Push him closer to me," shouted Kurodan. Horad was on his feet trying to reach out.

"Vae vivis," Feore shouted again, pushing Toradin back towards the dungeon wall

Toradin managed to dig his thumbs deep into Feore's lidless black eyes. Even as blood squirted out, Feore continued shouting, "Vae vivis!"

Keeping his hands on Feore's head, Toradin kicked hard off the wall, flinging Feore backwards. Kurodan leapt upon him, wrapping his chains around Feore's neck. He heaved backwards, falling to the ground and Feore's back now pressed against Kudoran's chest.

The two began thrashing on the ground. Kurodan struggled to contain Feore's frenzied movements. Next to them, Toradin was on all fours, gasping for air.

"Kill him," Horad shouted.

Feore's hands slithered upwards and began to claw Kurodan's face. "Grab his legs," Kurodan yelled.

Toradin threw himself on Feore's feet, barely able to reach them. Kurodan arched backwards, his veins bulging and spit flying from his mouth as he continued to tighten the chains. Feore's body twitched and twisted, contorting in an unnatural manner. Finally, Feore lay still, and an unsettling silence hung like a stench around them.

Kurodan rolled Feore's body off himself and sat up. No one spoke. Their captain had fallen and by his own hand. This final atrocity broke Kurodan's hope of survival. Now, now his courage had faded and gave way to madness.

The door was unlocked, and orcs made their way into the dungeon. One of the orcs laughed out loud at the sight of Feore's corpse, "Looks like the bloodsucker had his way with your captain, eh?"

Toradin scowled up at them, "After he already had his way with your leader, orc."

The orc scowled back. "On your feet, humans."

Some of the men slowly stood and others acted as if no one had even spoken.

"I said, on your feet!" the orc who had given the command approached closer, wielding a club. Kurodan remained seated next to Feore.

"And if we refuse? You will do what? Kill us?" Toradin said standing.

One of the other orcs delivered a harsh blow to Toradin's face, sending him onto his back.

"Enough of this," the orc with the club said.

"Your master wants us alive. If you kill us, your lives are forfeit," Toradin said, sitting back up and wiping the blood from his nose.

"There are things far worse than death, human," the orc retorted.

Kurodan laughed. "I know, we all know. Your threats no longer hold sway over us."

Now the orc also laughed. "Get them moving." The other orcs began to work some of the men's shackles. "One at a time," the leader demanded. "We will not risk them trying to escape again."

Kurodan watched as one by one the men were marched out of the dungeon and into the tunnels. The process was slow. *Are the orcs nervous, or even fearful?* Kurodan wondered. A group of the orcs would escort one prisoner while the others remained behind and watched them. Sometime later the orcs would return for the next.

"Where are you taking us?" Kurodan demanded.

"We do not answer to you, human. It is you who answers to us."

"You answer to the vampire," Kurodan challenged. "Say we force your hand, orc? Say we revolt right now and force you to slay us. How would you answer to the demon?"

The other men now looked at Kurodan in bewilderment.

"What are you doing, Kurodan?" Toradin hissed. Kurodan ignored him.

"You think you can fight us still in chains?" asked the orc.

"We have before."

"And you failed, human."

"We failed not because of any orc," Kurodan sneered. "Your master had to step in on your behalf."

The orc grew angry at this. "If you do not stop talking, I will bleed you."

"Do your worst," Kurodan said.

The orcs moved closer to him as heavy tension filled the dungeon.

Then Kurodan screamed, spurring them on, "Do it! Finish me, you cowards!"

The other orcs heard the commotion and returned to the room ready for a fight. But Kurodan's rage had inspired Toradin and Horad to join him in defiance. In the chaos, they shouted and challenged the orcs to end their miserable lives. Others begged to be spared, and one or two merely looked on with blank expressions.

"That is quite enough, paladin," the vampire said, descending the steps. His presence immediately hushed the men and the orcs. "If I tell you where I am taking you, will you go willingly?"

Kurodan spat on the ground.

"Very well. Leave the paladin here, Take the others."

The orcs began to work the chains and shackles. Kurodan thought of urging the men to fight, but at a grim glance from Toradin, he forced his mouth to stay shut. The orcs marched the men up the steps and left only Kurodan, the vampire, and Feore's corpse.

Kurodan's gaze shifted from the monster to Feore's body and back. He finally broke their silence.

"Well, scourge?"

Chapter XXVI:
The Book of the Dead

Crune guided Dramington through the forest. The lord tripped over frozen brush and struggled to catch himself against a tree. Crune crept along carefully, choosing exactly where he walked. With each step, his eyes darted back and forth, hoping he would not see what he already knew lay in wait. *None of this has gone according to plan*, he thought. His mind raced against all the possibilities of failure.

"How much farther?" Dramington asked. Crune paused and looked around as if searching for something. "Do you even know where we are?"

"Yes, my lord. We should be very close." Crune's voice was still a whisper.

Dramington seemed to care less and less about their noise the further they traveled. Tripping again, he stopped and leaned against a large tree to stop his fall.

"What, what's this?" Dramington asked in alarm as his hand traced a marking that was carved into the tree.

"Some of the trees are marked, my lord. It means we are almost there."

Dramington moved his face closer to the frozen bark on the tree. His eyes and fingers studied the symbol further.

"This way, my lord," Crune whispered. He could feel his heart and blood pumping, but his body was wet with a cold sweat. He had tried not to draw Dramington's attention to the numerous markings that now surrounded them on each tree. "So close," Crune murmured, "I need to—"

Dramington drew his sword. Crune stopped and slowly turned.

"Where have you led me, Crune? What have you done?" A brief silence filled the short distance between them. The lord continued, "I have seen these markings before. I have heard the rumors and the stories."

As the two men stared at one another, they heard the quiet crunch of snow nearby.

Dramington pointed his sword in the direction of the sound, still glancing over his shoulder at Crune. "Answer me." More footsteps disturbed the snow around them. Dramington turned again at the sound. "Who is out there?"

"My lord," Crune began, but Dramington caught a glimpse of movement. A dark, red-hooded figure quickly stepped out from behind a tree, only to hide behind another. Lights appeared around them, in the distance, as someone began to light torches.

Shadows danced across the dark, as more hooded figures stalked closer.

"What is this?" Dramington asked, clearly in disbelief at what he was seeing.

Crune's face was devoid of emotion, staring back at him like a corpse. He raised his light, and a slight smirk slithered across his face before he threw the torch into the snow and plunged them into darkness.

Dramington's fear surfaced as it slammed into him, forcing him to flee through the forest blindly. His heart pounded in his ears as he sprinted, struggling to find his footing through the snow and the blackness. He could not see his breath, but he could feel its warmth, as cold tears uncontrollably trickled from his eyes.

Branches tore at his clothing, slowing his escape. He could hear them. Hear Crune. Hear those people dressed in red. They no longer attempted to hide themselves. He could hear their heavy breathing and their footsteps running after him. Like a pack of dogs toying with a stray cat. His legs burned and his feet grew wet and cold, snow falling into his boots as he ran. He fought the urge to turn and fight. His hand gripped his sword tighter than he ever had in his life.

Rignor stopped when he heard the sound of men running. He could make out the other members' torches now, but they were running back in his direction. Then he saw them. Lord Dramington and Crune, that fool trying to catch him. Rignor chuckled.

Dramington could hear Crune only a few feet behind him. He turned and let loose a scream, raising his sword. Crune stopped, a knife in his hand. Dramington had no words, he could only scream in his anger and his fear. He took two steps forward, swinging his sword.

Crune moved quickly but slipped in the snow. He fell onto his back and raised his knife to try and defend against what would almost certainly be the strike that would end his life.

Dramington's screams were snuffed out as Rignor

clubbed the back of his head with the pommel of his own sword. Dramington fell face first in the snow next to him, and Crune quickly stood, attempting to regain his composure. One of the men dressed in red approached and handed his torch to Crune and began binding Dramington's hands behind his back.

"Good catch," Thrass said.

"You were supposed to wait," Crune muttered. Then, taking another deep breath, he said louder, "You were supposed to give me time."

"Shut up, you got him out, didn't you?" Rignor said.

"Yes, I did," Crune said, crowing, "I got him out. I got him here."

"And you almost let him get away," Rignor said dismissively. More of the hooded figures approached, watching the two argue.

Crune took a step forward, knife still in hand.

"What? You finally going to try and kill me?" Rignor challenged. Finished with the binding, Thrass stood and grabbed Crune, pushing him back slightly.

"We don't have time for this," Thrass told them. "He is waiting." The men looked down as Dramington rolled onto his side, moaning.

As he walked deeper into the forest, Crune was still furious at the entire situation. Only their torches lit the way. The stars and moon's light failed to penetrate the tall trees. They walked in silence, save for their one prisoner.

Blindfolded and gagged, Dramington was being strung along through the snow. The lord's hands were tied behind his back, and Thrass led him by a rope tied around his neck.

My prisoner, Crune thought. *I am the one who should be thanked. It was my doing. My work. My plan.*

More of the strange symbols appeared, some carved into the trees and others made from twigs hung from their branches. Their presence cast a foreboding feeling, one of dread and warning.

Now the group entered a denser part of the forest, trees and vegetation engulfing them in a strangled web. Ahead of Crune, the pace slowed. He watched each member trespass through the density careful not to disturb the web, perhaps for fear of awakening whatever foul abomination had constructed it.

Shortly thereafter, they emerged into a circular clearing that was entirely walled off by trees, save for above their heads. The night sky could now be clearly seen from where they stood. As Crune looked up, he noticed that the sky directly above them was devoid of moon and stars. It was as if something had forced them away, like a cold breeze blowing out the flame of a candle.

The ground was covered with fresh grass and its appearance seemed seasonless, considering the snow that blanketed the rest of their surroundings. In the center was a stone altar, covered in the symbols and markings that littered the forest. Torches stood erected in the ground around the altar. And there, standing at the unholy shrine, was a man dressed in blue robes.

Crune let out an audible gasp. Was it really him? After all this time, he knew fate had brought him back to the wizard at last. One of the members pushed Crune slightly forward. He had become motionless in his shock, but the members were forming themselves in front of the altar. In unison, they dropped to one knee, their heads bowed in reverence.

The man at the altar said nothing. Crune's eyes strained to glean a better look at the man. He had to know for sure—was it him? When Dramington was led forward, more light flickered in the center. It was him, Crune was sure.

The members stood and removed their red hoods. They forced Dramington to kneel and removed his blindfold. He looked up at the wizard with complete and utter confusion. As Dramington began to panic and look frantically around him, the wizard's face only revealed what Crune construed to be a slight smile.

Crune rolled his eyes at Dramington's muffled begging and pleading. Each member stared at him with what seemed a morbid curiosity. Like how a flock of carrion birds eagerly stare at a dying animal. He begged and pleaded as best he could, with his mouth still gagged. One of the members removed his gag so he could speak, though Crune knew it would not save him.

"Please," Dramington croaked. "Please whatever it is you want... I... I can get you. By the light, please do not kill me."

The wizard's eyes looked from the man to the audience standing before him. He then looked up and around the trees that encompassed them, as if almost confused, even turning his back to Dramington and the altar.

Finally, he looked up at the dead night that hung above them. He slowly turned to face the man. Placing his hands on the altar, he leaned close to Dramington and whispered, "Light? There is no light."

The wizard stepped back, and the closest members seized Dramington, placing him upon the altar. He shrieked and cried out. His body thrashed and twisted against the bindings.

Witnessing this, Crune began to tremble with an uncontrollable excitement. He looked down to see his hands trembling before he looked back up. The vision that the wizard had shown him all that time ago, Crune was sure now it was about to become a reality.

Another member approached the altar, knelt and produced a dagger. The wizard accepted the offered blade and examined it for a brief moment, before he drove the dagger into the man's chest. Not once, but over and over he stabbed, until Dramington's screams finally ceased. The wizard then quickly cut the rope that bound the corpse.

Lifting the dagger, now dripping with Dramington's blood, the wizard held his hands above his head. All around, the members stood and held their hands in the air, mimicking their leader. Crune awkwardly copied those around him.

Dramington's corpse lay flat against the altar that was stained with his blood. Crune watched as the wizard closed his eyes and remained perfectly still. No one uttered a sound.

Crune's mind was eating itself, waiting for what would happen next. He could feel something stirring, the same feeling he had felt all that time ago, when the wizard had first looked into his eyes.

The wizard reached down and produced a monstrous looking book. He held it aloft with one hand, with the other he opened the pages with the bloody knife. Crune watched in shock as the book seemed to come alive. Its pages fluttered wildly, almost licking at the blade.

Dramington's body twitched. Crune's eyes grew wide, and his mouth hung agape. The wizard's eyes were resolute. The corpse convulsed as if plagued by a terrible pain or burned by an invisible fire. The altar became increasingly red from the corpse's blood. Then, as quickly as it had begun, the movement ceased entirely.

After an instant of stillness, a scream unlike that of

any mortal poured forth from the corpse, and it sat up. The wizard walked around the altar, now joining the audience, to witness his own work. The corpse stood on the altar.

Crune knew Dramington was dead, but now the man was able to move.

The wizard turned to address the cult. "Behold the power of the one and true Dark God," the wizard said, pointing up at the undead thing on the altar. "There lies power within death. New life and new existence. Within this power is your reward—your potential. You must rise and seize it."

The members stood, and Crune quickly imitated them.

"Vae vivis," the wizard then shouted.

"Vae vivis," the members chanted in response. And Crune felt the words flow from his mouth as did every other member. "

"Vae vivis!"

Chapter XXVII: Hope

The vampire held aloft a golden chalice. He peered into its beauty and its purity, for he bore no reflection of his own.

"The evil that was believed vanquished shall be summoned once more," the vampire proclaimed. "A never-ending night shall consume all that inhabits the world, and all his creations will pour forth in legion."

As he continued to envision the destruction he sought to bring to the world, the vampire did not look at Kurodan.

"Behold, the war amongst the gods shall know no bounds, and the world of men shall be sieged in ruin. All faith shall be led astray unto them. And he shall wage war upon the world of men, and they shall make ready for battle."

It appeared he was acting his future role as messenger of doom and harbinger of death to all those who opposed the Dark God.

"The righteous will stand before the wicked, and the wicked will tear down the very gates of the heavens. And he shall rob peace from the world and set loose great suffering upon the innocent. The Dark God shall rule atop his throne and devour the flesh and blood of the living. And he shall meet out his eternal vengeance until only his image remains. Who then shall be saved?"

Listening to this declaration that foreshadowed the slaughtering of masses, Kurodan began to shake with anger. He lifted his head and said, "You truly are mad. Do you really believe that this god of yours will share his power? You will be but a pawn for him to move about his board as he pleases."

"That is where you are false," the vampire responded. "Yes, he will be the ruler of this new world, but I will be his emissary, his messenger, his general, his subjugator and minister. I will be the cruel instrument through which he wreaks havoc on those who oppose us. He will take his rightful throne as god over this world. I will share in his power, his kingdom, and reap more reward than you can possibly fathom."

The vampire held the chalice above his head, admiring it further. His dead eyes slowly shifted back to Kurodan.

"You still judge by the notion that my kind and I are a scourge. That our mere existence in this world is but a plague and that we are cursed. This is the greatest falsehood preached amongst men. I had once believed this lie as you do," the vampire smiled.

"Yes, I was once a devout warrior of your Holy Order. But now I possess more power than you paladins. Even more than the High Council, more than the few wizards still wandering the world. The dark gift we possess that you were taught to fear and hate since birth is simply that—a gift," he said simply.

"And when the Dark God awakens, we will evolve from that gift, growing forever stronger, while you humans will be fighting to exist."

They were now locked in each other's gaze, neither turning away. Kurodan was trying to hide his confusion. *How? How had this creature once been a paladin? How had someone who was held to the highest standards of the light, fallen... to this?* And then Kurodan remembered that this must be what Feore had spoken of—that he had known the vampire before, in life.

The vampire revealed his fangs slightly in a smirk. "I am almost tempted to offer you my blood, to bestow upon you this monumental blessing of rebirth. To embrace this enlightenment and elevate you by my side into the coming of the new night. But this you must choose willingly, for I will not grant such a blessing on those unworthy."

Kurodan found himself no longer able to find the words to defy the vampire. He spat in his face.

Laughter came in reply. "So sure of yourself, paladin?"

When Kurodan spoke, his voice was quiet, almost a whisper, but still clear and confident. "I would damn your soul to the deepest pits of hell, but I believe your soul was devoured when you were spawned into the miserable creature that now stands before my eyes."

"Trust me, you know nothing of my soul or what it has endured, this I can assure you" the vampire answered. He turned his back to Kurodan, letting the silence and hate simmer. Just when Kurodan thought the vampire would at long last feed on him, or finish his life, the creature turned back and knelt close to his face.

Placing his pale white hand on Kurodan's shoulder, he danced his clawed fingers delicately across bare skin. Kurodan fought the overwhelming urge to flinch away.

The touch was unsettling.

The vampire's gaunt face looked tired as he let out a sigh. "It is truly a travesty that you will not bear witness to our great conquest." He spoke with what seemed to be real sadness and genuine regret. "Alas, I will think of you when I feed upon your brethren's corpses."

Then he stood and turned to walk out of the dungeon. Kurodan tried to leap to his feet, but his shackles jerked him back down. He screamed in a rage, "I would rather suffer a thousand agonizing deaths than be an accomplice to your madness and senseless slaughter."

The vampire stopped and turned slightly before exiting. "That can be arranged, paladin."

Chained to the stone floor, Kurodan let his head drop, but then heard the footsteps of others approaching.

"He will be the last," the vampire spoke from beyond the door. "The one I have chosen. Bring him to the peak. It is time."

To Kurodan's astonishment, it was not orcs who had entered but men. They were dressed in dark red robes and had painted their faces with the same markings and runes that were in the vampire's throne room.

"If you fight us, we will have to take your life, and that will greatly displease our master," one said.

"I would welcome that death, for it would be a release from this hellish captivity, you traitors," Kurodan mocked. The red-robed man who had spoken unchained the links that were bolted to the stone floor, but left Kurodan's hands shackled.

"While that may be true, our master requires you for the ritual. On your feet," the man gestured with his spear.

As they walked him into the dark tunnels, Kurodan asked, "You think your master will spare your wretched lives? Or do you think his false god will?"

He was answered with a strike to his back.

"We will be rewarded for our faith."

Kurodan laughed aloud, "Faith? You do not know the meaning of the word."

They slowly made their way uphill through the tunnels, climbing to the top of the mountain. Their dim torches cast long shadows as they walked. They began to turn into tunnels he did not recognize. He was lost. Kurodan began to feign weariness or rather ceased hiding it, seeming to lose all his composure and strength. "Do not slow down, we are getting close," the man leading him said.

Kurodan raised his head to see in the faint light that they were coming to an opening that he had not seen before. A sense of pure terror gripped and overwhelmed him. He knew that even his worst nightmares could not conjure what awaited him.

This is it. Now or never, he told himself. *Die on your feet or forever stay the lamb being led to the slaughter.* Kurodan pretended to trip and stumble, but as he did, he pushed the man who was leading him to the ground and fell on top of him. The two behind Kurodan raised their weapons to cut him down but he wrapped his chains around the acolyte's neck and rolled onto his back. The choking man now faced the others, gripping at the chain.

"Kill hi— he tried to scream, but Kurodan stood and gripped the chains tighter. Kurodan slowly began walking backwards, keeping the traitor between him and the other two.

"Fool, release him or we will be forced to end you," one shouted while raising his sword. Kurodan tightened his grip on the shackles. The acolyte was now turning dark purple in the face and frantically trying to free himself.

Weapons at the ready, the other two acolytes

charged. Kurodan put his foot in the small of his captive's back and kicked with all his might, simultaneously lifting the shackles up. As the three acolytes crashed into each other in a heap, he turned and fled.

His chest and head pounded, his tongue and mouth were dry, his legs ached and strained as he opened his stride into a full sprint. He fought his instinct to slow down as his vision blurred and the light from the torches grew dim. He could hear the acolytes screaming and tearing after him. He knew if he stopped, he would die, but he had never been through these tunnels before. He was running blind in every sense.

He sprinted into a small room that was set alight with torches on the walls. Two tunnels seemed to continue upwards and a third looked as if it went back down further into the mountain. Kurodan began to charge at the first tunnel that continued upwards, but as the screams of the pursuing acolytes continued, he saw lights and shadows coming from the two tunnels that led upwards.

Kurodan stopped, the shouts and sounds of beating feet echoed in the tunnels. He panicked, turned and ran headlong into the tunnel that started at a slight decline.

As he continued to run, he thought he had already lost. There were tunnels branching off both left and right. He did not know which way was up or down in the dark. He thought every second that he would merely sprint down a new tunnel and into an army of orcs or worse. This tunnel clearly led back down into the mountain instead of to the peak where he had hoped he could escape. It was too dark to run at a full sprint now, but he could hear the acolytes entering the same tunnel to give chase.

He broke to the left and slowed to a jog in this new

tunnel. It quickly became so dark he was unable to witness his own hand in front of his face. *There is no escape*, he thought, stopping dead in his tracks. *It's over.* He was exhausted, gasping for air while trying to quiet his breathing. He began to turn to face his death, but something caught his eye.

Light. A faint hint of light. But it was different. It was not the same glow as a torch. He ran towards it like a madman hallucinating an oasis in the dying sands of a desert. The light was still faint when he reached it. It was coming from a smaller tunnel, almost a large hole that appeared to climb at a steep angle. Kurodan threw himself upwards, scrambling through the dirt on his stomach like some rodent or insect. His feet and legs fought as he continued to kick his way up. His hands clawed at the dirt as the light seemed to grow a bit brighter.

He could now see to the end of the small tunnel. The top seemed to be covered by branches and thorns. They cut into his body, drawing blood as he pushed his way through them. He finally broke free and was standing out in the open, on the side of the mountain. The cold brisk air took his very soul by surprise. He gazed up into the night sky and saw the largest full moon he had ever seen in his life, surrounded by bright stars. It seemed so much closer so high up on the mountain. The sight, with the realization that he was no longer trapped inside, stole his breath away.

He noticed scattered trees about him as he awoke from his trance and frantically looked around. He saw that the mountain peak was not far. He heard voices and saw bright lights flickering at the top.

He could make out some kind of tower, or pyramid, at the very top among all the fires' lights. Kurodan turned to face down the mountain and ran for his life.

He was sprinting as fast as his body would allow. He stumbled down a steep section of the mountain and as he regained his stride, looked up to see the trees around him were denser. The moon was still bright enough that he could make his way through them. His breathing was nigh out of control, but still he tried not to slow. All he could think about was getting as far from the mountain as fast as he could. One thought entered his mind and made him slow—*The others*. Could he abandon his brothers in arms to whatever unholy death awaited them?

No, Kurodan thought, *I will not leave them to perish here. But I cannot save them on my own.* These conflicting thoughts combined with the mountain's terrain forced him to slow his pace.

Boom.

A deep, loud sound echoed through the night air. Then again and again. It was coming from a drum at the peak of the mountain. Kurodan slowly turned to look back up the way he had come. The trees blocked his view of the mountain peak, but he could hear the drum booming from the top. It was a single drumbeat, slow, loud, and damning.

The drum now began to beat slightly faster, and more drums joined in. The noise seemed to echo through the entire mountain and slowly grew with each beat. Fear got the better of him. He turned back down the mountain and ran even faster. No matter how fast he ran, the drums seemed to beat loudly right behind him. His body trembled from the cold, and he broke out of the trees and into an open clearing. The moon revealed a cliff that gave way to more trees and a valley below

The drums were now raging in a furious crescendo of sound that demanded his attention. Looking up, he saw what looked like bonfires lit around the peak and small faint shadows dancing around the flames.

If I do not get off this mountain now, I will never leave, Kurodan thought. He started picking his way towards the steep drop-off, trying to carefully descend, but something else seized his attention. More lights, now coming from the trees ahead of the clearing.

Kurodan's first instinct was to try and shout, but the drums were so loud and the lights so far away, that it would have been in vain.

He stopped and watched, hoping that it was an army or scouting party from Mil'Thuras. *Maybe they have already been warned of the threat here and sent an army. How long have we been missing now?* he pondered. *They must have heard the drums.* Exhaustion and excitement overtook Kurodan and he had a vision of storming the mountain peak with his brothers in arms… rescuing any survivors and watching the vampire fall as he smote him into oblivion.

The forest now looked set ablaze by a sea of torchlight. The light was growing brighter as it drew closer and closer to the treeline. Then, suddenly, the drums ceased. Kurodan's head snapped back up to the peak, but he could not make anything out except for the fire at the top.

Then a horn blew, from within the trees and torches, in answer to the silenced drums. It was no human horn. Kurodan felt a chill crawl up his spine, as he slowly turned back to the sea of fire dancing through the forest. It was an orcish horn, booming, long, and terrible.

"Have I merely traded one doomed fate for another?" Kurodan whispered aloud to himself. The massive army before him that he had envisioned as his savior and avenging force, was yet another enemy.

The horn ended and there was a slight pause. Kurodan's body began to shake and tremble. The drums atop the mountain peak boomed again.

Kurodan, still against all odds, refused to accept defeat. Not after coming this close. He ran back up the way he had come. Tree branches whipped his face and tore at his ragged clothes. His chest began heaving, fighting for air. As the mountain became steeper, Kurodan was forced to a stumbling stupor. He fell to his hands and knees, clawing his way through the forest floor, like a decrepit animal. He began dry heaving, gasping, crying.

He tried lifting his head and willing his body to stand, but his vision blurred, leaving him as blind as though still trapped in the tunnels. He felt as if he was falling off the face of the mountain itself and into the night sky. He managed to roll onto his back, tears now streaming down his face. His vision faded, making the shadows around him come to life. Monstrous beings floated and danced down from that bright moon, to finally bring him face to face with death. All went dark.

Kurodan opened his eyes as he smelled something rancid. What had been killed and was decaying next to him. *Maybe I am dead and now my body is wasting away*, he thought. The noise around him was unrelenting as the drums from the mountain top continued beating. His mouth was so dry his throat felt swollen, and it made it difficult to breathe. He knew if he did not find water soon, he would perish whether he was captured or not. As his eyes began to focus, he noticed light flickering in the distance.

Kurodan started to sit up when he witnessed something crawling in the treetops high above him. He watched the shadow move from branch to branch, tree to tree. It seemed to be massive—the size of a wild horse— and yet it moved with grace.

As he propped himself up, he saw another large shape, and then another. Soon Kurodan was looking all around at the giant graceful creatures that moved so effortlessly in the forest, and realized he knew what they were.

Giant mountain arachnids. He had heard horror stories of them as a child, stories of warriors caught in a colossal web only to be consumed by these monsters. The stories had always told of entire broods of arachnids in the mountains around the Barren Lands.

Seeking a place to hide, Kurodan dragged himself under a mass of roots that jutted out from a nearby tree. The drums completely drowned out the sound of the creatures' movement, but Kurodan now could see them climbing overhead, a blanket of dark bodies and many legs spreading atop the trees.

Kurodan tried, with all the energy he had left, to make himself as small as possible under the roots. He wondered if they could see in the dark, if they could smell him. He now knew the rancid smell must be coming from these creatures. As he moved his attention away from the treetops, he saw torchlights moving through the forest.

Orcs. More orcs than Kurodan thought to have ever existed. He had thought that most of the orcs had been killed or disbanded at the end of the Great War. *How could such large an army go unnoticed?* Kurodan thought.

He willed himself into the damp cold earth as the closest orc approached the roots. The orc's skin was a deep green, that was almost entrancing in the torchlight. Kurodan held his breath and lay motionless.

He could not help but watch the orc. It was as tall as a man, its body muscular and defined from a lifetime of combat, survival, and fighting under harsh conditions.

It moved with the instincts of a predator. Inside the chainmail hood, the orc's face was menacing. Red war paint contrasted the green skin, its underbite held two large tusks, one whole and the other broken. Its eyes were yellow, like a large feline, cunning and calculated. A long scar started on the forehead and came over the left eye, tearing down its cheek. Kurodan recognized him. It was the orc that had slain the challenger, the leader who had brought them into the mountain. The drums atop the mountain still roared out like thunder across a storming sky.

Kurodan looked away as the orc stepped within arm's reach of the roots, hoping that if he did not look upon the orc, the orc would not look upon him. The orc stopped, and Kurodan knew in his heart he was found. He shut his eyes as hard as he could. He waited for the death blow from the orc's hideous dagger, or the shout sounding the alarm that they had found a prisoner. Kurodan waited for what seemed like an eternity but was not given the satisfaction of death.

He opened his eyes. The orc had raised his torch, looking at the treetops above them. They were alive with the arachnids. The orc gazed upon them, seeming to revel in their nightmarish forms. All through the forest, orcs marched and passed their position.

Kurodan was transfixed, looking at the orc now standing almost on top of him. Long black fur covered its legs from just below the knee down to the boot. A fur loincloth covered the orc's pelvis, where a human skull rested in the center of the belt line. The chainmail armor glinted in the torch's flame. It had obviously been taken from one of his previous victims. Kurodan stared into the black eye sockets of the skull that decorated the orc. *Perhaps this poor soul was the original wearer of the armor?* Kurodan thought.

The drums from the mountaintop ceased. Kurodan could now hear the full cacophony of evil that moved all around him. The orc reached for a horn that was slung across his side. The sling was fashioned from human hair and skin. He brought the horn to his mouth while lowering the torch. Kurodan was now barely exposed by the torch. But the orc looked up at the night sky and, with a deep breath, blew the terrible horn.

The noise was devastating. Kurodan, now with no care of being exposed, slammed his hands over his ears. The horn continued, relentlessly. Blood oozed between his fingers as he fought the sharp pain within his ears, writhing on the ground in agony. The ground he lay on shook from the sound.

When the horn finally ceased, Kurodan regained a shred of his sanity, his ears bloody and ringing. The drums from the mountaintop thundered in reply. The orc raised the torch and stepped off, continuing the march. Kurodan lay in utter disbelief. *How? Had it been pure luck or merely a curse to continue in existence within this hellish place*, he wondered. *Maybe one of the arachnids would spot him from above and crawl down the tree to feast on his flesh.*

He lay within the crevasse at the bottom of the tree and witnessed the rest of the army move through the forest. The rows of orcs seemed to never end. Kurodan thought the sun would soon be up and the army would still be marching. But at least the heat from the orc's torches gave his bones some small sense of warmth as they passed by. The drums continued from the mountain peak.

Kurodan's mind wandered. He thought of the vampire's offer, the golden chalice, the wizard, the orcs. As he pondered the horrors surrounding him, he no longer cared.

His exhaustion had finally broken him down. The army at last came to an end, and Kurodan squirmed underneath the roots, trying to raise his head to see. A few remaining orcs were moving up the forested mountain. Slowly, he crawled from his hiding place and stood. The forest floor had been trampled and decimated by the marching army, disturbing the ground into thick mud. He stumbled, making his way back to the cliff.

The scenery was hauntingly beautiful under the moonlight. He gazed across the valley and down the cliffside, considering if he had even the slightest amount of energy to try and make his way down. He looked up the mountain as the drums ceased once again. He could now see the bulk of the orc army and all their torches light up the mountainside. The orcish horn sounded once again, making Kurodan shudder and cover his ears. He expected the drums to echo across the air once more, but silence was the only reply.

He turned to face the cliffside. "I have failed. Please, Father, forgive me," Kurodan said as he lifted his foot over the cliff's edge.

"Stop!" a woman's voice shouted from behind him. Broken out of his trance, Kurodan stumbled backwards and fell away from the cliff's edge. He lay there on his back, unable to regain the strength to stand again. He heard running footsteps and hushed voices around him.

"You will get us all killed, surely there are orc scouts remaining behind that will have heard you," a man scolded.

"I was not going to let him throw himself off the cliff." the woman's voice hissed. "We need to find out who he is."

Kurodan could now make out figures standing all around him.

"Post scouts. We will need to move quickly if any part of that army backtracks," the man ordered.

He tried to ask for water but only coughed and choked. Weakly, he motioned towards his mouth. Someone knelt beside him and tilted his head forward. He felt something press against his lips and then cool water trickled into his mouth. Kurodan's eyes closed as he began gulping the water down. His throat still ached, but the water helped soothe his body.

"He looks and smells of death," the woman said.

"Yes, well how did he manage to evade that army?"

"Maybe they figured him already dead?"

"It does not matter right now. We need to move quickly," the man said sharply. "Pick him up."

Kurodan's body was almost completely limp, and he tried to motion for the water again. He heard a shout and opened his eyes. He was being carried over someone's shoulder.

Two orcs came charging forward, one holding what appeared to be a human head in his hand. Both had bloody swords raised as they sprinted toward Kurodan and his rescuers. He blinked and heard the whistling of arrows all around him. The arrows struck the two orcs and threw them to the ground.

"Move now," the man ordered.

"They killed the scouts," the woman warned.

Kurodan felt his body bouncing as whoever was carrying him began running. He tried to keep his eyes open and saw the two dead orcs grow distant. He heard the swishing of trees as they moved through the forest.

Kurodan could not tell where they were going but did not care. He felt something swell inside of him, something that ignited his fortitude and courage tenfold. Something that he had forgotten the feeling of,

Hope.

Chapter XXVIII:
The Offering

The vampire stood at the top of Mount Ruin. The ground had been flattened and sculpted with stones. He turned from the altar that lay in the center, his back now facing the large pyramid that had been constructed for the unholy ceremony.

The vampire's gaze looked up at the immense rock face that towered opposite the pyramid. It was the tallest point of the actual peak. The final call of the orc horn perverted the world. Its sound, an ominous warning, a challenge even, foretelling of the impending doom.

The fires set around the outer edges, raged as the acolytes continued to stoke them. The drums had ceased upon the arrival of the orc army, calling forth all those who would serve the Dark God, all those who would wage war against the world of mankind.

The vampire glanced at the prisoners who were chained and bound, kneeling. He only counted six. He looked for the third paladin.

The thought of offering him one last chance to accept his blood flickered through his mind. His eyes widened when they failed to find him.

"Where is he?" he shouted. The acolytes ceased their actions, exchanging uncomfortable looks amongst themselves. One of the acolytes walked forward, his head bowed slightly, as if to avoid eye contact and hopefully any consequence.

"My master, word was sent that he was lost in the tunnels on his ascent. We are still searching and will find him soon," he said.

"You thought it wise to just now bring this to my attention?"

"I thought it best to not disrupt the preparations of the ritual and summoning, my master. We will find him, but the tunnels are deep and many within the mountain," he replied.

"You will only find his corpse in one of the many tunnels if anything at all! Though you are correct. The summoning must not be delayed. Come, mortal, and reap your reward." The vampire motioned with one arm and beckoned the servant forward.

Toradin raised his head and grinned "Kurodan must have evaded your plans, scourge. He is probably on his way at this very moment to muster the armies of Mil'Thuras. We will erase your kind from existence. You may complete whatever foul ritual you speak of—it matters not. The world of men will never fall!"

Horad looked at Toradin with a solemn affirmation at his open defiance of the vampire.

The vampire turned from the acolyte and stood over Toradin. "I desired the other to be the final piece of the ritual, but now I see that you shall suffice. Whether he still lives matters not. Whether you believe the kingdoms of men will live through the coming storm matters not."

He pointed his pale clawed finger at Torading, "You will be the final key that unleashes the Dark God upon this world. You will bear that great responsibility, and yet you will also bear the same travesty. You will not be here to witness it all transpire."

Toradin stared into the vampire's eyes, challenging the demon to no longer wait and end his life now. The vampire's features remained emotionless and dead. "The only travesty we will face, is not witnessing you and your ilk being burned to ash." Horad said coldly.

"Reward, my master?" the acolyte asked, his curiosity outweighing his fear. The vampire turned and motioned to the altar. Its construction was immense and made of stone. The four corners were decorated with human skulls. The center had been carved into a giant bowl. The pyramid steps rose behind it. Across the stone courtyard loomed a giant black stone, the tallest point on the mountain.

The acolyte slowly approached the altar. Clawed fingertips found their way on his back and guided him closer. They both gazed into the bowl. "Search hard and you will find it," the vampire said.

The acolyte leaned in closer as if puzzled by the emptiness of it. There was an audible cracking sound as the vampire's jaw unhinged, like that of a snake. His fangs glistened, and his tongue elongated. His eyes dilated to pitch black. His cheeks stretched, growing taut and thin. His hand grasped tightly at the back of the man's robes while the other gripped his head.

Pure terror pulsed through his body, as he struggled to free himself, frantically pushing away from the altar. Only the emptiness inside bore true witness to man's full fear. The vampire sank his teeth into the acolyte's neck, his jaws clamping down like that of a large swamp reptilian.

The man released a scream that sounded like a wild animal being eaten alive. Both his scream and the taste of his blood seemed to intoxicate the monster. He bit down harder, chewing through the neck.

The screams were cut off as he began to asphyxiate, blood gurgling from his mouth. His eyes were sealed shut, tears streaming down his cheeks and into the blood.

The vampire's grip grew even tighter, forcing the man's head deeper into the altar. The horror of tearing flesh, spilling blood, and gurgling nauseated the prisoners. Toradin fought the urge to vomit from the noise alone. The acolyte's entire body began to tremble and twitch in unison with the movements of the vampire's jaws. Then a deep, guttural gulping sound, muted forth as his victim's blood was shared between the demon's mouth and the altar.

The vampire released his teeth and raised his head back, gasping for air. His pale white skin contrasted the dark red blood that soaked his face. The surrounding fires seemed to rise at the act of death, the flames craving to burn wood as the vampire craved to drink blood.

He let loose a laugh, delighted. Contorting the acolyte's neck, further exposing the grievous wound, he bit down again with such force that the man went limp. The vampire took his fill and gently released the body, leaving it dangling headfirst in the altar. Even with all the bloodshed, the deep bowl was still rather empty.

He turned from the altar, his eyes pitiless black chasms. His jaw reattached to his skull with a sickening sound, though his mouth remained agape, revealing reddened fangs. He was breathing heavily but appeared to be exhilarated from the horror he had just wrought. The men either bowed their heads or attempted to inch backwards, for fear of becoming the next victim.

There came a deep growling laughter near one of the

fires. An orc dressed in chainmail, with a scar above his left eye and a horn slung at his side, approached the altar. Everyone turned their attention to the orc.

"I see you have begun without us, vampire," the orc said in a deep voice.

The vampire approached the orc. "You are late, Korgath, but most welcome," he said.

Toradin watched as orcs began to swarm into the stone courtyard and form a massive circle at the edges. These orcs seemed to never cease in numbers. He wondered if they had found Kurodan or if he had truly managed to escape. He clung to the last thread of hope, deep within his soul. "Kurodan, if you still draw breath, return here with all the men you can muster. Avenge us and send these devils back to hell," he whispered.

Korgath pushed past the vampire and stared at the corpse splayed over the altar. He grabbed the dead body and flung it to the ground. Some of the orcs made a hole in their ranks, and two enormous spiders crawled through and clamored towards the body.

Toradin and the other prisoners recoiled in fear at the sight. The two monstrosities fought over the dead until one of the spiders, victorious, began spinning the corpse within its legs, wrapping it in a cocoon of webbing. The arachnid scurried away from the fires and onlookers, dragging its prize in tow.

The orcs broke out into whooping laughter at the sight of this. Korgath stuck his hand down into the altar's bowl and dipped his fingers into the blood. Pulling his hand back out, he looked from the dripping blood to the prisoners. "Let us finish this. The sun will rise soon."

The vampire nodded and pointed to the prisoners, "Get them up." The acolytes grabbed Toradin and the other prisoners, pulling them to their feet.

Pointing to Toradin, the vampire said, "Leave this

one. He will be the last."

Korgath grabbed Horad by the back of the neck and violently forced his head over the altar. Horad screamed and wrenched his body against the chains and the orc's grasp. Without any hesitation, Korgath pulled his long dagger from its sheath and slit Horad's throat.

Horad's body twitched and twisted as if possessed by some maddening spirit. His blood spilled into the altar as Korgath held him firmly with one outstretched hand. Paying no attention to the bleeding victim, he asked, "Who's next?"

The orcs erupted in a bellowing cheer, stomping their feet and clashing their weapons. Toradin watched in rage, as this orc butchered the four remaining prisoners, one by one, over the altar. Two struggled to fight or resist. One screamed and begged. The last accepted his fate willingly. Toradin felt a sickening guilt, knowing these nameless men were now gone and their lives would not be remembered.

With each victim's death, the surrounding orcs erupted into a frenzy. The vampire seemed to be in a trance watching the blood pool deeper and deeper.

As the orc drained the last victim dry, leaving only Toradin, one of acolytes knelt before the vampire and presented the golden chalice.

The vampire took the chalice to the altar and submerged it in the blood. Delicately, he placed it onto the edge of the altar. Korgath held his green hand over the goblet and carved a deep wound into it. The blood in the chalice splashed as the orc added his own.

The vampire motioned for the dagger and repeated the same process. One of the acolytes stepped forward and carefully offered a small lit torch. The vampire took it from him and said, "Strip the last prisoner bare and chain him to the top."

"Yes, master," he nodded, backing away. Three of the servants began to rip Toradin's clothes from his body. Toradin tried to fight but froze, as he watched in amazement, as the vampire held the torch's flame to the chalice, and the blood caught fire. *As if it were made of oil*, Toradin thought. Dropping the torch, the vampire carefully held the chalice in his hands as he and the orc eyed the bloody bubbling concoction.

Toradin felt the sting of the night air against his naked body. He stumbled as the acolytes dragged and pulled him up the steps. His arms and legs were outstretched as he was chained to two large pillars. The vampire and the orc ascended; the acolytes were careful not to impede them. Toradin could see the blood boiling in the chalice as the flame flickered atop it.

The vampire turned to face the orcs and acolytes down below. The giant black peak loomed over them all. Raising the chalice high above his head, he shouted, "Hear me now, Dark God. We offer you this sacrifice in the name of all that is unholy. Blood has been spilt this night in your deification. This world will submit and tremble at your whim."

Korgath grabbed Toradin's face and held his mouth open. Toradin's eyes widened as the vampire brought the chalice to his lips.

"The world of men has ended, human," Korgath said. "See you in hell!" The vampire poured the flames and blood into Toradin's mouth.

It burned. His mouth was on fire, and his entire body fought against the chains in torment. He tried to scream but began to choke and gag. His face felt as if it were going to melt from his skull. Korgath covered his nose and mouth forcing him to swallow.

After one swallow, Korgath released his grasp, both

the orc and vampire stepped back. Toradin screamed. He screamed louder than he had ever heard someone scream. He terrified himself. He screamed so loud he thought his lungs would burst. Blood began to flow from every pore of his body. In mere seconds, his entire being was drenched in his own blood. He looked down at the ground around him to see more blood than he had thought could flow inside him. It wet and warmed the cold chains, but he could not free himself.

Now the orcs were quiet. They and the acolytes stood silently watching this unspeakable death unfold. Toradin wanted to die. He wanted the pain to stop.

"Make it stop! Please," he begged.

His screams cut through the night as though the entire world would be able to hear them and shudder. Toradin finally began to feel his life fade. He hung limp, dangling from the chains. His flesh had become detached, drooping from his body. As if rotted from some hideous form of leprosy, leaving a dark, dripping, red-stained skeleton.

The mountain began to shake, unleashing an earthquake from within. The vampire and Korgath held onto the pillars. The orcs and acolytes below fell and stumbled. Toradin's skeleton dangled and danced in the chains, a hideous marionette made to perform by its insidious master.

A split formed down the middle of the giant black rockface. The crack widened and cascaded downwards, as if the peak would crumble and fall away. The mountain shook more, and the very center of the courtyard collapsed in on itself. The altar of blood fell, swallowed by the heart of the mountain. A darkened pit was all that remained.

The earthquake suddenly ceased, and the peak came to life. All watched in dread as two vast bat-like wings stretched outwards.

Between the wings, a black head with horns lifted, and then clawed hands raised high into the night sky, stretching from its lifetime of slumber. The demon opened its glowing yellow eyes. Its smile held sharp fangs and teeth. It stood to its full height, a great and terrible shadow, and flapped its wings. The howling wind threw them to the ground. The vampire and Korgath knelt by Toradin's chained corpse, their palms upward, worshipping the demon.

It stepped into the stone courtyard with a thunderous crash, sending the orcs and acolytes into a panicked frenzy. The pit lay at its clawed feet.

The vampire raised his head to see the demon's immense eyes staring back at him. It said nothing but a terrible voice thundered in his ears. The voice spoke an ancient language that soon became clear. It deafened the vampire and brought him to bend on all fours.

"I accept your offering and so begins your debt."

The sun was beginning to rise.

Chapter XXIX: Sun Devourer

When Kurodan came to, he was on his back staring up at the sky. It was still dark, but on the horizon, he could see a glimpse of the sunrise.

"He is awake," the woman said. Kurodan sat up to see a group of men and one woman. The woman approached and offered him water. Her straight brown hair and green eyes captivated him for a moment. Kurodan's attention then quickly went to the water pouch, grabbing it he sucked down long gulps.

"Who are you and what were you doing up on that mountain?" a man asked.

"My name is Kurodan, I am a paladin of the Holy Order. I have been kept prisoner by a vampire and the orcs. I managed to escape just before you found me."

Kurodan started to stand but the man drew his sword and held it against Kurodan's neck. The man's eyes squinted, calculating. "You escaped and just happened to avoid the largest orc army to ever be massed?"

Kurodan stood, slapping the blade away, "I have been held captive by those devils for long enough. I will not be held captive by my own people."

The woman stepped between them. "Kurodan, do you know why the orc army was going to the mountain top?" she asked.

"The vampire," Kurodan immediately answered. "He plans to awaken the Dark God. My party was sent to scout the mountain, but we were overtaken and captured. There were not many survivors when I managed to escape. I fear there may be none left."

"I am Andaria, and this is Captain Bravmond. We are with the queen's army of Mil'Thuras."

Bravmond sheathed his sword, "If what you say is true, paladin, we must make haste to warn the queen."

The ground shook and trembled. "Earthquake!" someone shouted. The group rushed to their nearby horses who were pulling at their reins and neighing wildly.

Kurodan turned to Mount Ruin. He saw a massive black creature at the crest, a demon that was birthed from the mountain itself. The earthquake slowly receded. "I fear we may be too late," he said, pointing to the peak.

"Gather our equipment," Bravmond ordered. "We make for Mil'Thuras. Now." The men rushed with ferocity around the camp grabbing equipment and saddlebags. Two men poured water onto a small fire. Bravmond motioned for Kurodan to follow him to the horses.

"I do not trust you," he said. "No man could have simply made it through that army by chance. Betray us and I will gut you where you stand."

Kurodan smiled. "I do not fear death, my soul died within that mountain."

They mounted the horses and started to ride. The

sunrise was above the horizon now; its warmth and beauty increased the small amount of hope stirring inside him.

His eyes shifted from the sunrise to the creature on the mountain, and his hope vanished. The creature raised one of its massive arms high into the sky. Kurodan could not believe the size of the creature. Even this far away he could make out its features. Its wings overshadowed the entire peak. Blue flame ignited from its outstretched hand.

"Look," Andaria shouted. Everyone stopped and turned, gaping. The flame appeared to take the shape of a spear.

"What is it doing?" Bravmond yelled. The creature pulled its arm back as if readying to throw a javelin.

"It's going to throw it," Kurodan said.

"At what?" one of the other men asked.

The creature hurled the flaming spear into the heavens above. All eyes followed the blue streak as it soared towards the sun. It came in direct line of the sunrise, and the party had to shield their eyes to not look directly into its rays.

Everyone stood in silence and wonder, trying to figure out what had just happened. "What was over there?" Bravmond asked.

Andaria turned her horse. "We need to mo—"

An enormous explosion erupted from the sun. Dark blue flames shot forth and shattered the sky itself. Darkness fell from these fissures, rippling like a torrent of water, casting an ocean of darkness.

It was the most awe-inducing sight Kurodan had ever witnessed. His mouth hung ajar as he turned in his saddle, watching the magic, from one horizon to the other.

The entire world was cast in a dark shadow. The sun had transformed into a full moon, but its color cast a dark deep blue.

"We must go now," Bravmond shouted. The party flew on their steeds. Kurodan could not tear his focus from the new moon as he galloped. *What evil magic is this?* he wondered. His mind flickered to Andazar at the thought of magic. He quietly damned the wizard to himself. The sky itself had warned the world what was to come. The queen needed to know the Dark God had returned.

The vampire and Korgath stood atop the pyramid in wonder and awe. The sky had darkened, and the sun had become a moon. The world had been transformed in a matter of moments. The vampire eyed Toradin's bloodied skeleton chained to the pillars. "Pity, only your remains will have the chance to see what unfolds henceforth," he muttered.

Korgath was staring up at the Dark God. It had not taken its gaze away from the sun since it had hurled the flaming spear into the sky. The orc army had given a wide berth to the stone courtyard as the Dark God now engulfed it.

It finally turned its gaze back to the two leaders standing atop the steps. Korgath bowed his head down as if wanting to avoid any interaction with it. The vampire smirked at the orc warlord, showing a hint of fear for the first time. His gaze shifted from the orc and stared directly up into the Dark God's eyes, almost defiant.

"What does the Dark God require?" he asked. Just as he finished asking, he felt a flicker of an answer in his own mind. It came from the Dark God, though it did not speak. A form of prophecy.

He bore witness to a vision: The Dark God raising

an army that would swallow up the world. He required time and souls of the living. More sacrifices to birth this unholy horde. The vision burned through his mind, bringing him to his knees. Fighting away the pain the vision had brought his mind; he stood and faced the Dark God once again.

"Your will is my command."

Korgath eyed the vampire with surprise as he understood the Dark God had communicated to him without speaking. The demon turned its attention back to the glowing moon. Its arms and massive wings folded, as if impatiently waiting.

Korgath followed the vampire down the pyramid steps. "What must we do?"

"Our task is great, and we have little time. Gather your army, march to the nearest human settlements. Raid them. Kill those who fight, enslave all those you can. We must bring more captives back here. As many as possible, Korgath. We must make haste."

"More captives? The ritual is complete," Korgath said. "What will more prisoners bring us?"

The vampire looked up at the black statuesque figure that towered above all. "The Dark God requires more offerings so that he may bring forth his true army. We must be the instrument to make this task happen. We go now. I will take my acolytes and aid you in this endeavor. Remember, Korgath, they must be alive to be offered."

Korgath turned to address his army. "We march back down the mountain. We make haste for the nearest human settlement. Enslave as many as you can. Kill the rest," he bellowed. The orcs turned and began to march down the mountain. Korgath could hear his chieftains' barking orders.

The Dark God paid no attention to the army

assembling around it. Its gaze was still fixed upon the moon.

Kurodan cursed as he could no longer sense the passing of time, just as it had been while held captive. The blue moon had not moved in the sky. They rode until their mounts could no longer gallop and had to slow down. Andaria and Bravmond led the formation. Neither had spoken a word since the party had fled from the mountain. The men were anxious, looking around nervously as if expecting more dark magic to unfold around them.

Some of the riders whispered to each other in hushed voices. The orc army could be seen in the distance moving down the mountain.

Kurodan broke the silence, "Where is our route taking us?"

Without turning around Bravmond replied, "Directly to Mil'Thuras."

"Yes, but what way? Surely, we must be passing nearby villages and settlements on the way?" Kurodan asked.

"Yes, we will be passing Avernost first. We will not travel through the town itself, nor on any main route. We must travel secretly and swiftly," Bravmond said.

"We must warn them. We must send word that they need to flee to Mil'Thuras," Kurodan argued.

Bravmond turned in his saddle, "We are out of time. If you have not noticed, the orc army is already on the move again. We must make for Mil'Thuras without distractions."

"Distractions? The people of this land are more than a mere distraction! You would all but abandon them to the hands of the orcs?"

Andaria intervened, "Bravmond is right, Kurodan.

The people in the surrounding settlements will have surely taken notice of the dark magic. They know that in times of crisis they are to make for Mil'Thuras."

"You truly believe the people will make sense of all that is happening when we can barely comprehend it ourselves?" Kurodan almost shouted. He was growing angrier by the second.

"How do you even know the nearest settlements are in danger? You cannot possibly guess the orcs' movements," Bravmond countered. "And if you were to try, I would guess they are headed to the same destination we are. We need to get there first."

"You said it yourself. Avernost is close to our route on the way to Mil'Thuras. Do you honestly believe that the orc army will merely pass them by? That the people in that town will go unmolested and be spared?" Kurodan questioned. The rest of the men had grown silent as Kurodan continued to press the issue.

"We head for Mil'Thuras. If you are so determined to warn the nearby settlements, I will not stop you," Bravmond said.

Andaria turned in her saddle again, "Kurodan, we need you with us. We will need you to aid in our explanation of these events to the queen. Your testimony and proof of life will hold more sway for her and the council's decision. The future of Mil'Thuras hangs on your choices."

Kurodan let his anger build, brooding now. He wanted vengeance more than anything. He wanted to warn anyone and everyone. He wanted to oppose the orcs, to rout them and see them destroyed. He wanted everyone to know the vampire still walked the earth. He wanted to inflict the pain he had suffered back onto his enemies. He thought of what Maldin had spoken of on the last day of his training.

"...It will be the wanting to wage battle when there are none to be waged or staying your sword when battle has begun but your services are required elsewhere."

Chapter XXX:
Unholy Harvest

Crune crept silently through the trees among the other acolytes. His eyes fixated on Andazar who was leading them away from Mount Ruin. Lord Dramington, or what remained of his physical form, awkwardly attempted to keep pace with the wizard until he finally slowed to a stop.

Crune broke his concentration from the wizard and looked about his surroundings. All of them instinctively stopped, patiently awaiting further instruction from their master.

He and some of the others startled, Andazar ignored the audible gasps, as two figures stepped out from the shadows. One was draped in black robes, his bald head and face were ghastly white. The other was no human either. An orc, dressed in hooded chainmail, his yellow eyes squinted at Crune and the others.

Are these more servants of the wizard? Crune thought to himself.

"So, you have succeeded in the ritual?" Andazar asked.

"The Dark God has been awoken and now requires living souls to bring forth his army," the vampire replied.

"I only require the dead," Andazar said simply.

Korgath looked from Andazar to Dramington. "You have the power of necromancy, wizard?"

"Among many others."

Crune watched as the pale figure stepped towards Andazar. He instinctively shrank back, now being able to make out the vampire's features. "The Dark God can wait no longer. We must make haste."

"So be it," Andazar said motioning back towards the town.

Crune fought to keep his composure, his hands shook with nervous anticipation and adrenaline. Orcs now walked among them, brandishing all manner of weapons.

Crune carefully eyed one of the monsters, that was almost within arms distance. The orc carried a large spear that had various war trophies decorating it. The orc met Crune's eyes, and his green face frowned and snorted, as if disgusted to be alongside humans. Crune quickly looked away to avoid the orc's stare.

They moved down the road, closing in on the town. Crune pushed his way past some of the others and saw Korgath make a fast motion with his hand. Two groups of orcs quickened their pace. They moved around the outskirts of Avernost and hid in position, waiting to capture any stragglers that might manage to flee.

The war party stopped. "Remember Korgath," the vampire said. The orc turned. "Capture as many as possible. Kill only those who fight."

Korgath's face broke into a smile so sinister that

Crune felt his heart skip a beat. The orc drew his dagger, placed the horn to lips and blew its terrible sound. All, save for Andazar, sprinted towards the village.

Tamerill shot up from his cot in the barracks, the orc horn blaring. Without thinking his hands went to his armor and weapons. He had taken refuge among Lord Dramington's men, after Crune and the others escaped. He had explained to them his station within the Silver Wardens, and his mission of uncovering the vampire worshipping cult, rumored to have roosted in Avernost.

Some of the men were hesitant at Tamerill's story, which turned to outright fear from the thing that appeared at the top of Mount Ruin. The thing that had devoured the sun...

But ultimately, they had accepted his offer, on the terms that they would still receive their usual wages even without Lord Dramington present.

Tamerill had convinced them to stay in Avernost, and that his superiors would pay them, if only they cooperated with his investigation. As he looked at the men frantically donning their equipment, he wondered if he had made a grave mistake staying in Avernost himself.

Tamerill and the other men burst from the barracks door, swords and shields at the ready. Women and children shrieked, dogs barked and whined, horses kicked and ran aimlessly. People flooded into the muddy streets as they tried to escape. Tamerill watched as orcs and men dressed in red hooded robes attacked without mercy.

Some of the other townspeople came with swords, torches, or mere farming tools. "To battle!" Tamerill cried.

He ran at the one of the men in red who was fighting

with an old man, armed only with a pitchfork. Tamerill swung his sword and struck the assailant in the side of the head, killing him outright.

The old man looked at Tamerill in bewilderment. "Get the women and children to Corenbundt," he screamed.

Crune recognized one of the men fighting in the street, remembering him drinking at The Broken Cup. *What was he doing fighting alongside Dramington's men?* he thought. Crune started to walk towards the unknown soldier and noticed he wore a strange silver emblem.

Tamerill turned to see an orc in chainmail, armed with a dagger. The beast slashed one of Dramington's men, forcing him to the ground. The orc grabbed a fistful of the man's hair and swept his blade across his scalp. Blood ran down the man's face as he screamed for mercy.

Crune watched as the soldier charged the orc warlord, lunging with his sword. The orc sidestepped, gripping the warrior's sword arm, he pulled the man onto his dagger. The soldier screamed as the blade sliced into and twisted his insides. The orc headbutted the man to the ground, raising his blade into the air, dangling with entrails.

"Take them," Korgath bellowed.

Crune moved through the chaos picking his fights carefully. Around him, orcs and acolytes descended on the townspeople like angry ants on carrion. Only small numbers attempted to stand and fight, knowing it was futile. He stopped almost in awe, when a single woman charged straight at the vampire with a stake.

The vampire quickly drew his sword and cut her arm apart at the elbow. She screamed as the vampire knelt beside her, bringing her neck to his lips.

Crune's attention was torn from the vampire when he found his next victim. His grip tightened around his dagger as he ran towards him.

Rignor swung his club hard, connecting with the back of a man's skull, who was trying to fend off a group of orcs. His head collapsed in on itself as brains, blood, and bone littered the ground. The orcs's expression changed from excited to surprised, as Crune tackled Rignor to the ground.

Crune stabbed wildly into Rignor's ribs, who had dropped his weapon. They struggled on the ground, wrestling in the mud for their lives.

Some of the orcs formed a semicircle, laughing and cheering as if at a gladiatorial event. Rignor, now realizing who his attacker was, fought even harder. He grabbed ahold of Crune's weapon hand, trapping the blade in his body, preventing Crune from stabbing again. "Shoulda' known you'd come for me," he laughed and spit blood in Crune's face.

With their free hands, they each tried to punch and grab one another. Crune twisted the blade as hard as he could, forcing Rignor to scream. Crune's eyes and veins were bulging from his face.

"For the Dark God," he screamed.

Rignor's body kicked and squirmed as his life drained away. Crune managed to rip the weapon free and stabbed maddeningly until Rignor stopped moving.

Sitting atop Rignor's corpse, Crune let out a sigh of relief. He calmly looked around. The orcs on the outskirts of the village gave out shrill war cries as they hunted down their prey.

Korgath was prying a child from its mother's arms. The mother was slapping wildly at the back of his head as he handed the child off.

"Not my baby, please," she begged.

Korgath turned, swiftly bringing his dagger around and across her throat. He was impressed at the woman's will. She held her grievous wound with both hands, as if choking herself. Blood spilled between her fingers. She stumbled after the orc who was dragging her child away in chains. She finally fell, clawing after them with her last breath.

They lit torches and set fire to the houses, smoke and flames billowing into the night sky. The orcs chained and shackled the survivors. Each of them screaming, crying, and begging.

Andazar walked among the horror as if on an evening stroll, stopping only to look upon the dead.

"To the mountain," the vampire commanded, pointing his red-stained sword into the air, and Korgath lifted his horn. Its sound blared, deafening.

Everyone covered their ears at the loud sound of the orc horn, save for Kurodan. He was too angry, too filled with rage. Their party grew silent, listening only to the screams. Kurodan rose immediately moving towards his horse.

"Where do you think you are headed?" Bravmond asked.

Kurodan ignored him. He sheathed a sword into the horse scabbard.

"Kurodan, we cannot risk it," Andaria said. "We must stay our course."

Kurodan turned, fury in his face, "You wish to sit here and do nothing? Listen to their screams. You all have the power to save them!"

"Kurodan—" Andaria's voice was cut off by another scream. Kurodan mounted and kicked his steed in the direction of the screams.

"Let him go," Bravmond said. "He has a death wish. The orcs are too many for our scouting party. Our mission is to warn Mil'Thuras."

The other men avoided each other's stares not wanting to speak. They could still hear the faint screaming off in the distance.

"Have you forgotten that we need him to speak to the queen? His voice must be heard," Andaria argued. "He knows more than all of us."

Bravmond merely shook his head. "If you go after him, I will not follow you."

Kurodan was galloping towards the town. He knew nothing about it, but he did not care.

"Listen to the people who you chose to forsake!" he said to himself. He spurred his horse faster, the trees whipping at him as they flew through the forest.

The cries became louder but less frequent. He could hear and smell burning wood. Smoke rose into the air. He stopped his horse, dismounted, and crept closer. As he slowly made his way to see the town, he heard twigs breaking. He whirled around to see an orc with an axe raised.

The orc let out a hideous noise and charged. Kurodan braced himself, his sword clutched in both hands. The orc came at him with bloodlust in his eyes. Kurodan charged at the last second as the orc brought the axe high over his head. His blade caught the orc dead center in the chest, driving him backwards.

Kurodan threw all his weight forward as he felt the blade pass through, falling on top of the orc. The orc was laughing and gurgling in its own blood.

It grabbed Kurodan by the neck, trying to choke him

before he died himself. Kurodan wrenched free of the orc's grasp and grabbed its axe lying in the grass next to them. He raised the axe high as the orc had done. He swung it down with all his might. The axe split the orc's head clean as if chopping firewood.

Kurodan sat back, trying to catch his breath. His head snapped up at the movement of another orc coming from the opposite direction. Kurodan struggled to pull his sword from the orc's chest cavity, then abandoned it and ripped the axe from the shattered skull.

The second orc had a club raised in one hand and chained shackles in the other. The shackles clanked and rattled as he ran. Kurodan brought up the axe, ready to end the creature's miserable existence. He heard a whistling sound and watched as an arrow soared past him and into the orc's face. The orc crumpled to the ground, dropping like a large stone.

Andaria emerged from the forest, bow raised and another arrow knocked. Kurodan placed his boot on the first orc and finally tore his sword free. He turned his attention to the village; it was engulfed in flames. The surviving townspeople were begging and crying for their lives as the orcs marched them forward into a single line formation. Bodies and blood paved the streets.

He saw him—the vampire. He was standing over the corpse of a one-armed woman. And the orc—the one with the horn. It was wrestling a child away from its mother, as she fought with near insanity. The orc turned lightning fast, cutting her throat. Kurodan marched towards them, jaw clenched, sweat beading from his forehead, mouth dry.

Bravmond tackled him to the ground. Kurodan wrestled with him as his eyes flashed back to the town.

"To the mountain," they heard the vampire call.

"You must be there with us to warn the queen," Bravmond grunted as they rolled in the dirt. "You will be the one to convince her and her council. Don't you understand?" Pulling away and standing, Bravmond slowly offered his hand to Kurodan. "Without your report, there is a chance everyone will fail to act. This would put into motion the death of all mankind." Then he added, "We have saved your life twice now, paladin. Do not expect a third. We ride at once."

Kurodan turned from him, fixing his eyes on the slaughter. In horror, he saw a bleeding woman attempt to crawl through the mud to reach her shackled child. His anger felt palpable, and he tensed when Andaria bent down and grabbed his shoulder. He noticed a silver bracelet she wore around her wrist.

"We will kill them. All of them," she whispered. "She will not go unavenged I promise you."

They rode their mounts back to the party's camp. Some of the men were asleep, weapons next to them or gripped in their hands. Bravmond's horse stopped at the fire pit, which had turned to small embers and coals. "Mount up," he called.

The men quickly jumped up, staring at Kurodan, as they brought their mounts closer.

Kurodan exchanged a glance with Andaria. He could not find the words to thank her for saving his life, but his face betrayed his thoughts, and she understood.

"Ambush," Bravmond screamed.

Kurodan turned his horse, wielding both axe and sword. The orcs had trailed them to their camp. War cries rang out from both the soldiers and orcs as they clashed together.

Andaria shot an orc in the chest from her horse. It

fell but another took its place. She threw down her bow and drew her sword.

"Shield wall," Kurodan screamed. The soldiers tried to form a line, but the orcs had set upon them too quickly.

"Hold," Bravmond shouted.

Kurodan charged his horse into two orcs trying to outnumber a soldier. His axe and sword swung around the horse's head, biting into their victims.

Andaria rode her horse even further into the fray, her sword quickly growing thick with blood. An orc's head flew from its shoulders as she flicked her blade downwards.

"They are too many," Bravmond tried to shout over the fighting.

The orcs swarmed Andaria as she had charged onwards. Kurodan tried to push his horse closer to her, but the fight was raging now. There was no room between orcs, soldiers, and trees. An orc grabbed at Kurodan, who swung the axe down hard. The orc caught the axe by the handle and dropped its body weight. Kurodan tried to bring his sword around to finish the orc, but it was too late. He felt his feet slip from the horse's stirrups and landed on his back.

"Andaria," Bravmond shouted, pain and fear plagued his words.

"Fall back," came the cry of another soldier.

Kurodan watched as the orc stood over him, swinging the axe. He had dropped his sword in the fall. *It's over*, he thought. Then an enormous spear took the orc in the side, raining blood down on Kurodan. Bravmond urged his horse alongside him.

"Get on your feet," he said, holding out a hand. Kurodan jumped up, and gripping Bravmond's hand, threw himself on the back of the horse.

As Bravmond turned his horse to follow the other

soldiers, Kurodan looked back and saw Andaria. She was alone, encircled by the orcs.

She swung her sword as if driven by madness. She caught one orc in the throat and another across the face.

Kurodan gripped Bravmond. "We must go back for Andaria," he shouted in Bravmond's ear. Bravmond did not turn to look back and spurred the horse into a gallop, tears wetting his eyes. Kurodan watched as Andaria was ripped from her horse and disappeared among the orcs.

They rode further and further into the never-ending night. The riders fought sleep in their saddles. When their horses began to falter from exhaustion, they would quickly stop and mount another horse in tow, allowing the first to travel with no rider. This was a trick many of the scouts and their horses had mastered to allow for longer and swifter travel.

When they crossed a stream or river, they were forced to stop for short durations. the men dismounted, trying to stretch and nurse their saddle-sore muscles, while the horses gorged themselves on the water. Travel such as this, even for the most seasoned men, was brutal.

None of the men spoke to each other. They had mastered the art of hand signals. Simple motions and looks given to each other sufficed. The night hung over them as if a dark rain cloud had followed their journey, not yet making their travel harder but foreshadowing it.

Most of the men were lost in their own thoughts staring up at it. *It was hard not to be enamored by its beauty*, Kurodan thought.

Bravmond's attention was on the horses. He motioned for his second in command, a man by the name of Hural. The two nodded to each other and motioned to the others. They quickly began to set up blankets on the ground.

Kurodan walked over to Bravmond. "Why are we stopping?"

Bravmond let out a heavy sigh, as if too tired to argue or explain. Without even looking at Kurodan, he said, "If we are to all make it back, we need to rest for short periods. At least a few hours, maybe more. If the horses do not rest, they will die from exhaustion and the men … if we are set upon in another ambush, we will be too tired to fight or run."

Kurodan knew Bravmond was right. "I will stand watch if needed," he said.

"That is generous of you, paladin. Make no mistake, our return is dire. We will not be able to tell how much time passes as we rest. I have no solid notion of how many hours we have travelled thus far. Judging by the terrain we have covered; I would wager two days.

Kurodan looked up, "But this unending night has warped all sense of time. It is like being trapped inside the mountain again."

Bravmond paused as he could plainly see the exhaustion and pain on Kurodan's face. "We have put distance between ourselves and Mount Ruin, but I am still wary of pursuers, and we still have many long hours of riding ahead of us. I will have you take the last watch. I trust you will be able to wake me when we are ready to move out again?"

Kurodan nodded in agreement.

"Try to get some rest. We will need your strength," Bravmond said. As Kurodan was preparing his sleeping arrangements, he noticed Bravmond staring at something he held in his hand. He squinted and realized it was the same silver bracelet Andaria had worn. Bravmond wiped away tears from his eyes as he walked off.

Kurodan lay down and his gaze drifted up to the faint silhouette of the Dark God on the peak of the mountain. He could still make out smallest features of the giant being. As he laid down and waited for sleep to take him, he grew anxious. *What horror would the devil conjure next?*

Chapter XXXI:
Dying Breath

The chains clanged and jingled as the prisoners swayed and stumbled up the mountain. At first, they had more or less been able to keep pace with the orcs. As the mountainside grew steeper and the top closer, they began to struggle, unable to fight their exhaustion.

"They will not make it," Korgath said. He turned from the head of the formation, eyeing their captives. Some of the children and elderly were being carried on the backs of men and women. "Let us kill the weak and keep the strong. Time is running short."

The vampire paused, "No. The more we kill the less we bring back for the army."

Korgath grew impatient, drawing his dagger. "At this rate the ascent up the mountain will claim all of them."

Andazar stepped forward, interrupting them. "They will make the climb. I will make it so."

"Halt," Korgath commanded.

Andazar pushed his way past Korgath and some of the orcs as he reached the first prisoner. He was a strong, tall man with a black beard. His hair and shirt were wet and gnarled from sweat. The orcs had placed him in front of the line in an effort to keep their pace. The man looked up from his shackled hands to see the wizard staring back at him. The man simply spit on the ground.

Andazar laughed. "Look at me, mortal." The two locked eyes but said nothing. Andazar slightly raised his staff, a light began to emanate from its tip. The man looked from the wizard to his staff and became lost in the light. A slight smile slithered across Andazar's mouth, as the vampire shielded himself from the light and moved away.

"Hear me, mortal. You serve me now. You will make haste to the top of the mountain. You serve me."

The man looked paled and appeared to almost lose his balance. When he regained some of his composure, his face had changed. His mouth hung slightly ajar; his breathing came in slow long drags. His eyes were dead on the inside.

"To the peak," Andazar said dismissively.

The wizard slowly moved down the line of prisoners, his light blinding them and binding them to his will. "The prisoners will be along shortly, do try and keep up," Andazar laughed.

Korgath snorted, his head shaking in disapproval, but before he could rebuttal the prisoners began to move again. The man in front took great long strides up the mountain, pushing past the other orcs. The man locked eyes with Korgath as he walked past.

"We serve him now," the man repeated.

Korgath was almost lost in a trance, frozen where he stood. The man turned from the orc and continued up the mountain.

Korgath remained stunned for a few long seconds while more and more prisoners made their way past him. Another orc, Grunedar, approached and raised a torch above their heads. The light revealed a blank stare on his face. Grunedar waved a hand in front of his eyes. Korgath immediately snapped out of the spell, shoving Grunedar away from him.

"Do not look into the prisoners' eyes, lest we become slaves ourselves," Korgath shouted.

Andazar heard him and grinned. The orcs kept their distance from the prisoners now while hiking upwards. There were no more shouts or cracks of whips from the orcs. Only the heavy breathing, the marching of feet, and the clanging of chains. The flames on top of the peak continued to grow.

The march climbed higher and higher; the prisoners now did not break stride but some of the weaker orcs struggled to keep the same pace. Andazar had caught up to the front, his staff no longer bearing the light.

"So, tell me, vampire, what did the Dark God speak to you?" he asked.

"It is what it showed me, not what it said, that is important."

Andazar remained quiet as if waiting for a further explanation. After a long pause and no reply, the wizard asked again, "What did it show you?"

The vampire looked up at the moon. "A new age."

Tears wet Kurodan's eyes as he looked upon the great gate of Mil'Thuras. He wiped them away quickly. Even in the unholy night, the city stood strong—a bastion of hope. He had thought he would not live to look upon its beauty again.

The gate opened and they made their way to the queen's throne room. Kurodan looked around to see the city's streets emptied, as if abandoned. All was eerily quiet. He could see and feel peoples' eyes on them from windows and homes as they rode. *This new night, it seemed, had succeeded in its magic. Terror gripped the great city,* he thought.

The party dismounted and approached the guards standing duty at the door leading to the throne room.

"Who goes there?" asked one.

"I am Captain Bravmond. I have urgent word for the queen."

The guards exchanged glances. "The queen has made no request for council."

"No request?" Kurodan pushed his way to the front of the party.

Bravmond placed his hand on Kurodan's shoulder. "He is a survivor of Mount Ruin. The queen must know he is alive," the captain said. A shocked look appeared on the guards' faces.

"Aye, captain."

As they opened the door to enter, one of the guards stopped them.

"I do not know what is happening, what evil has taken hold here," he said in a whispered hiss, forcing Kurodan and Bravmond to lean closer. "The queen does nothing… the city's people suffer, and she sits on her throne and does nothing. Please, I beg of you. Bring her news that will make her act."

"I will force her to act, by my hand," Kurodan said, leading the company forward. The throne room was empty save for the queen.

"I have ordered that no one is to step foot in here!" she said, immediately protesting their presence. Then she paused, recognizing Kurodan. "You? You survived?"

"Aye, your majesty," Kurodan said.

Around him, Bravmond and the rest of the party

knelt. Kurodan stayed standing as he began his report. "The captain and his scouting party rescued me. I have dire news you need to hear."

"What scouting party?" the queen asked. "I gave no such orders."

Bravmond stood "We were tasked with scouting Mount Ruin. To track any movement of the enemy, your majesty," he said.

"By whose order?"

"Mine," Bravmond replied.

"You dare give commands to undermine my authority, captain? I should have you stripped of your title and your lands."

"Enough," Kurodan interrupted. "I have not passed through death itself to sit here and listen to the ruler of Mil'Thuras bicker about titles and land. The Dark God has been awakened. Its forces mass around Mount Ruin. Orcs march freely across our lands, killing and slaughtering—"

"That is only—" the queen started to interrupt, but Kurodan had not finished.

"I am witness to all this destruction, and I have seen the vampire who leads their ground forces."

At this last statement, the queen suddenly looked fearful. "How… How do you know a vampire leads them?" she asked quietly.

Kurodan ignored her question. "Where are your armies my queen? Where are the armies of Mil'Thuras? Why do they not ride out to meet them in battle?"

Before she could answer, the throne room door burst open and Maldin and Gleed ran in.

"By the gods! Kurodan tell us everything," Maldin said.

"The Dark God is here; its armies march against the world of men, and we must go to battle," Kurodan urged.

"What happened at Bursben? What of the rest of your party?" Maldin asked.

The queen spoke before Kurodan could answer, "You think it wise to ride out and meet them in open war?"

"Open war is upon us," Kurodan retorted. "Where are our allies? Why have they not come to unite against our one common enemy?"

"We have riders headed towards every major city as we speak. Our army is not capable of dealing with this threat alone." the queen said.

"So, what is your plan, your majesty?" Bravmond interjected.

The queen sat atop her throne, staring blankly into nothing. She looked haggard and drained, almost like a captive herself. "Right now, we wait to see what armies can be formed and, by the gods, sent to our aid."

"Your plan is to sit here and do nothing?" Kurodan argued.

"What else can we do?" the queen shouted "Tell me?"

"You can lead your people and this city." Kurodan said and walked towards the door.

"Wait," the queen called. "How is it you survived? What has happened to the others?"

Kurodan stopped and turned, "Where is Andazar?" he slowly asked. No one gave an answer, for none probably knew. "Where is the wizard?"

Then Kurodan told them of the wizard's betrayal. He described the events in short order, trying to block out the horrors he had witnessed.

At the end of his report, the queen denied any knowledge of Andazar's intentions or whereabouts. She called for another meeting with her council. Maldin and

Gleed stayed to debate the best strategy moving forward.

Kurodan found himself unable to stomach it any further. Even after seeing his own mother, pure joy had overwhelmed her to know he survived, but he was completely and utterly lost.

He stood in the dark and quiet catacombs. A single torch lit his surroundings. *Odd*, he thought. *The dark, like the inside of the mountain, is now more comforting than anything else.* He gazed upon the sarcophagus of his father imbued with the emblem of the Holy Order. Sword and shield hung above it.

"Forgive me, Father. I have failed you," he whispered aloud. "It seems the world is ending and the very evil you died fighting is going to win… it feels as if your death was in vain." Kurodan fought back his almost uncontrollable emotions, choking them down.

"If you truly believe that, then you have failed him," came a voice.

Kurodan turned in surprise, wiping the tears from his eyes. Maldin walked up beside him, ignoring his embarrassment, and stared at the sarcophagus. His gaze turned upwards to the sword and shield. "Your father was one of the best men I have ever served alongside."

"So I've heard. He still fell nonetheless, and it appears his sacrifice might have been all for nothing," Kurodan said disdainfully.

"His sacrifice is why you are still here, is it not?"

"Yes, I suppose so."

Maldin set his hammer on the ground, the handle leaned against the stone. "Has anyone ever told you how he fell in battle?"

Kurodan was shocked. "No. Never."

"He saved many lives that day, including mine."

"How? How did he die?"

"We had gathered all our forces to meet the enemy in open battle—every able body that could fight. We were outnumbered, but our numbers in the Holy Order were still strong. Your father, as you well know, was my second in command. We thought it best to attack, drawing our enemy out during the night and fighting into the dawn.

"Krashnik the Terrible and the Warlord Morglain had amassed their armies, and we met them in open battle." Kurodan watched as Maldin paused, as if he could recall every moment from that battle, replaying the events in his mind.

"We charged into their ranks, and we slaughtered each other. Never have I seen fighting in all my battles like that one. We fought hard; our powers of the light proved to be more than many of their numbers could handle. The tide began to turn in our favor as dawn approached. We knew with the rise of the sun we would be able to destroy them. We only had to keep their forces there, make sure they could not be routed from the field of battle, but then..." Maldin's voice trailed off.

"Then what?" Kurodan asked.

Maldin drew in a deep breath, his stare empty and filled with emotion all at once. "It was their leaders. Krashnik and Morglain. They fought harder and harder. They killed so many men that the sight of those two beings struck fear into every heart, enemy and ally. Their actions spurred the orcs and vampires to fight on. I fought until I came face to face with them." Maldin eyed the weapon in front of him, and his hand gently touched the vampire's skull that hung chained to his hip.

"They had killed so many of us that I was left alone fighting those two. And I faltered, Kurodan. They had me ... but before they could deliver the killing blow, your father intervened. He sacrificed himself, giving me just enough time to finish them. I purged the vampire with holy fire and then, with his own weapon, I slew the orc. But I was not fast enough to save your father.

"With his last breath, he instilled in me the will to press on. With the enemy's leaders felled, we seized the tide of battle, and the sun finally rose. We killed them with the dawn and won."

Maldin grew still and silent after finishing his tale. But Kurodan still had a question. "What did my father say to you before he died?"

Maldin walked to the head of the coffin and pulled the sword and shield from the wall. Turning, he handed them to Kurodan. As he took them, their markings glowed white hot at his touch, before fading suddenly.

"That there is good in this world, and it is always worth fighting for. Even to your dying breath."

Chapter XXXII: Dance With the Devil

The Dark God now crouched over the crevasse in the courtyard like a monumental gargoyle. Its appearance resembled some of the statues that decorated the halls within the vampire's throne room. Its clawed hands danced through the air as if invisible music played in its ears. Fire began to rise from the pit. The flames danced and moved with the demon's fingers, responding to its will. As the fires grew, they animated the monster even more. The night was unending, and the dawn never arrived.

The vampire and Korgath approached as close as they could bear and knelt. The giant chasm of fire raged. The heat was so intense that the orcs dared not draw too close.

"Stand," burned the command in the vampire's head. He stood and locked eyes with the ancient demon.

"Into the flames," the voice demanded, and the great

demon pointed to the pit.

The vampire turned to Korgath. "Cast them in."

Korgath stood and faced his fellow orcs. Some whimpers and cries came from the prisoners; the fires had begun to break the Andazar's trance. Korgath motioned to the fire.

The orcs broke out into a frenzy, grabbing and shoving the prisoners forward. Their cries and pleas grew louder. Some of the orcs began beating on their drums made from skin, pounding a primal beat. Others began to play on fiddles, flutes, horns, and trumpets crafted from bone. The sounds spurred the orcs on even more.

The Dark God began to wave its hands in and around the great chasm. The flames came alive. Just before the man with the black beard was about to be cast in, the flames changed in color from orange to red. Then red to blue, blue to green. The man stopped fighting, and all the other prisoners stopped and stood still. The music died from a roaring trumpeting onslaught to a soft haunting melody. The orcs began to unchain the prisoners. The man's gaze never broke from the flames. The Dark God smiled, and the man threw himself from the edge.

The prisoners walked slowly as if each waited their turn at an executioner's block. One by one they threw themselves into the flames, smoke billowed up from the fires that continuously changed colors. The Dark God moved its hands and arms through the flames as if playing with sand. The smoke clouded the demon's form save for its great yellow eyes and enormous claws.

The great demon's audience watched as a creature spawned forth from the fire. It bore fangs, scales, and hooves. Its hair was wild and mangy. It had claws, horns, and a tail. Never had any living being bore witness to such villainy.

The Dark God began catching falling prisoners as they committed their acts of suicide. Its great hands held them aloft in the flames. The music grew and the drums and trumpets played once more. The flames engulfed man, woman, and child alike. Their forms contorted and mutated in the flames and gave birth to more nightmarish creatures. They danced and jumped in the demon's palms. They crawled over and through its fingers as the Dark God turned its hands over, watching with glee. The creatures fell into the flames and vanished. Then more crawled forth and spilled into the courtyard.

Soon every orc and demon raged and danced with the music and fire. The vampire and Korgath merely stood watching. As the last of the prisoners were nearing the edge, a group of orcs approached the courtyard. Korgath turned and motioned them closer. The orcs brought more prisoners in tow. Some of these last few had not fallen under the terrible trance of the flames.

Andaria wept with horror at witnessing this new hell birthed into the world. "This one has a lot of fight left in her," one of the orcs said. Korgath stepped closer to her. Andaria's gaze shifted from the prisoners walking towards their doom to the vampire.

"You!" she screamed.

Andaria thrashed against the orcs' clutches, but it was of no use. "This is your doing. You did this." Her screams carried such violence and hate that it made many of the orcs and demons pause.

"Bring her," the vampire commanded. The orcs carried her towards the flames, as the second-to-last prisoner was thrown from the edge.

She thrashed and fought, looking more in common

with the hellish beasts that surrounded her, then human. But just as they reached the edge, the vampire stopped them.

"Wait."

Andaria could feel her skin beginning to singe from the fires that rose from the pit. As the orcs turned her, her eyes met the demon's. Its yellow eyes and fanged smile peered through the smoke and fire. A fear washed over her, so strongly that her knees buckled. Her weight gave way, but the orcs held her in place.

The vampire now stood face to face with her, his smile rivaling the great demon's that watched from behind her. His voice was almost a whisper, "This is all my doing. You will thank me in time."

He grabbed Andaria's face and brought his other hand to his mouth. The vampire bit down on his wrist, spilling his baneful blood. He forced her mouth open and held his blood against her lips.

She fought still, coughing and spitting, but the poison made its way down her throat and into her chest. He gripped her by the throat, lifting her. As he raised her up, the orcs released their hold. Her feet now hung suspended from the edge as the flames licked her legs and body. Andaria coughed and choked up the blood onto his hand and arm, her own hands still trying to break his grasp.

"Fear not and be reborn," he said and released her.

Chapter XXXIII: Onslaught

Kurodan stood upon the tallest front wall of Mil'Thuras, gazing down into the darkness of the valley below. Staring at an army of death itself. Standing with his brothers in arms, knowing that what took place would decide the fate for the rest of the world. This battle could put into motion the very undoing of mankind. Few had truly heeded his warning that this moment was almost upon them, and now it had arrived. Here they all were, standing on the high walls ready to defend the kingdom of men until their last breath. Knowing full well, that that breath drew ever closer.

There were so many that the true number of the enemy's forces was nigh impossible to tell. A horde with fangs, claws, wings, swords, spears, horns, and all manner of other treacherous forms. Eager to spill blood in all their savagery.

Kurodan's heart ached, and his fury raged inside. His mind's eye flickered to Toradin and Horad. What unimaginable ends they must have faced. Now Kurodan prayed his brothers' souls rested in peace. Their army covered the entire valley. As they marched towards the front gate, the sound grew louder and louder, until they came to a halt.

Kurodan had never seen such numbers before. It was as if this demonic force had marched through a portal from some other world. All had grown quiet, the final breath held in anticipation of the coming onslaught.

Then the vampire appeared walking down the center of the army. He was just a small faint figure, growing slightly larger as he walked down the open aisle formed between two ranks. He walked to the front, standing at the head of the forces, he looked up at the city. His gaze glanced over the entire wall that towered over him and then almost fixated on Kurodan. Kurodan could not be entirely sure, but their eyes seemed to lock in just a brief instant. The vampire, too, somehow knew Kurodan was here.

Kurodan simmered with rage thinking of all he had endured before escaping the vampire's claws. This scourge had slaughtered and tortured his kinsmen. And now he had awoken the Dark God, the true master of this demonic army. Kurodan swore he would kill this scourge before his life was over.

The vampire did not utter a word, but merely raised his sword and held it high above his head. Standing there defiantly in face of the kingdom of men. Then the entire army erupted.

They began beating their armor and chests, bashing their weapons against shields, smashing spears into the ground, stomping feet onto the earth, all in unison. The sound echoed throughout the valley and off the wall. The beat drummed over the war cries, screams, and hellish battle chants. It was a horrifying and astounding display.

Kurodan could sense the dread and fear that spread across the men on the wall like a plague. His knuckles whitened as his hands clenched around his father's sword and shield. The men beside him grew tense and restless. The noise grew into a crescendo of rage and fury. In the very rear of the army, the Dark God approached

The vampire's voice could be heard: "Turn their world to ash." In response, the masses below began working their catapults and siege equipment. Constructed out of timber and stone, the contraptions were crude. The beams were pulled down and set into place. Kurodan felt his stomach tighten even more. He heard Bravmond's voice cut the air, giving a command.

"Load," the captain called.

Soldiers ran to and fro, working their own heavy weapons. The massive trebuchets did not merely fling boulders. The master craftsmen of Mil'Thuras had chiseled and shaped the enormous slabs of stone into the heads of their past kings. They were giant sculptures of the utmost beauty and magnificence. This was a battle tradition that was held sacred. Whenever the city should brave an attack and be forced to defend its own people, the kings of old would return to take up their oaths they had sworn in life and fulfill them even in death.

This attack could not be more fitting, Kurodan thought. *If we fail, there will be no more kings.*

Kurodan's attention was ripped from his thoughts, as he heard human cries.

"They have prisoners," one of the soldiers shouted.

Kurodan watched as men, women, and children were led in chains to the catapults. They were loaded into the massive buckets of the contraptions.

"No," a soldier cried.

"Steel your hearts," shouted Bravmond. "We will

cast these devils back to the hell from which they spawned. Now, release!" The enormous wood beams of the trebuchet swung through the air. The ropes snapped as they sent the kings of old to destroy their enemies.

Kurodan watched overhead as the giant kings hurled over the wall and came thundering down. Some of the demons and orcs tried to scatter while others stood vigilant. The stone heads fell into the ground with such force that they formed craters in the earth. Some of the heads rolled and tumbled causing even more death within their ranks. One of the old kings crashed into a catapult, causing it to erupt in splinters, bodies, and earth. Kurodan felt a surge of pride with his anger.

The captives' cries could be heard even louder now. The buckets of their catapults were filled with oil and came alight as orcs set torches to them.

"Set their people free," the vampire called from below.

Kurodan stood in shock as the catapults hurled the burning bodies. They lit up the night sky like shooting stars. Their screams echoed loudly, and then the bodies came apart as they struck.

Fire, oil and blood smeared and sprayed in explosions. Some of the bodies came down on the soldiers standing in formation. The soldiers struck were killed and others nearby caught fire. But the men scrambled to put their brothers out and not break bearing. Within moments of the impacts, only small flames lingered, and the damage was minimal.

Kurodan understood that this method was not used to destroy the city's defenses or kill the soldiers within. Its purpose was to inflict visual horror and fear. He watched as some soldiers vomited and wretched at the sights.

Others kept their attention towards the army,

refusing to break their gaze and glance at the broken bodies.

Then the world shook with a thunderous boom. It felt like an earthquake. Kurodan watched from the wall as the army before him tried to disperse. Orc and demon alike wildly began trying to move their ranks outwards, creating an empty path in the middle of their forces.

Behind the army, the Dark God approached. With each step, it shook the world beneath it. The vampire turned his back to the wall and knelt with his sword. Kurodan's fixation on the demon was broken by a single shout. An older man wielding a sword sprinted past Kurodan, towards the center of the wall.

"Stand! Stand your ground," he commanded.

Kurodan did not recognize him at first and approached him.

"Take courage. Depend on the man next to you." he urged.

Kurodan now recognized the man who spurred them on. It was the mad priest, Mathius. *What is he doing up here on the wall? He will get himself killed,* Kurodan thought.

Some of the other men must have had similar concerns. "What is this priest doing?" one called.

"Get him off the wall." another protested.

Mathius looked up at the sky and spoke. Kurodan thought he was praying at first but heard his voice, almost a whisper to himself, "I have stood by for far too long. If you will all be bound to inaction, so be it."

"Priest, what are you doing here?" Kurodan asked.

Mathius ignored Kurodan's question and the other soldiers' comments. His focus was on the task at hand.

He now stood facing the army, and the great demon. Mathius's face betrayed no emotion, void of thought and fear.

The Dark God stepped over the vampire, paying neither him nor the army attention.

Its great wings expanded as it stretched its arms outwards in challenge. The sheer being and form made Kurodan's stomach sink.

He felt that insidious feeling that had plagued him as a prisoner within the mountain. Helplessness. Despite his confusion of the priest, he ached for the battle to begin. To finish it, victorious or not. He watched as Mathius held the sword above his head and noticed the blade itself. Its craftsmanship surpassed anything he had ever witnessed, even his father's sword which he now carried. *Where did you get that blade?* He wondered.

Mathius spoke but his voice was no longer that of a mere man, it was deep and godlike. "By the power of the gods, and I as their messenger, I cast you back into ruination!"

Kurodan watched in amazement as Mathius's weapon glowed white hot. The light was so strong that it produced an aura around the priest. Kurodan now questioned the priest's true nature, *Had he once been a paladin, or was he something else entirely?*

The demon still stood unmoving, the army behind it had begun to shrink backwards. The white light grew, and Kurodan had to shield his vision, as did other soldiers nearby. It was like staring directly into the sun. Kurodan could now feel the heat of the light, as it grew hotter and brighter, the priest was almost completely swallowed by it.

Boom.

The Dark God took another step forward. But it was halted. Mathius flung the blade with a power not matched by any mortal.

It soared towards the demon, spiraling end over end.

Its light flew true, striking the demon in the chest.

Falling forward, the Dark God crumbled in on itself. It let out a bellowing scream so deep Kurodan thought it sounded like ten orc horns at once. Every being fell to the ground screaming, but no sound could be heard over the demon's agony.

When its cry of pain ended, Kurodan willed himself to stand. Mathius stood, now devoid of any light or magic. The demon was crouched on all fours, its massive wings covered most of its form as if to shield it from any further attacks. The entire world in that moment paused. Within that stillness, something stirred.

The Dark God made a noise. It seemed to be a single word in a language no mortal could decipher. Though it was a deep and guttural growl, it was almost quiet. As if by design, to make sure everyone was to listen carefully. It carried with it a most certain dread.

"Run!" Mathius screamed and grabbed ahold of Kurodan as he tried to flee.

Then the Dark God erupted into the sky, its wings expanding to their full length, one arm grasped high. A blue fire spawned forth from its fingertips and took the shape of a long spear. Suspended in the night, it looked like some ancient warrior about to perform the killing blow on a downed enemy.

With one swift movement, it hurled the spear downwards towards the wall. The flaming spear lit up the sky, then struck the front gate. Kurodan felt the world explode beneath him as everything turned to darkness.

Kurodan awoke to the sound of battle. Screams, steel against steel, the rending of flesh. His vision blurred, and he vomited.

Bodies lay broken and mangled around him. Rubble, debris, and dirt choked the air. Mathius lay within arm's reach, either dead or dying, he did not know.

He was still atop the wall, but as he looked across it, he saw a great chasm now where the gate had stood. Gone was the great gate of Mil'Thuras. Gone was the gate that had stood defiant, unopposed to all enemies. Gone was the great gate that had never been breached in all time. Now orcs and demons alike poured forth, smashing into the last and final shield wall of men.

The Dark God stood, towering over the destruction it had wrought. Its arms were outstretched, and the palms of its hands turned upwards. Its minions swarmed forwards. Kurodan watched as his brothers in arms held fast. He could see and hear Maldin below in the middle of the fray.

"Hold," came the shout of the familiar voice.

Kurodan watched as a sea of soldiers flooded the main courtyard. Archers began firing arrow after arrow until their quivers fell empty. The orcs answered back in kind, and their projectiles whistled overhead. A boulder from a catapult struck the side of the wall and Kurodan thought it would collapse; it shook so violently. His mouth was dry, and his chest heaved. His pulse pounded in his temple with adrenaline.

"Steady," he commanded, to himself as much as the other men around him. They were trying to survey the best way to get into the fight. A sea of armor-clad bodies stood shoulder to shoulder. There was no room, no way to get to the front of the battle.

Kurodan turned his attention down to Maldin. A light shone brightly as he wielded his great war-hammer. He raised the weapon high above his head and brought it thundering down.

The light turned into an enormous blinding flash. Many of the demons and orcs caught fire. Their screams were wild and vicious.

They tried to turn and flee, but those behind them merely trampled their own, cutting and hacking the burning monstrosities.

"Hold," came Maldin's voice again.

A deafening cheer rose from the soldiers all around. *We are holding*, Kurodan thought.

A single shout cried out from an archer atop the wall. "Defend the wall!"

Siege ladders, tall crude beams of wood held together by rope, were braced upwards.

"Ladders," Kurodan alerted.

The men around him readied themselves, standing shoulder to shoulder. Some of the archers were still firing their bows, almost at point-blank range now as the enemy climbed. Some had dropped their bows and drew their swords. But the enemy just kept coming in endless numbers.

Kurodan now witnessed men, orcs, and demons hack each other to pieces as the enemy spilled out onto the wall. One demon pulled its clawed hand from the chest of a soldier

It had the head, legs, and hooves of a goat. Its torso was black and muscular, and its face was etched in bloodred markings. Sharp jagged teeth lined its rotting mouth. It ran at Kurodan, hooves beating against the stone.

Kurodan hefted his shield as they made contact. He thrust with his sword underneath, hard. He felt the blade pierce flesh and sink deep into his foe. The demon screamed and reeled backwards. Kurodan pushed forward, slamming the edge of his shield into its ugly face, causing the bone to cave in. The beast fell backwards, already dead before it hit the ground. Soldiers all around him fought with the same savagery.

"Spears," came another shout Kurodan recognized. Across the chasm on the other side of the wall, Kurodan saw Gleed.

"Spears," Gleed shouted once more. Kurodan watched as Gleed stood in front of a ladder and thrust his spear into the next orc. His spear pierced through with ease and began to shimmer. Then blinding light erupted from Gleed's weapon, and the orc exploded in flames, sending fire and light outwards. The ladder caught fire and crumbled, the climbing orcs and demons falling to their death.

Another blinding flash from the bottom of the chasm thundered upwards from Maldin. Kurodan turned his attention to the ladders closest to him. Spearmen had heard Gleed's shouts and worked their way to the front, stabbing wildly. Kurodan pushed his way to the front of the closest ladder and slammed his shield in front of him.

"Stand back," he commanded.

His eyes turned white with fire. His whole shield began to shimmer and shake. Kurodan poured all his thoughts and emotions into his shield. His hate, fear, adrenaline, regret, and his love of his brothers in arms around him.

An orc slammed its axe against Kurodan's shield over and over. Kurodan's mind flashed to his father. He let out a scream as the shield erupted in its own blinding light. The explosion incinerated the orc and set the siege ladder flying from the wall in smoke and ash. The men shouted in cheers and excitement. Kurodan felt a fellow hand grasp his shoulder in adoration. His shield smoldered black with the orc's blood.

As Kurodan regained his senses and his eyes returned to normal, his gaze focused on the Dark God once more. It was still standing like a magnificent and terrible statue, arms outstretched.

Its horrible yellow eyes locked with Kurodan's. Its face broke into a smile of what seemed like horrific delight, freezing Kurodan to his core.

Kurodan snapped out of his fear, weaving his way through the chaos. Friend and foe flickered across his vision as he moved. Thundering lights echoed and boomed as more paladins had joined the fray. Kurodan felt his arms burning as he wielded both sword and shield in unison. Demon and orc fell before his prowess.

As Kurodan moved from the wall down to the courtyard, he fought towards where he had last seen Maldin. He saw Bravmond. His helmet was missing, his armor scarred and blood-soaked. Kurodan watched as the captain sidestepped an oncoming orc and swung his sword with both hands. The orc's torso seemed to levitate from its legs and fell to the ground.

"Drive them back," he screamed. His voice was hoarse but loud. His eyes were wild with bloodlust and anger. His men began to rally beside him.

Kurodan hacked another demon to pieces as it tried to rip his shield from his grasp. *Almost there*, he thought. He was getting closer with each felled enemy.

Black smoke carried by some foul wind drifted towards the captain and his men. The demons and orcs that witnessed the smoke let out war cries and shrieks. Then Kurodan watched as the vampire materialized from the smoke, swinging his sword. The blade found its mark, and a soldier's armored head was cleaved from his body.

"Vampire." screamed Kurodan.

He melted into ash and dust once more only to reappear closer to the captain and claim another victim. The demons and orcs rallied to the vampire and his black smoke as the men rallied to the captain. The vampire's black magic seethed with the battle as he became almost a figment of imagination.

Kurodan struggled to kill an orc in front of him as he tried to keep the black smoke in view. The vampire's sword swung as if the blade craved to drink blood as much as the one wielding it.

Every time a soldier would attempt to strike a killing blow, they would begin to choke and panic as he vanished, only to be stricken down in turn. The elegant speed with which he moved was like a forgotten dance. As his men were cut down, Bravmond held his position defiantly as the smoke was almost on him.

"No," Kurodan shouted.

His eyes turned into flames as he slammed his shield into the earth. Demons, orcs, and even allies were consumed in the eruption. Kurodan regained his shield and sprinted past burned and maimed bodies. His heart sank as he saw the captain laying on his back. To his surprise, the captain rose to his feet like an animal that had just freed itself from a snare.

Kurodan saw a brief moment of serenity wash over the captain's face as he reached him. The demons and orcs were now standing at bay, wary of Kurodan's holy light.

The captain smiled a devil's grin. "Shield wall," he shouted. Soldiers rushed to the command.

"Forward," came the next order. The wall began to move in unison to the sound of soldiers' war chants. The smoke drifted down to the earth, and the vampire emerged as if he could walk between worlds.

"Hold," Kurodan yelled.

The captain's eyes glared at Kurodan. "What are you doing?" he demanded.

Kurodan ignored the captain and stepped out of the formation. The vampire laughed, almost sounding relieved, at the sight of the paladin. Kurodan's eyes turned to flame as he screamed. He thrust his sword forward, a stream of light and fire bursting forth. The monster dissipated into smoke, drifting away, but the creatures behind it were consumed.

The vampire appeared again, "I thought you were surely dead by now."

"I am happy to disappoint you," Kurodan retorted.

"Disappointed? No, now I have the chance to feast on your blood just as I've done to your brothers." His hideous long tongue licked the blood from his sword.

"I will vanquish you to oblivion, demon."

Kurodan charged, his shield and sword blinding with white light. The vampire melted into shadow. As Kurodan tried to anticipate the dark magic, the smoke flew swiftly above him. He aimed his sword at the sky. Fire and light exploded once more, a beacon of fury. The armies surrounding them slowly began to move away, creating an almost gladiatorial battleground.

He materialized with a wrath Kurodan had not yet witnessed. His dead eyes beckoned to him. Kurodan's shield met the vampire's sword in a magnificent spectacle. Fire and light sparked with each blow. The sound of their weapons seemed to deafen everything around them.

The ground shook.

Kurodan caught a glimpse of Bravmond watching among the others, in almost a reverence, as the two danced their waltz of death. The fire and light from Kurodan's weapons grew more numerous as the vampire fought on, vanishing and materializing.

Some had to shield their eyes each time the light and fire roared from the holy weapon. The demons and orcs distanced themselves further as some still were claimed by the destruction.

The vampire shadow stepped behind Kurodan, his back now to the captain and the men. Before he could strike the paladin down, Kurodan brought his shield to bear. The captain gasped; he and his men braced for death. No light and fire claimed them. The captain opened his eyes to see the fight still raging.

The ground shook.

There was a pause as the vampire materialized further away from Kurodan. Their eyes fixed upon one another.

The ground shook.

"You cannot win. The light will purge your soul," Kurodan said defiantly.

"My soul is dead, and I will devour yours," the vampire screamed with hatred, but his words rang hollow.

The ground shook.

Witnessing doubt in the monster for the first time, Kurodan knew in that moment he had won. He felt it in his bone.

"Vae vivis," the vampire bellowed and charged.

Before Kurodan could raise his shield, his world ignited into a maelstrom of illumination. The vampire vanished into ash, flying away from the light. Kurodan fought to gain his bearing.

"Fallback," came a cry.

It was Maldin and Gleed. Kurodan ran forward as Maldin and Gleed both kept the demons and orcs at bay. Their weapons, alive, incinerating their enemies in a cacophony of sound and violence.

The ground shook.

"Get them back, Kurodan!" Gleed shouted.

Kurodan paused and turned his gaze upwards to see the Dark God approaching. It had already passed through the chasm in the wall.

"Defend the queen," Maldin ordered.

Kurodan ached to stay and stand alongside them in battle. But he turned and took charge of the remaining men, "Captain, get them moving to the throne room."

The captain nodded, echoing the call to fall back. Kurodan brought up the rear as Bravmond forced his way through the men, trying to lead them. Kurodan turned to see Gleed and Maldin in the distance.

They alone held back the onslaught. They were making a final stand, their weapons flashing in the night like lightning. They would not last.

The Dark God was here. Kurodan's gaze met the Dark God's a second time. Its face broke into the same evil smile as it towered over the very city itself. This time Kurodan did not freeze. He ran towards his doom.

"I will rid you of that smile before I die."

An old man sprinted into his view.

"Stop," he commanded.

Kurodan almost stumbled in surprise as Mathius grabbed him. "You must come with me at once," he said.

Kurodan pushed past the priest but felt a hand grab the back of his armor. Kurodan turned to strike the man off.

"We must save as many as we can," Mathias shouted. The priest pulled on his arm, running further away from the fighting. Kurodan did not put into words why, but he followed him.

Chapter XXXIV: The Mighty

Captain Bravmond slowed his pace to catch his breath. His eyes searched across the men filing out in front of the Great Hall. "Not enough ... not enough," he whispered. He knew their lives flickered like a candle about to be blown out. The enemy's numbers were too many.

"Shield wall," his hoarse voice commanded. The remaining soldiers held the courtyard—the last line of defense. As Bravmond watched the enemy rush towards them, his mind wandered for an instant. Memories of Andaria drifted in front of his eyes.

He squeezed them shut trying not to lose control. It was no use. He knew these visions would be the last time he saw her. He opened his eyes and looked down at her bracelet around his own wrist. "Forgive me, I will see you in the next life," he whispered

Then he shouted one last time, his voice rang long and loud. It unveiled every fragment of his pain, sorrow, pride, hate, and love.

The captain struck down the first two oncomers as his men fought and died next to him. He ripped his blade free of flesh and bone. A spear hurled through the air and struck the captain by surprise.

The tip hit its mark just beneath the breastplate. It punctured through his belly and out his back, just missing the spine. His body grew weak as he tasted coppery blood in his mouth. His shield dropped to the ground, but he refused to let go of his sword. He stumbled forward, one hand gripping the spear that impaled him, the other slashing wildly. He caught an orc across its chest and sent it reeling back, sharing in his same pain. A demon swung its large scimitar missing the captain's head, but the blade came down shattering part of the spear's shaft.

The captain's body convulsed violently as more blood pooled from his mouth. Before the demon could bring the sword back around, he plunged forward, stabbing his own into the unholy being. The demon collapsed, and the captain fell to his knees. All around him, the orcs and demons rushed past, pushing his men further and further back. His gaze lifted upwards from the spear.

An orc bearing red war paint and dressed in chainmail approached. His eyes pierced back into Bravmond's, and his smile grew wide with one broken tusk. The captain remained upright on one knee, but his body was failing. The orc, now standing in front of him, bent down and grabbed ahold of the broken spear.

The captain gasped in pain as Korgath hefted him to his feet. His vision blurred as the orc's face spoke to him.

"You have failed."

Bravmond struck the orc across the face. Both their faces twisted to rage as Korgath lifted him high into the air. When Korgath could not raise him any higher, he let go, dropping the captain. The broken spear smashed into the ground, and Bravmond's mangled body lay still.

The queen barked orders, "Brace the door. Whatever lies on the other side, you will stand your ground as members of the queen's royal guard," But only five of them remained. They moved quickly, their armor clanking as they began barricading the doors.

From the other side, a battering ram began a slow and steady cadence. Each crash rocked the doors with a horrendous sound, though the men continued their efforts. She knew it was inevitable. Jaw clenched and teeth gritted, *This is the end.* she thought, *I will be damned if I am killed on my knees.*

"It is no use. They will soon break through," one of the guards said.

"Then we will kill as many as we can. I command you to hold and stand your ground," she screamed. The guards slowly backed away and formed a line in front of the door. A large crack revealed the orcs on the other side, shouting in cadence as they heaved the battering ram.

Crack.

Another slam, then another. The guards gripped their swords and shields, holding their breath knowing they were about to die.

"Hold," the queen shouted once more.

The doors flung open with a thunderous crash.

"Stand back," came a command from an orc.

But the queen did not respond. She was stunned, staring at the single figure now approaching. He was dressed in black armor. His skin was pale as snow, and his sword dripped red with the blood of his enemies.As he entered the Great Hall, her guards rushed him.

He let out a bloodcurdling scream as he accepted the challenge. The queen had never seen such rage and eloquence in one being. The first two guards fell as his blade sang its abominable song. The second two guards came on strong, swinging blows that would have cleaved a normal man in half. He shadow-danced around their blades, countering with his own. The sound of steel smashing against steel echoed.

He felled another guard, slashing his blade across the helmeted face and cleaving to the bone. The last two men advanced at the same time, attempting to overwhelm their adversary. One raised his sword to hammer it back down. The other plunged forward towards the vampire's heart.

He parried the stabbing blade, whirling around and gripped the man's arm in place. The man's horrendous scream filled the hall as his arm was severed by the other guard's falling blow. The one-armed man fell backwards shrieking.

Now wielding the severed arm that still gripped the sword, the vampire turned and plunged the blade into the last guard's stomach, who fell to his knees holding the weapon and bloody limb. At this, the queen let out a fierce battle cry, running at him with her sword raised.

He grabbed ahold of the guard's helmet and tore it from his head. Slowly, he drug his own sword's edge across the guard's throat, staring into the eyes of the queen as he did it.

She stumbled, almost dropping her sword. "No," she gasped. "It cannot … it … you … how?"

The guard produced a horrific gurgling sound, as sharp steel carved its way across his jugular. Korgath and his lieutenants stepped into the hall, eyeing the trail of corpses.

Still staring at the queen, the vampire pointed his

blood-stained sword at her. His eyes were black-charred coals, his mouth and fangs splattered red. Veins bulged from his neck, his chest heaved. He was macabre incarnate.

The queen's face was stricken with terror. "You are dead," she declared.

"I still am."

Chapter XXXV:
Betrayal

Shortly after the last battle of the Great War

"My king, the remnants of the undead are scattered, leaderless, divided. Let us hunt them down to the last wretch. We must not let up while we have such an advantage. Even now, after such a costly victory, we must press on," Maldin said.

The king wearily rose from his throne. His left hand trembled uncontrollably from a wound he had sustained fighting. One of the many prices he had paid as king.

We all have paid a price, he thought. His other hand gripped the trembling one, forcing it into submission. He regained his composure, but his face still betrayed him. The heavy weight and exhaustion they had all endured had taken its toll.

"Maldin, with what forces do you propose we hunt them down with? The vampires and orcs fought till their dying breath, and we fought till ours to stop them.

While we achieved victory, what remains of our forces is broken," the king said. "We have stopped them and need time to regather our strength and resources."

Maldin turned his gaze to the floor as images of friend and foe being slaughtered on the battlefield crept into his mind, "You are right, my king, but ..." he trailed off, then looked back up into eyes that were remembering the same horrors. Still, he continued, "We do not have the luxury of time. Any respite we are given, so too, does our enemy have. If we do not finish this now, I fear that the suffering will be doomed to happen again."

The king sat back down on his throne. He stared blankly into the unknown of his wandering fears and doubts. The duties and responsibilities of being king had not been kind over the years. His blonde hair was grey and thin, his beard ragged. His body appeared frail underneath his robes.

Maldin took pity on him, for he had truly been the king his people needed in their darkest hour. Bending on one knee before him, Maldin said, "You have saved your kingdom and its people this far. I know better than most, the choices you have had to make, but I bid you heed me. I urge you, though the choice may seem nigh impossible, to assemble our troops once again. To march again. Raise our banners high as we finish this once and for all. We will not be safe until their kind has been erased of existence."

The king let out a heavy sigh. He knew Maldin was right. He just did not know if his people could stomach more battle—if he could stomach it any further. Then he heard the sound of running just before the throne room doors burst open.

"My king," Vannus shouted, out of breath.

Maldin and the king both rose to their feet. Vannus

approached them and knelt, lowering his head.

"Catch your breath, paladin, what is this sense of urgency?" the king asked.

Vannus stood, nodding to Maldin. His fierce blue eyes shown with seriousness, and his straight black hair fell to sides of his head, just above his chiseled jawline. "My king, I have news from our scouts."

"Scouts?" the king questioned, raising his voice in surprise. "What is the meaning of this?" Vannus looked surprised himself, not expecting this reaction.

Maldin stepped between them, "My king, we left a group of scouts near the mountain to remain—"

"You directly disobeyed my orders! I commanded every soldier to return to the city after the battle had finished. You left more good men out there alone. My orders were to regroup in case of a counterassault. We need every sword and shield here," he said. "Damn you."

"I thought it best—" Maldin began, but Vannus stepped forward.

"My lord, it was my doing. Maldin was giving your orders when I protested. I handpicked my most trusted men to stay behind. To track those that survived and fled. To send word as quickly as possible, when anything, if anything, was learned. That is why I have this information now."

The king was still visibly angry. "What news did they send?" Maldin's face grew concerned as he braced for the worst.

"They said there are only small bands of orcs left. They believe that no vampire was able to escape. The orc numbers are still enough to be a threat, but the bands are divided and now fight each other for dominance. The message reads that the time to strike is now, as they have no clear warlord, and we can use that to our advantage," Vannus said.

The king took all this into consideration. "How can their word be so easily trusted?" he began. "How can we be so certain no vampires still walk the earth? If the orcs find a leader to unite their bands while we march against them, we will have lost all advantage." The king was almost rambling now, "If we do not make it there in time to fight them in their current state of chaos, we could be overrun or ambushed. Our greatest advantage now lies within these walls. As you said yourself, Maldin, our casualties have been severe and great. If they come for us now, we will need the city's defenses."

"My king, that is precisely why time is of the essence," Vannus interjected. "This opportunity is that of sand in an hourglass. Every second we waste here lets our chance of winning this forever slip away. If we fail to act now, think of the repercussions. The orcs will eventually claim a new warlord. Morglain was slain," Vannus acknowledged, and both he and the king paused to glance at the orc's great war-hammer now held at Maldin's side.

Vannus continued, "My scouts also mentioned an orc they believed to be named Korgath. They believe this orc may be Morglain's successor. He will not stop, my king. If he is not killed by his followers in the pursuit of power and claims it for himself—"

"If he claims power, he will come for us all," the queen said, cutting off Vannus as she walked into the throne room. "Have you heard nothing that your king has said? You directly disobeyed him and now question him in his very own throne room. How dare you!" She did not hide the ferocity in her words.

"Your highness, we only want to provide the king with an accurate picture of our enemy. He must know everything we do, and more, in order to protect his people," Vannus said.

"This fight is not yet over. We must finish it." Maldin added.

"We will finish it how the king sees fit," the queen responded. "He has already told you his course of action. We will need our city's walls to win against the remaining orcs. The remnants of our forces are too badly wounded to win another full-scale battle out in the open, no less in the orcs' own territory."

"Enough," the king said, standing and raising his hands. "Hear me now," he said, eyeing all three of them.

"Maldin, you will take your most trusted men and organize the remnants of our forces. You will divide them in the best manner. One force for another assault, the other for some defenses. Vannus, you will send word back to your scouts immediately and tell them we are coming. Have them send strategy of the safest and quickest route. My queen, I am turning over the city into your hands. You will remain here and protect our people if need be. Once our forces are ready, I will lead them."

Maldin and Vannus bowed.

"As you wish, my king," she said. Maldin and Vannus both turned and quickly left the throne room.

"Once you send word back to the scouts, meet me in the armory. I need you to make an estimate of our weapons and armor before I make a final decision of how to divide our forces," Maldin ordered. Vannus nodded as they quickened their pace and then separated, exiting into the courtyard.

Vannus was preparing his messages when he looked up as Gleed shouted his name. The big man sprinted towards him, spear in hand.

"What is it?"

Gleed skidded to a halt in front of him. "Your scouts sent more word." He handed Vannus a miniature roll of paper. He unrolled it, his eyes scanning the message.

His face darkened as both men read the parchment.

"Find Maldin," Vannus said. "I will notify the king. And make haste."

Vannus sprinted back through the great hallways. Guards and servants moved out of his way as he ran past.

As he neared the throne room, the guards confronted him, "State your business, paladin," one demanded.

"I have more urgent news for the king. The battlefield has changed."

"The king and queen are in a private council. We are under strict orders to not allow—"

"Move or be moved," Vannus said. The guards gave each other a quick glance. Just then the king's voice could be heard shouting within the throne room.

"What treachery is this?"

Vannus burst through the doors, knocking one of the guards to the ground. Vannus froze when he saw the queen holding her sword to the king's throat. Andazar the wizard was standing by her with some of the royal guards. All of them seemed to gasp as Vannus barged in.

Vannus drew his sword but felt a hard blow to the back of his head. The guards rushed him while two more slammed the doors shut.

"Fools," the queen hissed.

Andazar quickly approached Vannus and kicked his holy weapon from his reach. Four guards punched and kicked him into submission, holding him down on his knees. Andazar bent down, eyeing him closely. Vannus glared into the wizard's eyes. Andazar reached down and picked up the miniature scroll of paper that lay on the ground in front of him. He unrolled it and read aloud:

DIRE ~
We have tracked down what we believe to be the last remaining vampire. Korgath and the orcs do not seem to

know of its existence. It is wounded and we have it trapped. We might be able to take it alive and find out if there are any others. If we should fail, I will make sure to bring the beast down with us. By the Holy Light, hurry.
—Paladin Dangrin.

"How could you?" the king said to his wife.

"How could I? How could you be so easily swayed by those who serve you? For years I have watched as you have fought to make the right choices for our people, only to fall short each and every time. No longer. Your weakness will not jeopardize us anymore," the queen said.

"Bring the orc," Andazar motioned with his hand. Two guards dragged an orc into the middle of the throne room. It had been bound and beaten severely. The orc looked around cautiously.

"What of the vampire?" the queen asked.

"There is no chance it will be taken alive, even if it is wounded. We will send word that it is too dangerous for us to come, and for them to kill the vampire," Andazar replied.

Vannus spit on the ground. "You truly think the orcs and vampires will stop?"

Andazar walked over to the guards standing over the orc. One of the guards held out an orcish sword and Andazar unsheathed it.

"You will bring doom upon us all," Vannus shouted.

The orc let out a hissing laugh.

"Be silent!" the queen ordered.

"You humans believe you are truly any different? Here you all stand, killing each other for power. You are no different," the orc said, ignoring her command. "We will come for you. Your world will burn to ash. Your people will be slaughtered and enslaved. The Dark God will rise again. His darkness will cover the world."

One of the guards struck the orc hard on the side of the face. The orc laughed louder, "You think you can just make deals with a devil, and he will not come back to collect his debt? You understand nothing, queen," he said, tainting her title with derision.

"If your kind ever comes here, they will be eradicated. Korgath knows this," she said.

"I will have your eyes put out; your tongues cut from your mouths. I will have every limb of your body paraded around the streets!" the king spoke harshly.

Andazar handed the orc blade to the queen.

"Mil'Thuras is now mine," she said, bringing the blade up quickly and driving it through the king's throat. He grasped at his neck, blood spurting out onto her and the stone floor. Then he fell to his knees gurgling. She casually walked up to the king and ripped the blade from his neck.

"What are you doing?" Andazar protested. The orc laughed at the butchered king.

The queen walked over to Vannus, and a trail of red drops followed the blade. "He will have died a hero who tried to save his king," she said.

Andazar stayed the queen's arm. "No one must know he was here."

"You truly believe you will not be found out? The paladins know I am here. They will see through your treason," Vannus said.

The queen's eyes darkened, and her lips pursed. Andazar moved in between them, approaching Vannus. "The paladins will act swiftly; we must be swifter," he said. Andazar placed his hand on the paladin's face.

"Sleep now."

Vannus's body shook so violently the guards struggled to hold him. Then his muscles relaxed, and he went limp.

The sound of horses' hooves and the jerk of wagon wheels shook Vannus awake. His eyes opened to nothing but darkness. He discovered his hands, feet, legs, and arms were bound as he struggled to sit upright. There was a bag or sack covering his head. His fingertips carefully caressed the thick ropes, probing like snakes looking for newborn rats. The ropes were tied with precision and gave no slack.

Vannus's body tensed, and his breath shortened. He began to squirm, jolting his arms. His legs fought and kicked as he rolled his body side to side. Yet his efforts were in vain. To his left was a wall. Vannus rolled into it again. To his right was something different.

He rolled his body again. It was hard and cold but not a wall. On the third roll he felt something move. "Is someone there?" he asked. His voice was so quiet, he wondered if he had actually said anything aloud. There was a moment of silence and then a reply came.

"Be still," came the voice of an orc.

Vannus lay there examining the variables of his predicament. His surroundings shook as the wagon wheels traveled from stone to dirt. There was no sound of men speaking, no hushed voices. Just the horses and the wagon.

We must make our escape if we are still inside the city, he thought. *Surely any nearby citizens or guards would react to a paladin and orc escaping from a wagon, bound as prisoners.*

He nudged the orc beside him. No response. Vannus nudged harder. The orc responded in kind, digging its elbow into Vannus's ribs.

"We must make our escape, orc," Vannus said.

"Easy for you to say, human," he hissed. "Either

way I am dead."

The horses broke into a full gallop and the wagon below the orc and Vannus quaked.

"Now," Vannus said, willing himself upright, feeling the cold rushing air bite into his skin. An armored boot slammed into his chest, knocking the wind out of him.

"Lie still," came a voice. "He is awake now."

"No matter, watch them both," Andazar said.

Vannus's mind was racing as fast as the horses that drove them onward. *I must escape*, he thought over and over. Time seemed to be unending as the horses never broke gallop to rest. It was as if they were spurred on by some fear or other worldly magic. The orc had not moved or spoken since his failed attempt.

When the horses stop, memorize your surroundings, he told himself. Just when he thought the horses could no longer go on, they would. They were galloping so fast he thought the wagon could fall to pieces at any moment. Vannus had lost sense of time but began to see light poking through the sack that blinded him.

Daybreak, he thought. They had ridden yesterday and through the night.

That still put them a few days' ride from any of the nearest towns—at the pace of a normal horse. Even the finest horses he had the privilege of riding would have to of stopped some time ago. It was impossible to tell how far they had traveled or in what direction.

The air grew warmer as the sun was no longer hidden behind the mountains; its rays lit up the world. And still they travelled at this unparalleled speed. Vannus thought that Andazar was taking them to the ends of the world, just as the horses slowed to a trot.

As the thunder of the horses and wagon quieted, Vannus heard a forest all around him. Wind blowing against trees, birds chirping, and the faint sound of people. They were close to a town or village. Vannus racked his mind, *But which town could it be?*

Then he heard it. The loud clanging of a church bell. Vannus did not recognize it immediately, but as it became familiar to him, his mind was plagued with wonder. Had they really reached Dirkholm in such a short amount of time.

The horses continued at a slow canter until they had at last reached whatever their destination was. Vannus listened as Andazar and at least two other men got out of the carriage.

"I'll stay," a third said. Vannus lay still to listen for any others. He tried to look down at his wrists that were rubbed raw. He could feel the warmth of his blood that had softened his restraints.

Vannus fought the urge to turn his head as he heard the sound of shovels. He worked his wrists slowly, each motion causing a shooting pain. The rope was still tight, but he might slip his hand free soon. He was careful, trying not to move when he thought the guard was watching though he could only make out his outline.

Slowly, he told himself again and again. *There it is, almost free.*

The sound of the shovels stopped.

"Bring the paladin first," Andazar said.

Vannus tried to see the soldiers as they half dragged, half carried him to Andazar.

"Remove his sack," the wizard ordered.

"Why?" one of the soldiers questioned.

"So we know he is dead," Andazar replied annoyed as if the answer was obvious.

Vannus immediately glanced at his surroundings as the sack was removed. Andazar stood next to a shallow grave, the shovels still stuck in the ground.

Two soldiers stood next to him; the horses and wagon were only a few yards away. The third soldier stood in the wagon watching them. There were trees all around. Vannus lay on the forest floor.

"Well?" Andazar said.

The two soldiers glanced at each other nervously. Vannus shouted as the men dragged him towards the grave. His screams for help were cut off as one of the soldiers struck him in the mouth. Vannus lifted his head to shout again, but then the men dropped him, rushing to the wagon.

The orc had freed himself and was hacking the third soldier to pieces with his own weapon. Vannus turned to Andazar, who did nothing. The two soldiers drew their swords, circling the orc.

"Help us, wizard!" one shouted angrily.

"Oh, do not tell me the finest of Mil'Thuras cannot handle one measly orc," Andazar scoffed.

"Free me and I will help you," Vannus pleaded to them.

One of the soldiers turned and glanced back at Vannus. The orc struck, stabbing the blade into the back of his neck, its point jutting forth from his throat.

The other soldier swung his blade but missed as the orc ducked. The orc wrenched his blade free just in time to parry the soldier's second blow. The sound of steel on steel clanged.

"Help, wizard," the soldier begged, fending off the orc's blows.

Andazar laughed, "Very well," he said and took a step towards them.

"No, he is mine," the orc protested. The soldier looked from the orc to Andazar, and then to Vannus. Vannus saw the confusion on the soldier's face turn to rage.

The soldier ran at the orc, raising his sword high.

The orc threw himself into the soldier, their swords clashed, and they collapsed on the ground. Andazar laughed again.

"Help him," Vannus urged.

The soldier and orc struggled; their weapons lay useless next to them. There was a loud thud as the soldier struck the orc with his iron gauntleted fist. Then the orc flew into a frenzy and drew a tiny blade from a hidden sheath. The orc began to carve wildly at the soldier's face and throat. The soldier's legs kicked madly, and his gurgled scream grew into a crescendo that sickened Vannus, battle-hardened though he was.

"Enough," Vannus shouted.

The orc looked back at Andazar and smiled, showing his sharp teeth. Turning again to the soldier, the orc brought the blade down hard into his forehead with a horrible thud.

Then the orc stood and took a deep breath. "Well, that was fun," he said.

"Bring me one of their swords," Andazar said.

The orc bent down, picking up the sword that would have slain him.

"Quickly," Andazar motioned again. The orc casually strode over to the wizard who held out his hand for the blade. The orc paused.

"You want me to kill this one as well, wizard?" it asked.

"You orcs, always have such an uncontrollable lust for bloodshed," Andazar mocked.

The orc smiled again. "What is the purpose of killing, if not for the thrill of it?" he asked.

"Come closer, orc, and I'll show you," Vannus said.

The orc took a step towards Vannus.

"Enough. Give me the sword," Andazar ordered.

"This one special to you, wizard?" the orc taunted him back.

"I should have let the soldiers kill you when they had the chance. The sword," Andazar said, growing impatient. The orc tossed the sword into the air and Andazar snatched it swiftly.

"Now, orc, go and tell your lord the king is dead. The queen will not push for your race's extinction, so long as you keep each other in check."

The orc looked from Vannus to Andazar. "What of the vampire?" the orc said.

"Should the paladins fail to kill it, finish what they could not. Under no circumstances must it be left alive. Is that understood?" Andazar replied.

The orc snorted, "Give me the paladin's note, as proof of the vampire's existence." Andazar tossed the note to the orc.

"Never in my days would I have thought one of the great wizards would turn their back on the world of men and doom us all," Vannus said.

"Quiet," Andazar commanded, holding the sword to Vannus's throat.

"Well, what are you waiting for?" the orc hissed.

"Begone now, orc, I'm sure you will have no trouble finding your way back to your own kind," Andazar said.

The orc eyed Andazar carefully, "You are not the only one with secrets, wizard."

Vannus watched as the orc turned and trotted off, eventually vanishing in the forest. His eyes moved to Andazar, who still pressed the blade's edge into his neck.

The wizard stood like a statue, watching as if he could still see the orc in the distance. Minutes passed and still Andazar did nothing.

"Either kill me now, wizard, or release me, but do

not waste my time," Vannus said, spitting at him.

Andazar still said nothing. Another minute passed and Vannus's curiosity grew, "Are you not going to kill me?"

Andazar finally removed the sword from Vannus's neck, driving it into the ground next to him. Vannus's gaze shifted from the sword to Andazar and back to the sword.

Andazar looked at him sternly. "You were not supposed to have witnessed this. You are not supposed to be here, paladin," he said.

"Well, I am here, wizard. You and the queen will be found out eventually," Vannus said assuredly.

Andazar sighed as he removed a small water pouch from his robes. As the wizard opened the pouch, a foul odor wafted out. "There are things now set in motion that are of greater magnitude than you can comprehend. I will call upon you to aid me in my efforts when the time comes."

Vannus tried to sit up at the audacity. "You think that I would serve you?" he asked.

Andazar ripped the sword from the ground and impaled it through Vannus's chest. Vannus twitched and spasmed as his mouth flew open, gasping for air. His body fell back into the shallow grave. Andazar placed his foot on Vannus and drew the blade back out of his body. Vannus writhed on the ground, the ropes still restraining him.

His vision began to blur as his eyes watered. Andazar's face came closer, fading in and out from his view.

Then Vannus tasted the foul poison from the pouch. He choked and spat as the liquid slid down his throat. It started to numb his entire body, and then he felt nothing.

Just cold. He drifted into the hell that awaited him. The sound of a shovel and dirt echoed faintly.

Chapter XXXVI:
The Nightmare

He awoke to darkness, gasping for air, the more he tried to breathe, the more he choked. His body was being crushed. Or perhaps he was drowning beneath the surface of a frozen lake. He tried to swim, but his arms were held in place. He began to writhe and squirm, trying to scream but only gagged more.

Fighting, his hands clawed their way above him. No thoughts entered his mind save one: he was dying. As he tore upwards, he felt whatever was holding him down give way. His hand broke free of the darkness, and he felt a gentle breeze graze his fingers. The other hand erupted forth like a geyser. He tried to bring his head to the surface but continued to struggle. When his hands came back down, they felt the cold earth.

He pushed his body up with all the strength he could muster, until at last his head surfaced. He coughed and spat, sucking in air where he could. His vision was blurred, but he could see the bleak moon that perched like an owl above the world that slumbered beneath it.

He ripped the rest of his body to the surface. As he viewed his surroundings, he saw a faint person in the distant trees. Someone dressed in a blue robe. The form grew smaller and smaller until it was out of sight. His insides churned and contorted. He squirmed on the ground and vomited. His head pounded and he shivered as the cold air cut to his core.

The wizard quickened his pace through the trees and into the town. All was quiet. The town's inhabitants were fast asleep, awaiting the new day that would soon awaken them from their slumber.

Andazar carefully approached the house he had selected. He slowed to a stop, looking up at the night sky. He turned back over his shoulder and paused. The faintest smell of dead flesh hung in the cold. Two words passed his lips, "Vae vivis."

He stalked to the window at the back of the house. All was dark inside. The wizard raised his staff to the window. It began to glow, brighter and brighter. The room inside illuminated, revealing a bed with a small sleeping girl. The light woke her, and she stared at the wizard through the window.

Andazar moved his hand around the glow, and the light began to form a shape. The little girl's eyes watched in amazement as the light turned into a giant butterfly. She smiled gleefully. He motioned for her to come outside.

The little girl was hesitant but watched as the amazing butterfly changed colors, from green to orange. Then pink to red, and purple to blue. *It's so pretty*, she thought.

The girl crept to the back door and opened it, bracing herself for the cold night. To her surprise, she was still warm. She saw the man in blue waving his hand around the butterfly as if playing with it.

He walked closer to her and stopped. The butterfly turned toward her, flapping its beautiful wings. Sparkling flecks of light flickered down from them and blew across the air. It smelt sweet like sugar. The man in blue turned and headed for the forest; the little girl followed.

Her bare feet crunched against the warm snow. Her gaze never broke as the butterfly swirled at the top of the staff. It was now a bright yellow. She tried to quicken her pace, but he was so tall and walked so fast!

A light appeared out of the darkness. He tried to call for help but could produce no sound from his throat. Then his insides twisted again. It drove him mad, forcing him to pant like some starved animal. He stumbled to his feet, watching the moving light float gracefully through the trees. He walked towards it.

Every few steps, he was forced to lean against a nearby tree, almost collapsing again. His insides burned; his mouth was dry with the taste of acid. His head pounded, ears ringing. *I've been poisoned*, he remembered. The light grew closer and closer.

The little girl was running to catch up to the light. The butterfly was fluttering and twirling. She wanted to catch it and keep it forever, but she broke her gaze from the butterfly for the first time to see how far her house was.

She saw only dark forest and felt the cold wind whip the back of her neck. She quickly turned back to the man to ask how to get back home. Darkness. The little girl stopped, her feet freezing in the snow.

Her lips began to quiver, and tears strolled down her

cold face. "Momma?" she whispered in panic. She wrapped her arms tightly around her shoulders for warmth. She took one more step and felt a thorn prick her foot. The warm blood turned cold in the snow.

The light went out. He stopped, searching the trees to see if the torch would reignite. He tried to call out into the darkness, but it was no use. There was still a horrible pounding in his ears. His hands, trying to stop the reeling pain, held his head. The pounding continued.

When his hands fell from his head, they were full of clumps of his own hair. As he raised his head, the beating sound seemed to be coming from the forest. He walked closer. A sweet aroma overtook him, instantly accompanied by hunger. His insides raged again. He took a deep breath, sniffing deeply as he moved closer.

Snap.

The little girl heard a twig break in the near distance. Fear slammed into her, making her squeal and run. She ran blindly, darting through the darkness and trees. The snow crunched loudly under her feet. Something was following her trail. She could hear an animal behind her, sniffing.

She hid behind a tree, her back pressed hard against its enormous bark. She could hear the sniffing. It grew louder and louder. Its footsteps crept closer and closer. She wanted her mother. She wanted to run and hide under her blanket in her bed. She wanted the man with the beautiful butterfly to come back and rescue her. Where had he gone?

The sniffing suddenly stopped. The forest fell under a hushed silence. She could hear nothing, save the slight breeze and her own breathing. Slowly, she poked one eye around the tree to see if the thing was gone.

The stars were bright, casting some light onto the forest floor, just enough for her to make out her surroundings. Trees. The large trees loomed over her and seemed to almost whisper to each other, to her.

She looked from left to right and then back again. Two glowing eyes met her gaze. The trees seemed to whisper louder now, urging her to run.

The monster lunged, releasing a bestial growl. She turned and ran as fast as her legs would carry her. The snow was so cold. Her feet burned. That thing, the monster with the eyes, was so close. She could hear its heavy footsteps crashing behind her. She let out a scream as she fell, turning on her back and throwing her arms up over her face.

She could not help but watch through her arms as the monster descended on her. Its skin was pale like the snow but covered in black mud and earth. Its mouth bore razor-sharp fangs, and the fingers were long claws. Its crow black hair was matted with dirt and snow. Its breath smelt of acid and smoke. Its body was skinny and malnourished, almost a fleshy skeleton.

The monster gripped her with its terrible hands and her piercing scream was silenced.

His mind awoke from the hellish nightmare. His eyes slowly opened to see the night sky fading away with the approach of the sun. His head throbbed and his bowels twisted. Bent over on his hands and knees, he vomited. His vision began to clear. He was still in the forest.

His eyes fell on his hands. They were the color of tainted snow. His nails were like daggers, and his skin was covered in mud and dried blood.

"No … no, please, no," he whimpered.

He slowly turned his head, following a brownish red

trail that painted the ground. "No!" he screamed, scrambling to his feet, moving away from the nightmare in his dreams.

He panicked, breathing heavily. Sunlight crested the mountain peaks, and his vision began to blur once more. His head began to spin, and his legs felt weak. He tore through the forest, frantically looking for anyone to help him.

As the sun rose, he felt as if he was going to die. He paused for a moment, considering it. *Would it be a release from this current abominable existence?*

Hooves. And shouting.

Through his delirious state he could make out the sound of people nearing him. Voices, horses, carts, and wagons. He willed himself forward in hopes of help. He soon came to the edge of the forest. There was a small town. A dirt road ran through the middle of houses and shops with a large monastery in the center. A crowd had gathered in front of it. A woman was crying hysterically while others tried to comfort her.

"Spread out and search the north," a man shouted.

Another shouted, "We will take the south."

The first man yelled, "Call her name. The instant anyone finds a sign, report back here at once. The clergy will ring the church bell to signal all search parties."

The crowd dispersed then, leaving the clergymen alone with some of the others. The hysterical woman collapsed in a crying heap at the sound of the shouts.

"Isabella!"

Men approached the forest, walking towards him. He was about to call out for their help as he braced himself against a tree, but he saw his hand again. Fear crept into the base of his skull.

How would they understand? he thought. *It was an accident. I don't even remember what happened.* A vision of skin being flayed and bones breaking pierced his mind. He turned, bracing his back against the tree and peered around it.

"Isabella!"

He saw a barn near one of the houses. Horses, chickens, sheep, and pigs roamed in a nearby pasture. He crept his way through the trees, stopping occasionally to hide himself. The barn grew closer, and he could see that there was no one around. It appeared that all the townspeople who stayed were still gathered at the monastery.

"Isabella!"

The shouts grew fainter but cut deep into his ears. Now he could not push the images out of his mind. The little girl had wailed in agony as he cannibalized her. He began to crawl on his hands and knees through the open pasture. The animals broke into a wild frenzy at his presence. The horses whinnied and galloped away, the pigs squealed, and the chickens flapped their wings. The sheep fled as a hound barked and tried to corral them away from the beast skulking on the ground.

"Isabella!"

He had reached the barn; he could smell hay and manure. He stared through a hole in the wooden boards. There were six horse stalls, three on each side. Shovels, saddles, reins, gardening tools, and a scythe hung on the interior walls. All was quiet and still.

"Isabella!"

The sun's rays had now broken through the sky and brought a new dawn. He felt as if he were being roasted alive over a giant campfire. He reached up to open the door and saw smoke rising from his skin.

Stifling a cry of pain, he fell into the barn and

crawled towards the furthest stall. He lay there, curled in mud and hay, as the burning slowly receded.

"Isabella!"

"Make it stop," he cried aloud. The images began to resurface. His mind painted his tongue licking, gorging on blood slathered on broken bones. He pounded his head with clawed fists. *The little girl's heart ... it had tasted ... so pure.* All seemed to grow dim and still. The shouts were almost too faint to hear now. Even the animals had stopped making noise and distanced themselves from the barn. He felt so weak. He lifted his hands and arms in front of him. Shock and horror etched his face.

"What have I become?" he whispered.

He knew what must be done. Grasping at the stall walls, he stood. He surveyed the tools that decorated the inside of the barn. There was a dirty black cloak draped over one of the opposite stalls. He forced his feet to drag across the dirt floor, as his hands worked their way along the walls. He now stood below the tools. The scythe hung above him, calling to him.

He pulled it from the wall, feeling the full weight of the blade. It was heavier than he had anticipated. *How could such a tool weigh so much more than the sword and shield he had carried into battle?* his mind questioned. This blade had been well kept. He gently ran his finger along the edge. A slight pain shot through his finger as the blade nicked it.

A small drop of blood emerged from the cut and his eyes widened. He felt it. The hunger. It clawed its way up from the depths of his being. He stood holding the scythe and watching the blood in a daze.

Shouting.

He turned his head quickly towards the noise. Men were shouting closer now, and he could hear running through the forest.

"Sound the bells! Sound the alarm! We found her!"

He heard the church bell ring out across the town. It drowned out the shouting. Then a slight pause of silence, and the bell tolled again. A single woman's cry of pain pierced through the ringing. The sound was maddening.

He wedged the scythe into the corner of the horse stall, the blade facing upwards. He stood over the blade, his eyes clamped shut and his hands slammed against his ears. The scream died and his eyes opened.

"End it now," he cried, and threw himself on top of the blade.

Chapter XXXVII: Rebirth

His chest ached and he coughed up blood. The taste was exquisite. He saw the shaft of the scythe underneath him. He could feel the blade as he tried to move. He felt stronger, save for the aching pain in his chest. He pushed his weight up, struggling as the blade made a tearing sound against the inside of his flesh.

He pulled the tip from his chest and watched as the gaping hole it had left began to close. The wound healed itself in a matter of seconds. He shut his eyes. Close by he could hear a horse snorting and kicking up dirt. Further away, he could hear the sound of water boiling, a clergyman's prayer, the pasture grass and trees fluttering in the breeze.

Night had descended upon the town. He felt alive. No more pain, no more sickness. He drew in a deep breath and opened his eyes. Then it struck him. The hunger. It was back. He could still taste the remnants of the girl, smell her blood in his nostrils. It consumed him.

Darius could not sleep. He lay in his bed listening to his parents whisper to each other. They were talking about Isabella. She had wandered off into the woods last night and had not returned this morning. All Darius wanted to do was go out to the pasture and play orcs and warriors with the other boys.

His mother had made him promise to stay in the house and do his chores all day. He did not understand why he was not allowed to play just because Isabella had gotten lost.

Why would she go out into the forest at night? he thought. He had never gone outside of the town at night, at least not by himself.

Darius knew the girl had died. He had heard his parents talking about it, but they had avoided discussing it around him. A little scared, he sat up in bed. He had remembered seeing the thing crawl into the barn from the house window. He wanted to run out of the house and find his parents, but he had promised them he would not leave all day. He could hear them now through his bedroom door.

"Why was he hiding under his bed when we came home from the monastery today?" his mother asked.

"He was probably just frightened, dear. He knows something bad happened today. He is young but not stupid," his father said.

"Well, how do we tell him what happened without scaring him further? Surely the other kids will spread stories of what happened. I do not want him hearing about it from them."

"I will talk to him tomorrow morning, dear."

Darius remembered Isabella's mother's scream. He had never heard someone scream like that before. *It was as if she was going to die of sadness*" he thought. He nervously got out of his bed, feeling sick to his stomach.

He started walking to his door when his eye caught a glimpse of something through his bedroom window. A hooded figure moved through the tall pasture grass. *It was the monster coming out of the barn*! He flung open his bedroom door, startling his parents.

"What is it?" his father almost shouted in alarm.

"I saw it," Darius stammered. "It went into the barn while you were looking for her. I didn't say anything because I thought it wasn't real. It's outside right now."

His father grabbed a sword that was lying near the table. He walked over to the window and looked outside. His mother grabbed Darius in both of her arms. "What did you see, sweetheart?" his mother asked.

"The monster that got Isabella," Darius said. His mother's face grew pale. She looked up to see her husband still staring out the window.

"Do you see anything?" she whispered.

"Get the holy books. Lock yourselves in the bedroom and pray until I return," he said. Darius began to whimper.

"What? Where are you going?" she asked.

"Do as I say," his father demanded. "Now. I need to warn the town." The three of them watched as someone approached the dirt road from the pasture. It was wearing the old, ragged cloak from inside the barn.

He could hear the man following him from down the road. His breathing was heavy, and his pulse elevated. He walked through the town hearing and sensing everything. The people who were awake, sleeping, lovemaking, crying, laughing, all of it. He could ... taste it.

The hunger drove him down the road. The monastery loomed high above him. He stopped and crossed the road.

"It cannot be," he heard the man behind him whisper. He weaved his way through the town until he stood at the front of a tavern. The wooden sign hanging out front read The Horse Tail's Tavern. He could hear the heartbeat of everyone inside.

There were multiple people following him now. Some with torches. The town was becoming aware of his presence. He walked up the steps, opened the door and stepped into the tavern. Everyone inside fell silent and turned to look at him.

He paid them no attention, walking to the front bar and sitting down on a stool. The walls were dimly lit with lanterns, and there were a few candles spread among the tables. There was a surprisingly large number of people inside. Ale, wine, and food littered the tables. One man, fat and balding with a stubby beard, moved away from him.

He could sense their breath, their blood flowing through their veins. He was becoming intoxicated just being in the mere presence of other living beings. He walked to the bar and sat on a stool. His cloak covered his hands, but his clawed bare feet became more visible as the cloak rose up. Hushed murmurs floated across the tables.

The barkeeper approached slowly, not being able to make out any of the new customer's features. "There something I can get you?" he asked, nervously drying a mug with a dirty towel as he spoke.

"I … I do not know," he replied.

The barkeeper looked puzzled. "You don't know what you want, or if I will be able to get you what you want?"

He let out a sigh and placed his hands on the bar, the black cloak falling away to reveal his claws. The barkeeper dropped the mug as he stepped backwards, slowly moving until he was against the wall.

The door burst open, and a group of men rushed inside. They held torches, swords, and holy books. There were harsh warnings and yelling as people pushed their way past and out of the tavern. He remained sitting with his back to them. He could taste it all. Their fear … he had never tasted anything so sweet.

"Wait," a man shouted, pushing his way into the inn. His eyes were bloodshot and his appearance disheveled. The man was drunk. The man approached, pointing with a stake.

"You took her from us. You butchered her," the man screamed. Tears were falling down the side of his cheeks. The man reached out with the stake and ripped the hood down. He did not flinch at the sight of the vampire.

His skin was a dark pale gray, his head bare, his face sunken and dead. Others tensed, gripping onto their weapons and their faith. The man leaned against the bar to get a closer look at him. His left still holding the stake.

"Look at me, devil," he demanded. "I am going to send you back to he—aaaaAAGGGH."

His hands moved like spiders, ripping the stake from the man's grasp. Then he brought it back down hard, driving clean through the man's hand and pinning it to the bar. The man's scream was like a symphony to his ears. Using his free hand, the man clawed at his mangled one.

The others shouted prayers and curses; some fled. He stood from the stool, lifting his head back. The cloak fell, revealing his hideous form. His eyes glossed over black like a shark's when it breaches the ocean waters.

His jaw made a cracking sound as it detached from his skull.

He hissed a low laugh. Some of the candles and torches blew out. The entire tavern seemed to moan and creak.

Then the mob charged him, the first raising his sword high overhead. Right as the blade came hurtling down, the figure erupted into a cloud of black smoke, as if vanishing in a magic act. The smoke made some of the attackers' cough and gag.

He reappeared to the side of the man and his fangs came down on his neck. He ripped his jaws away finally tasting the blood, heaving the screaming man into the next oncomer.

A third lunged with a sword but only stabbed a black mist. He appeared to his back; his clawed fingers tore the man's throat out. Blood flowed down the body, pooling, making the tavern floor slick. He let loose a roar that made the men cover their own ears.

One darted for the door only to stop as the black mist blocked his exit. He materialized, grabbing the man's head with both hands. His thumbs finding their way into the man's eye sockets, like worms finding fresh mud. He drove them deep, watching the blood ooze and squirt. As the man felt his eyes rupture, he howled.

The vengeful father had torn the stake from his bloody hand and charged madly towards him. He shoved the blinded man to the floor to welcome the challenge with open arms.

They made eye contact as the father charged; he did not see fear in his eyes. Only rage and hate.

The father brought the weapon down with enough conviction to kill, but he caught the father at the wrist and slammed his other hand into his throat. The father grunted as the blow lifted him from his feet.

He turned and held the father against the tavern door. The man was trying to yell. His body twitched as he kicked and tried to free his weapon.

"You killed her?" the father gasped out.

He looked into his eyes and answered, "She did not die in vain." Then he wrenched the father's arm, breaking it at the wrist, and drove the stake into his chest.

The last survivor, a clergyman, watched in horror as the vampire stepped back from the man who now hung suspended to the door. He clenched his holy book to his chest.

"Gods grant me strength," he yelled. The clergyman grabbed a torch from the wall and held it out in front of him. The vampire walked towards the man; his footsteps made no sound as he stepped over the mangled bodies.

"Gods grant me strength," the clergyman repeated, stepping away until his back was against the wall, still trying to ward off the vampire.

He bent down and retrieved a sword as he approached. His body was covered in the blood of his victims. He stood directly in front of the man gazing past the flame into his eyes. The clergyman was trembling now. The vampire smiled revealing sharp red fangs.

"Gods?" he paused, eyeing the clergyman with amusement. "Your gods have abandoned you."

"The gods will protect me!" the man shouted, swinging the torch as a weapon towards the vampire. The attack was uncoordinated but passionate, fearless even. But he simply swung the sword, severing the clergyman's arm. The man reeled back in shrieking agony, the butchered arm and torch falling to the ground.

He smiled as the clergyman dropped the book and, what he assumed was his faith, and clutched his dismembered limb. The man's screaming grew louder and more frightful as his body caught fire from the torch.

As he burned alive, the tavern itself began burning. Soon the interior erupted with crackling flames and billowing smoke.

Quickly he donned the black cloak once more, and then faced the father's corpse pinned to the door. The memories were clear. The nightmare was no longer a dream but a reality. He now had tasted a mere morsel of the powers he had been given. The curse was now a gift.

Onlookers panicked and shouted as they heard the screaming clergyman from within the tavern. "Get water. The whole place is on fire," someone yelled.

The door opened and a figure cloaked in black walked from the burning building. The door revealed the corpse of Isabella's father. Vannus walked slowly down the road away from the wreckage. Ahead he saw Andazar waiting for him.

Chapter XXXVIII: Cataclysm

The queen's throne room

The orcs continued to fill the Great Hall behind Korgath, who was pleased to see how quickly they had surrounded the queen in her own throne room. Hate etched her face as she backed away towards her throne.

"She looks like a trapped animal," Korgath chuckled. The orcs laughed, mocking her fear.

She faced the vampire. "How?" she asked.

"You had me killed, your highness. Death decided hell did not want me. Now I have been reborn," Vannus said, slowly walking towards her.

"How could you fall so far to siege your own kingdom and countrymen?"

"You dare lecture me?" Vannus screamed. "On the merits of loyalty, no less … the queen who betrayed her own warriors and people to stay in power.

I gave my life defending this forsaken city, and now in death I will claim it as my own."

The queen did not rebut him with an insult or bellow a warrior's shout. She charged him. Vannus raised his sword in both hands over his head and ran at her. The queen managed to sidestep and parry the weapon.

The sound of steel on steel was all that could be heard. She swung with all her strength, but Vannus merely dodged away and struck her across the face with his fist. The blow did not seem to slow the queen. She brought her sword back around with even more vigor.

Vannus ducked as the blade nearly took his head. He struck her again, this time kicking her in the stomach. The blow pushed the queen back slightly, but if it hurt her, she did not show it. She charged again, hurling herself at him. Vannus moved out of the sword's path with such grace and speed it made the queen's attempt look almost childlike. Still the vampire had refrained from shapeshifting into mist.

She pressed her attack, still showing no sign of weakness or fatigue. The orcs remained quiet as the duel pressed on. Korgath wanted to tell the blood drinker to quit toying with his prey and end it, but the queen's fighting spirit intrigued him. If there was one thing the orcish race placed above everything else, it was the will to fight.

Vannus caught her by the arm mid-swing. He raked his sword across the back of her elbow, mangling her arm. She merely snorted, exchanged the blade from hand to hand, and swung with her remaining good arm. Korgath could see the hate filling both their eyes.

Vannus moved out of her path and slowly circled her. The queen now waited for Vannus to strike in hopes of baiting him onto her sword.

He ran at her with his sword at the ready. She

feigned a strike and then quickly pulled her sword in close to her and plunged the blade directly into his stomach.

Korgath raised his eyebrows in surprise. His orcs were stunned as blood poured out of Vannus's wound.

The queen stared into his eyes as she tried to pull her sword free. Vannus grabbed her hand and the blade, pulling himself closer to her, sliding the sword further inside him. A metal clang rang out as he dropped his own sword onto the ground. The queen finally broke her bearing.

"No," she trembled.

Vannus gripped her by the shoulders, his nails digging deep into her armor. He brought his forehead down on hers with such force that it threw her to the ground. He pulled her sword from his body and dropped it, unfazed by the gaping wound left behind. Dazed, the queen started to scramble for the sword, but Vannus gripped her by the back of her hair and yanked her to her feet. Fear finally painted her eyes. He clutched the back of her armor as she struggled.

Still, she fought as Vannus lifted her high above his head. "I am your evil," he told her. He brought the queen down onto his knee, snapping her spine. She screamed in pain and forced herself onto her stomach. Her legs no longer worked as she tried to crawl away, pulling herself forwards with only her arms.

Vannus knelt beside her. "Sshhh," he whispered. His jaw detached, his tongue slithering forth. The fangs, they called out to her. No longer in control and overcome by dread, she whimpered.

Her screams were wracked with wretchedness as the vampire took his time with her. Even Korgath had to look away.

Kurodan sprinted to keep up with the priest. They

fought to push past the soldiers in front of them, but it was no use. Kurodan kept looking back over his shoulder. Maldin and Gleed were now out of his sight, but he could still hear their weapons thundering.

"They need my help," Kurodan shouted. The priest did not break his focus, still running forward. "I'm going back."

At this, Mathias turned to face him. "No. The queen is the one who will be able to rally other armies of men. We must secure her safety."

"How are we going to do that if we cannot even reach her throne room?" Kurodan asked.

"There," the priest pointed and ran into an alley that lay just off the stone road. Kurodan raced to catch up with him. "This is a dead end," he said as they came to a stone wall.

The priest gripped a stone in the wall and pulled it out, revealing a small hole. He then pulled a key from his cloak and thrust it inside and turned. Kurodan stood in amazement as the wall gave way into a door.

Mathias did not wait for him and ran inside. Kurodan looked behind him to see more soldiers pressing up the main road and then followed after the mad priest.

"Should we not have more men follow us?" he shouted. The secret door gave way to a long winding corridor. The stairs were not evenly spaced and far apart. Kurodan could not help but wonder what secrets had been kept hidden within this passageway over the years.

"There is no time," the priest replied sharply. Kurodan was breathing heavily by the time he caught Mathias, who was now standing at another door and fumbling with the same key.

"Where does this lead?" Kurodan asked.

"This passageway leads to many others that go throughout the city."

As the door opened, Kurodan saw multiple other corridors and stairs going up and down. The priest ran to the one directly in front of them and came to a third door.

He paused before unlocking it. "Be ready." Kurodan nodded and gripped his weapons. Mathias opened the door, and they stepped through. They entered a small chamber with what appeared to be a tomb. In the center, on top of a stone table, lay a beautiful coffin.

"What …" Kurodan began, but the priest quickly motioned for silence.

On the far wall there was another door, but it was slightly elevated from the ground, small steps leading up to it. Kurodan could hear noises coming from the other side of the stone. The priest crept close to the wall, placing his hands and ear alongside it. He felt his way until he reached a small crevice in the stone and peered into it. He then sat with his back against the stone staring blankly.

Kurodan approached the spot where Mathias had looked through. As he bent closer and peered out, he realized where he was. He was looking into the Great Hall. The door beside them was physically right behind the queen's throne itself. *This is a safe room for the king or queen*, Kurodan thought.

Orcs filled the throne room and Kurodan could not see the queen. "Where is the queen?" he whispered. The priest gave no reply.

Then, he saw the vampire rise, blood dripping from his lips. Faintly, Kurodan heard him say, "I claim this city in the name of the Dark God. All those who would defy him shall fall."

Kurodan made for the door though he didn't know how it worked or if it would even open. Mathias suddenly seized him and pulled him to the center of the chamber. They stood next to the coffin.

"Help me," Mathias said. He started to lift the coffin's lid. Kurodan was confused but helped anyway. Inside the empty coffin was a single flask that contained a brightly red colored liquid.

"Get in," the priest ordered.

"What?" Kurodan said sharply.

"The city is taken, we have lost. I must seek out the remaining magic before it is too late."

"Who are you, priest?"

Mathias let out a heavy sigh, "I will explain in due time. We cannot risk any more lives of the Holy Order now. You will be needed. Take this." The priest thrust him the potion.

"What am I supposed to do? Hide in this coffin until what end?" Noises could be heard again on the other side of the stone wall.

"When you wake, seek me out," Mathias pushed Kurodan towards the coffin until he climbed in, sitting there in disbelief at what he was doing.

"Drink," he commanded. Kurodan wanted to resist, he stared from the strange liquid back to Mathius. "You must trust me, paladin. This fight is still not over."

Kurodan opened the flask and drank its contents. The liquid was warm but had no taste to it. He struggled to lay flat, feeling lightheaded.

As Mathias closed the heavy stone lid, he whispered, "When you wake, find me."

Kurodan's world went black.

Chapter XXXIX: The Son of Man

Crune witnessed the vampire and orc warlord leading the army from the great hall, through the courtyard of the city, back towards the shattered wall.

He followed Andazar, who strode up and down the streets. The wizard held the Book of the Dead aloft in one hand, feverishly reading aloud the ancient passages. The pages made from skin turned by themselves as the wizard spoke words that none could understand.

As the words inscribed began to bleed, so too did Andazar bleed from his eyes, nose, and mouth. While he still held the tome of evil high in one hand, he began to point his other to and fro like a symphony maestro. Crune could hear no music. But soon it became apparent that the wizard orchestrated a song of death and decay.

The dead began to rise and followed their leader in an unholy procession. Crune ran alongside the dead, waving his arms in celebration, rejoicing, witnessing the power Andazar had shown him in his dreams so long ago.

Pausing, Crune stared at the great being that stood giant over the city. Arms and wings folded once more, the Dark God beheld the wrath that had sacked the city, waiting. As Vannus drew near, he struck the earth with his sword and knelt before the great terrible devil, as if to be knighted.

"Mil'Thuras has fallen in your name," he said. Then lifted his head and met its eyes.

The devil pointed to the west. It did not speak nor enter the vampire's mind. Vannus understood. The unholy procession made its way back through the crumbled city wall.

They marched out of the ruin, raising new black banners in the name of their god. They marched to end the rest of mankind. The night sky opened. Lightning came from the east, flashing to the west, and blood rained down upon the world.

End

Epilogue

Lying in the tomb, I awoke to the damp smell of decay and the turning of time. I fought the strain in my muscles, pushing and sliding the lid off the coffin. Stone grinded against stone until it fell away, crashing to the ground.

I sat up in the dark, a deep blue showing through holes in the crumbled walls and ceiling. The devil's moon still hung in the never-ending night. As my eyes adjusted, I readied my shield and sword.

Cobwebs, dust, and rubble littered the tomb. As I turned, I saw the stone wall hiding the coffin from the throne room had given way. Everything had been destroyed and forgotten, left for ghosts and the dead. The queen's throne was shattered into pieces.

As I approached, I saw her. Her bones lay strewn about what was left of the broken seat. Resting on the one unbroken arm, her skull sat staring back at me. Her crown rested precariously on its owner even in death. Covered in ancient, dried blood and grit, one small part still glinted brightly.

Walking about the remnants of the throne room, it was clear the world had been damned. They had won. I forced open one of the doors leading to the courtyard outside.

The terrain itself had been warped, as if earthquakes and storms had permanently wreaked havoc across the land. The once beautiful scenery of Gulgotha had been transformed into a barren wasteland. I recognized nothing and yet there, a small speck far off in fading distance, among all the destruction, it stood defiantly, mocking me. Mount Ruin.

Acknowledgments

If you have made it this far, thank you for reading to the very end. My hope is that this book, and any others I write in the future, will inspire people the same way that I have been inspired by all the stories that have come before mine. If you enjoyed this book, please leave a review somewhere—anywhere, really—and help spread the word.

I would also like to give thanks to the many people who have helped and supported me. There are far too many to name, but I will acknowledge a few here.

To my beautiful wife, Rachel: you have stood by me and never once doubted me. You are my rock, and I can't picture my life without you.

Nick, I still credit much of this to you. You were the first person to ever read the few pages I had written years ago. Your excitement and friendship gave me the nudge I needed to turn those few pages into a full-length book.

Mom and Dad, you have always been there for me. Mom, you were surprisingly the first person to read my completed draft in its entirety. Your support has also been amazing. And Dad, ever since I can remember, you have always shared your passion and love of reading with me. I will forever be grateful for that.